arma

I Found My Heart in San Francisco
Book Eleven

Susan X Meagher

Karma
I Found My Heart In San Francisco: Book Eleven
© 2011 by Susan X Meagher

ISBN (10) 09832758-0-7
ISBN (13) 978-0-9832758-0-0

THIS TRADE PAPERBACK ORIGINAL IS PUBLISHED BY BRISK PRESS, BRIELLE, NJ 08730

FIRST PRINTING: JULY 2011

THIS IS A WORK OF FICTION. NAMES, CHARACTERS, PLACES, AND INCIDENTS ARE THE PRODUCT OF THE AUTHOR'S IMAGINATION OR ARE USED FICTITIOUSLY. ANY RESEMBLANCE TO ACTUAL PERSONS, LIVING OR DEAD, BUSINESS ESTABLISHMENTS, EVENTS, OR LOCALES IS ENTIRELY COINCIDENTAL.

THIS BOOK, OR PARTS THEREOF, MAY NOT BE REPRODUCED IN ANY FORM WITHOUT PERMISSION.

Acknowledgment

My lovely and talented partner Carrie is the most supportive and encouraging woman I could ever hope to meet. I couldn't write without her.

By Susan X Meagher

Novels

Arbor Vitae
All That Matters
Cherry Grove
Girl Meets Girl
The Lies That Bind
The Legacy
Doublecrossed
Smooth Sailing

Serial Novel

I Found My Heart In San Francisco

Awakenings
Beginnings
Coalescence
Disclosures
Entwined
Fidelity
Getaway
Honesty
Intentions
Journeys
Karma

Anthologies

Undercover Tales
Outsiders

To purchase these books go to
www.briskpress.com

Chapter One

The sand-colored Lexus glided down the 101, the traffic almost non-existent. "There's something to be said for traveling on Thanksgiving afternoon." Ryan smiled to her partner when she turned off the freeway at the exit for the San Francisco International Airport. "Smooth sailing."

"You seem pretty darned happy," Jamie said. "I thought you'd be bummed that we had to leave the party so early."

Ryan spared a glance at her partner, her mouth twitching into a smile. "I hate to admit this, but sometimes I feel a huge sense of relief when we leave a party like that."

"You do?"

"Yep. It's not that I don't love them all, but it's draining to be around that many people—especially in such a small house."

Jamie shared an impish smile. "I also hate to admit it, but I feel the same. There are so many people, and so much noise, that it's like a blast of fresh air when you leave. It honestly takes me a while to relax after that kind of sensory onslaught."

"Me too. It's nice to be alone again."

Thoughtfully, Jamie said, "As much as the family re-charges me, I get my real sustenance from being alone with you. I'm really looking forward to this weekend."

Ryan shot her a glance and warned, "Most of my time has been scheduled for me. Coach Hayes doesn't like to leave much to the vagaries of chance. She's not the laid-back person that Coach Placer was."

"I know. But we'll get to sleep together, and we'll have our morning together, won't we?"

"Yeah. I think we meet at eleven tomorrow—but I didn't get a final schedule, yet."

"That's enough for me. Sleeping with you and cuddling you in the morning will be perfect. The rest of the time I can get caught up on my work."

"I'm looking forward to this too. Since I don't know the other players, and for the most part they don't seem very friendly, it'll be nice to have your sweet face greet me after the game."

"I'm friendly enough to make up for all of 'em," Jamie promised, smiling brightly at her.

"You're friendly enough to make up for a pack of snarling pit bulls."

※

Seven members of the team were already at the gate when Jamie and Ryan arrived. Each was dressed as Ryan was—in the Cal Basketball warm-up suit. Since they were going to Colorado, everyone also had a winter coat with them—in Ryan's case, a snowboarding jacket that had seen better days. Jamie was still trying to understand why the strip of duct tape that sealed a rip in the nylon was a source of pride for her partner, but she'd finally decided that some things were simply unknowable.

The crew was quite motley looking, and their attitudes didn't increase their attractiveness in Jamie's opinion. Each woman looked up, but only five of them bothered to acknowledge Ryan or Jamie's presence—and even they merely nodded.

Ryan looked totally out of her element, standing there awkwardly—and Jamie could tell she was trying to decide if she should bother to try to speak to her teammates. "Let's go sit down, and you can give me the run down on these characters," Jamie whispered.

Nodding briefly, Ryan went to the far corner of the seating area and flopped down onto one of the molded vinyl chairs. "Janae and I have our work cut out for us."

"If you're referring to your plan for gaining leadership of this crowd, I should say so." Jamie shot a glance at the women. "Who are they all?"

"The two sour-looking ones are Wendy and Janet. They don't speak to anyone else on the team, near as I can tell. Strangely enough, it seems like they're favorites of Coach Hayes—although I can't for the life of me figure out why."

"Nice," Jamie nodded, giving the women a glare.

"The tiny woman is Franny Sumitomo. Nice kid. She's a freshman from San Francisco. I think she can speak—but I've never heard her." She smirked wryly. "The two dark-haired ones are juniors, and their names are..." Ryan scrunched her eyebrows together and gave their names her best try. "Drzislava and Zeljka." She gave Jamie a look and added, "I'm not even gonna take a whack at their last names."

"Uhm...I'm guessing they're from out of town?"

Ryan chuckled and said, "They're both Croatians. I'm not sure how, but their families got out during the Balkan conflict, and they got permission to emigrate. They seem like a nice pair, but they don't appear to want to interact with the rest of the team. I suppose language is an issue for them." She smiled wanly and said, "I guess we should be glad that the two of them were on the same side during the conflict. Lord knows we don't need any more dissension."

"Who are the last two?"

"Oh, they are..." She was interrupted by a very tall, very large black woman, who flashed a warm smile and took the seat opposite them.

"Hey, Janae," Ryan beamed. "Meet my partner, Jamie Evans. Jamie, this is Janae Harris."

"Hi. Been here long?"

"Not very. I was introducing the cast of characters to Jamie. I was about to hit Jaleesa and La Trice. I don't know much about them, though. Have any insight?"

"Yeah, a little. They're locals—they're both from Oakland. Jaleesa is a junior, and La Trice is a sophomore. They've been close ever since La Trice joined the team."

"Are they friends of yours?" Jamie asked.

"Uhn-uh. The only things we have in common are skin color and a love of basketball. They're both very religious—and neither is very accepting of lesbians." Looking at Jamie she grinned and said, "I'm one of you, by the way."

"Duly noted," Jamie said, returning her smile.

"The bottom line is that we never hit it off—even though I tried when Jaleesa was a freshman. She spent a great deal of time trying to get me to repent." She flashed another grin and added, "It didn't work."

Another small knot of players approached, and took seats near the rest of the team. "Here comes the rest of our happy group," Janae observed. Jamie considered the threesome. Two blondes and a brunette, and they looked fairly friendly and upbeat. "Ella, Hilary and Lily," Janae announced. "Hilary and Lily are sophomores, and Ella is a freshman. They're nice enough, but they definitely stay in their own clique. They seem like typical party girls—they're the reason that a lot of guys come to the games. Hilary is dating one of the wide receivers on the football team, and Lily is seeing a guy from the swim team. If nothing else, they've helped attendance."

"Doesn't anyone hang around with Franny?" Jamie asked, seeing the young woman sitting alone.

"Nope. I've tried to talk to her," Ryan said, "but she's painfully shy. I felt like I was torturing her, trying to make her talk to me, so I've left her alone since then. It seems to be what she prefers."

"Ryan tells me that you two want to try to turn the team around," Jamie said to Janae. "Looks like you've got your hands full."

"And then some," Janae agreed, twitching her head in the direction of Coach Hayes, who had arrived on the scene. "She's the biggest part of the problem."

"Why is that? Ryan doesn't seem to have a good read on her."

"Well, primarily because she's an asshole." The look Janae gave their coach was dark and cold. "A real asshole."

Jamie shot Ryan a worried look. "And you two think you can overcome this?"

Ryan shrugged, and Janae spoke up. "Coach really doesn't interact much with us. Lynette is the one we have to work with most of the time—and she's great."

"Does the coach dislike you, Janae?" Jamie asked.

"Oh, yeah. Not for anything I've done, though. I was a good friend of a player named Deborah who stood up to Coach constantly.

There was a big controversy last year—you may have read about it in the Daily Californian. One of the seniors was accused of stealing from another student. The other student said that this player, Renee Watkins, stole a mini-stereo from her room. Coach had a meeting with the whole team, and said she was going to suspend Renee from the team until the charges were proved or disproved. Wendy and Janet—my two favorite people on the planet—vocally sided with the coach—to suck up, of course. Deborah and I argued—loudly—that kicking Renee off the team solely because of an allegation was plain wrong.

"Deborah was really angry about the whole thing and she let her temper get the best of her during one meeting, and she called Coach a racist. I'm still not sure if Deborah talked to the paper or not, but they printed a story that hinted at racial discord on the team. Now, Coach was a bitch before—but she got a lot worse after that. It seems like she started distrusting the players—like she was afraid that we were going to turn on her. That's when Lynette took over more and more. That's been a good thing—as far as I'm concerned."

"What happened to Renee and Deborah?" Jamie asked.

"Renee was cleared of all charges—it was case of mistaken identity," she said with a wry smirk. "Deborah graduated—after riding the bench for the remainder of the year."

"It sounds like a mess," Jamie said, her head shaking slowly.

"Oh, it was and is. But if we can get a few of the players to work with us, things might really improve."

Coach Hayes stood up and looked around the room, obviously counting heads. When the announcement was made that they could begin to board, Jamie stood up and slung her carryon over her shoulder. "Are you coming with us?" Janae asked.

"Yeah. Why?"

"Did Coach give permission for that, Ryan?"

Ryan shot her a startled look. "I didn't ask. Jamie made her own reservation for the flight, and she booked her own hotel room. Why would anyone care?"

"Coach Hayes cares about everything. Absolutely everything."

Lynette came up to the threesome before they boarded, and called Ryan aside. "You should have checked with me before you decided to bring Jamie along. We don't like surprises."

"I'm sorry if I did something wrong. I didn't know it'd be a problem. She's paying for herself, and getting her own room. We did this all the time with the volleyball team. I didn't think to ask."

"It's not the reality, it's how it looks. Coach doesn't like it to look like anyone is getting special treatment. It's no big deal—keep us informed, okay?"

"Okay. Again, I'm sorry, Lynette. I'm not a rule-breaker."

"Don't worry about it. It's a small issue." She gave Ryan a very serious look and added, "But don't let it happen again."

※

They were settled in their seats, a stranger taking up the third spot in their row. Jamie inclined her head towards Ryan and said, "I was thinking about our last photo opportunity this afternoon."

Ryan smiled, thinking about the elaborate photo set-up that Jamie had arranged at the Thanksgiving feast. "That was fun. We should do that more often."

"It was a lot more than I bargained for." She gave Ryan a lascivious wink.

"I thought you wanted to see the look on my face when I told you how much I loved you," Ryan reminded her in a whisper.

"Tiger, we nearly captured the look on your face when you make love to me. But it'll be kinda fun to see on film how we progress from a gentle kiss to near copulation in less than a minute."

※

After an uneventful flight and a bus ride to the motel, the two young women sat at a round Formica table, one of the pair resting her chin on her braced hands, staring in wonder at her partner, who was methodically consuming two pieces of pie—one pecan, one pumpkin.

"I was thinking about this pie during the entire flight," the dark-haired half of the couple mused.

Jamie smiled at her, her head wagging the entire time. "I know you love pie, but you can't possibly be hungry, honey. I've seen some prodigious displays of food intake, but today had to be some sort of record for gluttony."

Ryan batted her eyes and said, "I thought you wanted me to gain weight?"

"I do, but you don't have to do it all in one day. I don't want you to have nightmares."

"I never have nightmares from eating too much food. Too little? Definitely."

"Far be it from me to interfere with your well-oiled machine. You know what the beast can handle."

"I do indeed. Want some?" Ryan offered as she extended a fork carrying a tiny shard of the pecan pie.

"Nope. I'm gonna have to borrow your pants if I eat another bite. I'll never understand how everyone in your family is so thin."

"Well, most of them do manual labor, and that burns up the calories. But I also think the O'Flahertys have a pretty quick metabolism. As for the Ryan side, they're small boned and thin."

"Good genes once again." When Ryan was finished with her snack, she went into the bath to get ready for bed. Jamie followed close behind, and by ten-thirty they were snuggling together to try to get warm. "Jeez, it's cold here," Jamie complained.

"We might have to put on clothes. This blanket isn't very thick. I don't think we'll ever warm up."

"Why can't we leave the bedspread on?" Jamie asked, her whole body shivering.

Ryan cocked her head, giving her partner an amused look. "You haven't stayed in many motels, have you?"

"Nope. I've been in hotels on every continent, but when the golf team went to Oregon, that was my first motel. Why do you ask?"

"Motels are…different from what you're used to. The room rate card says this place costs thirty-nine dollars. That's not a lot of money—even for me. Now, I'm not saying that motels appeal to low-class people, but people tend to subject these places to a lot of…hard use."

"What's your point? I'm freezing here."

"All sorts of things go on in a bed, right?"

Grinning widely, Jamie agreed. "Yes, love. Lots of things. And we've done most of them."

"Right. And some of those things that we and lots of other people do on a bed cause bodily fluids to be exchanged, right?"

"Uhm…yeah, that's rather obvious."

"A lot of people don't take the bedspread off before they start playing," Ryan said, letting that thought hang in the air for a moment.

Jamie's head swiveled to look at the bedspread, now neatly folded over a chair.

"They don't wash them very often," Ryan added, smiling to herself when a visible shiver raced down her partner's body.

"That would never…ever have occurred to me," she said, a look of complete distaste on her face.

"That's why you have me. I'm your tour guide to the seedy side of life."

Jamie scampered out of bed and started hastily tossing garments from her suitcase. She put on a turtleneck, a sweatshirt and a pair of sweatpants, then tossed Ryan one of her volleyball T-shirts, knowing that her partner wouldn't need nearly as much clothing as she would. As she got into bed, she looked at the bedspread with revulsion and said, "I'm not even going to sit on that thing to tie my shoes."

Ryan cuddled her up, deciding not to tell her that many motels didn't wash the blankets very often either.

Despite the clothing, and the vigorous rubbing from her partner, Jamie was still decidedly cold. "My God, my nipples are so hard they could break off." She ran her hands over her breasts vigorously.

"Let me help," Ryan said with a grin as she tried to slip her hands under her partner's shirts.

"Don't you dare touch me with those ice cubes masquerading as hands."

"But it's a great way to warm up."

"It can be a nice way to wake up—in the morning," Jamie insisted. "I'm too cold to even think about taking anything off, and I don't want to have sex fully clothed."

"Have you ever?" Ryan asked, snuggling even closer.

"No, I have not. I'm a respectable woman who likes to have sex in a nice, big bed, with a nice, nude body."

"It can also be fun to get really hot…so hot you can't bear to wait," Ryan murmured, her breath finally warming one of Jamie's ears. "Then you find a quiet place and start touching each other—through your clothes…then under your clothes," she added, in case Jamie missed her point.

"Well, I hate to be closed-minded. We can try that—in the morning," she reiterated, unwilling to budge on that point. "When your hands are nice and warm." She grasped one of Ryan's hands and kissed the frosty digits, tucking them into her armpits to warm them.

"Okay," Ryan muttered as she snuggled into her partner's now warm embrace. "You're the boss."

※

Jamie woke when the sun peeked through the window, and when she went to the bathroom she tucked the curtains closed so they wouldn't be disturbed. Few things gave her more pleasure than cuddling with Ryan in the morning, and since they had time, she knew their cuddling would soon be very, very fulfilling.

It was six-thirty, and Ryan was still sleeping soundly. Smiling at her lovely countenance, Jamie snuck back into bed and wrapped her arms around the sleeping woman. A small moan was Ryan's only reply, and as the warmth enveloped her, Jamie slid back into slumber, looking forward to the next time they woke.

The shrill ringing of the phone ripped Ryan from a delightful dream. She fumbled for the receiver and croaked out, "Yeah?"

"Ryan? Lynette," she said, brusquely. "Team breakfast is in ten minutes. Did you forget about it?"

"Huh?" she gasped. "I didn't know about it."

"Well, you'd better hustle. You won't play tonight if you're late."

"Shit. Shit. Shit." she cried as she leapt from bed and jumped into her warm-ups. Jamie saw her shoving her bare feet into her high-tops, and rushed to lend a hand.

She ran into the bathroom and handed Ryan a brush, but the

irritated woman stormed into the bath, grabbed a covered band from the counter and tied it haphazardly around a ponytail. Her Cal baseball cap was shoved onto her head, and she jogged for the door, mumbling profanities to herself the entire time.

"Well, that was fun," Jamie said to the empty room as she collapsed onto the bed.

⁂

Ryan was in the middle of a full-scale rant, and Jamie sat on the bed and let her vent. "Lynette assumed Coach Hayes had given me the rule book," Ryan complained, slapping the plastic-covered notebook against her hand. "Coach Hayes assumed Lynette had given it to me. I look like a loser for breaking practically every rule on my first road trip." She shook the book at Jamie as she paced in a tight pattern. "I have chemistry textbooks with less information in them than this. Is this a basketball team, or boot camp?"

"I know this is disappointing. This isn't turning out at all like you'd hoped, has it?"

"No." Some of the starch left her sails, and she flopped down on the bed. "Nothing has gone right so far. I'm afraid I made a big mistake here."

Biting her tongue, Jamie didn't say the obvious. She hadn't thought that joining the team was a good idea; she didn't think that playing for a jerk was a good idea; and she didn't think that it would be possible for Ryan and Janae to create a more harmonious atmosphere. But Ryan had made her decision, so she wasn't about to share her trepidation at this point. Deciding that it was best to offer some reassurance, she said, "Maybe you did, but you won't really know for a while. Try to learn the rules and go along with the flow."

"I don't wanna learn the rules," Ryan whined, throwing the book at the wall with a quick snap of her wrist.

"Wanna come back to bed? I could help relieve some stress."

"Can't." Ryan got up and shook her head. "We've got a team meeting—unscheduled of course—and then we have to leave to go to the gym for a walk-through. I won't be free until after the game."

Karma

"What about dinner?" Jamie asked, her eyes going round.

"I'll have to eat mine before the game. I think it's scheduled for four. You're on your own." She came over to the bed and squatted down so that she could look Jamie in the eye. "Do you regret coming with me?"

"Not in the least. I'm going to go over to the campus to study, and then I'll grab a snack and come to the game. Being able to sleep with you is enough for me. Really, honey."

"You're too good a sport. I think I need to take a lesson from you."

"You're not usually upset by things like this. It's a lot—all at once. You'll be fine."

"I hope you have enough confidence for both of us," Ryan said, bending to place a soft kiss on her partner's lips.

※

The weekend produced not one, but two humiliating defeats, the only bright spot being that now the team could try to make an earlier flight home on Sunday, since they didn't qualify to play in even the consolation game of the tournament. Ryan didn't play much in either game, racking up a grand total of two and three minutes respectively.

"Dinner?" Jamie asked when she greeted her outside the visitors' locker room.

"Love to. But I can't go anywhere very nice in my warm ups."

"Okay. Let's go back to the hotel and you can change. Should we take a cab?"

"No, let's take the team bus. Maybe we can get some people to have dinner with us."

When they got to the bus, Lynette was standing by the door, and she motioned Ryan aside. "I assume you didn't have time to study the book yet, Ryan, but no outsiders are allowed on the bus."

"Sorry, I didn't know, but that's okay. We'll grab a cab."

"Again, sorry to be the heavy, but Coach requires the team to travel together. You can meet Jamie back at the hotel."

Ryan looked at her carefully to make sure she was serious, but the grim set to her mouth clearly said that she was. "Okay," she muttered as she turned to tell Jamie the news.

After making sure Jamie could find a cab, she ran back and hopped on the bus, receiving a narrowed look from Coach Hayes. "We leave thirty minutes after the game. I think you'd better spend some time with Lynette this week going over the rules."

"Yeah, I think I'd better," she muttered on her way to an empty seat. Jamie went down to the lobby to inquire about local restaurants, finding that the hotel dining room was the only game in the neighborhood. Some time later her partner joined her. She smiled when she saw her, decked out in a marine blue, wool cable-knit sweater, an ecru colored turtleneck and a pair of winter-white wide-wale corduroys. But Ryan didn't return her smile as she marched across the lobby. "How old am I?" she demanded, her face flushed with anger.

"Uhm…I'm guessing this is rhetorical—but you're twenty-four."

"Right," she fumed. "Isn't a twenty-four year-old woman old enough to be treated like an adult?"

"Yes, of course you are. Are you gonna tell me what's wrong?"

"We got special permission to eat wherever we want to tonight. Usually we are forced…forced…to eat with the team."

"Well that sucks," Jamie agreed. "That's not going to make traveling with you much fun."

"No, and I got a lecture about that, too," she groused. "Turns out Coach Hayes had to make a point about you traveling with me—even though Lynette already had."

"Why would they deny permission, honey? I pay for myself… you're staying in my room."

"How do I know?" Ryan said, her voice much louder than normal. "I hate this."

"Calm down, Tiger," she soothed. "Let's have some dinner. You'll feel better when you've had a good meal."

"It's so stupid," she grumbled, still talking about the team meal. "They had some skanky-looking buffet set up in one of the meeting rooms. Everything looked greasy and cold. I can't gain healthy weight eating that kind of crap."

"Honey, calm down," Jamie said again. "You can go to the buffet, and snack on something that looks okay, and then go order a meal later. They allow you to do what you want after the team meal, don't they?"

"Yeah, I guess," she said, unwilling to be mollified.

Once in the dining room they were shown to a table. After they scanned the menu, Jamie said, "I thought you were going to see if anyone wanted to join us."

"I did. I got a bunch of blank looks and a few 'no thanks'. Janae looked like she wanted to come, but she doesn't have two nickels to rub together. She has to eat the damned buffet. That's probably why she's twenty pounds overweight," she groused.

"Maybe everyone was tired," Jamie offered, but her theory was blown when four of the players came down to the dining room together. One of them made eye contact with Jamie, and even though they did an immediate about-face, Ryan saw them and raised an eyebrow at her partner.

"You were saying?"

"They don't know you well enough to dislike you," Jamie offered, but quickly realized the thought hadn't come out right. "You know what I mean."

"Yeah, I do. I don't think it's me, actually. It's always hard to come onto a team late. They didn't get to know me during the long fall practice sessions."

"Does it bother you a lot?"

"Yeah," she admitted quietly. "That's what I loved so much about volleyball. We were such a tight group that it made even the practices fun. I don't get that same feeling at all with the basketball team. The practices seem like work—only work."

Once again, Jamie shot her a worried glance that Ryan caught. "I'm grouchy—probably because I'm not playing—and we lost two games. I'll feel better soon."

It was after seven when they finished dinner, but neither was ready to go up to their room. "Wanna go for a walk or something?" Ryan offered feebly.

"It's twenty-five degrees outside. And the only thing around here is the freeway."

"Good point. They really do a good job of isolating us, don't they?"

"Yes, they do. I took the bus to campus today, and we passed at least six motels that were significantly closer. They intentionally put you next to the freeway. I don't get it."

"I think they're afraid we'll get into trouble if we're too close to campus. One more example of treating us like kids."

"Let's go hang out in the bar," Jamie suggested. "They've probably got a basketball game on."

"Okay. Maybe we can pick up some women and have a party," Ryan grinned as she waggled an eyebrow.

"Your pick up technique had better be very rusty."

"Wanna try me?" Ryan asked in challenge, her eyes dancing for the first time that night.

"Uhm…sure. How?"

Ryan pursed her lips and thought for a minute. Finally, she crossed her arms and nodded confidently. "You know what I've always been curious about?"

"Nope."

"I've always wondered if you would have given me a tumble if you hadn't been engaged, and you were more aware of your attraction for women. What do you think?"

Jamie grinned up at her and patted her on the side. "I think your womanly charms would have convinced me to do something very uncharacteristic. You would have had me out of my knickers in a matter of days if I hadn't been trying to repress my urges."

"Days?" Ryan's mouth gaped open. "I was thinking hours."

"The nerve." Jamie huffed playfully at her cocky lover. "I'll have you know that I'm not that kind of girl, Ryan O'Flaherty. I admit that you would have compromised my virtue—but it would have taken you a while."

"Let's play a game," Ryan suggested, the gleam in her eyes suggesting the naughty nature of her proposal. "Let's act like we've never met. I'll try my rusty technique out on you, and see if it still works."

"I'm willing to give it a try. Only one problem. I can't be myself, or this won't work. If I put myself in the mindset I had when I met you, I'd never allow you to pick me up—no matter how attracted I was to you."

"Fine. Then be someone else. I know," Ryan suggested. "Be Mia."

Jamie tossed her head back and laughed. "No way, sport. You and Mia would be doing it in the elevator on the way to your room. No, if we're gonna play a game, it's got to be a contest. You've gotta work."

"Surprise me," Ryan said as she placed a kiss on her cheek. "I'll be myself, and you be anyone your heart desires. You go on in, and find an isolated place at the bar. I'll come in and sweep you off your feet in a matter of moments." Her wildly waggling eyebrow indicated how excited she was at the thought of playing this game.

"You're on, Tiger, but I'm not going to give in as easily as you might think. You're going to have to use all of your charm to get me to give it up."

"I'm up to the challenge."

"We'll see about that. Now, I'm really going to try to play a role, okay? Don't try to mess with my concentration. I'm a method actor, you know."

"Whatever works. Now go get ready to meet your Princess Charming."

Chapter Two

After waiting a respectable amount of time to allow Jamie to get into character, Ryan strode into the bar in her inimitable, confident style. Regrettably, the first faces she recognized were Wendy and Janet. Trying to be the bigger person, she walked up to them and said, "Hi, guys. What's going on?"

"Nothing," Janet said abruptly. "Your friend's over there," she added, twitching her head dismissively in Jamie's direction.

"I knew that. I was trying to be friendly."

"Sure. Whatever," Janet said, turning back to face the bar—rudely dismissing Ryan.

Gathering her wits and deciding to let the insult go, Ryan focused on the game once again. She adopted a casual, relaxed pose as she glanced around the relatively empty bar for a moment. There were about two dozen stools at the long bar, but only eight were occupied. One lone businessman sat at the far right end of the bar watching the Denver Nuggets on television. Two men in flannel shirts and jeans sat a few stools from him, and another pair sat right in the middle of the bar. Wendy and Janet got up and left, much to Ryan's pleasure, leaving only one attractive young woman sitting alone at the far end.

Taking in a breath, Ryan tried to act as she would have over a year ago, doing her best to erase the image of her partner, and see her as she would have then.

Hmm, nice, she said to herself, nodding slightly. As Ryan spent a minute taking her in, the blonde turned around on her stool, as if looking for someone. Ryan noted the attractive cream-colored cashmere sweater set and the black corduroy slacks. *Mmm, nice dresser.* Making a decision to see what could happen, she walked over and pulled out a stool one away from hers.

"Hi," she said casually, trying to get a read on how aggressive she should be.

"Uhm…hi," the woman answered absently as she furrowed her brow a tiny bit and looked over Ryan's shoulder, obviously waiting for someone.

"You don't mind if I sit here, do you?"

"No, I uhm…guess not," she answered, casting another look around.

"It can be so intimidating to come into a place like this alone. Guys think they can immediately hit on you." Ryan shook her head in distaste, then shot the woman a smile.

She returned the smile and focused on Ryan. "Actually, it's nice to have someone to talk to. I was waiting for a date who looks like he's not going to show, and I've had to turn two guys away already." She let out a gentle laugh that rumbled rather low in her chest. There was something very attractive about the laugh, and Ryan decided she would see what her story was.

"I'm Ryan," she said as she stuck out her hand.

"Jamie."

"Good to meet you. Are you a local, or passing through like I am?"

"Local. Well, local during the school year," she amended.

"Oh, you go to Colorado State?"

"Yeah. I'm a senior this year."

"Oh, me too. Well, I'm a senior also, but not at CSU. I go to Cal."

"Ooo, UCLA, how cool."

"No, no. That's a bit of an insult," she chided her gently. "UCLA is in Los Angeles. Cal is in Berkeley, across the bay from San Francisco."

"Oh, wow," Jamie said ingenuously. "I've never been to San Francisco. Is it really as nice as they say it is?"

Ryan leaned back on her stool and gazed at her partner for a moment. She didn't know how Jamie managed it, but she gave off every indication that she'd never seen Ryan in her life, and had no more interest in her than she had in the bartender. Taking in a breath, she decided to make a small move. "San Francisco is nicer than they say it is," she replied as she slid over to the stool right next to Jamie. "Definitely nicer." She waited a beat and asked, "Who were you waiting for tonight?"

"A blind date." Shaking her head, she said, "I should know better by now. They never work out."

Ryan looked over at a nearly empty glass and offered, "Let me buy you another drink to cheer you up a little. I've had more bad first dates than I can count, so you have my complete sympathies." Before Jamie could even form a word, Ryan had signaled the bartender. "What would you like?" she asked as she locked eyes and gave her a dazzling grin.

"A white wine spritzer," she said slowly, still giving Ryan a puzzled look.

"Great. Two white wine spritzers," she instructed the bartender.

As the bartender walked away, Jamie glanced over at her companion and asked, "What are you in Ft. Collins for anyway? Not much here but the university."

"I'm here to play basketball. We're in a tournament."

"You're on the women's basketball team?"

"I couldn't make the men's," Ryan replied with another dazzling smile. Lowering her voice, she added, "I tried."

"Wow, I've never known anyone who played a sport in college," she said with obvious interest.

"Then I should introduce myself to you again," Ryan said, her smile growing. "I just finished the volleyball season."

"Really? Two sports?"

"Yeah. I really like to compete."

"Gosh, you must be very talented to play two sports for a big school like the University of California. It is a big school isn't it?" she asked suspiciously.

"Pretty big. About thirty thousand students."

"And with all of those students, they have to keep dipping into the same tiny talent pool?" A teasing smirk was firmly in place.

"Yeah, if I didn't play they were going to have to grab the first woman they saw who was over five foot seven."

Jamie tossed her head back and laughed in a thoroughly delightful manner. "You're really funny."

"Thank you. Many people don't get my sense of humor. It's kind of an acquired taste."

"So, where are all of your teammates tonight?"

"I get tired of them after a while. We've been here since Thursday evening, and not to insult your town, but there isn't a lot to do around here. So, I'm looking for someone new to talk to."

"Well, I'm about as new as you can get."

"Yep. I lucked out tonight. You're not only talkative, you're interesting too."

"Thanks," she said, smiling tentatively. "You're pretty interesting to talk to also." She cocked her head slightly, and looked at Ryan for a minute. "I was confused when you sat down next to me and offered to buy me a drink. That's never happened to me before."

Ryan dipped her head to take a sip of her drink, flashing Jamie a bright smile. Her bangs nearly covered her eyes, and she peered through them with an impish look—while managing not to comment on Jamie's statement.

"So, ahh…when do you go back?" Jamie asked, forgetting that she had been waiting for Ryan's reaction to her comment.

"We're leaving in the morning. The trip will waste the whole day, and we've got finals starting on Monday."

"Eeew, don't remind me. I've got two on Monday."

Ryan leaned close—close enough for Jamie to take in the sweet, clean scent of her recently-showered body. "So, you were going out to let off a steam before finals, huh?" she asked in a conspiratorial manner.

"I guess. I don't know. Sometimes it seems like there isn't a decent guy in all of Colorado. I keep trying, but it's getting to be depressing."

"Oh, come on, I can't imagine a woman like you has too much trouble finding dates."

"Hrumpf," she grumbled. "Dates I can get, but it's rare that I want a second. Either they're juvenile frat boys, or trying to score without too much trouble."

"That must be hard," Ryan said sympathetically as she leveled her gaze, and locked her eyes onto Jamie's.

"Oh, I don't really have anything to complain about," she said lightly. "Tell me about yourself. Are you seeing anyone?"

"No one exclusively. I'm not ready to settle down yet. I want to be out of grad school before I get serious."

"Are you going to law school like everyone else in the world?"

"No. I have no interest in that. My major's biology, but I'm considering programs in math, biology, chemistry and possibly medical school."

"Wow, those are subjects I've steered away from as much as possible. I'm an English major."

"What area?" Ryan asked, looking very interested.

"English literature. I've focused on the Victorian period."

"I don't have much knowledge of your subject, but I admire people who can manipulate the language. I bet it's fascinating to study a certain time period like that intensively."

"Yeah, it really is. I love my subject, but I don't know what I'll do with it."

"Does that really matter? Isn't it more important to do what you love? I've always found that sticking with what interests me works out best in the long run."

"I like your perspective, Ryan," she said, giving her another smile. "Hey, your drink's about gone. Let me buy you another." Her nose wrinkled as she said, "I've never bought a woman a drink before."

"Okay. I'd like that. You're a lot more entertaining than television."

"Really?" she asked, tilting her chin. "You'd better check your listings before you make a claim like that. You might even have HBO." Her green eyes were twinkling, and Ryan felt herself being drawn into this very attractive woman's aura.

"I'm absolutely certain," Ryan said softly as she leaned in a little, lightly brushing her shoulder against Jamie's. The light was dim, but she was pretty sure she saw a delicate shiver crawl up her neck. *Gotcha*, she mused happily as she leaned back into her own air space. *Now I just have to reel you in.*

After another half hour of pleasant conversation and two more spritzers, Jamie took a deep breath and said, "I guess I'd better get going."

"It's still early." Ryan glanced at her watch. "Only eight-thirty."

"Yeah, but I'm getting a buzz on, and I won't drive if I'm impaired."

"How many have you had?"

"Umm, I guess I've had four. I hope I'm okay to drive." She had a worried frown on her face, and Ryan saw her opening.

"That's nothing to play with. If there's any doubt in your mind, you should wait for a while. I know, let's go walk around the block a few times. That might give you a good indication of how sober you are."

"There aren't any blocks around here," she laughed. "The best we could do is a few laps around the parking lot."

"I'd gladly walk around the parking lot to make sure you were safe," she said as she leveled her gaze to stare right into those sea green eyes.

Jamie had a hard time making her mouth work, but she finally got out, "I really think I'll be okay. I don't want to put you out."

"Do you need to be home for anything special?"

"No, not really."

"Do you normally stay up past eight-thirty?"

"Yeah, I'm kind of a night owl."

"Then let's go up to my room, and watch that riveting HBO for a while," Ryan suggested calmly, as if it were the obvious solution.

"Oh, I don't know…"

"Jamie, it's eight-thirty on a Saturday night. There's nowhere to go around here, and we can't sit here for another hour without ordering more drinks. You won't go play outside, so why not go upstairs and waste a couple of hours? I swear I'd never forgive myself if you got into an accident on the way home."

"You wouldn't know," she said softly, stating the obvious.

"Well, that clinches it. I'm not going to stay up worrying about you all night. Either I drive you home, and take a cab back, or we hang out until I'm sure you're sober." Ryan was using the full force of her personality, and after a beat, the blonde head started to nod.

"Well, okay, I guess it would be all right." She gave Ryan a lopsided grin as she confided, "I don't normally go to strange people's hotel rooms."

"Well, that's where you're in luck," Ryan said, guiding Jamie out of the bar, her hand on the small of her back. "I've been called many things, but strange isn't one of them."

※

As they walked down the long corridor to her room, Ryan noticed that Jamie was walking unsteadily. *I've got to remember that a couple of drinks really does affect her.* When she opened the door, Jamie looked around at the suitcases neatly laid out on the luggage racks. "Nice room," she said idly. "I've never been up here before." As she walked by the open shelving near the bath she spotted the navy blue Cal warm ups. "You really are on the basketball team," she said with a giggle.

"I never lie." Ryan walked over to her suitcase and found the T-shirt that she had slept in the night before. "Further proof," she said triumphantly as she held it up to show the "Cal Volleyball" printed on the breast.

"You came prepared," Jamie said warmly.

"Yep. I'm glad I'm not a gymnast, though. You'd expect me to have a set of parallel bars in my suitcase."

"You really are funny," Jamie repeated as she sat down on one of the vinyl, barrel-style chairs, next to the small wooden table that was bolted to the floor.

"Thanks. So would you really like to watch TV, or talk some more?"

"Let's do both," she suggested as Ryan handed her the remote. "What programs do you like to watch?"

"I don't watch TV much. I don't even have one in my room."

"What do you do for fun?"

"Well, my sports do take up a lot of time, and my classes are pretty time consuming, but when I do have free time, I tend to play with my computer. It's not a lot more interactive than TV, but I feel like I'm more in charge of the programming."

Jamie looked up and noticed the laptop sitting on the bed and she asked, "Would you rather we played on your computer than watched television?"

Ryan looked at her and then looked at the computer. "Yeah, I would," she decided. She climbed onto the bed and booted up the machine, humming a tune the whole while. When it was up, she asked, "Internet?"

"Sure. You can show me some of your favorite sites."

"They don't have Wi-Fi and the cable isn't long enough to reach the table. Do you mind coming over here?"

"No, that's fine."

Ryan got up as Jamie sat tentatively on the edge of the bed. "Be right back," she said as she went into the bath. "Feel free to browse."

She returned a few minutes later to find Jamie sitting in a chair next to the table. Her face was clouded with what Ryan could only guess was suspicion or maybe even anger. "What's wrong?" she asked, siting on the edge of the bed right next to Jamie.

"I...I feel like you tricked me," she muttered softly. "I feel stupid."

"What? How did I trick you?"

Jamie shook her head and got to her feet, looking like she was about to cry. "I thought you were really concerned about me. It didn't cross my mind that you were trying to sleep with me."

She started to walk to the door, but Ryan dashed right in front of her. She didn't touch her, but she got in front of the door to prevent her from opening it. "I don't know what made you say that, but I think you owe me an explanation. An apology would be nice, while you're at it."

"I owe you an explanation? That's a laugh. How about an explanation from you? You're the one who has something to apologize for."

"I still don't know what in the hell you're talking about," Ryan said, voice rising. "Will you at least tell me what has you so upset?"

"You're obviously a lesbian," she said in an accusatory tone. "Every other site on your favorites page was gay this or lesbian that."

Ryan gaped at her for a moment, shocked at not only the statement, but also the implication. "And being gay means not only that I want to sleep with you," she said slowly, "it also means that I'd have to trick you into it?"

"Well, don't you?" she demanded with her face still flushed with anger.

"I've slept with a lot of women in my life, and if I tricked you into it, you'd be the first," she said curtly. "Even lesbians are concerned about drunk driving, you know." A look of pained hurt crossed her features, and she backed away from the door as she added, "I don't know what your image of lesbians is, but I'm not a rapist. I suggest waiting to drive until you're sober, but if you want to leave, be my guest."

Jamie picked up her purse and stalked out of the room, closing the door firmly behind her.

Ryan leaned against the door for a moment, her heart racing, actually feeling deeply hurt. *How in the hell did this turn out to be so realistic?* In her heart, she knew it was ridiculous to be upset about having been accused of wanting to sleep with the woman—since that was the whole point of the game. Shaking her head, she went into her closet, removed her sweater and turtleneck, and folded them neatly. *Jamie's so good at this that she really hit me in a vulnerable spot.* After removing her bra, she put on her volleyball T-shirt and shucked her slacks. She was hanging them up when she heard a very quiet knock on the door. "Yes?" she called out.

"Uhm…it's Jamie." Her voice was so soft that Ryan had a hard time picking it up. "Can I talk to you?"

Ryan opened the door a crack and said, "I've got my pajamas on. I can't guarantee that won't exacerbate my rapist tendencies."

Jamie's voice gained volume, and she said, "Look, I'm sorry I overreacted. I want to apologize to you. If you want me to do that from the hall, I will."

Relenting, Ryan opened the door and allowed her to enter. Jamie cast a quick glance down to see what her companion was wearing, and was pleased to see that the big T-shirt went a third of the way down her thighs. "I'm getting into bed," Ryan stated decisively. "It's too cold to be standing around in my underwear." She marched over to the bed and pulled the covers back, then slid in and settled the laptop on her legs. "You were saying?" she asked, looking up at Jamie impassively.

"I wanted to apologize. It was unfair to assume you wanted to sleep with me because you're gay. I'm also sorry that I stormed out, but I wanted to make sure I really could leave if I wanted to."

"Obviously you don't know me at all," Ryan said, "but I meant it when I said I don't lie. I wanted to be sure you were sober before you left."

Jamie sat down on the second bed and looked at Ryan carefully, swallowing before she asked, "Can you honestly say that sleeping with me didn't cross your mind?"

Ryan shifted slightly, then took a deep breath and said, "To be completely honest, I approached you because I thought you were really attractive." A blonde eyebrow rose, and Ryan continued her explanation. "It's kinda hard for lesbians. I mean, if a guy sees a good-looking woman, the odds are that she's straight. It's not that easy for me, though. It's hard to tell if women are gay or not until you spend time with them. After being with you for a while, it was pretty clear to me that you were straight. But I really did like talking to you, and I was lonely, so I thought it would be fun to hang out. I suggested you come up here to make sure you didn't harm yourself or anyone else with your driving—not to try to seduce you. But if you want to throw yourself at me, I promise I won't scream," she added soberly.

Jamie graced her with her gentle laugh and said, "You are such a tease. But thank you for forgiving me."

"Your reaction really surprised me. Don't you know any other lesbians?"

"No, well, none that I know of. Maybe it's the people I hang out with, but we're a pretty straight bunch."

"Want an education?" Ryan asked, a tiny hint of a dare in her tone.

"Ahh...what do you have in mind?" She backed towards the door once again.

"Let me show you some of the sites I monitor. The wonderful world of lesbianism is really pretty interesting, and you sound like you could use some honest information about my people."

Jamie hesitated for a long while, gazing at Ryan until she convinced herself to take a leap of faith and trust her. "Okay," she said gamely, climbing onto the bed.

By nine-thirty Jamie was wearing Ryan's basketball sweatshirt and a tremendously large pair of sweatpants. She was under the covers, but they weren't touching in any way—mostly because Ryan was being hypersensitive about their personal space. Jamie had been peppering her new friend with questions about lesbian life for the better part of a half hour, and to Ryan's experienced eye, she was no longer tipsy.

Over the course of their conversation, Ryan briefly told her of her first experience with Sara; she told her how it felt to be gay at a young age; she explained that she had never been with a man; and she told her about her current dating practices. After all of the questions being hurled her way, she decided it was time to probe the stranger's psyche for a bit.

"You now know everything about me but my hat size. But I'm the only one answering questions. Tell me about your love life."

"There's not much to tell," she admitted. "I've dated a lot of guys, but I've never gotten serious about any of them."

"You've never had a steady boyfriend?" When Jamie shook her head, she persisted, "That seems funny to me. I'd think that guys would absolutely love you."

"Why do you say that?" she asked, unable to suppress a delighted smile.

Ryan felt her stomach flip at the shy grin, and she recognized the early-warning signs her libido was sending out. "I've got three older brothers and a dozen older cousins, and I guarantee every one of them would flip for you. You're the kind of girl they like. Besides being very attractive, you're smart, and witty, and you look like you can take a lot of teasing. You're not one of those real 'girly' girls."

"I'm not girly?" she asked with an even bigger smile.

"You don't look like you'd be real high maintenance," she amended. "You look like you'd be a lot of fun."

Jamie looked thoughtful for a moment. "Men are pretty interested in me, but I haven't ever felt the spark for any one guy. I know I'm picky, but sometimes I wonder what the problem is."

Ryan turned her entire torso so that they were face to face. She didn't say a word, looked deeply into Jamie's eyes—holding her gaze for endless moments. Her eyes slid from the sea-green orbs flecked with specks of gold, to the perfectly arched brows that framed them so attractively. Sliding down, her eyes landed on the cupid's-bow mouth, the moist coral lips begging to be kissed. She wasn't sure this was the time to make her move, but her heart was starting to beat loudly in her chest, and she could feel the first signs of arousal start to thrum in her body. From long experience, she knew that when she felt this way, the object of her attentions was usually traveling right along with her.

When her eyes flicked back to Jamie's, she saw the dilated pupils and noticed a slight flaring of her nostrils. *Oh yeah…you're ready.* Her voice was smooth, and warm, and so matter-of-fact that the question she posed seemed entirely natural. "Have you ever thought you might be gay?"

The pupils dilated even more, this time with alarm. "No, I don't think so," she said quickly, biting her lower lip nervously. "Uhm… I've asked myself that question a few times, but it doesn't seem like that's it." She looked away briefly, seemingly gathering her courage. After a few slow blinks of those mesmerizing eyes, she looked back to find Ryan's deep blue gaze still locked upon her face. Her eyes lowered under the penetrating regard, and she heard herself speak the secret that she had never revealed to another soul. "Uhm…I have had some fantasies about women, though."

Ryan's voice dropped to its lowest register. "Fantasies? Do you want to talk about them?"

Jamie looked away again as she began to blush. "I…I've never told anyone about them," she said very softly. Her hesitant gaze met Ryan's briefly, and she whispered, "Do you really want to hear them?"

"If you want to tell me."

"I think I do," she began, but she seemed unable to get started, her voice quavering as she stammered helplessly. "I…I…uhm…"

Ryan tried to ease her way as much as she could. "I remember what it was like when I had my first attractions to girls. Want me to tell you what it was like for me?"

"Yes," Jamie agreed, her relief obvious.

"I used to fantasize about the feel of a woman's lips." Ryan sighed, rolling onto her back. "I'd never kissed anyone romantically, but somehow I knew it would be wonderful. It was," she said, a fond smile forming on her mouth.

"I think about that, too."

"The softness, the resiliency, the way you melt together," Ryan dreamily mused. "It's wonderful."

"It sounds like it," Jamie sighed as she flopped onto her back as well and stared up at the ceiling.

"Have you ever wondered what it would be like to have a woman touch you?" Ryan asked quietly, after allowing her friend some time to let her imagination transport her.

Jamie's reply was a very small nod.

"That's wonderful, too. I've never been with a man, so this is a guess, but I'd assume that they're usually pretty forceful and determined in bed—especially if you don't know them very well."

"Well, I don't have much experience either. I'm sure that many guys are great lovers—but I haven't met them yet. The guys I've played around with have been all about getting me into bed as quickly as possible. Not very romantic."

"Some women are like that, too. But that hasn't been the norm for me. Most of the women I've been with are foreplay junkies." She chuckled. "That's my favorite kind of obsession."

"I can imagine."

Her eyes were closed, and Ryan knew she was imagining it right at that moment, so she decided to add a few images to her fantasy. "I love it when a woman undresses me slowly, letting me see how much she wants me. Then, when we're both naked, I love to have her touch me from head to toe—first with her hands—then with her mouth."

Jamie let out a soft, strangled cry, and Ryan urged, "It's okay. You can trust me. Tell me what you dream about."

Jamie stared up at the ceiling for a few moments, then gathered her courage and said, "I don't do it very often," she warned, "but once in a while when I'm with a guy, I kind of…replace him…with a woman. Like if he's kissing me, and his beard starts to irritate my face, or if he kisses too forcefully, I let my mind wander, and imagine what it would feel like to have someone soft and smooth take his place."

"Do you only think about being kissed, or do you do more than that?" Ryan asked, rolling onto her side to rest her head on her braced hand.

Karma

As Jamie considered the question, she unconsciously imitated the posture. When she was ready to reply, they were facing each other, with about a foot of distance between them. "I think about other things too." Her gaze traveled everywhere but Ryan's eyes. She was unable to continue, and Ryan didn't push her.

"Having those thoughts is no big deal. I bet nearly everyone would fantasize a bit if they didn't try to fit into a rigid box that defines their sexuality."

"I like being in a box," Jamie gulped. "I like having a label for how I feel—and I don't want that label to read 'lesbian'."

Ryan nodded thoughtfully. She tilted her head and asked, "Would you consider yourself a lesbian if you dipped a toe into the pool? You know…to see if you had any interest."

"Well, uhm…no, I wouldn't," she decided. "I've tried to think of a way I could do that, to tell you the truth. But it always felt like it'd be too complicated. I don't know any lesbians, and that's not the kind of thing you ask your straight friends to do with you." She laughed wryly. "I'm also afraid of the repercussions if I experimented with someone I knew. I mean, what if she liked it more than I did, or vice versa, you know?"

"I understand completely," Ryan said solemnly. "The perfect opportunity has never come up."

"Yeah, I guess that's it."

Ryan's face broke into an amused grin as she postulated, "I guess the perfect opportunity would be with a stranger, probably in a place where no one knew you, ideally with someone from out of town, and with someone who wouldn't expect anything from you in the future." She shook her head slowly as she leaned in a bit. "That's a very tough order to fill. You might never get the chance." At the end of the sentence, she raised one eyebrow in challenge, maintaining her calm, open gaze.

Jamie slowly leaned in at a similar cant. The bedclothes rustled gently as she moved, and a single spring creaked. Her voice was thin and tremulous, but she gathered up her courage and asked, "If I ever found the right opportunity, what should I do?"

As Ryan's voice dropped even lower, she continued to move towards the center of the bed. Her eyes were half closed as she stared right at Jamie's lips. "I think you should make your dreams come true."

"But I don't know what to do," Jamie whispered. Her eyes closed, and she took in a breath to try to calm her racing heart.

"I'd love to help you fulfill your fantasies," Ryan murmured gently. "But I don't want to frighten you, or talk you into doing anything that you're not comfortable with. Tell me what you want."

"I want to kiss you." The words were out before she could pull them back in. Jamie was shaking from anticipation, and Ryan could feel the nervous energy rolling off her body.

"I want that, too," Ryan said, her voice confident and warm. "You have the most amazing lips. So soft and full. They're about the most kissable lips I've ever seen."

Jamie smiled at her serene expression and scooted over until their breasts touched lightly. Ryan was still on her side, but she had dropped her head onto the pillow, waiting for Jamie to reach for her. Her eyes were closed, but her lips were parted enough to cause them to look moist and warm and inviting. As Jamie hovered over her, she slid her hand into Ryan's dark hair, and lowered her mouth until their lips were micrometers apart. She could feel her own heart thudding in her chest, as she closed the remaining gap and lightly brushed her lips against Ryan's. "Ooo…nice," she murmured as she went back for another slightly longer caress.

"Mmm-hmm," Ryan agreed as she rolled over onto her back and sighed deeply.

"Does this feel good to you?" Jamie asked softly, her confidence building. She shifted to lean over and lightly nibble on Ryan's bottom lip.

"Very, very good," Ryan whispered. "But I've been kissed by more women than I can count. The important question is: how does it feel to you?" Her hands were softly stroking Jamie's back as she looked up into those warm, green eyes.

"It feels very nice. But in my fantasies I was being kissed. Can you…help me out?" She was still lying very close, and Ryan could feel her breath when she spoke.

"I'll do anything you ask me to do. Just tell me what you want."

"I want you to kiss me," she asked softly, leaning in even closer.

With an amazingly quick and powerful move, Jamie was suddenly lying on her back, one long, muscular woman braced over her body—clear blue eyes gazing right into her soul. Ryan dipped her head and covered Jamie's soft, warm lips with her own, pressing insistently until the lips began to yield. The tiny groan that escaped her mouth was echoed by her partner as they parted. "Like you imagined?" she asked in a volume just above a whisper.

"Exactly." Jamie breathed, her eyes still closed. Her mouth quirked into a grin, and a bit of the real Jamie peeked out. "But in my fantasy there are many kisses, and they're never interrupted by a question and answer period."

Ryan chuckled as she brought her hand up and lightly tweaked her partner's nose. "Now who's the tease?" But as her hand passed by her visitor's face, she stroked Jamie's cheek with the tips of her fingers and reminded her. "I said I'd do anything you asked. I meant that. But if you don't ask for it, I won't do it."

"Then let me be more clear," she whispered. "Kiss me again."

With a confident smile, Ryan leaned over and lowered her mouth. She started to nibble, barely touching the coral-tinted lips, smiling to herself as Jamie sought to increase the contact.

"Like that?"

"More," Jamie begged, her eyes still tightly closed.

"How many more?"

"I want you to kiss me senseless." She pulled Ryan against her, her mouth opening slightly as her eyes closed in anticipation of the assault.

Ryan came in close and whispered, "I'm gonna kiss you 'til your eyes cross." The smirk that curled up on the corners of Jamie's mouth lasted only a minute until it was replaced by Ryan's smooth lips covering every inch.

The kisses varied in duration and intensity, and they were accompanied by ever more frenzied sounds that came from deep within Jamie's chest. Ryan had obviously kissed many women, and she had certainly learned a great deal from her varied experiences. She had an unerring ability to slowly increase the passion of her attack until Jamie was nearly faint with arousal, but when she was sure she couldn't take another moment of the sensual embrace, Ryan would back off and slowly lower the heat.

During these lighter moments, she would kiss down Jamie's jaw line, lightly flicking her pulse point with her tongue. After Ryan was sure that Jamie was able to breathe again, she would dive right back in, and whip her into another frenzy.

After the third cycle, she waited until Ryan was working on the hollow between her collar bones to gasp out, "I can't take much more. You've got to touch me."

"You know the rules," she hummed against the soft skin as she licked a wet path back up to a very sensitive pink ear. "You ask—you get."

"Oh God." Jamie moaned pathetically. "I don't know what I want you to do."

"Sure you do," Ryan purred. "It's no different than being with a man. You have certain parts of your body that you like to have touched…and kissed…and fondled. Give me direction and I'll get right on it."

"But I…I've never asked for what I want," she groaned. "This is hard."

"No rush," Ryan said easily as she started to kiss her again. "If you think of something, shout it out."

After another five minutes of incendiary kisses, Jamie yanked her head away forcefully and moaned, "My breasts. God, please touch my breasts."

"Love to," Ryan purred as her hand slid up under the enormous sweatshirt. Jamie's bra was still in place, so Ryan ran her short fingernails over the aching nipples—teasing them through the silky fabric.

"Touch my skin," She implored after a few moments of the torture.

"Do you want me to undress you?"

"God, yes." she cried as she thrust her hips against the air.

Ryan smiled down at her as she helped her into a sitting position, then gently removed her sweatshirt and slipped the bra off her shoulders without Jamie even knowing it had been unhooked. Her head dropped until it was less than an inch from the deep mauve tip of Jamie's right nipple. But instead of taking it into her mouth, she used her hands to once again tease and torture the incredibly sensitive mound. Jamie could feel the warm breath glide across her responsive nipple, but Ryan made no move to touch it with her mouth.

After enduring more torture than she thought possible, Jamie finally begged shamelessly, "Please, Ryan, please kiss my breasts."

Immediately the dark head closed the distance and began to plant light kisses all over every inch of flesh. Those tender, teasing kisses only made her need grow and before she even knew what she was doing, she roughly grabbed Ryan's head and forcibly pushed it onto her throbbing breast. "Suck me," she growled deep in her throat, as Ryan began to feed hungrily on the hot flesh. Ryan's hands and her mouth worked as one to excite her partner until she thought Jamie would explode from sensation. "Harder," Jamie urged, pushing against her tormentor's wide-open mouth. "Bite my nipples. Oh, God. Yes. Yes."

As Ryan's teeth found the throbbing nipples again and again, Jamie's legs spread wide and she shifted her body until one of Ryan's thighs was right between her legs. Her hips were never still as she rubbed against her partner furiously, still holding the voracious mouth to her breast with both hands.

When the suckling became overpowering, she pushed Ryan's mouth away so abruptly that a loud pop broke the silence as the suction was severed. Finally at the end of her rope, Jamie grasped Ryan by the face and stared at her with a gaze so heated it could smelt iron. "Make me come. Make me come now."

"You're the boss," Ryan smirked as she slid down the lithe body, maintaining eye contact the whole while. Jamie's remaining clothing was removed so effortlessly that she assumed Ryan had accomplished the feat by telepathy, but seconds after she issued her demand, her legs were spread wide with Ryan's dark head moving slowly as she greedily consumed her.

Ryan barely had time to enter her before her partner screamed out her release, thrilling Ryan to the core, the rough moans continuing unabated. Jamie maintained her vise-like grip on Ryan's head as the spasms continued to thrum through her body, her fingers never relaxing. Her breathing was starting to calm, but after working so hard, she had no desire to abandon her pleasure so quickly. "Stay with me," she urged gently. Meeting Ryan's eyes, she smiled and said, "You're good at this."

"Well, I don't like to brag…"

"Enough chitchat. Back to work." Jamie grasped Ryan's hand and slid it between her legs. "Gently…" she urged, gazing up into Ryan's love-filled expression. Her fantasy over, she lay back and let the love and devotion she saw there fill her soul. As many times as they had made love, she had never failed to be completely charmed by the deep pleasure that she could see in Ryan's eyes as she brought her to orgasm. Jamie knew that her lover got nearly as much satisfaction from the experience as she did, and she tried to hold her gaze to share the sensation as long as she could. Their eyes locked together, Ryan touched her with a whisper-soft pressure, searching her face for the first signs of climax. She didn't have to wait long. Unable to keep her eyes open, Jamie moaned out another debilitating orgasm, and lay limply in Ryan's arms.

"Damn, you're good," Jamie mumbled. "What was your name again, honey?"

"Princess Charming." Ryan said, gloating. "And I've still got it, ba-bee."

The warm water beat down on the two women, their embrace protecting Jamie from the sharp spray. Her voice was muffled by a good deal of warm, wet flesh, but Ryan could easily understand her. "Did you enjoy yourself last night?"

"Oh, yeah," Ryan growled, her voice low and rough. "We're gonna have to do that more often."

"I think the thrill will wear off over time, but I'll give it another whirl sometime. Heck, you turned me on so much I might have gone with you if I was acting like myself from a year ago. Maybe I didn't need to be in character at all."

"Aww, you're trying to butter me up. It's working, by the way." She dipped her head to make eye contact. "I was positively blown away by how realistic the whole thing was. I was really angry when you accused me of trying to jump you."

"And I was really hurt," Jamie chuckled. "I guess that part of my personality is easily accessible, huh? I really felt like myself—in a different locale and a different timeline."

"I love you in any timeline. I could fall for Colorado Jamie in a snap. Although in reality I wouldn't have slept with you last night."

"What?" Jamie's face turned up so quickly that she got a mouth full of warm water. Spluttering, she repeated, "What?"

"I wouldn't have. You were sending off all sorts of 'I'm afraid I'm a lesbian' signals. I never slept with women who did that. I only slept with the 'I'm mostly straight, but I'll try anyone once' types."

"Well, if we play the game again, I guess I'll have to act like Mia."

"We can buy you some different wigs to alter your look. I'd like to see if I can snare you under a variety of situations."

"Face it, Tiger, I'd fall for you in any situation possible. But, speaking of falling, I was surprised that you feel asleep so quickly. Weren't you frustrated?"

"Huh-uh. I was in my old way of thinking. My goal was to give women pleasure. That's how I got my pleasure. When you let me start to taste you, I was fully satisfied."

"That's so odd. You never do that now."

"I know, honey. We have a partnership—a mutually satisfying partnership. That's not what I used to strive for…but I'm glad I've got it now."

"Me too. You deserve to receive pleasure." She slid her hands down and cupped two firm, slippery cheeks. "Can I interest you in some now?"

Ryan lifted her arm, and cast a quick glance at her watch. "Team breakfast at eight. Then we leave for the airport. Business before pleasure, babe."

"Lord! Who says athletes have all the fun?"

Chapter Three

It was nearly five when they returned home to Berkeley that night, and Ryan began to unleash her frustrations as soon as they entered the house. "I'm not saying I'm better than the starting forwards, but when you're getting your asses kicked, it's time to try a different substitution pattern. How does the coach know I can't help if she won't give me a try?"

Jamie waited a second to make sure Ryan was finished. "Maybe you should speak to her."

"Coaches hate it when you take up their time to whine about playing time. I have to make the most out of my three fucking minutes."

Jamie came up and slid her arms around her grouchy partner's waist. "This has never happened to you before, has it?"

"What?"

"That you don't get to play much."

Ryan lifted her head as she considered the question. "I guess it hasn't, now that you mention it. But this is what happens—the competition gets stiffer as you go up in class."

"Do you really think the other forwards are more talented than you are?"

"Uhm, I can't really say. That's Coach Hayes' call. They're obviously doing what she wants, or she'd give me more of a chance."

"Well, I still think you should talk to her. At least let her know that you want to contribute more."

"We'll see," she said absently as she looked at the list of phone messages scribbled in Mia's nearly indecipherable hand. "Does this say Rich Placer or Mick Jagger?"

"Do you know Mick Jagger?" Jamie chuckled.

"How can I know him if he won't call?" Ryan conceded absently as she carried her bag up the stairs.

They were both too tired to cook, so Ryan offered to go pick up a pizza from Zachary's, leaving Jamie to unpack while she was gone. When she pulled into the driveway, she was surprised to see Catherine's Mercedes.

"Hi there," Ryan said as her mother-in-law rose to greet her. "This is a nice surprise." Ryan's eyes darted from Catherine to Jamie, and she knew immediately that something was very, very wrong.

A second, longer look revealed that Catherine was obviously upset, and had been crying. Ryan opened her arms and Catherine nestled into her embrace, leaning against her heavily while Ryan's eyes frantically searched Jamie's face—seeing the same desolate sadness that filled her mother's eyes.

Catherine lifted her head and said, "I've had Jim served with papers, and I'm going to file for divorce."

Jamie looked over at her partner with an ineffably wounded look, hearing the news for the second time not making it any more palatable.

"But I thought…" Ryan started to say, but Catherine shook her head.

"I thought so, too, dear, but things haven't worked out like I had hoped." She pursed her lips while shaking her head a little, looking like she was arguing with herself. "I wouldn't normally tell you details like this, but it won't make any sense if I don't." She lifted her head and squared her shoulders, saying, "I was watching the congressional session on C-SPAN on Wednesday and saw the woman Jim has been having the affair with. She's still with him," she added in clarification, her lower lip quivering.

"Are you sure, Mom?" Jamie asked, her tone bordering on frantic. "Maybe there's a reasonable explanation…"

"I spoke with your father, honey. He claims they're no longer involved, but I can't let myself believe that. He might be telling the truth, but I don't trust him enough to believe him."

"But what if he is telling the truth? Is it fair to let him try to work towards reconciliation, and then dump him because of a suspicion?" Jamie realized that her words sounded harsh, but she wanted to make sure her mother was thinking this through thoroughly.

"Maybe it's not fair," she admitted softly, "but life isn't fair. I was committed to giving this my best effort, and I think I have. It seems to me that my best isn't good enough." She sank into a chair, looking as if every iota of energy had been drained from her body. She fell silent. A silence that lengthened as Jamie and Ryan processed what was going on, and struggled for an appropriate, supportive response.

After her original question, Ryan hadn't ventured another word. She finally walked over to Catherine and sank to her knees in front of her. Catherine's head cocked slightly in question, and Ryan silently extended her arms, offering an embrace. Leaning forward, Catherine fell against her, while Ryan held her tightly, saying simply, "I'm so sorry."

Though Jamie was devastated by the unexpected turn of events, she took the cue from her partner, and stopped trying to cross-examine her mother. She moved across the room and joined Ryan, cuddling up against her mother's side as she hugged her tight. "I'm sorry, too, Mom. I know you tried your best. He got more chances than he deserved."

Catherine sniffed a little, trying to maintain her composure, drawing comfort from the obvious love in the embraces encircling her. "I couldn't have gotten through this a year ago. You've helped me find strength I didn't know I had."

The younger woman kept her arms tight around her mother. "We'll get through this, Mom. We'll be there for you whenever you need us."

"You already have been, sweetheart." Catherine smiled, focusing not on what she had lost, but rather on what she still had. "You already have been."

❖

They convinced Catherine to stay while they ate, but she had no appetite, and didn't join them. The hours passed slowly, since none of the women had much to say—each of them struggling with her own feelings. At around nine, Catherine stood and said, "I'd better get going."

She looked so lost and alone, that Jamie immediately protested. "I don't want you to be alone tonight, Mom. Please stay with us."

"No, honey, I've taken up your whole evening. There's nothing more to say, anyway."

"It doesn't matter if we talk," Jamie insisted. "I don't want you driving home tonight." She walked over to her chair and sat on the arm. "Please?"

Catherine shook her head decisively. "I'm really fine. You needn't worry about me."

Ryan finally spoke up. "We do worry about you, Catherine. Both of us do. I'd feel better if you'd spend the night, but if you won't do that, we'll drive you home. Whatever you prefer."

"Oh, I wish I had just called. I hate to be a burden."

"That's so far from the truth that it's not even in the ballpark," Jamie said. "You're not burdening us. We're sharing this with you. That's a very different thing. We're all sad…let's spend the evening supporting each other, okay?"

"Okay," Catherine finally agreed, the tiniest of smiles curving her lips. "We'll have a sleepover."

❧

"How ya doing?" Ryan asked gently as she sat down on the bed after they had Catherine squared away in Ryan's room.

Jamie looked at her for a second, and then climbed onto her lap. "I'm sad…I'm disappointed…I'm angry with my father for his inability to control himself…I'm angry with Mother for starting down this path if she was going to give up so soon…I'm sad for both of them." She rested her head against Ryan's neck and sighed. "I'm sad for myself, too. I want my parents to love each other."

"Of course you do," Ryan soothed. "That's a very natural reaction, honey. Every child is affected by divorce…no matter how old you are."

"I guess that's true. I'm disappointed in myself too. I want to be there for my mom…I don't want to be so wrapped up in my own feelings right now. She's the one who's in pain."

"So are you," Ryan reminded her. "And if you let yourself experience whatever feelings you have—even the bad ones—you'll be able to be there for her when she needs you."

"How'd you get so smart?" Jamie asked softly as she leaned back in her partner's embrace and settled a few flyaway strands of her hair.

"I learned that in my grief support group after Michael died. I was having terrible nightmares for a while, and one day the group leader got me to admit that I was furious with him for dying. As soon as I let that out, the nightmares stopped, and I was able to get past my anger and let myself feel the loss."

"That was a long time ago, and you were a kid," Jamie marveled. "How'd you remember that all of this time?"

"I use it a lot. It was honestly one of the most important lessons I've ever learned. If I can allow myself to feel the dark, ugly emotions that always come up when something upsetting happens, I'm able to let my gentle feelings come up, too. It's like the bad ones have to come out to let the good ones flow."

"Do you have bad feelings about my parents' divorce?"

"Yeah, I do," Ryan said, "but I don't want to share them. It works better for me if I keep them to myself." She waited a second and said, "But feel free to share yours if it helps. It just doesn't work for me."

"Okay, if something comes up I might, but this is probably the kind of thing it's best to share with Anna. It's nice to have a therapist at times like this."

"You might need to see her a few extra times. The holidays are gonna be hard for you if there's a lot of strife between your parents."

"Okay. I might do that."

"Are you going to call your dad?"

"Yeah," Jamie said softly. "I'll call him before I leave for class. I'm not looking forward to it," she added needlessly.

Karma

When Ryan emerged from the bath the next morning, Jamie was sitting at her desk chair, her head in her hands. "Well, the deed is done," she declared, looking up when she heard Ryan enter.

"How was he?"

"Not good. He was going to come home for Thanksgiving to surprise me. Mother called him on Wednesday night to tell him to stay in Washington."

"Oh, Jamie, I'm so sorry. He must really be in pain."

"He is. He swears that he hasn't slept with his…mistress…since the weekend of the Stanford game. I believe him, I really do. I think he was making a totally sincere effort here."

Ryan gave her a sympathetic look, trying not to allow her own grave doubts to show. "I guess it doesn't matter if he's telling the truth at this point. It's your mom's decision, and only her opinion matters."

"I know, I know, and I'm going to try my best not to get in the middle. Daddy actually begged me to try to get Mother to listen to him—but I can't. This has to be between them."

"I know it'll be tough to stay neutral, babe, but I really think it would be a mistake to get involved. You have no power here—you can only be pulled in both directions."

"I know, but it's hard to say no when I hear him crying on the phone. He was sitting in his office on Thanksgiving—with no one to talk to. We were all having a blast, and he was alone." She looked out the window as she bit her lip to keep from crying. "It doesn't seem fair."

"It's not. Especially if he's telling the truth."

"Especially then," Jamie agreed.

Jamie's focus was far from sharp when she showed up for golf practice. The morning was crisp, cold, and windier than she liked, so she spent some extra time stretching before she started to work. Scott Godfrey, the head coach, nodded at her, and she gave him as warm a smile as she could muster. "Have a nice Thanksgiving?" he asked.

"Yeah, it was fine. How about yours?"

"Great. This was Elizabeth's first Thanksgiving, so we had more than the usual supply of relatives show up. I think my wife is really glad that it's over." He rubbed his hands together and said, "It's really freezing today, isn't it?"

"I got back from Colorado Springs last night, and compared to that, this weather feels positively balmy."

"Were you skiing?"

"No. My partner, Ryan, is on the basketball team. They had to go all the way to Colorado to get their butts kicked."

He cocked his head and commented, "Basketball? I've been reading about her on the volleyball team."

"Oh, yeah. She was on the volleyball team. But the season's over, and she jumped right into another sport."

"You certainly don't sound very happy about that."

"No," she said, shaking her head. "I'm not. I didn't mind when she agreed to play, but I don't care for the chemistry on the team. She thinks she can help improve that, though, so we'll see."

After a moment, he asked, "What do you think of ours?"

"Our…what?"

"Our chemistry. How does it compare with what you've seen with Ryan's teams."

"Mmm…I'd say we're right in the middle of the two extremes that she's experienced this year. The volleyball team was a very tightly knit group. They really liked one another, and they socialized quite a bit as well as playing together. But the basketball team is very cliquish, and I get the impression they don't like to be around one another more than is absolutely necessary."

"The middle of those two extremes doesn't sound very good."

"Well, I don't detect a lot of camaraderie, and I don't think many of the girls socialize, but I also don't see any antagonism or jealousy. We're all polite to one another, and we joke around in the locker room, but that's it. To be honest, we don't know each other well enough to have much to talk about."

He shook his head. "I wish we had the budget to do some things to build team spirit. All I can afford is the one weekend before our first tournament in Vallejo."

"It's really an individual sport, Scott. I don't see that it's possible to do much to bring the team together. For what it's worth, this is no different than my high school team was."

"Things were different last year. We had three seniors who were all very gregarious. The younger girls really followed their lead."

"This is a pretty quiet group."

"Yeah, and it doesn't help that the team is so young. With four freshman and only two seniors it's been hard to keep the spirit from last year going. You're brand new, and Juliet is…well, she's not the type to spend her time getting to know the other players."

Jamie chuckled. "I don't think I've ever heard her speak."

"I'd guess that she's the most focused player I've ever been around," Scott mused. "Her goal is to turn pro as soon as she graduates, and I think she's honestly got a chance."

"I haven't seen her course management skills, but she's a heck of a ball striker. She has one of the most beautiful swings I've ever seen, too."

"Yeah, I wish I could take credit for helping her build that swing, but she had it when she got here," he chuckled.

"I'd better get busy if I want to build my own swing. I'll try to think of some ways to promote harmony, Scott. It's hard when we have to practice at the beginning of the day. Not having our own course makes things tough."

"It does," he agreed. "But we're never going to get a course, so we'll have to be more creative."

Scott had spent time with Jamie the previous week, giving her a few tips on improving her draw shot. She worked on that diligently, then spent another hour going through her entire bag, hitting fifteen to twenty balls with each club. Scott and his assistant, Evan Foster, split their time among all of the women, spending a few minutes watching each and offering tips where needed. By the time Jamie was finished, only Juliet remained. It was not quite eight, and she didn't have class until ten, so Jamie sat down at the base of a practice bunker to watch her teammate.

Even though they'd been practicing at the same facility for nearly three months, Jamie couldn't remember saying more than a total of twenty words to Juliet. However, after talking with Scott, she decided that she needed to start being more aggressive about making friends on the team. She felt a little guilty about putting so little effort into building the team, but she selfishly wanted to spend every minute of her free time with Ryan. But after talking with Scott she knew it was important to make an effort to help turn it into a real team, rather than a collection of individuals.

She spent at least a half hour watching Juliet's nearly perfect swing. When the woman finally stopped and began to stretch, catching Jamie out of the corner of her eye, she turned around in surprise and said, "Uhm…hi." Looking over her shoulder to make sure Jamie wasn't looking at someone else, she asked, "Are you… waiting for me?"

"No, not really." Jamie smiled warmly. "I don't have class until ten, so I thought I'd hang out for a while."

"You've…been watching me?" Juliet asked, obviously puzzled.

"Well, if I'm going to sit and watch a teammate, you're the one I'm going to choose. Might as well try to learn from the best."

"You uhm…think I'm the best?" Juliet asked, a small smile forming.

"I know you don't pay a lot of attention to what's going on around here, but you don't seem oblivious," Jamie chuckled. "It's no secret that you're the best player on the team."

The woman shrugged, looking uncharacteristically shy. "I work hard."

"A lot of talent and hard work are a great combo." Looking at her watch, she asked, "Do you have time to get some coffee?"

"Uhm…not today," Juliet said. "I have class at nine." She hesitated a beat, then added, "I could tomorrow, though. My first class is at eleven."

"Eleven, huh? My first is at eleven, too. Why don't we come out early and play a round after we practice for a while. I'm sure Scott would let us cut practice short."

Juliet nodded. "I'd like that. It's getting tough to get eighteen in after class, now that it gets dark so early."

"Where do you usually play?"

"Here at Tilden, mostly. I usually go home to Sacramento on the weekends, though. I can get in a lot more holes, since the course is much less crowded. On a good day, I can play three rounds."

Jamie gave her a warm smile and said, "You do work hard, doncha?"

"Yep. I know what I want. I might not get it, but I swear I won't fail because of a lack of effort." Her watch alarm went off and she hefted her bag onto her shoulder. "Gotta go. See you bright and early tomorrow, okay?"

"It's a date." She watched Juliet practically sprint for the parking lot, thinking that even though it hadn't been a huge gesture, she felt good about at least trying to form a friendship.

Jamie stopped back by the house after practice to find her mother and Mia in the kitchen, chatting companionably. "How are you feeling?" Jamie asked when she crossed the room to offer a kiss.

"Better," Catherine said. "A good night's rest made a big difference. You were right, as usual, honey. I'm sure I slept better knowing that you were close by. I only woke up once, which is a big improvement. When I couldn't get back to sleep I almost took a crack at playing that elaborate drum set that I assume must be Ryan's." She chuckled, showing that her mood had definitely improved.

"How'd you guess?" Jamie asked wryly. "I gave it to her for her birthday, but she's barely had time to break it in."

Mia stood and walked over to her friend. "I've got to get going now. I'm really sorry to hear the news," she said, meeting Jamie's eyes.

"Thanks. We'll get through this, won't we, Mom?"

"We will. We're tougher than we look."

"That's a relief," Mia joked, kissing Catherine's cheek.

As she was walking out of her morning class, Jamie reached down to her waistband to retrieve her ringing phone. "Yesss," she drawled.

"How do you always know it's me?" Ryan asked. "Or do you use that sexy drawl with everyone?"

"No, only you. And I know it's you, despite the fact that you have caller ID disabled, because you're the only person who knows my schedule so intimately. What's up, babe?"

"I have good and bad news." There was a note of mystery in her voice.

"Hmm, give me the bad first."

"I've been asked to try out for the national volleyball team." She was unable to keep the enthusiasm out of her voice.

"That's the bad news?" Jamie almost shouted, unable to control her excitement.

"Well, it's both," Ryan said. "It's good news since it's a huge honor, but it's bad news since it requires me to make some hard choices."

"Are you at home?"

"Yeah, why?"

"I'm coming home for lunch," she said decisively. "I have to congratulate you properly."

A half hour later, Jamie rode up to the house on her bike and matched the grin on her beaming partner's face. She trotted over to Ryan and threw her arms around her neck. "I am so proud of you."

"Thanks, honey," Ryan mumbled into her shoulder. "I'm pretty excited myself."

"Well you should be. I guarantee you're the only woman invited who played just two years at this level. Not to insult USF."

"Actually, a couple of freshmen got invited, including that cutie from Stanford, but I am the only twenty-four year-old."

"It makes me so happy that you were able to play this year," Jamie said, her eyes bright with tears. "It's wonderful to see you this excited about something."

Ryan grasped her hand, and pulled her into the house. They jointly prepared soup and sandwiches, and a half hour later when Mia came wandering in, she had to laugh at the scene. Jamie was perched on Ryan's lap feeding her spoonfuls of soup like a bird feeding her young. "You two are so cute," she said affectionately as she ruffled Jamie's hair.

"Have you seen Jordan?" Ryan asked, craning her head around to make eye contact.

"Not in the last fifteen seconds or so." Jordan came strolling into the kitchen beaming a smile.

Ryan urged Jamie off her lap as she jumped up and threw her arms around her teammate. "Congratulations," she said, giving her a rough squeeze.

Jordan leaned back in the embrace and asked suspiciously, "How did you know?"

"Coach told me when I talked to him this morning."

"Why were you talking to Coach?"

"'Cause I got invited too," she said, her eyebrows bouncing wildly.

Jordan let out a joyous cry and jumped into Ryan's arms. "That's so cool. That rat didn't say a word about you."

"He wanted to tell me first, and since I was out of town he didn't get hold of me until this morning. But since he'd already talked to you, he was free to tell me about you."

"We're going to have so much fun," Jordan cried again, but another look showed that Ryan didn't share her exuberance. "What's wrong?"

Ryan put her back on the ground and said, "Well, we're not sure that I'm going to accept."

"Not accept? Are you nuts? You'll never get another chance to go to the Olympics. How can you possibly not accept?"

"There are a ton of repercussions to trying out. I'm not sure if I can turn my life upside down right now."

Jordan sank down heavily into a chair as she let out a breath. "Boy, you jacked me up awfully high only to cut me right back down."

"I'm sorry, but we have to spend some time discussing this. It's not an obvious choice for me."

"You two can discuss it, but I have to get back to school," Jamie announced. "I love you, Tiger," she said softly as she kissed Ryan's lips gently. "And I'm very, very proud of you." Walking over to Jordan she bent to offer her a kiss also. "You're not so bad yourself," she said affectionately, patting her cheek.

Jordan looked at Ryan as soon as Jamie left the room and asked, "Doesn't she want you to go?"

"No, that's not it at all. She's totally supportive. I think she's confused by my reluctance, too. I guess it's hard for me because this isn't something I was planning for. I mean, I'd been scouted for the national team in soccer since I was fourteen. I'm pretty sure I would have made the team after my freshman year in college if I'd gone to Cal first. That was always my goal, and after that died I put thoughts of the Olympics and World Cup aside. I'll admit it was hard to let it die, but once it did, I didn't expect to resurrect it again."

"But this fell into your lap. It's a tremendous gift."

"I know. But I'd have to drop out of school for at least a semester—even if I didn't make the darned team. If I did that, I wouldn't only not graduate this year, I'd have to put graduate school off another year."

"But what's your rush? It'll all be here when we get back with our gold medal."

"There are things I want to do," she explained. "We want to wait to have a baby until I'm out of grad school. Delaying that a year slows our time table down."

"Jamie could go first."

"I know, but I like the way we've planned things. Besides, if I do this, Jamie will have to drop out and come with me. I couldn't be away from her for almost nine months."

"But it's the Olympics," she moaned, dropping her head onto the table. "This isn't some small thing."

"I know, but I'm also tied to the basketball team. It's not fair to ditch them."

"That's a joke," Jordan scoffed. "The equipment manager plays as much as you do." Ryan was stunned and hurt. Jordan rose to come stand behind her chair putting her hands on the strong shoulders and giving her a gentle massage. "I know how good you are, Boom, and it kills me that your stupid coach doesn't. I listened to your game on the Internet on Sunday, and there was a good ten-minute period where you would have sparked them in a big way. What in the hell is wrong with her anyway?"

"Thanks for the vote of confidence, but she doesn't seem to share your enthusiasm," Ryan said glumly.

"Well if you're going to let that be a big factor in your decision, you'd better ask her if she's going to use you. It's dumb to pass up the Olympics to ride the pine."

"You've got a point there, but that's not the only problem. I loved playing volleyball this year, but now that I'm on a team I don't really like, it reminds me of how much chemistry matters. What we had this year was really special, and that's why I loved it. I'm not sure I love volleyball enough to devote nine months of my life to it if I'm not crazy about my teammates."

"You're crazy about me," Jordan reminded her with a shy grin.

"Now that's the absolute truth."

Mia had been silently observing this entire dialogue, but she finally got up and took Jordan's hand. "Excuse us, but I promised Jordan lunch, and we've only got an hour to spare."

As they started for the door, Ryan pointed out. "Food's in the kitchen, girls."

"That's not what Jordan has a craving for," Mia said lightly as she tossed her curly brown hair and shot Ryan a wink.

After practice, Ryan decided that Jordan and Jamie were right—she had to get some indication from Coach Hayes as to her plans for the season, as well as take care of some special arrangements she needed to make. "Hey, Coach?" she called as the woman started to walk back to her office.

"Yes?"

"Do you have a few minutes to discuss a couple of things?"

She looked at her watch and scowled, "My family's waiting for me for dinner. Is it quick?"

"Uhm, probably not," she said honestly. "I'll make an appointment."

Coach Hayes looked at the concerned face for a moment and relented. "Come on, if it's important enough to make that face, I guess I can spare a few minutes."

"I'm not very good at hiding my feelings," Ryan admitted as she tagged along beside her. When they reached the office, Ryan asked, "Do you mind if I get out of my wet jersey?"

"Go ahead. I'll call home while you change."

A few minutes later, Ryan walked back into the office in a dry T-shirt and her warm up jacket. She sat down in the chair facing the desk, and waited for the coach to hang up the phone. When she did, she gazed at the younger woman and said, "You're right when you say you don't hide your feelings well. It's obvious you're unhappy with your playing time, but I need you to know that I don't explain my decisions to every unhappy player."

Ryan was a bit taken aback by those comments, but she immediately regained her poise and said, "I do want to ask what your plans for me are, but not because of playing time. I've been asked to try out for the volleyball national team, but I have no intention of doing that if it'd let the basketball team down. So my real question is, do you think you need me enough to give up this opportunity?"

Coach Hayes leaned back in her chair and stared at Ryan for a moment. "I didn't realize you were that talented at volleyball."

"I'm not sure I am, but it's nice to be asked to try out. And for the record, Coach, I never would question your judgment about playing time. I admit I'm disappointed that I haven't been allowed to contribute more, but I trust you to make the right decisions for the benefit of the entire team."

"Good," the older woman said briskly. "Now, how can I help you?"

"Well, as I said, I like to play basketball. I made a commitment to play for this team, and I intend to honor that commitment if you're relying on me."

"I don't understand how my input affects your commitment. A commitment is that. If you want to break your promise to the team, that's your decision. I'm not going to make it easy for you by telling you it doesn't matter."

Ryan blew out a frustrated breath and lowered her head, staring at the floor for a moment. "Look, Ryan," the older woman said, "I appreciate the spot you're in, but I don't want to be the one to make this decision for you. I can't promise you that you'll play much—if at all. There's a good chance that you'll end up being the best player on the team, but things could as easily go the other way. You have to do what you think is right."

Ryan forced her mouth into a smile. "Thanks for being honest with me. I need to decide within the next day or two, so I'll let you know."

"Good," the older woman said as she stood.

Karma

"One more thing," Ryan spoke up. "I'm scheduled to take a math test on the day of our game down at Fresno State. It's a national thing, and it's scheduled for that morning. I can get the okay for a delayed start, but I have to take it that day—and that day only."

"And?" the coach asked, arching an eyebrow.

"And…I wanted to know if I could fly home, rather than take the bus. There's a five o'clock flight that would let me to get to school by around six-thirty, if it's on time."

Narrowing her gaze, the coach asked, "What makes you so sure that the game will be over in time for you to make the flight?"

"Well," she said, flushing under the gray-eyed scrutiny, "I don't really play that many minutes. I thought I could leave at four, whether or not the game's over."

The older woman drew in a breath and said, "Ryan, if that's your attitude, you may as well quit. Either you're a member of the team, or you're not. Making your own schedules and traveling separately indicate a real inability to understand what a team is all about." She stood to go, arching her eyebrow again as she cocked her head. "Is there anything else?"

Ryan stood, shaking her head the entire time. "I'll stay for the game and ride home with the team," she said quietly. "I have to be accompanied by a faculty member for the entire time period of the test. Are you willing to keep an eye on me from nine to noon, and one to three on that day?"

"That's my job," she said, giving her a small, insincere smile. "I keep my eye on everyone."

Being in a bit of a fog when she left the office, Ryan's distraction caused her to slam into Lynette, who was trying to enter. "Oh, shit," she cried, immediately reaching out to grab the assistant coach's shoulders and steady her.

"Jesus. No wonder you play such good defense. If I ran into you on a pick, I wouldn't be in a hurry to repeat the experience."

"I'm really sorry, Lynette." Ryan looked at the assistant carefully to assess the damage. "I wasn't paying attention."

Lynette returned her look of concern, and nodded her head in the direction of the office. "Were you speaking to the coach?"

"Yeah."

"Is anything wrong? You didn't quit did you?"

"Ah, no, why assume something is wrong?"

"Well, she doesn't spend much time talking to players. That's our job," she explained, meaning she and the other assistant coaches.

"I got that impression. Do you have time to talk to me for a few minutes?"

Lynette gave her a genuine smile and said, "I always have time. That *is* my job."

"Is it against your policy to fraternize with players?"

"No," she said with a gentle laugh. "I don't know of any other way to get to know people."

"How about dinner at my house?"

"Tonight?"

"Yeah. Let me call Jamie and see if she minds," she said as she pulled her phone out of her gym bag.

Lynette waited patiently as a grin spread across Ryan's face. "I still don't know how you always know it's me," she chuckled.

After a pause she smirked and said, "I do not believe that the phone rings differently when I call, but it's sweet that you think so." Her smile grew bigger as she said, "I'll tell you. Would you mind if I brought Lynette Dix home for dinner?" She looked at Lynette and nodded as she said, "I knew you wouldn't mind, but I think it's polite to check. We'll be there in ten minutes, honey. I love you."

As she hung up she smiled and said, "I skated to school today. Do you want to run alongside or drive me home?"

Ten minutes later they were sitting in the cozy kitchen, preparing to eat the delightful coq au vin that Jamie had prepared. Ryan had filled Lynette in on her conversation with Coach Hayes on the way to the house, but she took a minute to bring Jamie up to speed.

"So what are you really looking for?" Lynette asked as she took a sip of the wine Ryan had poured for her. "Do you want advice on whether to accept the offer from the volleyball program, or do you want my opinion on whether we'll use you more this season?"

Karma

Ryan leaned back in her chair and took a sip from her glass as she gazed at the coach thoughtfully. "Neither, actually. I want your opinion on whether I'm an addition to the team, or a distraction."

"That's it?" she asked in surprise.

"Yeah. If I decide not to try out for the Olympic team, I want to stay and contribute if I'm wanted. But I have no interest in investing my time if it'll make things worse."

"Coach didn't give you any feedback, did she?"

Ryan shook her head. "None."

"Okay, I'll give you my take. We'll be a better team when you get more minutes. And nothing makes a team gel as well as winning. So I predict that if you stay, things will get substantially better on the court. But I can't guarantee that will translate to off the court."

Jamie brought the heavy cast iron Dutch oven over to the table as she asked, "Why do you think the team is so fragmented?"

"Boy, this smells delicious, Jamie," Lynette said appreciatively. "I don't get many home cooked meals." She leaned over her bowl and took another deep whiff as she smiled again. "I don't even want to wait until it cools, so I'll answer your question to distract myself. Obviously I can't tell you too much, since some of the things I know are confidential. Let's say that the team has gotten more cliquish in each of the five years I've been here. We haven't had much leadership from the upperclassmen, and, as you know, they set the tone for a team. But I honestly don't see much of that changing. I worry because I can see the freshmen already being infected by it."

"I see that too. It seems like Franny's afraid to speak."

"Yeah. Blacks, whites, freshmen and Eastern Europeans," she said wryly. "It must seem like back home in the Balkans for the Croatian girls."

"So only Janae, Franny and I are not in a clique?"

"Pretty much."

Ryan nodded her head slowly, looking as if she had made up her mind. "That's what I thought. It looks like we'll have to either take over one of the other cliques or start one of our own."

"You're gonna need some luck," the older woman warned. "The team's not only fragmented, I think most of the players like being in their groups. I don't see that they're motivated to leave them."

"Ryan's very persuasive," Jamie assured her, exchanging a fond look with her partner.

"I don't doubt that," Lynette agreed, "but this task could be beyond even Ryan's skills."

We'll see about that, Ryan decided, already trying to figure out how to appeal to the small groups.

❦

"Did it help to get Lynette's perspective on the team?" Jamie asked when they were getting ready for bed.

"Yeah, I guess so. I know we have our work cut out for us, but I still think Janae and I can make a difference."

"Correct me if I'm wrong, but it sounds like you've made up your mind about volleyball."

"No, I really haven't. I won't make that decision without you."

"No way. I don't want any part in this one," Jamie said, shaking her head decisively. "This has to be your decision. You're the one who'll have to put out the effort, so you're the one that needs to decide."

"But your life will be thrown upside down, too," Ryan insisted, wide-eyed.

"I know it will, but not as radically as yours will be." She put her arms around her partner, and said, "I'm not in as big a hurry to graduate, and I'm not in a hurry to start working. Living in Colorado Springs for a year could be a kick." She smiled. "I love to ski, and I could really work on my technique while you're jumping through the roof of the gym." She gave Ryan such a look of devotion that Ryan felt her heart swell with love.

"You're such a wonderful partner," she sighed. "So supportive... so caring."

"All true. And you'll be there for me if ever the situation is reversed."

"All true as well," Ryan confidently agreed. She placed a gentle kiss on the top of Jamie's head and said, "I should be able to decide about the Olympics once I get some more information. Then I need to decide if I want to stay on the basketball team if I don't go to Colorado."

"How are you feeling about that?"

"It's one thing if I quit the team to join the Olympic team. It's a very different thing to quit because I don't like it. As much as it pissed me off, Coach Hayes had a good point. I did make a commitment, and I have to decide if my word is worth more than my happiness."

Jamie rubbed Ryan's back and said, "They have a commitment to you too. Are they living up to it?" Ryan blinked at her, an almost vacant look in her blue eyes. Jamie explained, "They have a commitment to make the team as good as it can possibly be. That includes taking the time to figure out that you're a fantastic player, and can help them a great deal."

Ryan nodded, a confused look on her face. "I guess that's true," she mused.

"They have a commitment to help you develop as a player. They have an obligation to treat you with some respect. They can't throw a group of people together and expect them to survive. They have to do their jobs, so the players can do theirs."

Looking absolutely stunned by Jamie's words, she said, "I've never thought of it like that. I guess it does go both ways."

"Look, I know that your word means a great deal to you, but don't let your promise stop you from getting something that you really want."

Ryan nodded tentatively, "I'll try not to." She sighed, then yawned loudly. "This has been a bitch of a day."

"Oh, I noticed that you got a note from Moira. How is she?"

"Good," Ryan said, slipping into bed and cuddling up to Jamie when she joined her. "She wanted to thank us for the hospitality. Boy, I hate that we spent so little time together. Normally, I'm like her shadow when she's here."

"She's really special to you, isn't she?"

"Oh, yeah," Ryan sighed. Turning to look closely at her partner, a note of concern in her blue eyes, she asked, "Didn't you think she was special?"

"Yes, I did. I was particularly charmed by how much she seems to love you, but even without that vital trait, she was a very cool woman. Not very much like Maeve at all, much to my surprise."

"No, she's really not. She's much more like my mom," Ryan

agreed. "I think that's why she and my mom weren't overly close—they were too much alike."

"But she and your mom got on well, didn't they?"

"Oh, sure. They were friends, but they weren't as close as my mom and my Aunt Maeve—they were inseparable." Ryan paused thoughtfully and said, "You know, my mom didn't really want to come to America. She was perfectly happy in Ireland. As a matter of fact, I think she would have worked on my father to return if she'd lived. She wasn't all that crazy about the United States. She thought it was a very dangerous place to raise kids."

"Did she come only because of your aunt?"

"Yeah, pretty much. Well, my aunt and my father," Ryan grinned. "She apparently fell in love with him at first sight."

"I know exactly how she felt," Jamie sighed as she scooted closer, and wrapped her arm around Ryan's waist. "I can still remember the flip my stomach did the first time you turned around, and I got a look into those baby blues."

"Aww, you say the sweetest things."

"I speak the truth. I still get the same flutter when you look at me now, you know."

"Like this?" Ryan asked softly, as she locked her eyes upon her partner and gave her a sexy smile.

"Works every time," Jamie insisted, capturing the pink lips with her own.

Chapter Four

When the alarm went off the next morning, at five, two groggy women struggled to their feet. "You don't have to get up yet, honey," Ryan said, yawning loudly.

"Yeah, I do. I'm gonna try to do the same thing with my team that you're doing with yours. Today I'm going to play a round with the only other senior. I thought I might be able to work on her to see if we can try to be leaders."

"That's kinda cool. What's her name?"

"Juliet. She's the one who wants to try to make it on the pro tour."

"Oh, yeah, you've mentioned her. Is she nice?"

"From what I know of her, she is. Yesterday was the first time we've really spoken. I should have a better feel for her after today."

"Wanna shower together?" Ryan asked. "If we've got to get up this early, we might as well have something to look forward to."

"Sounds like a plan, but you keep those Irish hands to yourself, or we'll never make it."

"I will if you will. You're usually the naughty one."

"My secret is out." Jamie wrapped her arms around her naked lover and gave her a very friendly hug. "I'll save my naughty thoughts for tonight."

Later that morning, Ryan walked through the deserted halls of the athletic department offices, and found Coach Placer just opening his door. "Well, well, to what do I owe the honor?" he asked happily when he caught sight of her.

She yawned cavernously, then apologized. "Sorry about that. I've been getting up extra early to study for a math competition." She smiled and said, "I've been staring at formulas since six."

He shook his head and patted her on the back, guiding her into the office. "Nobody can say you're not a hard worker. It's women like you that make this job so rewarding."

"Thanks," she beamed. "Given how much I respect you, that really means a lot." She sat down in the chair in front of his desk and waited for him to take his seat. "I've got some questions, and I think you're the only person who might have the answers."

"Sure. Tell me what's on your mind."

"It's the volleyball tryouts. I'm betting that you know more than you've told me about them. I'm gonna guess that you even have a pretty good idea of what my chances are of actually making the team."

"Why would you think that?"

"I think that coaches are a pretty tight lot. I bet you've heard some rumors, or have some idea of what the outcome might be, but you don't want to tell me."

"Hmm, now why would I do that?" he asked with a sly smile.

"Probably because you wanted me to enjoy the thrill of being asked, and you think I might enjoy going out there for the experience."

"I see," he said somberly. "Well, let's say you're correct. Would my assumptions have been incorrect?"

"In my case, yes. I'd have to defer a lot of my plans if I go, not the least of which is graduating this year. I'm really only interested in attending if I have a good shot at making the team."

"What do you know about the team?"

"I know that most of the players have been together for years. And I don't know how many players they can carry, but I can only imagine that not many slots are open. I think they invite a lot of college players to keep good relations with the college coaches, and reward people for having a good season. But my guess is that they've identified who they want while the player is still in high school. If they progress like they expect them to, they pull them onto the team after they graduate and have really proven themselves for four years."

"How'd you get so savvy?" he asked with a smile.

"I was one of those people that the soccer federation had hand picked while I was in high school. That's how it seemed to work."

"You're about dead on correct," he admitted. "I think they might take three women from this tryout."

"How many were invited?"

"Twenty-five," he said gravely. "And I can also tell you that their biggest need is at middle blocker."

"What do you think Jordan's chances are?"

"I think they're good, but she's gonna have to put on a show when she gets to Colorado. That freshman from Stanford gets all the press—so much so that they'll probably have to take her, even though I think she'll be much better when she grows into her body a little. Jordan's a very talented player, and she's been to every major training camp that's been offered. A lot of people on the national level know her, and she's proven herself at the international level too. She played in Europe for six weeks last summer and did very well."

"What's the chance of both of us making it?" she asked, already knowing the answer.

"You're the mathematician, but I'd say you have a better chance of being struck by lightning simultaneously. And I'm not saying that I think you aren't both talented enough. But they're not going to take three new outside hitters—no matter how good you all are. Besides, it'd look funny to add two women from the same school, especially when we didn't even make the NCAAs."

"So you don't think they're only looking at how well we perform at the tryout?"

"No. Like everything else, politics plays a big part. You haven't paid your dues. I was actually amazed that you were even invited—but your numbers were too good to pass up."

"So you don't think there's any way I could impress them enough to add me to the roster?"

"Let me say this, if they add you, they'll probably subtract Jordan," he said with finality. "I think they'll take the Stanford freshman, even if she doesn't play that well. That leaves one slot—max—for another outside hitter." He gave her a sober stare and added, "I think they have to take a middle blocker, and there's a very good setter from Hawaii that they're very hot on. So, for either of you to have a chance you'd have to outplay the other."

She leaned back in her chair and said, "It was so pleasurable to play for you, Coach. I really wish it were still volleyball season." She shook her head and said, "It's so refreshing to talk to someone who'll give you the straight scoop."

"Things aren't working out so well in basketball, are they."

"No. I don't get to play much, and the team is very divided. Practices aren't any fun, and I haven't been able to make many friends. It makes me appreciate what we had this past season. And it makes me appreciate you too, Coach," she said fondly as she got up. "Well, maybe I'll come back as a fifth year player, if you'll have me."

"Have you? That's a laugh. The welcome mat would be so long it would go all the way to your house."

Over dinner, Ryan asked, "So, how did your golf match go this morning?"

"Good, as far as golf is concerned. But my goal was to get to know Juliet a little. That's obviously going to take more work."

"How come?"

"Well, we played eighteen holes of golf, and all she said was, 'you're away' and 'nice shot'. She's obviously not into wasting a word."

"Did you try to talk to her?"

"Yeah, but I stopped trying after she made it clear that she wasn't paying attention. I think this might be a very slow process. The good news is that I could learn a lot from her. She concentrates as fiercely as you do, honey, and she really knows how to think her way around a course. We decided to play again on Thursday morning." Jamie shrugged and added, "Whether or not we get to be friends, I think I can benefit from hanging out and watching her play."

"You'll wear her down," Ryan predicted. "No one can resist that adorable face for long."

Karma

That night, as they snuggled in bed, Ryan said, "Oh, I talked to my favorite math professor, and she agreed to proctor the Putnam exam for me."

"That's great. Will you take it on Sunday, or what?"

"Kinda," Ryan said, knowing that Jamie would explode when she told her the truth. "Kinda Saturday and uhm…kinda Sunday."

All vestiges of sleep now gone from her body, Jamie sat up and looked at her partner, one eyebrow arched dramatically.

"I have to take it on Saturday. It was hard enough to get the committee to allow me to take it at the end of the day."

"Explain," she wearily demanded.

Ryan rolled her shoulders and said, "I have to take it when I get back from Fresno."

"So you're going to play in a game in Fresno, ride a bus for three or four hours, and then take a six hour test?" Her expression gave Ryan the distinct impression that she didn't think this was a wonderful idea.

"That's the plan," she said, her mouth set in a grim line. "I don't have many options. It's either quit the team, or waste the months of preparation I've put into the test."

"Ryan," Jamie with said as much patience as she could summon, "taking it under those conditions means that you've wasted your preparation anyway. You can't possibly do well at the end of a day like that."

"Sometimes you do what you have to do. This is what I have to do."

"You've already made up your mind to refuse the tryout and stick with basketball, haven't you?"

Ryan was lying on her side, plastered up against her lover's body. Her arm was tucked tightly around her waist, and their heads shared the same pillow. When she spoke, her warm breath fluttered against Jamie's cheek. "Have I no secrets from you?" she chuckled deep in her chest.

"No, none at all. Spill it."

"I haven't made up my mind completely, but I'm leaning that way. How do you feel about it?"

"I've told you before that I want this to be your decision. You're the one who'll have to do the work. I want to make sure you're doing this for the right reason. Are you sure this is what you want?"

"Honey, if this was the soccer team, you couldn't hold me back. But it's not important enough to me to throw our lives into an uproar for the chance."

"Do you think Jordan will make it? It means so much to her."

"I think her chances are decent," Ryan said, "but not excellent. Coach told me some things that indicated that we'd never both make it, and she deserves it so much more than I do."

Jamie didn't think that was necessarily true, and when she turned to look at Ryan her expression telegraphed her feelings.

"She does," Ryan insisted. "She's been working for this since she was twelve. For me, it would be a gift. For Jordan, well, for Jordan, it's the most important thing in her life right now."

Nodding slightly, Jamie acknowledged those facts. "I still think you'd be a great addition to the team. You rule."

"I appreciate the vote of confidence." She stuck her arm out and grandly gestured towards their room. "But I think I'll make this my kingdom—with you as my queen." She collapsed with laughter as Jamie dramatically made the gesture that signaled forced vomiting.

When Jamie woke the next morning, she rolled over to cuddle, her eyes opening when all she found was a cool mattress. "Ryan?" she asked, getting no reply. The bathroom door was open, so Jamie figured her partner was already downstairs. She got up and tugged on a robe against the chill, then made her way downstairs, calling Ryan's name again. She was met with silence, and stood in the kitchen for a moment, idly looking around for a note. She opened the refrigerator and noticed that the orange juice container was missing. *Okay...one missing lover, one missing juice bottle. They both have to be around here somewhere.* As her eyes scanned the kitchen for clues, she noted the key was dangling from the deadbolt on the door to the backyard. *Ah-hah.* Smiling, she poked her head out the door to see Ryan sitting on the bench that rested under the arbor.

Wearing sweats, her hair mussed from sleep, Ryan was staring blankly across the yard, her face etched in pain. "Honey?" Jamie said softly, not wanting to startle her. Ryan didn't answer, deep in some form of contemplative state, and likely not wanting to be disturbed. Jamie turned around and went upstairs to take her shower, mildly concerned. Once dressed, she went back downstairs, deciding to leave a note for Ryan rather than break her mood. But Ryan was walking back into the house as Jamie entered the kitchen. To her surprise, Ryan's eyes were red rimmed and swollen, and she wiped at them with the sleeve of her shirt. "Sweetheart, what's wrong?"

"Something hit me this morning," Ryan sniffed. "I was lying in bed, sound asleep, and it was like a hand reached out and grabbed my heart, giving it a good shake. I woke up totally filled with dread, and I realized that this is the anniversary of my mother's death." Shaking her head, she closed her eyes tightly and muttered, "How could I be too busy to remember something like that?"

"Honey, you did remember. It must have been in the back of your mind for it to come to you like that."

"But I didn't think about it early enough," she insisted. "I normally commemorate it. Last year I had a Mass said for her at Newman Hall."

At Jamie's puzzled look, Ryan said, "That's the Catholic student center on campus."

"Oh, I see. You have to plan something like that ahead of time, huh?"

"Yes. I've been so damned busy lately." A few more tears slid down her cheeks, and she said, "How can I be too busy to remember my mother?"

Giving her a stern look, Jamie said, "You're being silly. You remember your mother every day. I know you do."

Giving her partner a sheepish look in return, Ryan nodded. "I do, but this is different. Being remembered at Mass would mean a lot to her. I know it would."

"Ryan, honey, it wouldn't matter to your mother to have the priest remember her. What would mean something to her is to have you remember her at Mass. I'll meet you after your last morning class, and we'll go together. I'll call and make sure they have a lunchtime service."

Ryan threw her arms around her partner and held her tightly.

"Thanks for loving me," she whispered. "I'll call you later this morning."

※

When Jamie arrived at the golf course she started to warm up, surprised that she was the first one there. After a few minutes, Scott showed up, and after chatting for a moment she said, "Juliet and I were speaking yesterday, and we decided it might be nice to play eighteen on Tuesday and Thursday mornings. Would you have any problem with our shortening our usual practice to get in some holes?"

"No, that's fine. I certainly don't have to supervise you two. Feel free to do that any time you want."

"Will do," she smiled, waving to the rest of the players as they arrived. "Shuttle bus must have been late again," she commented, feeling only slightly guilty for being able to drive herself to practice.

She worked for the required two hours, and as she was finishing up, an idea hit her and she sought Scott out again. "How would you feel if I could get more players to agree to play a round twice a week? I know that almost everyone plays several times during the week, but they all saunter over here when they can spare four hours. I was thinking that it might help team spirit if we could make it a more organized."

"That would be great," he agreed. "If you can get a decent sized group, I could have Evan go with you to provide a playing lesson."

"I'm gonna give it a whirl." She spent the next twenty minutes proposing her idea to every other player, and they all decided to bring their registration materials for spring semester on Friday so they could try to work together to arrange their schedules to accommodate the plan. *This is going pretty darned well,* she decided, pleased with her progress.

※

Picking Ryan up after her last morning class, they arrived at Mass a few minutes late. Ryan usually liked to sit near the front, but this time she took the last pew, staying right by the back door.

The priest flew through the noon mass, since most of the very small crowd consisted of students on their lunch hour. At one point, the priest asked the congregants to remember the souls of the dead, then mentioned the person that the Mass was being said for. Ryan was already kneeling; but after the priest mentioned the stranger's name, her head dropped even lower, and her shoulders began to shake noticeably. Jamie knelt down next to her, wrapped her arm around Ryan's waist, and held on tight. It quickly became obvious that Ryan was truly overcome with emotion, so Jamie tugged on her sleeve until she followed her outside. Grasping Ryan's hand, she led her to the small outdoor patio on the side of the church.

They sat together on a small bench, and Ryan immediately dropped her head onto Jamie's chest and cried so hard that Jamie feared she'd be sick. She'd seen Ryan cry on many, many occasions, but she had never witnessed an outpouring of emotion like this. As luck would have it, she was wearing a coppery brown cotton blouse with wheat colored jeans, and after five minutes of inconsolable crying, there were large dark streaks from her collarbone down past her breast. But her attire was the last thing on Jamie's mind at the moment. She was solely focused on her disconsolate lover and the pathetic cries that were coming from her.

As the sobs quieted down, Ryan lifted her head and sucked in a few shaky breaths. She had no tissues, and Jamie's were long since exhausted, so Ryan was forced to pull her T-shirt up to wipe her eyes.

Jamie had been patting or rubbing some part of her since they sat down, and as she wrapped her arm even tighter around her partner, she simply said, "Tell me, baby."

A few more deep breaths preceded her first words. "I realized today why I've agreed to hold off having children," she said softly. "I've been afraid to have a baby because I couldn't bear to cause my child this kind of pain. I don't think I can ever explain it fully. It feels like the pain is lodged in my bones. It's like it's an intrinsic part of me."

She leaned her head back and sucked in another breath before she said, "My mother probably had cancer when she gave birth to me, and as happy as I am to have been born, I know she wouldn't have willingly gotten pregnant if she'd known she was ill. I'm…I'm terrified to have a baby. What if the same thing happened to me?" Her face was stark white, and her whole body was shaking.

"Oh, honey, I know you worry, but there's every indication that you're perfectly healthy. Alison examined your breasts a short while ago, and she told you that your risk of developing cancer isn't higher because of your mother's illness."

"I know that logically," Ryan said tiredly. "This isn't about logic. This is pure fear. It makes me sick to my stomach to even think about having a child and being taken from him or her." She shivered again and in a shaky voice said, "I don't have the kind of strength that my mother had. I'll never have the kind of strength that she had." Ryan's eyes were tightly closed. "She was the bravest person I ever met. She was a small woman, but she had enough courage for an army. And not because of the way she bore the intense pain she was in. The bravest thing she did was to keep her fear from us. When we were with her, she was always upbeat and optimistic. How hard must that have been? How could she avoid grabbing us and holding on with every ounce of strength she had, while she cursed the fates that were taking her from us? I'll never understand how she was so brave, but if I had half of her courage, I'd be happy."

Ryan dropped her head again, struggling to hold the tears at bay. "Her birthday wasn't long before she died. We had all of the furniture moved out of the living room for her hospital bed. There were tubes and needles and IVs and God knows what else stuck in every part of her body. She couldn't have weighed eighty pounds, but I still remember all of us sitting on that bed with her on her birthday. She sang songs with us, and even managed to eat some cake. After everybody else went to bed, she held me in those bony arms and sang that sweet lullaby to me in her angelic voice. As much pain as she had to be in—and all she cared about was that I felt loved and comforted. I slept with her on that tiny bed most of her last week. It must have been terribly painful for her to have me plastered all over her, but she seemed to need it as much as I did. I was in her arms when she died…" Ryan rested her elbows on her knees, dropped her head into her hands and sobbed violently. "God, I miss her," she choked out as Jamie rubbed her back.

Karma

"I know how much you miss her," Jamie murmured. "And I know how it frightens you to think about repeating what happened to her. But what I've heard from you about your mom makes me sure that she wouldn't want you to let your fears get in the way of living your life." Jamie reached up and grasped Ryan by the shoulders, holding her until the blue eyes rotated to meet her. "You're a very brave woman, too, even though you have your doubts sometimes. You are, sweetheart. You're brave enough to face your fears, and you're brave enough to live your life. Some day we'll leave our children, but I'm supremely confident that our kids are going to be in their seventies or eighties by that time. We're going to live to be very, very old women. You and me, together."

"I wanna believe that," Ryan sobbed. "I can see you as an adorable old lady, but I never have an image of myself like that." She started to cry even harder and said, "I don't want to leave you alone."

"You can change the way you think about this. This is your fear talking." She lifted her hands and grasped Ryan's face, gazing deeply into her eyes. "Visualize this with me," she begged. Sighing, Ryan closed her eyes and listened to Jamie's voice soothe her soul. "It's seventy-five years from now and we're getting ready for your big 100th birthday party. You and I are in our bedroom, and you're pitching a bitch about wearing a dress, as usual," she chuckled. "You're still devastatingly handsome in my eyes," Jamie said softly. "Hair as white as snow, you wear it short now, and the cut shows off that strong jaw you still have. Your eyes seem even bluer, contrasting with your white hair." Jamie leaned forward and kissed the closed eyes gently. "Your skin is paler, but it's still fairly dark, since you're still outside so often, playing with our great-great-grandchildren."

Ryan couldn't help but chuckle at that image; heartened, Jamie continued, "Your shoulders are still broad, but you've lost most of your muscle." She laughed softly and said, "You're still in shape, even though you can't pick up a few hundred pounds like you could when you were only eighty."

Eyes still tightly shuttered, Ryan leaned forward and unerringly found her lover's lips. "In my mind, you're still blonde," she whispered. "I can see you sitting on the bed, deciding what I should wear to the party, making sure I don't look too casual."

"Of course I'll still be blonde," Jamie giggled. "It might take all of my millions, but I'm never going to look a day over seventy-five."

Tilting her chin, Ryan started to place tiny kisses all over her partner's face, murmuring between each kiss, "I…love…you…with…all…my…heart."

"And I love you, too." Jamie kissed her gently and vowed, "We're going to have our babies, and we're going to raise them to be happy, healthy adults. Then we're going to help our babies raise their babies. Then we'll help our grand babies raise their babies. We're gonna be around for a very, very long time. I'm certain of that."

"I'm not certain," Ryan said, "but with your help, I'm sure gonna try to believe."

"You've gotta believe, baby," Jamie urged. "Believing can make it happen."

※

Jamie spent the evening tenderly caring for her still fragile partner. As usual, when Ryan was in a vulnerable mood, she gratefully accepted all forms of physical attention, but generally avoided talking about her feelings. Even though that wasn't Jamie's way, she had learned to respect Ryan's needs, and had eventually stopped trying to get her to talk. Instead, she made it a point to study in the same room; repeatedly finding an excuse to get up and kiss the back of Ryan's neck, or give her a short massage. Her gentle ministering continued through the evening, extending to their bedtime with Jamie holding her lover tenderly through the night.

※

Caring, loving, tender Jamie was nowhere to be seen when the alarm went off at five on Thursday morning. She looked at Ryan through bleary eyes and grumbled a faint acknowledgment of her presence. "You first," she decided, putting the pillow over her head. Ryan dutifully got up and showered, then spent a few minutes dragging her partner from the warm bed.

"I don't wanna," Jamie moaned.

"Honey, you made a date to meet your teammate. You can't stand her up. Now, come on. Be a good girl, and I'll make you some oatmeal."

One green eye opened warily. "With bananas?"

"Of course. Bananas and lots of brown sugar, like you like it."

"Okay," she said, a tiny smile forming on her lips. "Only you can make five in the morning appealing." She got up and stretched for a few moments, then asked, "What's on your agenda for today?"

"Big day," she said, rolling her eyes. "I've got to meet my study group at six, then I have class. I'm gonna come home after that and get on the phone and start investigating private schools for Jen. It's not going to be easy at this late date; time is slipping away if I'm going to find a spot for her for second semester. I could kick myself for waiting this long. I swear I don't know where the fall went."

"I don't either. You've been sitting around here on your cute butt. I didn't realize what a lazy woman you were when I married you."

"Funny," Ryan said, ruffling her disordered hair. "Don't forget we play St. Mary's tonight. The bus leaves at three, so I doubt I'll see you before I go. Now let me get my cute butt in gear or you won't get breakfast."

When Jamie met up with Juliet in the parking lot of the always-crowded municipal course, they were both puzzled to see several dozen cars already in the lot. "The sun has barely risen," Juliet muttered, sitting on the bumper of her small car to put on her spikes. "Do people sleep here overnight to get a good tee time?"

A car pulled in next to them and two elderly women got out, chatting companionably. Another car honked, and the women waved to their friends, while Juliet gave Jamie a scowl. One of the elderly women called out, "Hurry on, girls. You won't have any time to warm up."

The younger women hurriedly finished getting ready, then went over to the starter, their eyes wide as they took in the large number of women ready to tee off. "Hi," Juliet said. "We're on the Cal golf team. Any chance of sneaking in before this crowd?"

The man gave her a wink and said, "This is our ladies league. You two are ladies…why don't you join them?"

"Sounds appealing," Juliet said, eking out a smile, "but we only have about two and a half hours."

"Oh, well, the ladies generally take five, and that's only if they're first out in the morning." He started to chuckle. "I'm teasing you. They go off on ten rather than one. You'll likely still catch them, but probably not until fifteen or sixteen."

"Would anyone complain if we played two balls?" Juliet asked, now showing a warm, friendly smile.

"I think we could bend the rules a little. Do you girls have your passes with you?"

"Sure do," Juliet said, and Jamie produced hers as well.

"Hard to tell if you two are on the golf team or the modeling team," the elderly man teased. "Girls as pretty as you two didn't play golf when I was a young buck."

"Why, thank you," Juliet said. "You should sneak out and join us for a few holes. We play pretty, too."

"I bet you do," he chuckled. "Have a good round, girls."

As they walked away, Juliet joked, "I never have to flirt with the starter at my home course. Of course, my dad would throttle the guy if he ever tried to come on to me." She shrugged and added, "The joys of public courses."

"We should have gone to Stanford," Jamie agreed, chuckling softly. "Of course, I never would have made the team there." She gave Juliet an appraising look and asked, "Why didn't you go to Stanford? You're clearly good enough."

Juliet looked a embarrassed and said, "Uhm…don't take this the wrong way, but, coming here was part of my long term strategy."

"And that was…?"

"My dad and I decided that I'd stand out more on a more mediocre team. There are at least three players on Stanford that are as good, if not better than I am, and I was afraid of getting lost in the crowd over there. Cal's program is new, and we thought it would look better for me to help put a new program on the map than help an existing one stay excellent." Shrugging, she asked, "Does that sound as manipulative to you as it does to me?"

"You're planning your future. You have to consider all of the angles. I'm glad you're here."

"So am I," Juliet said, smiling. "Besides, gold and navy blue go better with my coloring. That cardinal red doesn't do a thing for me."

Her eyes were smiling as she said this, but Jamie detected a hint of truth in her statement. She briefly wondering if she inadvertently happened upon goal-obsessed women or unconsciously sought them out.

Ryan began to think her morning search for schools for Jennie had been a complete waste. She was not in the least surprised to find that most of the good schools in the East Bay were not very interested in a child that had been suspended three times in one year, had recently run away from home, and had changed schools three times in a six month period. She was running out of ideas when the phone rang, jolting her out of her reverie. "Hello?"

"Hello, Ryan, it's Catherine. I wanted to get in touch to tell you about a few calls I made today."

"Phone calls?"

"Yes. Jamie called this morning and told me that you were getting busy on finding a school for Jennie. So I made a few calls to the schools that we looked at when Jamie was young."

"Oh, Catherine, that's so thoughtful of you to get involved."

"Nonsense. That child needs help, and I'm only too glad to do what I can. I called every good school from the Peninsula to the South Bay, and the only one that will even give her an interview is Jamie's old high school. And I'm certain that's only because the headmaster knows how much money we have."

"Do you think Jennie would fit in down there?" Ryan asked as delicately as possible.

"That's a difficult question. I didn't tell the headmaster that Jennie is a lesbian, since I wasn't sure if she'd want them to know. Aside from her sexual orientation, I'm sure she would be the poorest child in the school. And my guess is that she'd be picked on for that more than anything else."

"I know from experience that being poor in a rich kids' school can be tough."

"Was that your experience, dear?"

"Yes. I went to a Catholic girls school in Pacific Heights. The saving grace was that they had five or six scholarship students in my class, so I didn't stick out too badly. And since my family had always stressed that money wasn't really important, I didn't get caught up in it. I chose my friends carefully, and got so involved in sports that I gained some popularity from that. But some of the other scholarship students didn't fare as well. A lot of them felt totally out of place."

"Adolescents can be so cruel to one another," Catherine sympathized.

"It worked out for me. And it helped me to see early on that money doesn't make people happier. That was a very valuable lesson."

"I couldn't agree more when I look at the depressive personalities in my family."

"You've given me an idea, Catherine. I think I'll go pay a visit to Sister Mary Magdalene."

"Is that someone from your old school?"

"Yes. The Mother Superior," she said. "And she owes me a huge favor."

Luckily, Sister's secretary found a spot for Ryan to speak with her at noon, so after making herself presentable, she took off for the city.

"Well, well, I didn't expect to see you so soon, Ryan," Sister Mary Magdalene said as she extended her graceful hand.

"Thank you for seeing me, Sister. I've come to speak to you about a young girl that I mentor."

"What a lovely thing to do. It's so rewarding to help influence a young woman's life."

"It's been rewarding and challenging," she admitted. "The young woman in question is a freshman at a high school in Oakland. She's bright and very creative, and I firmly believe that she could be an excellent student—given the right environment."

"But she's not an excellent student now," Sister said perceptively, getting to the root of the problem.

"That's hard to say, honestly. The girl has identified as a lesbian since she was twelve years old, Sister. Her mother is a follower of a very conservative minister, and she has tried to force my young friend to change her sexual orientation. As I'm sure you know, that's a losing battle."

Sister nodded patiently as Ryan continued. "That isn't the big problem, though. Her mother has a very, very strict set of rules; but when she breaks one, hew mom throws her out onto the street and expects her to fend for herself until the mom decides to let her back in. Because of this she's been forced to live in a group home, and that move required her to change high schools. Then the state decided that she should live with her father and stepmother in San Diego, making her change again. That didn't work out," she said massively understating the situation, "so she's now back in the group home. Obviously, she hasn't had much classroom work this year, and the school has thrown her into a program that sounds more like a holding cell than a high school. I know she'll be lost if she isn't challenged academically."

"This sounds like a very troubled child. And you should know that Sacred Heart is not equipped to deal with girls with severe behavioral problems. Our girls are very high achievers."

"I'm aware of that," she said with a smile. "I was one myself not very long ago."

"You certainly were," she agreed. "I'd say you were one of the most talented students ever to attend our school."

"Thank you, Sister. I know that I don't have to remind you that one of the tenets of Sacred Heart is to offer a quality education to girls who couldn't otherwise afford it on their own."

"Yes, you of all people know that's true. But girls from less affluent homes must qualify academically, and it sounds like your young friend couldn't do that."

"I'm not so sure of that, but I'm not asking you to consider her as a scholarship student. She can afford the tuition. And strange as it sounds, I don't consider her a troubled child. Strong willed and independent, but not troubled. She's actually an incredibly sweet girl that needs to see that there's a better way to live. But I can't convince you of this in the abstract. I'd like to bring her over here to meet you. Will you do me that favor?"

She pursed her lips together and looked suspicious, but she finally nodded and said, "I will. Can you bring her tomorrow?"

"If I can't, I can have a friend bring her. I'll check with your secretary and find a time when you're free." Ryan stood and extended her hand as she said, "Thank you very much for your time, Sister." As she walked out, she poked her head back into the office to warn, "She dresses casually, so be prepared."

※

That night, after another humiliating basketball defeat, Ryan came barreling out of the visitors' locker room to find her fans patiently waiting for her.

"Here's our star of the game," Catherine said as she made her way over for a hug.

"Star of the bench, but thanks anyway, Catherine," Ryan said with a good-natured smile. "I got to speak to the Mother Superior at my old school today. She's agreed to talk to Jen, but she wants to see her tomorrow at two. I've got to leave for Fresno at four, and I can't risk being late. Is there any way you could do it?"

"I'd be happy to. Does Jennie know I'll come for her?"

"Yeah. I spoke to her before I came down here this afternoon. Then I called the housemother and asked her to call Jennie's school and get her excused for the day. Given what she told us about her course of instruction, or lack thereof, she won't be missing anything anyway." Ryan pulled a sheet of paper from the organizer in her gym bag. "I've written her address down, and included directions from the freeway. The directions to the school are there, too."

"I'm sure it will all go fine. Don't worry about a thing." Turning to Jamie she asked, "Will you stop for a cup of coffee before you head back?"

"Ryan has to go on the bus," she grumbled. "Her coach isn't terribly flexible."

"Jamie's angry because we're taking the bus to Fresno, and Coach won't let her come with us."

"Well, it's stupid," she pouted.

"So you're not going, dear?" Catherine asked.

"No, it doesn't make much sense to fly down there to spend the evening alone in a hotel room."

"Alone? Why would you be alone?"

"They're having a team dinner tomorrow night to review some game films, and I obviously can't attend that. I've got plenty of studying to do since my first final is Wednesday, so we decided that I should stay home this time."

"Why don't you come down to the house on Saturday?" Catherine suggested. "You could lounge by the pool while you study."

"Good idea. It's a date."

"I've got to go, or I'll have to run sprints as punishment," Ryan said. "Why don't you two go out for coffee? This bus takes forever."

"Good idea. See you at home."

"Thanks a million, Catherine," Ryan said as she gave her a kiss.

"I'll call you tomorrow night with a full report," she promised. "Play well in Fresno, dear."

"Thanks a lot," she replied as she bent to kiss Jamie lightly. "Thanks for coming all the way down here, babe. It means a lot to me to see you in the stands."

"I'm your groupie through thick and thin. You're as cute on the bench as you are on the court." She wrinkled up her nose and added, "Cuter, really, since you get to wear that perfectly attractive warm-up suit when you're on the bench."

※

Catherine rang the doorbell at the group home at ten on the dot. She smiled to herself as she heard eager young footsteps flying down the stairs from the second floor. Jennie flung the door open, and said, "Hi, Mrs. Evans. Do you want to come in and meet Sandy?"

"I'd love to." She smiled back at the girl's infectious grin. She entered the haphazardly furnished, but neat and clean two-story Craftsman style home, and paused in the entryway while Jennie ran to fetch the housemother. Seconds later she came back, holding a middle-aged woman's hand.

"Mrs. Evans, this is Sandy. She's the housemother here."

"Good to meet you," Catherine said as she extended her hand.

"It's always nice to meet Jennie's friends," she said warmly. "I really think it's wonderful of you and Ryan to try to get Jennie into a decent school. Her high school is fine if you're in a regular class, but they're not very flexible when a child isn't able to attend consistently."

"This is a preliminary interview," Catherine warned. "Jennie might not like the atmosphere at the school."

"Let's go find out," Jennie said optimistically.

※

On the way to the car, Catherine surveyed Jennie's outfit. It was the same one she had worn on Thanksgiving, and even though it was an improvement over her normal attire, it would be perfectly clear that she was not of the same social class as the other girls.

After ogling Catherine's car for a while, Jennie turned to her and asked, "Do you think I look all right? Ryan said that mostly rich kids go to this school."

"I think you look very nice," Catherine said with a big smile. "But one of my favorite activities is to go shopping. What do you say we buy you another nice outfit for your next interview?" Jennie looked hesitant, albeit hopeful. Catherine immediately assured her, "My treat."

Her sweet face nearly exploded with delight as she said, "Are you sure you want to? You really don't have to do that, Mrs. Evans."

"Definitely. I never get to shop for Jamie anymore, and I really do love it."

"Okay," she said with a giddy laugh.

Catherine decided to take her to a department store, since she didn't want to overwhelm her with her normal elegant boutiques. She shied away from the area that catered to Jennie's ago group, and took her to the area for young professionals. A friendly young woman came over and asked, "Can I help you today?"

"Yes," Catherine said. "This young woman is interviewing with some exclusive prep schools in the area, and she wants to make sure she fits in."

"You've come to the right place," the clerk replied with a smile as she led Jennie to the attractively displayed racks of merchandise.

Karma

An hour later Jennie emerged from the dressing room looking absolutely fabulous, if a little stunned. She wore an elegant, stylish navy blue double-breasted blazer, a short sleeved white cashmere shell and a pair of slate gray pleated slacks held up by a thin black leather belt. Thin black trouser socks and highly polished black leather flats completed the ensemble that gave every indication that this was a young woman from old money, who was recovering from some sort of injury that had regrettably required her head to be shaved. Catherine wished once again that the interview could take place in a week or so since Jennie's brush cut was nearly at the point of lying down, but even her unconventional haircut didn't detract from how lovely she looked. "I knew there was a beautiful young woman hiding under those baggy clothes," Catherine teased her.

"I don't know what to say, Mrs. Evans—"

Catherine placed a hand on her shoulder and asked, "Do you like the clothes?"

"Yeah. Of course. I've never had anything that fit me like this."

"That's all that matters," she said firmly. Looking up at the sales clerk she advised, "We'll take these, and I want to add the long-sleeved gray turtleneck sweater in the same shade as the slacks."

"Great, would you like hangers or boxes?"

"Jennie, would you like your things on hangers?"

"Can't I wear them?" she asked tentatively.

Catherine let out a silent *"hooray."* "You can if you want to, dear. They're your clothes."

After lunch in the store's café, they headed over to the school. "I've never been over here, except to go to Ryan's a couple of times," Jennie commented. "It's cool."

"To Pacific Heights?"

"No, to San Francisco."

"Maybe we'll have to remedy that," Catherine said, once she'd recovered from the shock of hearing that the girl lived minutes away from one of the most beautiful cities in the world and had never visited.

When they arrived, one of the younger teachers was enlisted to take them on a thorough tour of the facility. The school was not at all large, and was mostly contained in one building, a former mansion that had been beautifully converted to classroom space. The high tuition, and "A list" of alumnae worked to provide top quality facilities. Catherine thought she would have to carry her young friend when she spied the beautifully equipped art studio. Jennie reverently moved about the room lightly touching the potter's wheels, mounds of modeling clay, tubes of oils and watercolors, stacks of canvasses and piles of sketchbooks. Their tour guide made eye contact with Catherine, and they both smiled at the ecstatic look on Jennie's face.

As luck would have it, they were able to observe a lesson being conducted in the large music studio. Several girls were playing electric keyboards while they wore headphones so they could hear only themselves. Tiny soundproof booths surrounded the large space, and each room held a student playing a woodwind. The instructor sat at a console outside of the rooms and listened to each girl in turn. She could speak to them, and they could reply, but other than her soft voice, the space was absolutely quiet.

As they walked back to the office, Catherine pulled Jennie over to the large trophy case near the front entrance. "Someone you know is mentioned a few times on these trophies," she said, having been clued in by Jamie.

Jennie looked at the trophies, her smile growing wider by the minute. She looked up at Catherine with near adoration in her blue eyes and gushed, "She's really something, isn't she, Mrs. Evans?"

"She is indeed," the older woman agreed wholeheartedly.

Just before they entered the office to meet Sister Mary Magdalene, Jennie asked if she could use the rest room. When she emerged, every hoop and stud was removed from every obvious piercing, making Catherine sigh with relief.

The interview went well, to Catherine's experienced ear, and when it was over Sister suggested that Jennie go back down to the art studio and observe the class that was being conducted. "I'll come fetch you in a few minutes," Catherine assured her.

As soon as they were alone, Sister Mary Magdalene smiled at Catherine and said, "Ryan was right. She seems like a very sweet girl, but I don't see her fitting in here."

"Why not?"

"Despite her outward demeanor, she has had some serious behavior problems, Mrs. Evans. Her grades have not been good, and she's basically learned nothing so far this year. She would be seriously behind the other freshmen, and I doubt that she could keep up without substantial outside help."

"What type of help?"

"She would need a private tutor at the very least. And even though she's beautifully dressed, I think it's obvious that she's from very humble circumstances."

"Your point being?"

"We couldn't afford to provide tutoring for her. I don't know how her family can afford tuition, but I can't imagine they could afford a private tutor also."

"Money need not enter into this discussion, Sister. Jennie will have everything she needs."

"But it's unfair to allow her to enter when her grades are so suspect. She'll be taking the place of a girl who'd be more deserving academically."

"Others might be more deserving academically, Sister, but I guarantee no other girl would benefit more from this experience. Isn't it worth the risk to have a hand in actually saving this child's life?"

Sister blinked slowly. "Do you honestly think she's in that much danger?"

"She was in terrible danger a few weeks ago. But Ryan has made a commitment to protect her, and she will do that—one way or another. Jennie seems to like it here, and I think the structure would be very good for her. She's far too worldly about some aspects of life, but incredibly naïve about others. I think this atmosphere will allow her to regain her innocence."

"I'd need to be assured that she will receive all of the outside help she needs, including psychotherapy if necessary," she said as Catherine felt her begin to cave in.

"She will have it. I'll personally see to it."

Sister nodded her head, and closed her eyes for a moment. Looking up, she tilted her head and asked, "What led you to become involved with Jennie, Mrs. Evans?"

"Ryan introduced us. And if Ryan believes in her, that's good enough for me."

"And what is your relationship with Ryan, if I may ask?"

"She's my daughter-in-law," Catherine said proudly.

Sister's eyes nearly popped from her head at that response, then her smile returned as recognition dawned, and she said, "I met your daughter this summer. She seems like a fine young woman."

"She is, and I believe Jennie can also become a fine young woman, with some help." She stood and fixed her gaze on the older woman as she asked, "What shall I tell her?"

"If she wants to attend, she may start on January the tenth."

Catherine grinned, nodding her head slightly. "I noticed that the lighting in the art studio is not very good quality."

"No, regrettably that's been a luxury we haven't been able to afford. The florescent lights leave quite a bit to be desired."

"How long are you closed for winter holiday?"

"Two weeks. Why do you ask?"

"That should be long enough to have professional quality studio lighting installed. Do you mind if I have my electrician contact you about upgrading? I'll pay for anything you choose."

"N…N…No, of course not, Mrs. Evans. That would be wonderful."

"His name is Kevin Driscoll, Sister. I'll have him call you on Monday."

Arriving back at the art studio, Catherine peeked in and saw Jennie sitting on a stool, absently fingering a pile of gray modeling clay. Her eyes were so fixed on the instructor that she didn't see or hear Catherine until she came up behind her. "Ready?" she asked quietly.

Jennie started, but scampered off the stool and joined her in the hall.

"Do you have plans for January the tenth?"

"No, not that I know about."

"How would you like to start school here on that day?"

Jennie stopped dead in her tracks and stared at Catherine with her mouth gaping open. "Really? Really?" she cried with a huge grin.

"If your mother gives her permission, Sister would love to have you."

"Mrs. Evans I'd give anything to come here," she said with wide eyes. "It's the coolest place I've ever been. But I don't think my mom will let me," she said as her face fell. "I talked to her on the weekend, and I told her that Ryan was going to try to help me go to a better school." She looked embarrassed as she said, "She told me that it didn't matter what kind of school I went to. All that's important is that I'm going to hell if I don't stop being gay." Her watery blue eyes looked up at Catherine. "Do you think that's true? Do you think that about Jamie?"

Catherine draped an arm around her small shoulders and said, "I don't believe the same things your mother does. I believe in a God who loves everything that he created. I think he did a very good job when he created you," she said softly as she brushed her hand along the side of Jennie's face. "If your mother does give her permission, would you mind coming this far to school?"

"How would I get here?" she asked, her practical side taking over.

"Don't worry about that. I want to know if you want to come here."

"Yes, I do," she said decisively. "I...I don't think I'm ever going to be able to go home, so I won't be able to go to my old school."

"Do you want to go home?"

Her head nodded briefly. "I miss my mom," she said softly. "But us living together is gonna get me killed," she added as a tear slipped down her cheek.

"Not a chance," Catherine assured her as she gave her a hug. "You have some very powerful protectors in your corner now."

Chapter Five

As soon as she dropped Jennie off, Catherine drove to Jamie's to apprise her of the events of the afternoon. Jamie had stopped at home before her last class and she was on her way out when Catherine pulled up. She leaned into the passenger window when Catherine rolled it down. "Mom, I've got to go."

"That's all right, dear. I have quite a few phone calls to make. Do you mind if I make them from here?"

"Of course not. I'll be home by six-fifteen. Do you want to stay that late? If you do, we could have dinner."

"I'll take you out to dinner, honey. Maybe Mia will join us. I haven't spent any time with her in an age."

"She usually has a date, but if you see her, ask her, okay?"

"I thought her boyfriend went to UCLA."

"Long story," she said as she kissed her mother goodbye, "but he's history."

Catherine went to make her calls from the kitchen table so she could make notes while she talked.

After calls to Kevin about the electrical work, a friend whose husband ran the department in City Hall that approved building permits, her lighting designer, and Ryan, she was absolutely talked out. It was after six when she heard the front door open, but instead of Jamie's voice, she heard Mia giggling as she ran across the parlor. "No," she screamed. "Stop it. Stop it." It sounded as if she was running away from someone, but her voice was giddy and playful, so Catherine didn't worry. "At least let me get a soda before you ravage me."

Catherine scrambled to her feet, deciding that she had to call out before they were all embarrassed. But as she started to speak, Mia came sliding across the kitchen floor followed by a wildly grinning Jordan. Catherine was shocked into silence as Jordan backed her prey up against the sink, and started to kiss her passionately as she ground her hips against her. Mia threw her arms around the strong neck and returned her heated kisses as a low moan escaped her. "I guess I don't really need a soda," she murmured sexily, trying to catch her breath. Her shrieks resumed as Jordan picked her up, and tossed her over her shoulder and started to make her way back to the parlor. Mia's head was facing away from the kitchen table now, and since Jordan was so focused on her captive, she didn't notice Catherine, either. As they made their way up the stairs, Catherine sat down, trying to get her mind around this development. She decided that the long story Jamie promised wasn't necessary, and that the old boyfriend was most definitely history.

Ryan lined up with the other players waiting to board the bus to Fresno on Friday afternoon. Since most of the players' legs were too long to fit into a bus seat in the traditional fashion, most of them took a seat alone and sat sideways. Ryan was one of the last to board, and as she passed row after row of solitary women she thought it was a good thing she'd brought her laptop with her. She nodded to Janae, but the large woman would never be able to share a seat—even if she wanted to, so Ryan kept going until she found a vacant one. The trip was expected to take about four and a half hours; she knew they could shave an hour off if they flew, but the athletic department tried to cut corners wherever possible, and bus trips were one way to do so.

Since she was blessed with the ability to be able to concentrate fully for long time periods, she hardly noticed the passing hours. A gentle hand on her shoulder caused her to look up with a start into the eyes of Lynette Dix. "Do you want to sleep on the bus?"

Karma

"We're here?" Ryan asked in amazement. "I had no idea."

"Studying for your test?" Lynette asked, craning her neck to get a look at the laptop.

"Yeah. I'm not sure how much help it will be at this point, but it keeps my mind occupied and makes the trip go faster."

"Well, you'd better get moving or they won't save a room for you."

"Don't we have assignments?"

"Nope. First come, first served."

"Oh, there you are," Shelly, the student manager said when she spotted Ryan in the lobby. "I guess it pays to be last. You get the single," she informed her as she held out the key. Before Ryan's hand reached hers, Janet Vitale, the senior point guard, and one of the pair that seemed most antagonistic to Ryan, grasped Shelly by the arm and hissed, "May I speak with you, in private?"

Shelly withdrew her arm from the firm grip and allowed Janet to lead her a few feet away. Ryan cooled her heels while the discussion continued, but she couldn't help overhearing words like "newcomer", "paying her dues", and "playing favorites" coming from Janet's mouth. Ryan felt bad for Shelly, but decided to let them work it out however they saw fit. A few minutes later, the red-faced manager approached Ryan tentatively and opened her mouth to speak, but Ryan graciously cut her off. "I don't care where I sleep, or how many people I share a room with. I could actually be okay on the bus."

Shelly's face relaxed into a grateful smile as she whispered, "Thank you. They're not paying me enough to take this crap."

"They don't pay you at all, do they?"

"Not a dime," she admitted. "Be right back with your key."

She walked over to Janet and handed her the key to the single and accepted the previously allotted key in return. As she started back towards Ryan, Janet's friend and starting forward, Wendy Dakin, grabbed Shelly and pulled her back next to Janet. Wendy was much more animated than Janet had been, and it quickly became obvious that she was incensed—not only at being dumped by Janet, but also at the thought of sharing with Ryan. Her face was clouded with anger, and she had the temerity to actually point at Ryan several times. Once again, Ryan tried to let Shelly do her job, but when she heard Wendy spit out the word "lesbian", she decided that she'd had enough.

She marched over to the front desk and quickly paid for an available room for herself. Strolling back over to Shelly, she dangled her key and said, "I got my own room."

The team manager looked like she wanted to kiss her, but her professional ethics reasserted themselves immediately as she said, "You don't have to do that. I can handle this."

"I'm sure you can, but I'll feel more comfortable if I don't have to worry about my ostensibly straight roommate 'accidentally' climbing into bed with me. I've always found that the people who act like they hate lesbianism the most are dying to try it." She gave both Wendy and Janet a big smile as she turned on her heel and strode off in her supremely confident style. An even wider grin graced her face when she heard the sputtering women unsuccessfully trying to form their outrage into words.

❦

The next afternoon Cal and Fresno State were knotted at sixty points when Wendy was called for her fourth foul. Ryan was itching to get out there and help, but with eight minutes left, she'd not yet been called on. She knew they should be beating Fresno State by twenty points, and having no opportunity to contribute was about to drive her wild. She'd been staring a hole in the back of Coach Hayes' head as the coach paced in front of the bench, but she knew it wouldn't do any good. As a matter of fact, it seemed that the more she indicated her eagerness to play, the less she was called on. As the coach turned around, she forced herself to look bored and, to her amazement, the woman knelt down in front of her and said, "We need offense. I know that defense is your specialty, but they've been double-teaming Drzislava all afternoon. Do you think you can knock down some jumpers?"

"I'll do my best," she said as she ripped off her warm ups. She ran over to the scorer's table and announced herself, indicating that she was to replace Wendy. It was the practice to take a towel with you and hand it off to the person you replaced, as a token of appreciation for their contribution. But when the whistle blew and Ryan pointed at Wendy, she watched in amazement as the player deliberately cut across the court to avoid Ryan's outstretched hand. She was forced to dash back to the sideline to deposit the towel she had carried. As she ran back to her position, she decided that Wendy would pay dearly for that slight.

Her intense focus and well-contained rage allowed Ryan to put on a show that amazed everyone—herself included. The first time she touched the ball, she dropped back and canned a trey, grinning and pointing at Franny Sumitomo who had fed her. As Fresno brought the ball down court, she easily stripped it, and was waiting under the basket to bank it in when Franny fed her again. During the next seven minutes, the double team switched from Drzislava to Ryan; but even with two defenders on her, she readily head faked both of them out of their shoes for one bucket after another. She noticed that Janet did not throw the ball her way once in the entire seven minutes, but every other player focused on her exclusively. At the end of the game, she had racked up sixteen points, and was the high scorer of the afternoon. In a somewhat surprising display of unity, every player except Janet and Wendy congratulated her enthusiastically as they made their way to the visitors' locker room. Janae draped her massive arm around her shoulders and said, "I've never seen a performance like that. Especially when the point guard won't throw you the damn ball."

"She's not a fan," Ryan said.

"Well, I am," Janae drawled, giving her a squeeze.

She had stripped off her uniform and was toweling off when Coach Hayes walked by and said, "Sleep well on Sunday night. You're starting Monday."

I guess that's code for "good job", she thought wryly as the enigmatic woman walked away.

This time Ryan rushed to be the first on the bus. She scrambled down the aisle until she reached the back row, and waited until she had Janae's eye. Janae took the seat across the aisle from Ryan's and they watched in amusement as the three rows in front of theirs remained empty. This fit Ryan's plans perfectly, because now they could talk without being heard.

"Well, partner, got any ideas about how to approach our reluctant teammates?"

Janae shrugged and said, "Not really, to tell you the truth. I know we've got to start somewhere, but it's going to be an uphill climb."

"I take it that approaching Wendy and Janet is futile," Ryan commented wryly.

"I've been with those two bitches since freshman year. It wasn't too bad then, but it's gotten worse every year. This year they think they run the team, and so far they've been right."

"Are they as homophobic as they seem?"

"I'm not sure. Part of me thinks it's not the gay thing as much as it is any difference. They treat the women from Europe like shit too, and they're straight. They don't even like Lily, Hilary and Ella, and I don't get that at all. All five of them are suburban, white, upper middle class women, and they're all straight. I think they look for something to dislike and focus on that."

"Maybe we should approach Hilary and Lily and Ella," Ryan suggested. "They've been around for a while, and they don't seem like complete assholes."

"Okay. How about Tuesday after practice?"

"Oh, right, we're at USF on Monday. Coach says I'll finally get to start."

"Wow, maybe she isn't as stupid as she looks." Janae grinned at her friend. "But I doubt it."

Jamie had driven down to Hillsborough on Friday evening, rising early on Saturday morning to start her studying. Aside from a two-hour break to listen to Ryan's game on the Internet, she'd been concentrating since eight. At around five, she looked up from the world's most boring accounting textbook to find her mother approaching with a small tray that held a pair of mugs. "Are you here on a humanitarian mission?" she asked.

"Pardon?"

"I thought the Red Cross had sent you to ease my suffering," she joked. "You know, I'm interested in knowing the concepts in this book, but getting there is not pleasant."

"I wish you were enjoying yourself more." She sat down on the chaise next to her daughter and handed her a mug of cocoa. "I appreciate that you're trying to make yourself more business savvy, but you could always hire a talented accountant, you know. You don't have to be able to do the work yourself."

"I know that. But I need to understand enough to know if my financial advisors are blowing smoke at me." She looked at her mother thoughtfully and said, "I learned a lot from the skirmishes Daddy and I had this fall. One thing that I'll never forget is that it's dangerous to trust someone to make all of your decisions for you. I won't do that again."

Catherine smiled warmly at her and commented. "You've learned quickly how to deal with your father. If I could have been more like you, we'd probably still be together."

"What do you mean by that?"

"You quickly learned that confronting him and giving him an ultimatum is the only way to reach him. He's used to wielding his power, and sometimes the only thing he responds to is a threat from an equally powerful opponent."

Jamie nodded, acknowledging that her father always tried to exploit weakness—in all of his relationships.

"I should have laid down the law and stuck to it. If I had thrown him out of the house after his first affair, it well might have been his last."

"Why didn't you?" Did you even consider it?"

"Of course I did. I...I didn't have the self-confidence I needed. I was a very confused young woman at the time. I think I let his affair erode my already shaky self-esteem to the point that he would have known I was bluffing if I'd threatened to leave." She shook her head and added, "From then on I didn't trust him. He knew it, but he also knew that I wouldn't do anything about it. Once you lose that trust, you no longer have a marriage." Patting Jamie on the leg she said, "That's one of the things I most admire about you and Ryan."

"What part of that is like us?"

"I admire how much confidence you have in her and in your relationship. The way you welcome her former lovers into your life speaks volumes about the trust you place in her."

Jamie shifted in her seat and gave her mother a sheepish look. "Don't put too much stock in the way I treat Sara and Ally."

"What do you mean, honey?"

"Well, uhm…let's say that my reasons for welcoming them aren't exactly noble."

Furrowing her brow, Catherine asked, "What are they, if not noble?"

"Practical. They're purely practical."

"You've lost me, honey. How can having Ryan's ex-lovers in your life be a practical move?"

She looked thoughtful and took another sip of her cocoa. "It's like this. I know my Ryan well. Spending as much time together and learning so much about her before we became lovers was the best thing that could have possibly happened. During that time I watched her try to start a relationship with another woman, and I also saw how she was with her more casual liaisons. One thing I learned was that she can't stand to be dictated to. She needs a lot of autonomy, and she needs to make her own decisions."

"Yes," Catherine said, "that sounds like Ryan."

"So, when her ex-lovers started popping up, I let her set the tone. She acted like it made her happy to maintain relationships with them, so I encouraged."

"Encouraged her?"

"Yes. I wanted to make it clear that I fully supported her choice to have an ongoing relationship with each of them—if that's what she wanted."

"But you wouldn't have chosen to have them be in your circle, if not for Ryan?"

"Hell no." She laughed. "Nobody wants to be reminded of her partner's past. I hate to recognize how much Sara shares with her. They went through so many things together, Mom, so many things that helped form Ryan. I despise that she knew the completely innocent young girl that will never reappear. I desperately wish I knew Ryan then—but I never can. It really sucks," she said, shaking her head.

"What about Ally?"

Rolling her eyes, Jamie said, "She's even worse. I know full well that half of Ryan's sexual repertoire comes from her. Every once in a while Ryan will do something to me and I think, 'Thank you, Ally.'" She started to laugh and said, "It's silly, because she's as marvelous a lover as she is partially because of the time they spent together. But I hate the fact that she was there first. That naïve young woman is also gone forever, and even though I love who she's become, it bugs the hell out of me that Ally's the one who made her who she is—in the sexual arena, at least."

"I had no idea," Catherine said slowly. "You acted so cordial to them both on Thanksgiving."

"Oh, don't get me wrong. I like them both. I don't think I could put that on. But I'm resentful of the place they hold in Ryan's life. Sometimes it bothers me to be reminded of it."

"But honey, if it bothers you, maybe it's not a good idea to try to form a friendship with them. You might start resenting them—and Ryan—because of it."

"No, I don't think so. I'm willing to tolerate my discomfort to give Ryan the autonomy she needs." She gave her mother another thoughtful look and said, "I knew who Ryan was when I fell in love with her. I knew she'd been deeply in love with Sara, and I knew that it tore at her to be estranged from her. How could I be the one to stand in the way of them having a connection again?"

Catherine nodded. "I see your point."

"But even though I know it's the right thing to do, I don't have to like it," she chuckled. "I'm trying to be generous, but sometimes I wish we could move to France. I'm sure she doesn't have any French ex-lovers."

"Well, at least you know who hers are," Catherine said, looking tired.

"Yes, I do. I know who each and every one is if they meant anything to her." She reached across to capture her mother's hand. "I think you probably do too, Mom. I don't think Daddy was ever in love with anyone other than you."

She gave her a wan smile and said, "You might be right. But I think the last one on his long list might have changed that. I think he really cares for her." Sparing a small smile, she added, "I should send her my condolences."

Jamie nodded and said, "I rather doubt she's the last woman in his life."

"I hope she knows that," Catherine sighed. She rose and said, "I'll leave you to your work. Hope the jolt of caffeine will help."

"Thanks, Mom." She grasped her hand and brought it to her lips, giving it a kiss. "Thanks for being there for me. It feels good to be able to talk about Sara and Ally with you."

"Anytime, sweetheart. I've always wanted to be your confidant." She gave her a wistful sigh and squeezed her hand, then turned and went back into the house, Jamie staring after her with a pensive gaze.

After stretching out on the bus and chatting with Janae, Ryan curled up in the corner of her seat and managed to snag a nearly three-hour nap, not waking until they hit a pothole in Berkeley. Since the bus passed a block from her house, she walked up to Lynette and asked, "You know how I said I had to be supervised today?"

"Yeah."

"Would you be willing to get off and go to my house for a second before I head over to school? I'm dying for a shower and something to eat, and I know Coach Hayes won't go with me."

"Sure. No problem. I can't imagine that you'll be able to stay awake through the darned thing at this point, so you'd better get some coffee, too."

Ryan walked up to the front and asked the driver if he could let her out when they passed the street. Coach Hayes heard the request, and her low voice floated up to Ryan over the noise of the engine, "This isn't a city bus. We don't make intermediate stops; and frankly I'm getting tired of you trying to manipulate things for your own convenience."

Ryan turned to face her in shocked silence. With all of the trouble and dissension on the team, she was absolutely amazed to have the coach single her out for criticism for wanting to get off a bus. The pragmatic part of her knew she should ignore the comment and go back to her seat, but she was sick of the coach's attitude, and she was not in the mood to suffer in silence.

Sliding into the seat beside her, she cocked her head and asked, "Would you care to expand on your statement?"

The older woman looked slightly surprised to have a player confront her, but she quickly leveled her gaze and said, "We've taken two road trips, and you had to have a private room both times. Then you try to get permission to fly back from Fresno so you can take a test. It doesn't help morale when you insist on special favors," she scowled. "Especially when you flaunt your money to get what you want."

"Flaunt?" Ryan blinked slowly, her mind refusing to comprehend the ridiculous statement. "Did you say flaunt?"

"This is a team. Obviously you can afford to have your girlfriend travel with us, and you can afford to turn up your nose at the team buffet and eat in the dining room. You can apparently pay for a private room without blinking an eye. But no one else around here can do that—and it's very divisive. You're clearly used to traveling in style, but you're going to have to lower your standards to fit in."

"There was a problem with room assignments," Ryan snarled, her anger at the boiling point. "I was trying to make things easy. I do not like to throw my money away on a room…and I don't flaunt it."

"Don't you ever raise your voice to me, Ryan O'Flaherty," the coach growled, her anger flaring. "If you want to get your hands on a ball again, you'll calm down and take your seat." Her steel-gray eyes were boring into Ryan, and the younger woman had to force herself to get up and put some distance between them.

She slunk back to her seat and pulled her knees up to her chin, cursing under her breath, refusing to even respond to Janae's curious inquiry about what had happened. Grabbing her cell phone, she called Jamie and growled, "Will you bring me a sandwich and a gallon of coffee?"

"Honey," she said with concern, "what's up? You sound furious."

"I am. Please bring me something—anything—to eat, and some form of caffeine. I'm about to blow months of work here, and I'd like a fighting chance. I'll be in front of Haas…trying to cool off." She disconnected without another word, leaving Jamie to stare at the receiver for a moment before she ran downstairs to rustle up something for her partner to eat.

When Jamie arrived, Ryan was sitting on the steps near the main entrance of Haas Pavilion, a somber Coach Hayes standing a few feet away. Leaving the car running, Jamie jumped out and handed her partner a bag with two sandwiches, two bananas, and two peeled, sectioned oranges. A giant latte was in her other hand, and Ryan grabbed it and started chugging it, something Jamie had never seen a human do. "Ryan?" she said softly, placing a hand on her arm, "do you want to tell me what's going on?"

"Let's go," the coach said brusquely. "My family's waiting for me."

Not uttering a word, Ryan gave her partner a squeeze and turned to follow the taciturn woman, shoveling bites of her sandwich into her mouth, washing it down with the coffee as she walked.

Ryan's anger at Coach Hayes merged with the rancor she still held towards the math professor who'd refused to let her join Cal's Putnam team, and she let it grow, knowing that she didn't have enough reserves to get through the test on her own. Deciding to harness the anger for motivation, she took her seat, thanking Professor Berkowitz for agreeing to proctor the exam at the ridiculous hour of nine in the evening.

Concentrating with every available bit of focus she could summon, Ryan took a deep breath and opened the test booklet, keeping her inner fires stoked with the mental image of pummeling her two main adversaries with her bare hands.

"Five minutes," Professor Berkowitz mumbled as her watch alarm roused her from the nap she'd been taking. The woman had arranged for a couch from a nearby office to be brought into the classroom, and she'd been out cold for an hour. The professor was duty-bound to keep an eye on Ryan, but the fact that Ryan had nothing but a spent coffee cup and plastic wrap from her sandwiches with her made the odds of her cheating infinitesimal.

As much as Ryan appreciated that the professor had readily agreed to proctor for her, she had to admit that hearing her snore softly was not really helping her stay awake. It was merely one more annoyance that demanded she sink into a deeper level of concentration.

At midnight, the professor took the papers away. "You're allowed a two hour break, you know, but it's optional. How long do you want?"

"I need to go to the bathroom and throw some water on my face."

They walked out together, since she wasn't allowed to be alone for any reason. As the door swung open, it hit a wicker picnic basket that had been placed right in their path. "What in the heck?"

"You need to check it out," Ryan said, "but I'm sure there aren't any test answers in there, just food from my sainted girlfriend."

The professor gave her a smile and picked it up, taking a note from the top. She read it quickly and handed it to Ryan, a big smile covering her face as she said, "Somebody loves you."

> *Hi sweetheart,*
> *I didn't know what you might need, so I've included a thermos of coffee, another of Pepsi, some sandwiches, cookies, fruit and some raw veggies. There's plenty for your professor too, so don't be greedy.*
> *I love you madly,*
> *J*

Ryan smiled back, and nodded agreeably. "Someone does indeed."

"Time's up," Professor Berkowitz said through a yawn as the alarm chimed 3:15 a.m.

Ryan's head dropped to the desk as her arm shot out, extending the test and her blue books dramatically.

After gathering up her supplies, the woman patted Ryan on the back and said, "Need a ride home?"

"Thanks for asking, but I have a feeling that a certain someone is going to be right outside," Ryan said, fatigue etching her face.

The professor laughed and said, "My certain someone's likely been asleep for five hours by now. After you're married for a couple of years, the picnic baskets don't show up with any regularity."

"We're gonna try to keep the magic going."

"With your determination, I wouldn't put anything past you. I hope you're pampering each other into your dotage."

They walked out of the building together, and were immediately hit with a set of flashing headlights. The professor gave Ryan a smirk, which was returned. "Like clockwork," Ryan said as she shook the woman's hand to thank her one last time.

To Ryan's surprise, Jamie, Jordan and Mia were all in the Lexus, and from the aroma that hit her when she entered, they had been at a bar. "Well, well, well, where were you girls while I was draining years of information from my poor brain?"

Jamie kissed her and gave her a squeeze. "We closed up the White Horse, then we went out for pancakes. We figured that if you had to stay up all night—we did too."

"I love you all," Ryan said, feeling all of the tension and anger leave her body. "One of you in particular," she added, giving her partner a fond pat.

When they reached the house, Jamie said, "Mom and I listened to the whole game on the Internet. I was soooo proud of you, baby. I called your father every fifteen minutes or so to give him an update for the first half, then he went over to Brendan's, and they listened too. He called me when it was over, and he was crowing with pride about how well you played."

"That really makes me feel good," she mumbled as she started to climb the stairs. "Coach told me that I can start on Monday." She flashed a brief smile.

Karma

"That's wonderful. Aren't you excited?"

"Maybe I'll be tomorrow," she said, yawning widely.

"Great game, slugger," Jordan said as she ruffled Ryan's hair. "We'll all be there to root you on at USF on Monday night."

"Thanks," she said, stifling another yawn. "I'll see you there, if I get up in time." Jamie shot a concerned glance at her and shared another with Jordan, as Ryan climbed the rest of the stairs with an uncharacteristic slump to her shoulders.

It was nearly ten when Jamie looked up from her income tax textbook to see Ryan begin to stir. "Hi," she said quietly. She got up and went to sit on the edge of the bed. "How are you feeling?"

Ryan blinked and rubbed her eyes while she made mewing noises for a few moments. This persona was one of Jamie's favorites, and she looked forward to the rare occasions that she saw this childlike behavior. As expected, Ryan's voice was small and rather high pitched as she squeaked out, "I feel gooder."

"Ohh, my cuddle bear looks like she needs some hugs. Does she?"

"Uh-huh." She happily nodded her dark head and extended her arms. Jamie got back into bed, and cuddled with her partner's warm body. She could feel her begin to wake fully, it was like watching a complex mechanical system warming up; she could feel muscular tension move up the long body from her toes to her head. By the time Ryan launched into her stretching routine, her mind was fully functioning, and she looked at the clock in amazement. "God, I'm setting some new records for laziness here."

"Not laziness—sanity," Jamie reminded her. "When your body conks out like that, it's because it needs it, honey. It's really not optional."

"I've gotten better at seeing that, but it's still hard to get the guilt feelings to go away."

"I know, but it's important to sleep when you need it, even if it does make you feel guilty."

"I guess things could be worse," she teased her partner as she snuggled her nose against her chest. "Being forced to be in bed with a beautiful creature like you is not such a bad thing."

"Hey, if you want to spend any time with your beautiful family, it's time to put your sweet butt in gear," she admonished as she patted the bare bottom.

"Be ready in ten," Ryan promised as her feet hit the floor.

Even though they spent the afternoon and evening with the family, it wasn't quality time, since Ryan spent much of the day dozing in front of the television in Conor's room. After dinner they retired to the bedroom so that Jamie could get some studying done. Ryan was still so fatigued that she didn't even pretend to study. She put some soft music on, and lay down on her bed next to her lover.

Jamie was determined to get in a few solid hours of work for her income tax final, since it was scheduled for bright and early Wednesday morning. It took all of her powers of concentration to be able to study with her partner dozing lightly and curled up next to her, but by ten o'clock she'd managed to make a sizable dent in her preparations. She had been idly running her fingers through Ryan's dark hair for the last half hour or so, but she wasn't actually paying much attention to her. "Well, I guess we should get going," she said, stretching the kinks out of her back.

Ryan was as deeply asleep as Jamie had ever seen her. She didn't even stir when Jamie got off the bed, something that never happened. Deciding they'd better stay the night, Jamie called Mia to tell her, then went to brush her teeth. Ryan was still out, so she went to the closet and took out a heavy blanket. After lying next to Ryan she tossed the end of the blanket so it covered them both. Still out, Ryan immediately turned on her side, seeking the warmth of Jamie's body. It wasn't the same as a good-night kiss, but it still counted.

Karma

Despite finals week Scott wanted the golf team to meet for practice, so Jamie dutifully drove over to Berkeley early on Monday morning, then went back to Noe Valley. Upon her orders, Ryan had reluctantly agreed to sleep in, and Jamie was pleased to find her still horizontal when she returned. "You can get up now, princess," she announced, sitting on the edge of the bed.

"I'm awake. I've been dawdling."

"It's nine-thirty," Jamie told her. "Take your shower and I'll get us a snack. Then I've got to start working on that income tax stuff again."

They both worked for a couple of hours, and after a quick lunch, Jamie pushed her partner back towards the bed. "But I don't want to take a nap," Ryan's childlike voice protested.

"I don't remember asking you if you wanted a nap, sweetheart. I'm ordering you. So lay your sweet self down, and rest your head on my lap."

"Do I get a head rub?" she asked, as she looked up at her partner through half-lidded eyes.

"Yes, you do," Jamie replied indulgently. "But only if you stick that pouty lip in." She bent and kissed the protuberant lower lip.

"Why do I hafta lie down? It's only one o'clock. I've only been up for three and a half hours."

"I know. But you need to be at the gym by five, and I want you to have a good long nap and a good meal before you leave. I don't want you collapsing again tonight."

"Okay," Ryan agreed as she got into bed. She shuffled around in the big bed for a moment before she looked up at her partner with a sexy grin. "I think I need a sedative," she drawled in a deep voice.

Jamie smiled and spent a moment regarding the child/woman who gazed up at her. When Ryan was in this mood, she tended to skitter between pouty five year-old and horny twenty-four year-old with startling frequency. "I'll make you a deal," she promised as she leaned over and kissed her lightly. "I'll make dinner for you at four. If you go to sleep right away, I'll please you in any way that you want if you wake up before then."

"Any way?" the very sexy older version asked with a devastating leer.

Jamie gulped audibly and nodded slowly, hoping that she could handle whatever she was getting into.

She never got to find out what Ryan's sexy leer represented, since she almost had to throw cold water on her partner to get her out of bed at four. "I don't wanna get up," she groaned as Jamie grasped her hands and tried to pull her into a sitting position.

"If you don't get up, you won't have time to eat. You haven't had much fuel today."

"I've been asleep the whole time," she complained. "When did I have time to eat?"

"Come on," Jamie cajoled. "I have something good for you…"

"What?"

"Italian comb—" she began; but before she could finish the word, Ryan was scooting across the bed and running for the bath. "You're welcome!"

Ryan had not actually spoken to Coach Hayes, but she had left a message for her as soon as her brain was functioning that morning. She left her home number, and her pager, and asked the coach to call her if she had a problem with Ryan getting to the game on her own. Her message was quite detailed, explaining that her family's home was minutes from USF, and that she was still fighting a serious bout of fatigue brought on by her having to stay up all night to take her math test. She didn't hear from the coach, so she assumed that the woman realized the folly of traveling to Berkeley to ride on a bus to return to where she had started from.

Jamie had never been to USF, so she decided to accompany Ryan and wander around the campus while they did their warm-ups. The gym wasn't even open when they arrived, so they walked over to a campus map where Ryan explained the layout of the plant. At a few minutes to five the Cal bus pulled up, and they walked back to the players' entrance to wait for the team. Most of the players were polite, and a few were even friendly as they milled around to wait for entrance. Jamie was about to kiss her goodbye when Coach Hayes walked up. "Twenty-five lengths of the gym," she said conversationally. "You can do them before or after the game."

"P...Pardon me?"

"You missed the bus. You know the rules," she replied flatly.

"But I called you..." she started to say, but the coach held her hand up to cut her off.

"Everyone rides the bus. That's the rule. Calling me to tell me you're going to break a rule is no excuse. I expect better behavior from a senior," she said dismissively.

Ryan shot a look at Jamie and, with a second to spare, firmly clamped her hand over her fuming partner's mouth. "Am I still starting?" she asked while Jamie squirmed under her grip.

"Yes."

"I'll do the laps after the game. I don't want to wear my legs out."

"Fine," Coach Hayes replied. "But you'd better make them quick. We leave thirty minutes after the final buzzer." She turned on her heel, and strode into the entrance, leaving them standing right where they were.

"Of all the bone headed..." Jamie started, but Ryan leaned over and kissed her lightly.

"I can take care of myself. I knew she had a bug up her ass about the bus, but I figured she'd be decent enough to call me back if there was a problem."

"Stupid fu..." she began again, but Ryan bent once more to cover her lips with a kiss.

"If I don't get in there, it's going to be fifty," she warned. "Let me get out while I'm ahead."

"So you can't even ride home with me?"

"Ride home together? Ha! She has a rule about us making eye contact with people in the stands. This is all part of her odd ideas about discipline. I'll see you when I get home," she said softly, giving her a tender kiss. Jamie's eyes were burning with anger, but Ryan gently reminded her, "This is my first time starting, honey. I don't want to screw it up."

Reluctantly, Jamie's expression softened, and she nodded. "You'll do great. I'm proud of you, Tiger."

The largest O'Flaherty rooting section of the season was on hand for the tip off. Since the game was so close to home, nearly all of the uncles, aunts and cousins were in attendance, as well as Catherine. The entire volleyball team also made the short drive, after stopping to pick up a delighted Jennie. When everyone had arrived, they comprised at least a quarter of the total crowd, and the buzz was audible.

Jamie sat with Conor on her left and her mother on her right. Jordan and Mia were right in front of her, along with the rest of the volleyball team. Catherine placed her hand on Jordan's shoulder and said, "I was so pleased to hear that you were given the chance to try out for the national team."

"Thanks, Catherine," she said with a big smile as she turned in her seat. "I'm pretty excited about it."

"When do you leave?"

"I'm taking off next Monday morning. I got permission to take two of my finals early, so I'll be finished with school as of Friday."

"Oh my, that's so soon," Catherine said.

"You're telling me," she heard Mia mutter glumly. Catherine bit back a smile and refrained from commenting. She knew the young women were physically intimate, but she didn't feel comfortable revealing her knowledge to either of them.

"It's exciting to see Ryan finally start isn't it, honey?" Catherine asked, turning to her daughter.

Conor poked his head out to comment. "This might be her first start, but it won't be her last. I don't know what the normal starting forward did to her, but Ryan's made it a personal vendetta to keep her butt on the bench."

Jamie and Catherine were taking Caitlin for a spin around the gym when the teams came back out for their short warm up before the opening tip-off. Jennie had not seen Ryan since she got the

Karma

good news about Sacred Heart, and her childish enthusiasm got the best of her. She scampered down the stands as the players went to their benches for final instructions. The starting players sat down, with the rest of the team and the coaches all gathered around them. The band was playing very loudly, and Coach Hayes paused impatiently to let them finish their number. Jennie came bounding up behind Ryan's seated form and poked her head around to give her an enthusiastic kiss on the cheek. As Ryan turned around she graced her with a wide smile, and patted her hand. She was still wiping the grin off her face as she watched the young woman turn and run back to her seat. Coach was still waiting for the band, but as Ryan turned around to face her she encountered a fierce scowl leveled at her. The coach made a hand signal that was punctuated by one word that she mouthed. "Fifty."

Her play left no doubt that Ryan was not only trying to secure a starting job, but was also making an emphatic point. She was not only a human scoring machine, she played defense with an intensity that was truly stunning. Conor and Brendan had been keeping up such a running commentary on her game that after ten minutes had passed, Jamie and Catherine got up and put Conor right next to Brendan so they could converse without leaning over them. "One thing I love about Ryan's game is that she's the only woman I've ever seen who uses head fakes on defense," Conor said. "That's kick-ass."

Maggie had watched more basketball games than she could count, and she joined in on the conversation. "Her defensive skills are head and shoulders above any other woman on the court."

"It helps to have twelve older cousins and three older brothers," Conor said with a chuckle. "We all played basketball, and since she was always the shortest player she had to develop her ball handling skills and learn to play very aggressive defense. She played at the point in all of our pick up games, so even though she plays forward at Cal, she still has the instincts of a point guard."

"My favorite part of her game is when she gets her volleyball and basketball skills mixed up," Maggie chucked. "I thought the woman she was guarding was going to swallow her tongue when Ryan slapped the ball back at her like she was serving a volleyball. There's nothing I like more than watching a single player disrupt the rhythm of a whole team, and Ryan does that beautifully," she said with admiration. "Too bad she doesn't want to go to law school. She could be a lethal trial attorney."

Conor bit his tongue before he was tempted to tell Maggie where on her list of potential careers his baby sister would place "attorney". Instead he forced a smile onto his face and nodded.

As the halftime buzzer sounded, Catherine stood and stretched for a moment, then turned to Jamie. "Would you girls like to go to a football game on Sunday?" She reached into her purse and pulled out some tickets.

"Uhm…sure. Are the 49ers home?"

"No, but your father left his Raider's tickets with me. He has eight of them. Would you like them, dear?"

"Sure."

"Conor?" Jamie teased as she held out the tickets and tickled his nose.

"Yeah, I'd like to go."

"Go where?" Mia asked as she turned around. "I want to go, too."

"You don't know where we're going."

"No, but you only go cool places, so I want to go, too."

"We've got eight tickets," Jamie said. "Jordan? Would you like to spend your last day in town at a Raider's game?"

"Yeah," she said after a moment's consideration. "It'll help me not miss the Bay Area so much."

Jamie turned to Conor and asked, "Would the other boys like to see the Raiders?"

"Sure. Rory likes them more than Brendan, but Brendan likes them well enough."

"Works for me," she said as she scampered down the row to propose the event to Rory, Brendan and Maggie.

The second half quickly turned into a rout, and the subs got into the game with almost ten minutes left. Ryan was replaced by Wendy—who, as expected, did not offer Ryan a towel or acknowledge her in any way. Jamie noticed the tiny smirk that crossed her lover's face as she went to take her seat and said, "That jerk will never play again if Ryan has her way."

When the game was nearly over everyone started to say their goodbyes. "Uhm, I can't leave for a while," Jamie said. "Ryan has to run twenty-five laps for missing the bus."

"She what?" Martin shouted.

"She has to run twenty-five laps of the gym," Jamie repeated tentatively.

"That is the stupidest, most asinine, imbecilic…"

"I know, Martin," she soothed. "But she wants to play, and she wants to be able to start, so she needs to go along—no matter how stupid it is."

"Where did this idiot learn to coach? In reform school?"

The family was getting antsy, waiting for the end of the game to watch Ryan run her laps. By now Janae was the only starter playing, and that was mostly because they didn't have an adequate backup center.

Play was getting sloppy this late in the rout, and the players seemed less focused than normal. Cal had Janae, Wendy, Lily, Hilary, and La Trice on the court, a team that had never played as a group. They looked pretty ragged on their first possession, and La Trice threw the ball out of bounds on a fairly simple pass to Wendy. As usual, Wendy was the soul of graciousness, barking out a loud criticism at La Trice as they ran back down the court to defend their goal.

Ryan didn't know much about La Trice, but the woman seemed very ruffled by the incident. La Trice was a senior, and she didn't seem to have the fire that a good point guard needed. Ryan had noticed that she played tentatively, even in practice, and this evening's production didn't do much to change Ryan's opinion.

On the next trip down the floor, the guard tried to thread a pass through some traffic and hit Janae for a shot from the post. Ryan could see her friend's eyes widen as the ball came to her. The pass was a good two feet too high, and Janae jumped as high as she could to snare it. Her defender went up with her, while another player cut behind them to guard Wendy. There was a lot of traffic under the basket, and somehow Janae caught her foot on someone as she came down. Ryan felt all of the moisture leave her mouth as she saw the inevitable collision play out in front of her eyes. Janae landed on her butt at the same time the other player hit the floor, and their heads banged together so hard that the crack was audible throughout the gym.

The student trainer was on her feet, running across the court before the two women slumped onto the unyielding floor. Coach Hayes was right behind her, while Lynette got to her feet and tried to keep the rest of the team on the bench. The anxious players strained against her, but she held them back so the medical staff could work uninterrupted.

Ryan turned and caught Jamie's eye, and Jamie's heart immediately clutched in pain for her partner. Ryan looked both frightened and powerless—two emotions that she didn't handle particularly well. She mouthed two words. "It's bad." Jamie nodded somberly, watching Ryan turn around stiffly to watch the scene unfold.

It was obvious that both players were unconscious, since neither had moved a muscle in the moments that passed like weeks. Jaleesa turned to the women on the bench and said, "We have to pray for them." She reached out, and every player except for Janet joined hands and bowed their heads, letting Jaleesa's words of praise and blessing calm their souls, if not their emotions. Janet broke away from the group and stood on the court with Wendy. The pair looked concerned, even frightened, but they clearly didn't want to remain with the group.

Two rolling gurneys were brought out, and cervical collars were carefully attached to both women to circumvent any additional spinal damage. Ryan was beside herself with worry—mostly because she'd been the recipient of so many similar injuries and she knew it was a very bad sign to be out for this long.

Everyone on the Cal sideline breathed a collective sigh of relief when Janae's fingers began to move as she was wheeled away. She was having a tough time, but Ryan realized that she wasn't twitching—she was trying to wave—and the gesture became even clearer a moment later. "She's awake!" Jaleesa cried. "Thank you, God."

Coach Hayes came back to the bench and said, "She's awake,

and she can move her hands and feet. The other girl looks like she's coming around, too. I think she'll be okay—probably a concussion, but nothing too serious."

Ryan gave her a look—knowing how serious a concussion could be. She was surprised when the coach returned her glance and said, "Go in for Janae."

Her surprise was so great that Ryan actually looked over her shoulder to make sure that one of the centers wasn't standing behind her. "Me?" she asked weakly.

"Yes, you," the coach said sharply.

With more than a little trepidation, Ryan walked over to the scorer's table and checked in. She shot a glance at her family and met Conor and Brendan's puzzled looks, adding one of her own. "Is she going in for Janae?" Jamie asked the boys.

"I hope not," Conor said. "She can't play center—especially in this league."

"Why not?" Jamie asked. "Ryan's as tall as anyone but Janae."

"That's not her style," Conor said. "Especially with the way Cal runs their offense. They want a true low-post player—and that's not what Ryan's built for."

Jamie gave him a suspicious look, having a feeling that her partner could play quarterback for the football team if she had a mind to. The game finally resumed, and it wasn't pretty. The team was even more disordered with Ryan's addition, and everything seemed to fall apart. Cal still won, but their last few minutes were such a mess that everyone realized the outcome would have been very different if much more time had remained.

Afterward, the team sat in the locker room, heads down, and their spirits as low. Coach Hayes tried to rally them, but her words fell flat. Jaleesa looked up at her and asked the only question that anyone cared about. "Any word on Janae?"

"She's at the hospital, and they're going to do a CAT scan on her to make sure there's no significant damage. I really think she'll be fine, people. Let's keep a good thought, and go on."

"Ryan, can I have a word?"

Ryan stood and waited for her to indicate where she wanted her. Coach led her back out onto the court and said, "This has been a tough night for all of us. You can do your laps after practice tomorrow if you want."

Surprised at this largesse, Ryan thought about it for a minute and said, "I'm so wiped after practice that I don't think I could do fifty. If that's my only option, I'd better do them now."

"Your choice. Did you weigh in before warm-ups?"

"Yeah," Ryan nodded.

"Go weigh in again. If you've lost more than a pound I won't allow you to do them tonight."

Ryan jogged to the locker room and weighed herself, noting that she hadn't lost any weight during the game. Trotting back out, she announced, "No loss. I was very careful to keep drinking."

"Okay, then let's go. We don't have all night."

Ryan ran over to the cart that the student trainer carried water and sports drink in. She took a big gulp from a fresh bottle, and set it down on the floor near the end line and took off. Her pace was quick, what Jamie would call a fast jog—but that wasn't good enough for Coach Hayes. "I said sprints," she reminded her loudly. "Start over."

The tension around Ryan's mouth became more pronounced, but she walked to the other end line and took off at full speed. She was moving so quickly that she had to put both hands out to stop herself against the other wall, and when she got there the coach called out loudly, "That's one."

The torture went on until all of the O'Flahertys were staring holes in the back of Coach Hayes' head. Ryan was sweating so profusely that Jamie could actually see the fluid running into her eyes. But she didn't stop once during the entire twenty-five lengths. On the last one the Coach yelled. "That's twenty-five. Take a break."

"Break?" Martin shouted so loudly that both Ryan and the coach heard him. The older woman looked up into the stands, seemingly for the first time, and blinked her eyes—obviously nonplussed at the large crowd. With a pleading look on her face, Ryan lifted her eyes for the first time, and shook her head. Martin met her gaze and nodded, silently agreeing to stay out of it.

The first twenty-five laps had taken less than ten minutes, but the entire time was spent in full out sprinting—and it had taken an obvious toll. When the water bottle was drained, she leaned over at the waist and grasped the hems of her shorts, pulling hard on them as she tried to suck in air. "This is torture," Jordan hissed as she watched her friend struggle. "What the hell is wrong with that woman?"

"I don't know," Jamie answered slowly. "She has very odd notions about discipline."

"I don't care what her notions are," Jordan maintained. "You don't do something like this to a player who has played a full game."

Ryan lifted her head after her one-minute break and asked loudly, "Can I take off my uniform?"

The coach nodded, but Jamie knew that for Ryan to ask for a concession, she must be dying. Ryan jerked the navy blue road shorts off to reveal navy blue compression shorts underneath, then removed her jersey. Jamie actually felt sick to her stomach as she watched the pained expression on her lover's face as she braced for another round.

"Hold up," the coach called out, then grabbed a towel and walked briskly over to Ryan. When she reached her she asked, "Can you continue?" Ryan nodded, not willing to risk the energy to speak. Sweat was running down her face in rivulets and she accepted the towel to wipe herself down. "You're obviously still sweating," the coach observed. "If you stop, that means you're getting overheated. Can I trust you to monitor yourself?"

"Yeah."

"Okay, let's go," Coach Hayes said grimly.

By the time Ryan was on lap thirty, a few of the players had sauntered back into the gym. It was obvious from the surprised looks on their faces that Ryan hadn't mentioned her punishment to anyone. They gathered in a small knot and spoke quietly for a few minutes, and it was apparent from their expressions that they felt empathy for their teammate.

Martin was standing in front of Jamie, and she could feel the coiled tension radiating from his body as he glared menacingly at the coach. She was going to ask one of the boys to make sure he didn't go down onto the court to give the coach a tongue-lashing, but when she looked at their faces they looked easily as outraged as he did. Scanning the crowd, she failed to find a calm looking face, and she prayed that no one would mouth off and make it worse for her partner. Even Mia looked irate, and Jamie knew that it was very hard to make Mia angry when watching Ryan run around in her skintight underwear.

At her thirty-second lap, Ryan paused at the end line, and Jamie immediately recognized the signal of imminent vomiting. "Don't look," she warned loudly, but most of the crowd wasn't quick enough. Ryan tried to get to the large plastic trashcan by the entrance, but she missed it by about two feet. Luckily she didn't hit her own shoes, and she stood slowly when she was done heaving, a disgusted look on her face.

The student trainer ran over to her and spoke to her for a few minutes, every eye in the gym watching the pair. Ryan was nodding her head forcefully, and Jamie knew she was determined to make it through, no matter how sick she felt. She had to put her hands on Martin's shoulders to stop him from rushing the court, and when she leaned over and said, "Martin, don't make it worse for her," she felt him lean against her in frustration.

"She's torturing her," he growled.

"I know. But Ryan's an adult. She can take care of herself."

He blinked slowly a few times and finally said, "I don't know if that's true."

The trainer had placed a probe in Ryan's ear, and the coach came over to consult with her. Ryan's temperature was found to be only slightly elevated, and the trainer commented, "If you can get two bottles of sports drink down and keep them down, you should be okay."

"Ryan?" the coach asked, raising her eyebrow. "Do you need to quit, or can you gut it out?"

Now that the coach had called her fortitude into question, the determined woman didn't give a second thought to how she felt. She glared at her, taking a bottle of sports drink and draining it in seconds, forcing her stomach to obey her command to behave. She gagged the second bottle down, and actually began to feel better when it settled in her stomach. "I won't quit."

"You can take it slow if you have to," Coach Hayes told her. "I'm sure you're not used to this kind of stress."

The words "fuck" and "you" were poised on her tongue, but she didn't let her temper control her. Instead, she narrowed her eyes and growled, "You know no such thing." She turned and jumped up and down a few times, to make sure she didn't feel nauseous again, and when she felt confident, she went back to the end line and inclined her head in the coach's direction.

At the signal to continue, Jamie saw the rest of the team remove their warm-ups without a word. As Ryan took off for lap thirty-three, every other member of the team—except for Janet and Wendy—went right along with her. Shaking her head to clear the sweat from her eyes, Ryan's mouth curled up into a small smile at the generous act of solidarity. Even the O'Flaherty clan was somewhat comforted by the gesture, but Jordan was muttering to herself, "What took them so damned long?"

Both Janet and Wendy looked like they'd eaten a bunch of sour grapes, but the rest of the team seemed more cohesive than Jamie had ever seen them. Most were actually smiling as they did their laps, and she could hear a few of them quietly urging Ryan on as she stumbled through her final ten.

Jamie had seen her lover put her body through many difficult trials, but she mused that this was the most debilitated she had ever seen her, beating out her exhausted state on the final day of the AIDS Ride. She was huffing and gasping for air with every agonizing lap, but she still managing to beat a few of her slower teammates down the court. When the coach finally called out "fifty" in a strong voice, most of the team bent over at the waist to catch their breath; but Ryan sank to the floor in a heap, collapsing so quickly that she looked absolutely boneless. Once again, Martin tried to make a run for her, but Jamie held him back. "It'll embarrass her if we go out there. Let her handle it. I'm sure she'll be fine," she said as calmly as she could manage. But even though her words were calm, she was seething with an anger so intense that it actually shocked her. She had only managed to remain in her seat during the last twenty-five laps by picturing various forms of medieval torture being performed on the lanky coach, and she was amazed at the pleasure she got from picturing the woman stretched out on the rack, with tendons and bones breaking with gruesomely loud snaps.

Ryan was lying flat on her back with her arms and legs spread out limply when Angela, the student trainer, approached her. "Ryan," she said softly as she squatted beside her and touched her clammy leg, "can you hear me?"

That brought a chuckle from the panting woman as she gasped out, "I'm exhausted, Angela, not deaf."

She gathered herself and managed to sit up after Angela extended a hand to aid her. In all this time she had not looked into the stands, and Jamie guessed that she was afraid of another rules infraction if she did so. She allowed the trainer to rub her body with a towel filled with ice, then got to her shaky legs and gulped down another two full bottles of Gatorade. Angela patted her on the back and handed her the navy blue warm-up suit that she had fetched from the locker room, but instead of putting it on Ryan started to walk slowly back into the locker room. Suddenly she took off again, covering the last twenty-five feet in moments.

"How does she have the strength to run?" Catherine asked, clearly amazed.

"Given how she looks, she's gonna barf that Gatorade right back up," Jamie predicted. "She absolutely hates to throw up in public."

"I should think that's a universal reaction," Catherine mused worriedly.

Ryan came shuffling out moments later with her warm ups on, and a towel draped around her neck. She looked very flushed, very tired and very wet, but there was still a proud grace to her walk that commanded both attention and respect. Once again she didn't lift her head, quietly following the rest of the team out to the bus.

Angry rumblings from the O'Flahertys eventually gave way to goodbye kisses and hugs, as the volleyball team, Jennie, Mia and Jamie got ready to leave. As they made their way out to the parking lot, each of the drivers announced, "See you at the parking lot by the gym," as they got into their cars.

"What did they mean by that?" Jamie asked Jordan.

A delighted grin and an exaggerated shrugging of shoulders was her only reply as she closed the door to Mia's car.

When she arrived at the parking lot, Jamie was enormously pleased to find all of the members of the volleyball team huddled together in the damp, cold fog, waiting for the bus to arrive. "You guys are too sweet," she said fondly as she joined them.

"We want Ryan to know that we're proud of her for not letting that asshole break her," Amy said.

"She'll appreciate it." True to her prediction, when the bus pulled up a few minutes later, Ryan smiled as broadly as she could. She chuckled as the group pulled her into the middle of their huddle, and patted her roughly on the back in a show of support.

"You guys rock," she said as she popped out of the huddle to wrap her arms around Jamie. "Hey, we need to get together this weekend to give Jordan a send off. What do you say?"

Everyone agreed, and they cemented plans to meet on Saturday night at the Berkeley house.

The foursome walked into the house almost simultaneously. Ryan chuckled at the sight of her friend walking along the sidewalk, affectionately holding Mia's hand. "Have you moved in?" she asked when she noticed Jordan's big gym bag.

"I wish I could," she said wistfully. "But instead I get to move into a dorm with five other women. Oops, I forgot to add that I'll be freezing my sweet ass off."

"I'll miss your sweet ass," Mia said softly as she faced her and palmed the body part in question.

Jordan turned her head to smirk at her friends, "Wish we could stay and chat girls, but duty calls and time's a wasting." Mia gave her an indulgent grin as she forcefully pulled Jordan up the stairs.

"Ahh, I recall my younger days when I was able to make love all night long," Ryan mused.

Jamie chuckled. "I remember when you used to be able to make love after six in the evening."

"Those days are over, babe. Now a couple of hours of basketball and fifty laps of the gym, and I'm inexplicably exhausted."

Ryan was lying in bed stark naked when Jamie came out of the bath. Her long body was uncovered, and Jamie noted some blotchiness on her sides. "What's this?" she asked, trailing her fingers over the spots.

"Mmm, probably a heat rash," Ryan ventured, not bothering to look.

Placing a hand on Ryan's belly, Jamie commented, "This feels like touching an oven."

"My core temperature gets elevated when I run that much. It takes a while to bring it down."

"Should I give you an ice bath?" she asked worriedly. "Maybe we should call the doctor."

"I'm fine, sweetheart," Ryan insisted. "Really. I'm only hot."

"How about a massage?" Jamie asked. "I have some nice aloe based lotion."

"You really don't have to, babe."

"I know, I don't." Placing her hand on Ryan's leg, she looked down at it while she drew patterns on her skin. "I want to be close to you. I was so worried about you tonight."

Ryan grasped her hand and squeezed it. "I'd love a massage. Being close to you might make me stop wishing I could go kick Coach Hayes' ass."

"If there's a line forming, I'd really like to be first."

Chapter Six

"Ryan, sweetheart," Jamie said quietly. "I've got to leave for practice now. Are you awake?"

Stretching languidly, Ryan nodded and mumbled, "I'm fine. Don't worry about me."

"I am worried about you. You've never slept through my getting ready in the morning. I didn't even get a response out of you when my alarm went off."

"I'm tired. No big deal." She kicked off the covers and placed her feet on the floor, pushing the hair from her eyes with a swipe of her hand. She caught hold of Jamie's sleeve and pulled her over to stand between her legs. "Now give me a kiss and scoot. You'll be late."

She did so and then grasped her partner's chin and lifted it so she could look directly into her eyes. "Are you sure you're awake?"

"Of course I am. We're having a coherent conversation, aren't we?"

"Just checking." She kissed her again and said, "See you tonight."

"Okay," Ryan said, adding a wave. She got up and went to the bathroom, and when she was done relieving herself stood in the doorway for a moment. "Fuck it," she muttered, then climbed back into bed and was asleep before she could change her mind.

Mia came home for lunch, puzzled when she heard some muffled sounds coming from the second floor. Walking upstairs cautiously, she detected that the noise was coming from her own room. "Jordan?" she asked.

"Nope. me."

She poked her head into her room to find Ryan lying atop the neatly made bed, watching TV and eating dry cereal directly from the box. She was clad in a black T-shirt and a pair of gray knit boxers. "Are you sick?"

"Nope," Ryan said, shaking her head. "Too tired for school. Do you mind that I'm in your room?"

"No, especially not since you made the bed. Why don't you plug your TV in?"

"Too tired," she sighed.

"Did you just get up? It's almost noon."

"I got up about a half hour ago. I should be studying for my chemistry final, but I couldn't force myself to answer the bell. I felt like I'd been ridden hard and put away wet."

"You were and you were," she teased, sitting on the edge of the bed. "Jamie was beside herself last night, buddy. I thought she was gonna run down there and throttle that woman."

"Do me a favor?"

"Sure."

"Don't tell Jamie I stayed in bed all morning. She's upset enough about last night. If she thinks I was too zonked to study, she'll make me go to the doctor."

Mia looked at Ryan carefully and said, "Maybe you should. It's not like you to lie in bed all morning."

"I'm fine," Ryan insisted. "I knew I couldn't get up and drag through a whole day and then be able to practice tonight. And there's no way that I'm going to ask out of practice. Mary Hayes has her head up her arse if she thinks I'm gonna ask for any slack."

Mia scooted closer and laid the back of her hand on Ryan's forehead. "No fever?"

"No, really, Mia, I'm fine. I was bone tired and dehydrated when I woke up. Being dehydrated gives me a headache, so I took some pills when I finally got up and I feel better now. I'm gonna force fluids down and chill a little. I should feel fine by tonight."

"Okay. I'm gonna go make lunch. I'm bringing you some, too."

"Thanks, pal," Ryan smiled warmly. "What are we having?"

"Whatever I can stick in the microwave. If we don't have leftovers around, it might be popcorn."

⁂

When Jamie got home from her long day Mia was already poking around in the kitchen looking for dinner. "So what's on the agenda for tonight?" she asked as Jamie set down a couple of big grocery bags.

"Do you mean the menu?"

"Well, I was getting hungry," Mia admitted. "I was almost reduced to making something for myself."

"Oh, Mia, I want you to promise you'll call me if you ever get a crazy notion like that again." She wrapped her arms around her friend, and tossed her back and forth roughly.

"Okay, okay," she giggled. "You might think I'm helpless in the kitchen, but I'll have you know I made lunch for your girlfriend today."

Jamie gave her a quizzical look and said, "You made lunch for Ryan? I thought she was planning on staying at the library all day."

Mia gave her a wry smile. "For as smart as she is, she's really a dope sometimes. She slept in because she was so tired, and then asked me not to tell you. Does she really think I'd keep something like that from you? Lord, she needs a full time supervisor."

Striding purposefully to the phone, Jamie muttered, "I'm calling my doctor."

"No, you don't need to, James. She didn't have a fever and she was acting totally normally. She was just bone tired and had a headache."

"For her to voluntarily stay in bed all morning…"

"She did that so she'd be rested enough to go to practice. It was apparently some big deal for her to show that last night didn't bother her." She rolled her eyes and said in exasperation, "Jocks."

Shaking her head slowly, Jamie muttered, "What am I going to do with her?"

"You'd better not tell her that I told you. If she thinks she can trust me, she might tell me things that you'd never learn otherwise."

"Good point," Jamie mused. "Okay, I'll keep my mouth shut." She walked over and gave her a hug. "Thanks for telling me. I need all the help I can get in watching out for my girl."

"Our girls do need a lot of pampering," Mia agreed. She looked at the bags of groceries and offered, "Let me help you make dinner."

"Help? What on earth has come over you?"

Mia looked slightly embarrassed She hemmed and hawed for a moment. Finally she looked up through her dark brown eyelashes and said, "I need to talk to you. And this is probably the only time we'll have alone today."

"I don't really need help, since I'm only going to put things out for sandwiches. I have my first final tomorrow and I'm stressing, not cooking. But I've got time to spend a few minutes with you. Come in the living room and tell me what's bothering you."

Mia allowed herself to be led into the room, where she flopped down into an overstuffed chair. "I'm kinda freaking about Jordan leaving," she said quietly. "I…I…I'm really gonna miss her." She was blankly staring at a spot on the coffee table, but Jamie recaptured her attention when she patted the love-seat beside her.

"Come sit by me," she urged. Mia shot her a grateful look, and scampered over to curl up under Jamie's outstretched arm. Jamie hugged her tightly, then brought a hand up to trail through the curly brown hair. "You've fallen in love with her."

There was a long silence as Mia tried to organize her thoughts. "I shouldn't…or I mean…I don't know…oh, shit. I have fallen in love with her. But I know she doesn't feel the same about me." Her head grew heavier against Jamie's shoulder, as soft sobs began to flow from her shaking body. "I know she doesn't love me."

"How do you know?" Jamie asked as she began to rock her gently. "Have you told her how you feel?"

"No," she said, shaking her head forcefully against Jamie's cotton-clad shoulder. "I mean, it's so stupid. She likes me because she thinks I'm safe. She doesn't want to get tied down for at least five years. She's told me that a number of times. She knows I've been with guys almost exclusively, and I think she thought there wasn't a chance in the world that I'd stop seeing guys for her. But I would, Jamie," she said earnestly. "I'd give up guys permanently for Jordan.

She's everything I've ever wanted in a lover."

Jamie squeezed Mia tighter. "I think you need to tell her. You'll never know what's going on in her mind if you don't talk to her about it."

"I can't do that to her. She's got six finals jammed into the next three days, and then we have the weekend together, and then she's gone. I want to be with her this weekend even if she doesn't love me," she sighed. "And if I told her, she wouldn't want to make love to me anymore. I know her. She's very honorable like that."

"Oh, Mia, I hate to have you keep this to yourself if there's a chance she feels the same way…"

"That wouldn't be fair to her. She needs to be able to concentrate when she gets to Colorado Springs. You don't know how much this means to her. I mean, if she makes the team, I might be able to tell her, but until then I really think I have to back off and let her have her freedom…even though it's killing me," she said through her tears.

"You poor baby," Jamie said softly. "I really do know how you feel."

Mia sat up and wiped at her eyes with the back of her hand. "I'll be okay," she said stoically. "I never expected that a woman would throw me for a loop like this. I thought only guys messed with your mind."

"I'm afraid not. Women are as good at mind-messing as men are."

❧

They went into the kitchen together and started to arrange the cold cuts and cheeses that Jamie had purchased on her way home. "Do you feel like talking about why you love her?" she asked as Mia leaned over her work, concentrating fiercely.

She dropped the cheese she was slicing and got a faraway look on her face. "I don't know, James. It's really snuck up on me." She bent to focus on her task again. "I do know that I've never felt more special than I do when I'm in her arms. She makes me feel cherished. That's never happened to me before." She let out in a strangled cry. "Never." She placed her hands on the counter and let her head drop down while struggling to regain her composure. "I thought I was in love before James, but it felt nothing like this. Jason said he loved me, and in some ways I think he did, but it always felt like he loved having sex with me more than he loved me. Do you know what I mean?"

"Yeah, I think I do."

"It's not like that with Jordan. I mean, we obviously love to have sex, and she's as horny as Jason ever was, but there's something so different about it." She grew thoughtful and paused for a minute, trying to put her feelings into words. "Jason wanted to have sex because he needed the release. He wanted me to have fun too, and he was always concerned with my pleasure, but it was mostly a way for both of us to get off." She lifted her head and stared out the kitchen window for a moment. "Jordan wants to have sex to show me how she feels about me. She's a very physical person. I guess all jocks are," she said, shrugging her shoulders. "I think she finds it easier to express herself with her body than with words." Wiping at her eyes again she continued, "Damn, Jamie, she makes me feel like she treasures me. That's such a powerful feeling."

Her tears returned in earnest, and Jamie went to her to offer comfort. It took a long while for Mia to calm down, but she eventually sucked in a shaky breath, and stood up tall. "She's so gentle and sweet with me, and so totally concerned with my pleasure. She's so kind...I guess that's what I find most lovable about her," she said reflectively. "I mean, I know she teases Ryan all the time, and she tries to act like she's cool, but that's not how she is when we're alone." Pausing to come up with the right term she blinked slowly a few times and said, "She's very fragile. Very open and accessible—even though it's obvious that it's hard for her. But she risks it when we're together. It's such a gift to be able to see her fragility. I can't hurt her, or put any more pressure on her right now. Do you understand?"

"I do, Mia, I really do." She brushed the curls from the dark eyes. "But you're describing someone who loves you, Mia, not someone who's marking time until she leaves for Colorado."

"I...I...I think she might love me," she admitted quietly. "But I don't think she wants to. I don't know what would be more painful, James—having her not love me, or having her try to deny her feelings."

"You're trying to deny yours too," Jamie reminded her.

"Yeah, but only because she's been so adamant about not falling in love or having attachments."

"Hey, you still insist that you're straight. You haven't given her much to go on, either."

"Shit," she mumbled. "We've managed to screw this up massively. This couldn't come at a worse fucking time."

"You still have time. I can see that you don't want to talk about this during her finals, but you have the weekend."

"Yeah. I don't know, I guess I'll see how things go. I've got to get myself under control," Mia mumbled. "She's coming over soon, and I don't want her to know anything is wrong."

Just then they heard the door open, and Ryan and Jordan's voices sounded in the parlor. Mia ran over to the sink to splash water on her reddened eyes, and was wiping them dry when the twosome entered. Jordan immediately looked at her with concern. "What's wrong?" she asked, swiftly crossing the kitchen.

Mia pasted on her normally sunny disposition and answered lightly. "The first time I volunteer to help get dinner ready, and Jamie makes me slice onions." She tossed her arms around her lover's neck and said, "Dinner's almost ready. Hungry?"

"Famished," she replied with a grin as she nibbled on Mia's lips, "for you."

Giving Ryan a small frown, Jamie demanded, "Come over here and kiss me like you love me." Ryan dutifully did so, adding a tender squeeze of her own volition. Their friends went into the dining room to set out the platters, and Ryan leaned down and whispered, "There aren't any onions here. What's really wrong with Mia?"

Jamie hated to be disingenuous with her lover, but she felt that Mia would want her secret kept. "Oh, stress, you know…end of term…PMS."

"Is she okay?"

"Yeah, but she's very sensitive. Be nice to her tonight," Jamie warned.

"When am I not nice?" she asked, standing up abruptly.

"Oh, you're always nice, you big dope. Be nicer."

"I'm going to be so busy with you that I won't even know they're here," Ryan murmured, grabbing Jamie from behind and grinding her pelvis into the tempting butt.

"Mmm," Jamie murmured as she reached back with a free hand and grabbed a handy cheek. "Hey, you're making me lose my train of thought…how's Janae?"

Ryan shook her head. "It doesn't look good. She has a severe concussion. She was kept overnight, and they claim she'll be fine, but my bet is that she's done for the season. I got her address—I'm gonna go by tomorrow before practice."

"The poor thing," Jamie sighed. "Is there anything we can do? Anything she needs?"

"I don't think so. When I've had a concussion, all I wanted to do was sleep."

"If there's anything she needs, you make sure she gets it, okay?"

"I will."

Jamie took a long look at her partner and said, "You look like you're all recovered. Are you feeling okay?"

"Yep," she whispered as she nibbled on a tasty ear lobe. "I actually feel great. My thighs are stiff, but I bet you could help me work out the kinks." Ryan grasped her lover's hand and placed it on her thigh, then started to thrust her hips a little. "Mmm, feels better already. They need love."

"Not tonight. Just because you're able to get by without cramming, doesn't mean I can. I've got a final in the morning, and I've got to study."

Ryan gave her an injured look. "I'm always supportive of your scholastic efforts."

"Yeah, yeah," she said, patting her on the butt. "Now go get some warm clothes on. It's cold in here tonight."

"Be right back," she promised as she gave Jamie a devastatingly sexy kiss along with a firm two-handed squeeze of her butt.

"Give me strength," Jamie muttered, trying to remind herself that her studies had to come before she did.

※

"So, Ryan," Jordan asked after they had been munching on their sandwiches for a few minutes, "what's up with that ignoramus coach of yours?"

"Don't remind me when I'm eating. She's got this really inflexible set of rules, and when you break one, she makes you take twenty-five wind sprints."

"What in the hell did you do? Jamie told us about getting twenty-five for not taking the bus, which is stupid enough. What else did you do, slug her?"

"No, not yet at least. I got another set because Jennie came down to hug me."

At that, Jordan nearly spat the food out of her mouth. "Are you shitting me?"

"Nope. No making contact with people in the stands before the game. She thinks it destroys your focus."

"That sucks," Mia said sympathetically. "How are you supposed to control what people in the stands do?"

"She's a control freak," Ryan said, shrugging her shoulders. "She believes you should have a chat with your friends and family members and tell them that you can't make contact with them. She thinks that we spend as much time obsessing about the game as she does."

"It's ridiculous," Mia decided.

"What's really ironic is that I went out of my way to stop by the USF locker room before warm-ups, since I know the coaches and the seniors on the team from when I played there. I knew Coach Hayes would go ballistic if any of them even acknowledged my presence. I'm really trying not to hit her hot buttons," she said with a wan smile. "I hope I've finally learned all of them."

"That's my Tiger, always seeing the bright side," Jamie said, giving her a sweet smile.

"In her defense, she did give me the option of doing the laps after practice, but our practices are much harder than our games. I was afraid of hurting myself if I did them when I was really exhausted."

"I'm glad you did what you thought was safest. Although it was torture to watch you."

"Thanks again for not making a scene. I'm not sure I would have been able to control myself if I'd been in your shoes."

Jamie grinned at her. "It would have been harder if I'd been alone.

Trying to keep a handle on your father and brothers helped focus me. I love the family, but I didn't want us all to have to go to jail together."

Ryan gave her a smile, and made the small announcement she'd been saving. "I'm not sure why, but I guess I'm the starting center now."

"That's great, right?" Jamie said. "You're the tallest."

"True. Jaleesa is shorter than I am, but as you can tell, she weighs more."

"Yeah, her hips and thighs are massive. I'd think that would make you a better player, though. You're obviously in much better shape."

"As long as you can get up and down the court, conditioning isn't the key for a center. Her lower center of gravity is a big plus."

"Is your coach an escapee from a mental asylum?" Jordan asked, her face contorted in anger. "You'll get tossed around like a doll in the PAC-10."

"That's a definite possibility. And if I don't get beaten up by the other centers, the ones on my own team might take me out. Jaleesa was not happy about the announcement, and La Trice didn't look like she thought it was a good idea, either."

"Just what you need," Jamie muttered, "more enemies."

"Yeah, I sure don't need help in that department," she mused. "You know, I think Coach tried to cut me a break today. After she made the announcement that I was going to start, she had me spend the entire time in Andrea Scoggins' office going over plays. I think she did that so I didn't have to exercise today."

"Is Andrea the really tall coach?"

"Yeah," Ryan nodded. "She's actually my age. She was a pretty good center when she played, and when she graduated two years ago she stayed on as an assistant. I haven't really worked with her up until now, but from here on in we'll be joined at the hip. Lynette mainly works with the forwards, so I have to get used to a new coach, too."

"Do you think you'll get along with her?"

"Oh, sure, she seems fine. I don't think she agrees with Coach Hayes that I should be the starter, but that shouldn't interfere."

Jamie gave her a worried look, thinking that nothing was ever as

Karma

it seemed with this team.

Ryan cleaned up after dinner, since she was the only one who didn't have a final the next day. Mia was pretty calm about her tests, but Jordan and Jamie were both stressed. Jordan even more so than Jamie. Ryan padded back out to the library where Jamie was ensconced, and slid across the leather surface to sit next to her. "Are you going to behave?" Jamie asked. She looked up through her dark blonde eyelashes and batted her eyes at her partner

"Me?" Ryan asked in amazement, jerking her thumb sharply towards herself. "Me?" she asked again in a higher voice.

"Yes, you sexy thing. You," Jamie whispered fondly as she leaned in close for a long kiss.

"I think you should spend a moment looking in a mirror, my sweet," Ryan grinned when Jamie backed up an inch. They were so close together that Ryan felt her eyes cross slightly trying to keep her lover in focus.

"Good point," she smirked and settled back on her own cushion. "We haven't…you know…in a couple of days," she murmured with an embarrassed chuckle.

Ryan dropped her half-lidded eyes and gazed at her partner. "It's so cute that you're too shy to put a name to it. But for the record, it's more than a few days. What with going to bed early so I can study in the morning, and my road trip, we haven't had sex in a week."

"God, Ryan, I don't know how we can keep these schedules and still have time for love. How do people manage?" She let out a frustrated growl.

"Well, I guess the good news is that we still have desire," she soothed softly as she nuzzled against the soft skin on Jamie's neck. "You do have desire, don't you?" she purred, her voice in its deepest register.

Jamie tilted her head back to give Ryan better access to her always-sensitive neck. "Mmm-hmm," she purred as the assault continued. "I'm hungry for you, baby," she whispered. Her hand snuck under Ryan's shirt and started to tease her skin.

"You guys want any coffee?" Mia's voice drifted through the house.

Shaken from their embrace, Jamie gently lifted Ryan's head with both hands and gave her a tender kiss. "I think I can use some, Mia," she called back. "And you can use a cold shower," she decided, kissing the tip of her partner's nose.

※

It was after eight before Jamie really began to concentrate, and she puttered along until ten without another break. Ryan got out her chemistry text and reviewed some problems for her Friday exam, but she wasn't very concerned. Her mind easily grasped the fine points of chemical properties and their interactions, and she found the undergraduate level classes to be almost childishly simplistic, even if she would never admit that to another soul.

Her mind began to wander and immediately turned to sex, as she felt Jamie shift against her.

To give herself a better full-length view, Ryan slid back across the long sofa and stuck a pillow behind her back. She tucked her feet under Jamie's thigh, smirking when her partner idly patted her leg.

Jamie was really concentrating, which allowed Ryan to spend some time gazing at her intently. As usual, what attracted her most was the way Jamie's nose wrinkled up when she was really puzzled by something. It was all Ryan could do to stop herself from scampering across the sofa to kiss the adorable nose, but she behaved herself admirably.

When Jamie would solve a problem that was vexing, her coral-hued lips would curl up in the most delighted smile, sending Ryan's heart into overdrive.

She found herself beginning to hum a low, slow tune, and after a few moments noticed that her hips had started to move very slowly against the leather surface. It was quite cool in the house, so she was fairly bundled up, wearing a turtleneck with a hooded sweatshirt and sweatpants. But since she wasn't planning on going out she had omitted any undergarments, and as her hips moved, she felt the fleece of her pants rub against her sensitive skin sending chills down her spine. She decided that she was going to have sex. Solo if need be. But sex was so much better with Jamie that she decided it would help clear her mind for her exam. *At least that sounded like as good an excuse as any.*

She continued to hum the song in her deep alto. The chemistry book was placed neatly on the side table, and she spread her legs apart, sinking down into the leather. When Jamie glanced out of the corner of her eye, Ryan twitched her hips a couple of times in an opening volley. She noted the grin that graced her lover's sweet lips, and decided that she was at least moderately receptive to a intimate connection.

To her surprise, Jamie didn't make any move to acknowledge her gyrations. Maybe she was feeling voyeuristic, a quite compelling idea.

Ryan had never masturbated in front of another woman, even though she had helped in one way or another innumerable times. As she had mentioned to Jamie a few weeks earlier, her childhood feelings about her grandmother's censure concerning masturbation had never really vanished, and she was embarrassed to show her need. But Jamie was so completely trustworthy that she felt she could push the boundaries and demonstrate how she performed this most private act.

She wasn't really sure where to start, since she was trying to entertain as well as excite herself. When she was alone, she usually fantasized, waited until she was wet and then started to touch herself. But she didn't think that would create enough visual interest for her partner. She knew this was as much about pleasing Jamie as it was getting off, so she decided to add a few flourishes that she didn't usually partake in.

She continued to hum the low song as she wet her index finger and thumb and slid her left hand under her shirt. A small gasp snuck out of her mouth as her cold fingers hit her warm nipple, and her mouth curled into a sexy grin. After a few tentative squeezes, she opened her hand and grasped her breast firmly, tugging on it with increasing pressure. A low moan escaped as her right hand joined the left, and she began to play with both breasts simultaneously. Still not a word from Jamie, but she noticed that a page had not been turned since she had begun her tease.

Ryan caressed herself through her sweatpants. She could feel her heartbeat pick up as she pushed her hand forcefully against herself, her hips grinding hard against the leather.

She was getting into the act now, but she remained mindful of her engrossed though silent audience. Jamie's eyes were burning into her, but she acted as though she were all alone, satisfying only her own needs.

Her feet came up onto the coffee table and her left hand slipped under her waistband. "Oh, yeah," she mumbled as her head dropped back and her eyes languidly blinked closed. Her fingers slipped down to gather the blossoming moisture, and she heard the leather squeak loudly when Jamie slid off the sofa. The rough scrape of shoes against the carpet was next, as her partner scooted across the floor to settle right in front of her.

Ryan took the opportunity to slide around and lie down, with Jamie still in place next to her hip. Now that she had room to move, she slipped her sweats down, sighing when her legs fell wide open. The satisfied growl that arose from her when her hand touched moist flesh was almost too much for Jamie to take. Watching Ryan pleasure herself was more exciting than she would have thought possible, and keeping her hands to herself was remarkably difficult. She finally stuck her hands under her thighs, to prevent an involuntary grab.

Ryan's fingers slipped gently over her own skin, and Jamie watched the pink flesh turn darker. It was mesmerizing, and she watched avidly, controlling herself perfectly until Ryan let out a long, low growl. In a moment, Jamie lost her struggle and grasped Ryan's shirt, tugging it up above her breasts. Her hungry mouth latched onto a full breast, suckling greedily while Ryan continued to purr.

Ryan was so into acting out the role of performing solo sex, that she didn't tacitly acknowledge the warm, wet mouth that was practically swallowing her breast. Jamie was making an incredible variety of sexy sounds, smacking her lips noisily while she fed, and Ryan lay back to enjoy them fully.

Ryan could feel the desire and heat that radiated from her lover, and she felt herself crest unexpectedly—the feeling rushing through her body like wildfire. She was pulsing and throbbing against her own fingers, the feelings magnified by the rabid desire she felt flowing from Jamie.

Without warning, Jamie was on top of her, pinning her to the sofa. "You make me so hot," she whispered roughly.

They wrestled around on the supple surface for a few minutes, kissing madly as they shared the unbridled passion that was flowing between them.

Jamie's hands flew to her own fly, fumbling with the zipper while her mouth remained locked upon Ryan's. She groaned in frustration, unable to contain her need for her partner's touch.

Ryan's hands joined hers, aiding her quest. Soon Jamie's jeans were pushed down, and Ryan's strong fingers effortlessly snapped the thin bit of fabric over each hip, flicking the panties to the floor. She raised her leg, grasped Jamie by the hips and settled her against her muscular thigh. Jamie let out a satisfied growl as her sizzling flesh met the smooth, toned column of skin, bone and muscle.

Questing hands reached down, both to steady herself and eagerly cup Ryan's breasts, squeezing the flesh rapaciously. Ryan's hands covered Jamie's, urging her on with whispered entreaties and a smolderingly hot gaze.

The curvaceous hips were beating out a strong rhythm, the friction building swiftly. Jamie began to grunt with each thrust, her breasts swaying tantalizingly before Ryan's gaze. Ryan reached up and grasped them hard—giving a powerful squeeze. Jamie's eyes saucered, then she cried out lustily, her voice finally drowning out the persistent squeak of wet bodies sliding against well-worn leather.

She collapsed abruptly, knocking the wind from Ryan's lungs. Ryan recovered quickly and wrapped her partner in strong arms, rocking her gently. "Damn, that was fun," she murmured into Jamie's ear.

"Umm-hmm," Jamie murmured. "I love to make love, but every once in a while it's nice to have sex. Nice, hot sex."

"Mmm…hearing you say that makes me want to have it again," Ryan murmured while she tried to position Jamie's hand right where she needed it.

Jamie beamed at her lover and wiggled her fingers teasingly, "Far be it from me to ever quash a good idea. Can you go twice?"

"Or die trying," Ryan said, grinning lecherously.

※

On Wednesday afternoon, Ryan knocked lightly on the door in a surprisingly quiet dormitory, and waited patiently for her friend to answer. It took her a while, and Ryan correctly guessed that she'd been sleeping. "Hi," Janae mumbled, immediately turning to head back to her bed. "Come on in." she added. She fell onto the bed heavily, the springs creaking loudly. "I've never been this tired in my whole life."

"I know the feeling," Ryan said, grabbing a desk chair and straddling it. "I've had a few concussions myself. They suck."

"Yeah. That about sums it up," Janae agreed. She looked at Ryan through her droopy lids and said, "During my moments of wakefulness, I decided I'm not coming back—even if they clear me to."

"I don't blame you. That team is a virtual hornet's nest."

"It is, but my bigger reason is that I'm not going to risk another concussion. My scholarship is paid for the year, as well as my room and board. That's the whole reason that I play at this point—so it's silly to even try to come back."

"I can understand that," Ryan nodded. "If I had a brain in my head, I'd quit too. I guess I'm too stubborn to know when to stop."

"You're not stubborn. You're a jock. It's hard to walk away from a team, no matter how much they suck."

Ryan nodded. "There's some truth to that."

"You'll make some headway. You're easy to like."

"Thanks," she smiled. "So are you. I'm really gonna miss you. You were the only person I looked forward to seeing on a daily basis."

"Well, I'll still be around, and if I get into med school, I'll stay in the Bay Area after graduation."

"Med school? I didn't know you wanted to be a doctor."

"Oh, yeah. Always have. I've already got my applications in to UCSF and Stanford."

Ryan rolled her eyes and said, "I wish I could say the same. I still can't force myself to get going on mine."

"Where are you applying?"

"My main problem is that I can't decide. I think I've finally decided that I don't want to be a physician. I think research suits me better. The only problem is that it looks like I'd have many more opportunities if I were a medical doctor. But I hate the thought of going to med school when I don't want to practice medicine."

"What field are you most interested in?"

"Honestly?" Ryan asked. At Janae's nod she said, "That's another problem. I like biology as well as math. I really can't decide. I know that if I get my Ph.D. in math, I'd be giving up biology permanently, and I don't want to do that."

"Why not get your Ph.D. in bio, then? You could focus more on the mathematical aspects of biology."

"I guess I could do that," Ryan mused. "I'm getting a lot of pressure from the math department to continue on—and that's where my real talents lie." She shrugged and said, "I get so confused that I try to put it out of my mind."

"But what do you like? What would make you happy?"

Rocking in the chair for a few moments, Ryan said, "I'd love to work on some basic research in genetics. Since the human genome has been unlocked I think there will be some fantastic opportunities in the next few years. I'd really love to help unlock the building blocks of our species," she said, her eyes bright with interest. "Part of the reason I don't want to be a physician is that I want to help as many people as possible. Doing some basic, pure research seems like the best way to do that. One day we'll be able to cure dozens of diseases with genetic engineering—and I'd love to help make that possible."

Janae looked at her for a long while, finally nodding her head. "Looks to me like you only have one option. You're gonna have to go for a joint M.D./Ph.D."

Ryan grabbed her head with her hands and moaned, "I've really tried to avoid thinking about that. Must you pull me from my denial?"

Laughing softly, Janae joked, "Hey, it's only a six or seven year commitment. Then, of course, you have to do a residency. Piece o' cake."

"Jamie's not gonna like this," Ryan predicted. "She's not gonna like this one bit."

When Ryan entered the locker room later that day, the place was empty. She went to use the rest room, and when she returned to the main room she heard her name mentioned. She wasn't sure, but she thought she recognized the voices as Lily and Hilary from over the tops of the lockers that separated them. "She's been with the team for like two seconds," one of the voices said. "Why would you put someone with no experience in over someone like Ella?"

"I don't have a clue," the other woman whispered loudly. "How's Ella supposed to get any experience if she doesn't get to play?"

"Ella's really pissed. She thinks it looks really bad to put a forward in over her and Jaleesa."

"It does." the other woman agreed. "I mean, how bad must you be if someone who doesn't know how to play your position gets to start over you? Ella's humiliated."

"Derrick says he heard that 'you know who' was gay. Do you think she is?"

"Oh, yeah," the other woman chuckled. "That was her girlfriend with her on the Colorado trip. They're like married or something."

"Good." The first speaker laughed. "Jarret keeps saying how hot he thinks she is. That ought to shut him up."

"Maybe he'd like it," the other one giggled. "Guys love to fantasize about lesbians."

Ryan rolled her eyes, having heard the comment too many times to count. "No way," the voice that Ryan assumed was Lily, said. "Jarret's old girlfriend turned lesbian. He's totally weirded out about dykes. Once he finds out, he won't even want me in the locker room with her. I'm staying as far away from her as I can get."

"Oh, she's not interested in you," Hilary chuckled. "She's all over that girlfriend of hers. I'm really glad coach doesn't let her go on trips with us any more, though. I don't mind being around gay people, but I hate it when they insist on shoving it in your face. They should keep that kinda thing private."

Since Ryan was separated from the women by a set of lockers, they would have never known she was there had Lynette not come in right then. "Hi, Ryan," she said loudly. "Ready to get to work?"

Karma

There was immediate silence from the other side of the lockers. Ryan rolled her eyes, she really had her work cut out for her to win over this clique as well.

※

Practice did not go well. Everyone was lethargic, and play was sloppy at best. They worked on a set of plays with Janet at point guard, Franny as the off guard, Drzislava and Wendy playing forward, and Ryan in at center. No matter how many times they tried to execute one particular play, the ball never got to Ryan. She had a sneaking suspicion that Janet was intentionally trying to screw with her, but Ryan wasn't about to say so. Janet wasn't as considerate, however. She pointed the finger at Ryan continually, until Coach Hayes finally asked her what the problem was.

"She's not in position," Janet complained. "Every time I try to throw the ball to her, all I see is her back."

"Concentrate on getting into position, Ryan," the coach reminded her. "Janet has a point. You look like you're still playing forward out there."

Ryan nodded and tried to change her style, but she wasn't doing very well at it. The practice dragged on, with everyone growing more frustrated. Seven o'clock finally rolled around, and Ryan breathed a heavy sigh of relief. She went into the locker room and tossed her wet jersey and shorts into the laundry, and slipped into a dry set of clothes. On her way out she made eye contact with the coach, and saw the disappointment in her eyes. She wasn't sure why she did it, but she approached her and asked, "Got a few minutes?"

Shrugging her shoulders wearily, Coach Hayes motioned Ryan towards her office. She sat down and nodded towards the empty chair, and Ryan sat and faced her. "Coach, if you want me to play the low-post, I promise to do whatever I can to learn the position. I know it's not going to be easy, and I know you'll be frustrated with me—but I promise I'll do my best."

The older woman nodded. "I think I know that. No one works harder than you do at practice."

"I've gotta say that I'm puzzled you chose me. I think I'd make a better point guard than a center."

For the first time since she met her, Mary Hayes actually laughed. "It must be late, because I'm slap-happy. The thought of your seventy-five inches dribbling that ball up the court is too funny."

"It is," Ryan chuckled. "But I always play point guard when I play with my family. I'm the short one."

"I assume there's a point to this story?"

"Yep. I'm wondering if you'd have any interest in mixing things up a little."

"Such as?"

"Well, you must have a good reason for playing me over Jaleesa and Ella, and I know it's not because you think I'm going to be good. I saw your face tonight, and you looked profoundly disappointed in me."

She nodded, saying, "I was hoping for a miracle. I know this isn't your position, but I still feel more comfortable with you than with either of them."

"Okay," Ryan said, her enthusiasm growing. "Then why not let me do what I'm best at?"

"And that would be…?"

"Let me play center like a third forward," Ryan suggested. "I'm never going to be able to bang bodies with the really big girls in the league, and I have no experience playing with my back to the basket. That's a skill that takes years to learn, and we don't have time for that."

"But if you played as a third forward…?"

"Then I could use the skills I already have. And not only that, it would confuse the hell out of our opponents until they got used to it."

Mary Hayes leaned back in her chair and gazed at the earnest young woman who had pled her case. She nodded her head slightly and said grudgingly, "Well, given how you practiced this afternoon, I suppose we don't have many options. I'm willing to give it a try. Will you work your ass off between now and this weekend's tournament?"

"I'll come early, I'll stay late, I'll sweep the floor when we're done."

"Don't go crazy," the coach insisted, a very small grin curling her mouth. "You have your work cut out for you just doing your own job."

"I can't tell you how much I'm going to miss this," Jordan said wistfully from her perch on the stair landing overlooking the neat back yard of the Berkeley house. She and Ryan were both sitting with their long legs dangling over the side, watching their friends dance to the music provided by the massive boom box that Mia had brought down from her room.

"Yeah, it's tough to have a party outdoors in December in Colorado Springs."

"That's the last thing I care about," she said somberly as Ryan straightened up a bit to look at her. Jordan had been giving off depressed vibes all week, but didn't seem as if she wanted to talk, so Ryan had let it be. Tonight, however, she was in one of her introspective moods, and it was obvious that she had some things to get off her chest.

Ryan placed her hand on her friend's smoothly-muscled thigh and asked, "What do you care about?"

She chuckled as she took a long draught of her beer. "I feel like a kid leaving home for the first time. It sounds funny, but I really feel like we've created our own family in these last few months. I really feel like I belong."

Ryan snaked an arm around her shoulders as Jordan dropped her head onto her friend's chest. "It doesn't sound funny at all. I feel exactly the same." After a moment she added, "I have a lot of people in my life that I'm close to, but it's always been hard for me to have close friendships with women—well, those that I don't sleep with."

Jordan blinked slowly then shook her head. "It's too weird to think of sleeping with you. I mean…I had a crush on you when we first met, but in no time at all I stopped thinking of you like that."

Ryan smiled and said, "Well, since I was with Jamie when you and I met, I never got the crush thing. It's funny though—I started to think of you as a sister. I think it's because we're so much alike it seems like we share a common gene pool."

"Yeah, it does seem like that. I'm really going to miss you. You've been a great friend, and if I got to pick a sister—it'd be you."

"Hey, you sound like this is the end of our friendship. You'd better not be trying to dump me."

"I have no intention of dumping you. But we probably won't see each other for the better part of a year if I make the team. We play almost straight through until the Olympics finish in October."

"You won't come home for Christmas?"

"The schedule only gives us two days off," she said glumly. "I don't think I can justify the cost for two days."

"Well, maybe something will turn up," Ryan said obliquely. "So, besides me, what will you miss?"

"Well, Jamie of course," she drawled, giving Ryan a sidelong look.

"Anyone else?"

She shook her head unhappily. "I had such firm ideas about not getting involved with anyone. I knew that volleyball was my focus, and I should have kept to my plan." She looked up at Ryan helplessly as she held her graceful hands out in front of her. "How did I let this happen?"

"I told you, pal, you don't have much choice when it hits you." She leaned back and gazed at her friend for a moment, then asked, "Do you love her?"

"Of course I do," she said with a note of resignation in her voice. "I mean, I guess it could be the fact that I'm leaving, but I feel sick about leaving her. I didn't think this could happen so suddenly. I have plans."

"Have you told her?" Jordan shook her head briskly, and Ryan could see the chills run up her body. "Hey, it's not like being in love is a bad thing. Would it be so awful to have a steady girlfriend?"

"It's not how I planned things. I wanted to be free this year. I didn't want to be pining for someone a thousand miles away."

"We don't always get to choose the timetable for our lives." She gave Jordan another squeeze. "Don't you think you owe it to each other to at least talk about it?"

"I don't know. If I were going to be here permanently, I think we might have a chance. But Mia's…you know how Mia is," she said smiling. "I think she might need close supervision."

"I think you're selling her short. She was completely faithful to her boyfriend until they were about broken up."

"Oh, I don't mean that she'd cheat on me," Jordan said quickly. "She hasn't been in a relationship with a woman before, and people tend to need a lot of hand holding to get comfortable with that. I'm afraid that she might waver in her lesbian resolve if I'm not here to work things through with her."

Ryan cocked her head and gave her friend a wry smirk. "When did you become the lesbian voice of experience?"

"I'm not," she agreed, blushing. "But I think I know who I am now. It feels right to call myself a lesbian, even if I'm not willing for the world to know. But Mia's in a very different space. She's a visitor to our land. I'm afraid she might want to go back to her home country if I'm not around."

"Shouldn't she be able to decide if she's willing to give it a try?"

"Yeah, and if I were going to be here, I'd trust that she'd be able to make that decision. But I'm not going to be here. I'm going to be very far away, and it feels unfair to expect her to wait around for me. God knows how long I'll be gone," she said glumly.

"I guess I see your point," Ryan mused, "and it would be hard to carry on a long distance relationship, but is it fair to give up without trying?"

Jordan rubbed her face with her hands. "I've been kicking that around in my mind all week. It was so hard to focus on my exams, when she was all I could think about." She leaned back and sighed, "This is too much. We're both really upset about my leaving. Things are too emotionally volatile right now for me to think clearly. I think it's safer to see how things go. I should be able to get a read on her after I've been gone for a while."

"You could ask her," Ryan pointed out. "Or bite the bullet and tell her how you feel."

"Now where's the challenge in that?" She gracefully rose to her feet. "Come on, Boomer," she said, extending a hand. "Let me show you how to dance."

There were about forty people jammed into the small yard. Many of the players had brought dates, but the dancing had been very free form, with everyone dancing together, rather than pairing off. As the evening wore on, the volunteer DJs had mixed in an occasional slow, romantic song, and when one such song began, Mia found the guest of honor and took her hand. "Dance with me?"

With a puzzled look, Jordan said, "Uhm…I don't think this is a very good one to dance to."

"Why not? We like this song."

"I know, but…" she looked around at the five heterosexual couples moving to the beat. "We won't be able to blend in, baby."

Standing very close and looking up into Jordan's clear, blue eyes, Mia said, "Do you honestly think I care?"

"Well…uhm…yeah, I do." Tilting her head, she asked, "Don't you?"

"There's only one thing I care about." Mia stared right into Jordan's eyes. "And that's staying as close to you as I can until Monday morning."

"But…but," Jordan protested softly, "there are a lot of people here that we don't know. You don't know that these guys will keep their mouths shut."

"I only care about your mouth. And after I take a taste of it, I'm going to dance with you." She slipped her hand up Jordan's arm, slowly moving over her skin until she caressed the back of her neck and pulled her down with gentle pressure. Jordan's eyes grew wide as their lips met, but Mia was oblivious to the few surprised looks shot their way. She released her hold and took Jordan's hand, leading her to the small knot of dancers. Jordan's eyes started to shift around the space, trying to see who was watching them, but Mia reached up and held her face between her hands, forcibly capturing her attention. "No one else matters. Only you and me."

Jordan took in a deep breath and let Mia's words sink in. "All right. Only you and me."

Mia slid one arm around her back, and placed the other against Jordan's shoulder blade, holding her in a snug embrace. Jordan responded by draping her forearms across Mia's shoulders and loosely linking her hands behind her back. "How's that?" she asked, moving their bodies closer together.

"That's perfect." Mia's chin lifted, her warm, brown eyes met Jordan's, and a flash of deep sadness passed between them. "I don't want you to go," she whispered, her voice catching.

Pulling her even closer, Jordan's lips pressed against her curls. "I don't want to go. I want to stay right here with you." Pulling back a little, she looked into the watery eyes and said, "Oh, please don't cry. Please don't."

"I'm sorry," Mia sniffed. "I can't help it." She dashed into the house, tears streaming down her face, Jordan in hot pursuit.

Jamie saw them run up the back stairs, but she had no idea what had happened. Looking around the dimly lit backyard, she spotted her partner, sitting in an Adirondack chair that she had maneuvered into a quiet, dark corner. "Honey?" she asked as she approached from the side.

Ryan sniffed and wiped at her eyes, turning to meet Jamie's concerned gaze. "Hi."

Climbing into her lap, Jamie draped an arm around her shoulders and hugged her close. "What's wrong, sweetheart?"

"Nothing…really. I was watching Mia and Jordan dance, and I started to feel so damned sad." She rested her head against her partner's breast and cried for a few moments. "This is so hard for them, and it breaks my heart to see them both in pain."

"You poor, sweet, baby," Jamie sighed, rocking Ryan in her arms. "It's really hard for you, too, isn't it."

"Yeah. Harder than I thought it would be. It really hit me tonight, Jamers. I mean, I knew that Jordan was important to me, but it dawned on me how much I've come to think of her as family."

"She's the sister you never had, isn't she?"

"Yeah. That's what it feels like. She 'gets me' as much as my brothers do. I mean, God knows that you know me intimately, but Jordan understands my motivations…what drives me."

"I know," Jamie soothed. "I know she has a role that I can't fill, and I know that it'll be very hard for you not to have her here. But you can still stay close, baby. You can call her, and e-mail her. You don't have to let the distance keep you from getting what you both need from each other."

Ryan nodded. "I know it's possible, but it won't be like it has been. We have our best chats when we're running together or working out. We both talk better when we're active."

"You talk fine when you're sitting in a chair in the back yard,"

Jamie teased gently. "You're gonna have to work at it, but staying connected to Jordan is worth it, isn't it?"

"Uh-huh." Ryan nodded. "It's definitely worth it." She offered up a weak smile, and said, "Sisters don't come along every day."

Chapter Seven

"We're leaving in one half hour," Ryan threatened from outside of Mia's closed door late the next morning. "I know you're in there, you two. I can hear you grunting."

She flinched as a shoe hit the door with a thunk, but she at least knew that they had gotten the message. Jamie was already downstairs, studying with deep concentration. "Did you make contact?" she asked idly.

"I got something thrown at the door, so I know they're conscious." Ryan sat down next to her partner to read the paper. With ten minutes to spare they heard the shower start, and at noon on the button the pair came flying down the stairs—hair wet and only partially dressed, but they were present.

"Coffee," Jordan choked out. "Gotta have coffee."

"We drank ours hours ago," Jamie chided her. "But if you get in the car like good girls, I'll stop for you."

"You're a goddess," Jordan intoned reverently.

"Why did you waste all that time in the shower?" Ryan asked.

Jordan turned and stared at her in shock. "Do you really think we'd go to a Raider game covered with the scents we were covered in? That's like throwing a pork chop to a pack of hungry dogs."

Ryan laughed, "There was a boy in my grandmother's town that no one liked because he was such a cuss. She used to say that his mother had to tie a pork chop around his neck to get his dog to play with him."

"Your grandmother sounds like quite the character," Jamie said with an amused grin.

"That she is."

"Enough reminiscing," Jordan said. "There's a triple latte with my name on it just waiting for me."

Traffic was congested around the stadium, but they got to bypass most of the gridlock with their valet parking pass. "Have you guys ever been to a game?" Ryan asked as the red-jacketed valet accepted the Lexus from her.

"I went to a Raiders game when I was little, and they were in L.A.," Jordan recalled. "How about you, Mia?"

"Nope. I've been to the Niners, but never the Raiders. I hear the crowd is kinda wild."

"You might say that," Ryan chuckled. "But we've got the Stadium Club pass, so we can hide out up there."

"Where's the fun in that?" Mia asked. "I want to soak up the local ambiance."

"You might change your mind," Ryan predicted as they presented their tickets at the gate.

"Metal detectors and hand frisking everyone?" Jamie asked as they were funneled along. "What are they looking for? Uzis?"

"Nope. Your average Raider fan comes packing heat." A yellow jacketed security woman did a thorough pat-down of each of them.

"Remind you of your recent altercation with the Oakland police?" Jamie asked loudly.

"If I see one of them snap on a rubber glove, I'm bolting."

The boys and Maggie were already in their seats when they finally located them. "We've been here about twenty minutes, and the crowd is already out of control," Brendan said. "I think we should go up to the Stadium Club."

"I agree," Ryan said looking around. "We're the only women around here so we'll be targeted."

"Oh, come on," Jordan said. "We're not at San Quentin. How bad can it be?"

Jamie agreed. "I think it feels more like a football game to be out in the stands. I hate it when we sit in the luxury boxes at Candlestick."

"Let's give it a go," Conor said, looking to his brothers for support. "We can protect the girls."

"Against all these guys?" Brendan asked, his eyes wide.

"We can take care of ourselves," Jordan said confidently. "Don't you boys worry about us."

"Okay," Brendan said, shrugging his shoulders. "I'll make a run for beer. Who wants one?"

Since everyone wanted one, four people had to go as there was a two-beer limit. So, Ryan, Conor and Brendan and Rory went to get in line for beer, while Jordan got in the longer food line.

"So, things are still hot and heavy between Jordan and Mia?" Conor asked as they waited.

"Yeah, I think so," Ryan said, not wanting to get into that particular discussion with her brother.

"I still say Mia's my type," he muttered.

"I don't know her very well," Brendan said, "but she seems like she's a lot of people's type."

"Yeah, she's a cutie all right," Ryan agreed.

"Come to think of it," Rory decided, "I think she could be my type."

"She's busy, boys," Ryan reminded them. "Give the girl a little room, will ya?"

"You know, I shouldn't admit this, but she's even more attractive to me now," Conor said. "Knowing she sleeps with Jordan…"

All three sets of O'Flaherty brothers' eyes rotated and fixed onto Jordan as the oblivious woman waited in line. She was looking particularly attractive, wearing bright red jeans that hugged her curves, and a creamy white angora turtleneck that highlighted her breasts to very good effect. "I'm gonna pop the first one who drools," Ryan threatened as the men ineffectually tried to wipe their conjured xxx-rated images of Jordan and Mia from their minds.

After they had procured the beer, they went over to the food line and waited patiently for Jordan to finally be served. "God. The prices are bad enough," she grumbled, "but it takes twenty minutes to get a hot dog."

The game against the Chiefs started after they got in line. Luckily there were TV monitors all over the concession area, since most of the crowd spent at least a quarter of the game waiting in the obnoxiously long lines.

Their seats were, of course, excellent ones. Located off the fifty-yard line in the lower deck, Ryan assumed that they would be surrounded by lawyers and businessmen. Even though she knew the crowd tended to be rough, she had assumed that most of the rowdies would be confined to the cheap seats. But since Raider games had garnered such a well-deserved reputation for drunken fights, most businesses had a hard time getting clients to even accept the tickets. It was unclear to Ryan whether the corporations and law firms had given the tickets to the drunken men around them, or if they'd migrated from the upper deck, but by the time they got to their seats, she was on the verge of punching a few guys. She and Jordan had been whistled at, leered at, and ogled during the long walk, and she knew her friend had a very limited tolerance for that sort of thing. To Ryan's amazement, Brendan had actually shouted at one particularly offensive patron, and she began to wish they had gone directly to the Stadium Club.

They were almost at their section, and she was watching the game with one eye as Oakland was churning down the field in an impressive drive. They passed in front of the metal railing that guarded the front of their box, and handed the food and drinks up to Jamie and Mia. Even though they were in the front of the section, Jamie and Mia had to stand to see above the crowd that constantly snaked in front of them. "I can't see," Mia complained for the tenth time. "I need to be taller."

The drunks in the seats behind them immediately offered a clever solution to her plight. As Jordan, Ryan, Conor, Rory and Brendan watched helplessly, the laughing brutes grabbed Mia around the waist and picked her up high into the air. "How's that?" the largest one asked.

"Put her down." Jamie shouted in outrage as she impulsively

reared back and popped the man in his ample gut.

"Oh, shit!" Ryan grabbed the railing and hoisted herself up, but before she could swing her leg over, the other man had grabbed Jamie in much the same fashion, and her sturdy legs began kicking violently as she screamed. Ryan made a leap for her, but the man was at least six foot three inches tall, and one whole stair higher than she was. Jamie's boot caught the guy right in the chest, and he quickly decided that he wanted to get rid of his trophy. But rather than putting her back down, he acceded to the wishes of the assembled multitude who were chanting, *"Pass 'em up! Pass 'em up!"*

The man and his companion decided that was a fine idea, so they handed their squirming, kicking prizes up and over their heads to the laughing pair of men behind them. Jordan had scrambled up after Ryan, and they stood helplessly as their girlfriends rose through the crowd. "Fuck!" Ryan shouted, her face red with anger. "Jordan, you and Conor take the right aisle, I'll take the left with Brendan. Maggie, you go get security. Rory, go to the top of the section and try to grab them if they get that far." Jordan jumped back down and grabbed Conor's hand and they took off. Ryan jumped back down too, and ran around to the left aisle. They couldn't hear each other with the crowd noise, but they communicated with hand signals. Ryan indicated that Jordan should go up a few rows and try to intercept Mia as she was passed up. Jordan dashed up three rows and snaked through the raucous crowd, trying to be in position to grab her lover, but the men who were participating in the game altered their path and started passing Mia up at a diagonal. As Jordan tried to run back to the aisle, her ass was grabbed so many times she felt like a pincushion, but she ignored the assaults to focus on her goal.

It didn't take long for the yellow jacketed security officers to start swarming all over their section, but they only served to get in the way. There was really no way to make the ebullient men stop, and the loudly barked orders to do so were met with derision, profanity and raucous laughter. The captives were still fighting valiantly, and it became clear that many of the men who passed them did so to avoid being kicked or punched. The lead officer on Mia's side yelled at her, "If you relax and stop fighting, they'll let you go."

To Jordan's complete astonishment, Mia cried, "Fuck you."

"They haven't broken her spirit," Jordan said in admiration.

Ryan was at the boiling point as dozens of men grabbed her precious lover in the most inappropriate of ways. She could see a few of the particularly lecherous ones grab her ass firmly, but when a guy only three spots in from the aisle leaned way over to squeeze one of her breasts, Ryan snapped and leapt for him. He was straightening up with a stupid, leering grin when his big dumb face met her powerful right hand. As soon as that happened, the crowd went wild. Fists started flying as Ryan and Brendan were both pulled into the melee. The crowd loved a fight much more than they liked to grab unwilling women, and by the time Jamie and Mia reached the top row of their section, the security guards were in position to reach over and grasp them by the shoulders. Jamie's last captor didn't want to let her go, and she was pulled from both ends until she finally wrestled one foot free and kicked the man right in the head. He let go immediately, but the guards who held her shoulders didn't realize it and kept pulling. When the resistance on her legs was released, she went shooting over and landed on a pile of yellow-jacketed flesh with a loud thump. Mia scrambled over and helped her to her feet as Jordan and Conor arrived. Jamie threw her arms around Conor with Mia doing the same to Jordan, much to the delight of the frenzied crowd. "Dykes! Lezzies!" they shouted. "Kiss her, baby. Give her a hot one."

Jordan had reached her capacity for insults, but she had one left in her arsenal. "Suck my *dick*!" she bellowed as she grabbed her crotch in a very obscene fashion.

"Uhm, ma'am," the calm voice of an Oakland police officer interjected.

"What?" she growled.

"It might be a good idea not to incite them. Once they know they've upset you, they get a lot worse."

"Fine," she groused. "But you'd better give us an escort, or somebody's gonna get kicked in the nuts."

"Yes, ma'am," he said with a smirk as he and his partner tried to clear the aisle.

Jamie had come to her senses, and she looked around wildly, her hair flying around her head. "Where's Ryan?"

"I don't know," Conor said. "They were right down there a

moment ago." He pointed down the aisle they were trying to traverse, and his impressive height allowed him to catch a glimpse of his sister's dark head flying around in the crowd. "Oh, shit!" He took off running, leaving Jamie behind.

She started to take off after him, but the police officers had seen enough of her feistiness, and they grabbed her and Mia by their collars and ordered a security guard to do the same to Jordan. All three women tried to wrestle out of their holds, but an officer said, "If you three get down in that mess we'll never get you back."

"But that's my girlfriend!" Just then Ryan jumped onto a seat and let loose with a roundhouse punch against some jerk's head.

"She looks like she's doing all right," the other officer said dryly.

Conor jumped onto the seat next to her, and seconds later Brendan's dark head, then Rory's fairer one, popped up. The four of them stood back to back to back to back, with such fierce glowers on their faces that the crowd actually backed off, looking for easier targets. There were at least fifty security guards on the scene by this time, and Jamie watched helplessly as the police ordered the O'Flahertys down from their seats. Bright yellow plastic bands were snugged around their wrists, binding them behind their backs. "You can't arrest them!" Jamie shouted. "They were attacked."

"We'll sort it all out in the lockup downstairs, ma'am," the officer next to her assured her.

When it became clear that the melee had calmed down, the officers allowed the women their freedom with the admonition, "Don't start any more trouble, you three. You can come down to the lockup to claim your friends."

"Start trouble my ass," Jordan fumed under her breath as they walked away. "Let's go get our food at least. Being mauled really works up an appetite."

Mia scrambled down the stairs to catch up with Jordan. "Hey, are you all right? I've never seen you get so angry."

"Yeah, yeah. I guess I'm just tense about leaving. I feel out of control."

Mia took her hand and gave it a squeeze, making a few of the men shout their approval. She stuck her middle finger up and kept walking. "I didn't know you had such a long list of profanity. Good game."

Jordan gave her a fond look, but when the reached their seats and saw eight empty beer cups, eight wax paper wrappers smeared with condiments, four empty bags of peanuts and four empty Cracker Jacks boxes all neatly lined up in their cardboard carriers, she almost started the entire fight up again. "Which of you motherfu…" she started, but both Jamie and Mia clamped hands over her mouth and pushed her back down the aisle.

They endured constant catcalls as they tried to exit, since they were now the celebrities of their section, but they got to the lockup without further trouble.

Luckily the officers who had been holding the O'Flahertys immediately let them go free. Still, when Jamie saw them emerge from the lockup with sheepish grins, she nearly burst into tears. Brendan's lip was split, with blood running down his chin onto his white golf shirt. A large red mark marred Rory's cheek, Conor's left eye was rapidly turning some interesting shades of blue, and Ryan had angry red marks on both cheeks and her chin, not to mention the bloody nose she was trying to control. "Anybody for the emergency room?" she asked lightly as Jamie threw herself at her. "Watch the ribs, babe, watch the ribs," she said, wincing audibly.

"What happened? How did you get hit?"

"Hard to say," Ryan said. "I saw some asshole grab your breast, and everything after that is a blur."

"My heroes." She hugged each of the battered warriors. "You're idiots, but you're still heroic."

⁂

They decided their injuries weren't serious enough to merit a trip to the emergency room. Doctor Terry was at home and didn't mind making the short walk over to the house for an impromptu check-up and a beer. He pronounced them all fit, but chided them for trying to take on the entire Oakland Coliseum.

Once the doctor had given them proper lectures, he couldn't help but compliment the crew. "I bet that lot of rowdies didn't know what hit them when the O'Flahertys got involved."

"No one messes with the fightin' O'Flahertys," Conor boasted.

"Our women are tougher than their strongest men."

Ryan took a look at her friends and suggested to Doctor Terry, "Now that you've checked us out, maybe you should have a look at Jamie and Mia."

"No, all we have is a few bruises. Although I do feel like a truck hit me."

"You were fighting with every ounce of power you have, honey. That was a tremendous strain on your body."

"Yeah, I guess it was, but you guys have to feel worse than we do. You were getting pummeled."

"Nah," Ryan assured her, "a few scrapes. It takes more than a bunch of hooligans to get the best of us."

"Well I think we should head home and soak in the tub for a while. I hate to miss Sunday dinner," Jamie said, "but I've gotta soak."

"I've got a better idea," Ryan said.

An hour later found Jamie and Ryan at the Olympic Club, lounging in the massive whirlpool. The O'Flaherty men were in their separate locker room, waiting to take Ryan up on her offer of massages for everyone. Jordan, Mia and Maggie were already undergoing their treatments, and Ryan and Jamie were patiently waiting their turn. "Feels good, doesn't it?" Ryan asked lazily as she allowed her arms to float to the surface of the bubbling water.

"Divine," Jamie agreed. "I'm proud of you for spending real money on something you'd normally consider frivolous."

"We deserve it. The boys were right there when we needed them, and you and Mia literally got manhandled."

"Like you just sat there and hoped for the best."

"I didn't do much," she said, her modesty making her lie.

"Well, even if we don't deserve it you'd better get used to this. Until classes start again, you're allowed to do four things: play basketball, relax, sleep and have wild, passionate sex."

"Gosh," she said reflectively, "I'm trying to think of who on earth would argue with that? Only one thing you missed on your list. I've got to get my grad school applications in soon, or I might as well not bother."

"Okay. By the time school starts you're going to be very well rested, weigh at least five pounds more, have all of your applications in, and be absolutely sick of my constant sexual attentions."

"Well then, school had better not start for many, many years, 'cause that last requirement is gonna take a very long time to fulfill."

※

Jordan relaxed against the headboard of Mia's bed, several fluffy pillows supporting her back. Mia lay sprawled against her body, her head resting on her lover's chest. "You know, I bet that when most people say they're gonna make love all night long, they're exaggerating," Jordan mused.

Mia laughed softly, and said, "We haven't been making love all night long. We had some very long breaks."

"You're right. But when I think of this night, I'll always remember it as the first night we made love 'til dawn."

Something about the way Jordan's voice sounded made Mia look up quickly. What she saw made her heart melt and, with a trembling voice, she asked, "Will you think about tonight?"

"Of course." Jordan shifted so that Mia fell into her strong right arm. She cradled her like a child, pressing Mia's head against her breast. "Of course I will," she whispered roughly.

Throwing her arms around Jordan's back, Mia hugged her with every ounce of strength she possessed. She fought valiantly to keep her emotions in check, but when she heard a great, wracking sob and felt hot tears drop onto her back, she lost her battle and cried piteously.

They cried until neither had tears left to shed. Both were weak from the outpouring of emotion, and Jordan slowly loosened her grip. Mia lay back and looked up at her with a face full of sorrow. Jordan's brow furrowed briefly, then, lower lip quivering, she said, "I don't have to go. I can stay…stay here with you."

In a flash, Mia was sitting up, staring at her with alarm. "This is what you've worked for your whole life! How can you even think of giving it up?"

The broad shoulders shrugged, and the vivid blue eyes shifted to stare, unfocused, at the rumpled sheets.

Mia's voice grew strong and fierce. "I can't let you even think of it. You'd never forgive yourself for letting this opportunity go." She held her lover at arm's length, and forced her to look into her eyes. "Promise me that you'll give this tryout your all." Shaking her lightly, she demanded, "Promise me."

"I will," she muttered, her darting eyes having a tough time remaining on Mia's face. "I promise I will."

Holding her close once again, Mia said, "You have to do this. You have to try your best. This is your only chance to achieve your dream."

Finally focusing on the warm, brown eyes, Jordan nodded again, wishing she could say what was in her breaking heart. She might be throwing away the only chance she ever would have to be with Mia, and that meant more to her than volleyball ever could.

Since Mia had an early final, Ryan was tapped to take Jordan to the airport. It was six-thirty when Ryan headed for the kitchen, looking for some breakfast. She hadn't seen Jordan since late afternoon of the previous day, so they hadn't worked out a timetable for when they would leave. It was time to get going, but she knew she'd have a devil of a time getting Jordan out of Mia's bed.

When she pushed the swinging door open, she nearly gasped in shock to see both Jordan and Mia standing in the kitchen. It was unclear whether they knew she was in the room, or they didn't care. Jordan was leaning against the built-in baking counter, with Mia leaning heavily against her. The taller woman was murmuring quiet 'shushing' sounds as she ran her fingers through Mia's curly brown hair. It was obvious that Mia was quietly crying, and Jordan's eyes were red-rimmed also. She rotated her head slowly, and made eye contact with Ryan, nodding her head and holding up a finger to indicate she needed another minute.

Ryan backed out, leaving them alone. Jamie came down the stairs as the kitchen door swung open. Mia ran out and scampered up the stairs past her, tears rolling down her cheeks. Jordan slowly walked up to Jamie and wrapped her in a tight hug, holding on for a long time. As she pulled away, she placed a gentle kiss on her lips and patted her cheek, still without a word. Turning to Ryan she nodded briefly and went to the door and exited. "Is she okay?" Jamie asked quietly.

"I don't know, but I'm sure Mia isn't. Good luck on your exam today."

"Thanks. I should be home by noon. Wanna have lunch?"

"It's a date."

Jordan was leaning against the Lexus, wiping furiously at her eyes when Ryan approached. The doors unlocked remotely, and Ryan reached into the back seat to grab some tissues. Jordan dabbed at her eyes and blew her nose as Ryan started up the car and drove to the coffee shop. She pulled up right in front and said, "I'll run. Triple latte?"

"Yeah," Jordan said gratefully, "and something to eat."

"Did you have anything last night?"

"Not a bite."

When they got to her apartment, it became obvious that Jordan was not in the proper mind frame to pack. She took a big nylon duffel and went through her drawers, hurling in all of her bras, panties and socks. Another drawer surrendered a few T-shirts, and a third gave up some sweat pants and two pairs of jeans. Jordan looked up and said, "I have to take a quick shower, Boomer."

"Go ahead. We can spare about twenty minutes."

Jordan gave her a grateful look as she made for the shower. She emerged ten minutes later, rubbing her long blonde hair energetically with a towel. She dropped the towel onto the bed, then broke into helpless tears when she saw what Ryan had done in her absence. Her friend had removed everything from her bag, and had neatly folded and organized every single item. She had also laid out Jordan's favorite black jeans and a thin black turtleneck. A bra, panties and a pair of black socks were placed on top of the sweater, and Jordan's short black boots were lying neatly on the floor in front of the clothing.

Wordlessly, Jordan collapsed into Ryan's arms, sobbing. "I don't want to leave. I'm so happy here. I feel so close to having what I've always wanted," she croaked out. "I'm giving up so much."

"I'm sorry this is so hard for you. But you can come back when you're done. You aren't losing anything. We'll all be waiting for you."

"You can't guarantee Mia will wait for me," she sobbed. "God, I don't want to lose her."

"She didn't look like someone who didn't care this morning. She was awfully upset."

"I know," she sniffed. "I know she cares for me. And if I were staying, I think we could make a go of it. But I don't think she's ready to commit to a long distance relationship. I think she's most upset by the loss of our unrealized potential."

"I don't know. I've known Mia for a while, and I've rarely seen her cry. She's not easily upset."

Jordan shook her head and started to dress. "I think we're both afraid to stick our necks out right now. This couldn't have come at a worse time. If we had another month, or even a few more weeks, I think we'd have more to go on. But it's still so new that neither of us has much confidence."

"I can see that, but don't give up. Promise me that you'll try to stay connected with her."

"I'll try. I really don't have any choice."

"I know that feeling," Ryan empathized as she gave her another hug.

She had Jordan settled at her gate when Ryan said, "I'm going to go get another cup of coffee. Join me?"

Jordan barked out a laugh. "I'll take all you've got."

"You didn't get much sleep did you?"

"I got exactly zero sleep," she admitted. "We were either crying or making love all night long. And we have our first run through today at four. They're going to think I'm some sort of zombie."

"I'll fix you right up. And I'll get you another snack."
"I won't move a muscle."

❧

By the time Ryan returned, Jordan was pacing furiously back and forth in front of her seat. "Jeez, where have you been?"

"Long line. But you can take it on with you."

"They already called us to board, so I'd better scoot." Her lower lip started to tremble again.

Ryan handed her the coffee and a scone, after Jordan lifted her carry-on onto her shoulder. Once her hands were full, Ryan folded up some papers and slipped them into Jordan's back pocket. "What's that?" She jerked her head around, ineffectually trying to see her own back.

"You'll find out when you sit down. Just don't throw it away before you look at it."

"Okay," she said with a dubious look, "but it better not be anything to make me cry, like some sappy goodbye card."

"No guarantees." Ryan wrapped her in a hug. "You've become awfully emotional lately. I'm not sure what might set you off."

"That's the truth," she conceded wryly. "I've lost a quart of fluid in the last twenty-four hours."

"Well, you could have lost a few teeth at the Raider game. Count your blessings."

"I do count them," she said soberly. "And you're one of the ones I count every day."

Ryan beamed a smile at her and leaned in for a kiss. Jordan gave her several, then turned and purposefully strode away.

❧

It took her until they had been in the air for twenty minutes to compose herself enough to pull the packet of paper from her pocket. She carefully unfolded it and had to hold back tears once again as she looked at the round trip ticket from Denver to San Francisco leaving on December the twenty-fourth and returning on the twenty-sixth. A hastily written note in Ryan's bold hand stated,

> *You're the gift I want for Christmas.*
> *Love, Boomer.*

When Ryan returned home, groceries in hand, Jamie came bounding out of the house to greet her. "Another exam finished!"

Ryan caught her in a hug, managing to maintain her control of the groceries at the same time. "Good thing for you I'm coordinated, or we'd have a dozen eggs on the ground."

"But you are coordinated. And strong, and soft and beautiful and…"

"What's on your mind, as if I couldn't tell?" Ryan asked with an indulgent grin.

"Well, we've got almost three hours until your practice, nobody's home, and you're the prettiest girl I've ever laid eyes on…" she teased seductively as she took Ryan's hand and led her into the house.

"Only too glad to perform my spousal obligations, but I need to have some lunch first, or I won't have my normal stamina."

"I'm only too happy to oblige." As they went into the kitchen she asked, "Did everything go okay at the airport?"

"Yeah, I suppose it did. But Jordan was devastated. You know, I think she felt like she belonged with Mia and us more than she ever has anywhere else in her life. This is really going to be hard for her."

"God, you should have seen Mia. I've known her for eight years, and this is the most upset she's ever been. The poor thing had to take a final first thing this morning, and her eyes were nearly swollen shut from crying."

"I hope you don't mind my spending our money without asking first, but I got an idea when I was at Jordan's this morning. I called the training site in Colorado Springs when she was in the shower, and found out when their practice was over on Christmas Eve and when they had to be back on the twenty-sixth. Then, when we were waiting for her plane, I ran back to the ticket window and bought her a ticket to come home for Christmas."

"Ryan, honey, I want you to understand something. You never have to explain where the money you spend goes, and you never have to ask my permission to spend it. This is our money, babe, and your decisions are as valid as mine. But for the record, I think it was a scathingly brilliant idea. Especially since Mia's birthday is the twenty-sixth."

"If Jordan gives me a hard time, I'm going to tell her the tickets are really Mia's birthday present," Ryan chuckled.

"Huh? Why would she give you a hard time later?"

"Oh, I snuck the tickets in her pocket. Her hands were both full and she was late getting on the plane, so we didn't have time to discuss them."

"Are you gonna tell Mia?"

"No, let's surprise her."

※

"Aren't you going to compliment me on sticking to your agenda for my free time?" Ryan asked as she and Jamie slowly woke from a long nap.

"What's that, sweetie?"

"I'm due at basketball in twenty minutes, so that's one item I'm allowed. I had an almost two-hour nap, a very good lunch, and very passionate, very satisfying sex," she added with a waggling eyebrow. "If I'd been able to squeeze in a little work on my grad school applications, I'd be golden."

"You're a very compliant patient. Now you scoot while I get some studying done. When you come home, I'll have dinner ready for you and take you to bed nice and early."

"I'll rush home as quickly as I'm able. Dallying is not allowed on my rigid schedule."

※

"How ya doing, buddy?" Jamie asked her roommate as she came trudging in the front door a few days later.

"I'm done." Mia let out a heavy breath. She pointed at the texts she'd dropped onto the floor. "As soon as I burn those books, I can flush everything from this semester so my brain's nice and empty again."

"How about some lunch?"

"Mmm, I don't really care. Any calls?"

"She has practice from eight until noon, honey."

"I know, I thought she might call as soon as she was done."

"She's probably hungry," Jamie said, but she was interrupted by the ringing phone.

Mia jumped for it, showing more energy than she had all week. A blissful smile covered her face. "Hi," she said, in a wistful, breathy voice.

Jamie took her cue and went into the kitchen to make lunch.

When Ryan returned from practice that night, Jamie was waiting to leave for the city. "I'm done. I'm done. I'm done. I'm done," Jamie cried as she leapt into her lover's arms.

Ryan smirked down at her, blowing away the long strands of her own hair that had settled onto Jamie's face. "If I ever hurt an arm or a hand, I've got to remember to call and tell you before I get home. I never know when a substantial weight is unexpectedly going to be hurled at me with a great deal of force."

"Hey, whose weight are you calling substantial?"

"At this point in the day—yours," Ryan said, exhausted from a very intense afternoon of practice. "As the day goes on, Caitlin starts to look like more than I can handle."

Sliding down the long body, Jamie patted her side and said, "Hey, I've got good news. If you'd been in my class, you would have won the portfolio challenge."

"Cool. So how did you do?"

"I came in third. Not bad for someone who was taking her first business class, huh?"

"Very good indeed." Placing a gentle, warm kiss on Jamie's lips, she added, "I'm really proud of you. You worked very hard this term—at courses that don't come naturally to you."

"Thanks. Now I have to see how I did."

"Mmm…in my opinion, that's the wrong attitude. You worked hard—you learned a lot—everything else is someone's subjective opinion of what you learned."

"Not really. We had a very objective final."

"Yeah, but a human wrote the test. The way they frame the questions; the topics they cover; the terms they use—all of those elements increase the subjectivity of the most objective test. What's important is that you got a lot out of the course—and that you're proud of your accomplishments. Other than that—let it go."

Jamie gave her a beaming grin, once again considering herself unbelievably lucky to have fallen for such a supportive woman. "I'll try to follow your advice. I agree that it's important to reward myself—rather than wait for someone else to do it."

"Hey, I know of a fun reward. Let's stop and buy a Christmas tree for the house. I'm sure the boys won't think of it."

"That would be nice. Do you have everything else?"

"Well, it's probably not of the same caliber as your family's, but we have plenty of ornaments to fill a tree."

"Ryan," Jamie gently rebuked her, "it's not important how much the ornaments cost. You know that, baby."

Ryan shot her a glance. "Ornaments cost money?"

⁂

After spending a ridiculously long time picking out the perfect tree and supervising the high school kid who lashed it to the roof of the Lexus, they arrived home in full darkness. Conor and Rory were both home, and the men ran out to help them bring the noble fir into the house. "Beauty," Conor said with approval. He held it out at arm's length and cut the string with his always-present pocketknife. Duffy approved too, scampering around the tree for a moment while Conor held it steady. Ryan had gone to the garage for the boxes of ornaments and lights, and after three trips they had everything assembled. A quick call for a pizza, and another to invite Brendan and Maggie over, and they started to unpack the carefully wrapped decorations.

Jamie was amazed to find that every single ornament in the box had been made by one of the children. All of the ones made by the boys were marked in an inconspicuous spot by a delicate hand, obviously Fionnuala's. But each of Ryan's bore Martin's European-style cursive, indicating her name and the grade she was in when the ornament was crafted. She noted without comment that one snowman made from Styrofoam balls indicated that Ryan was in the second grade. It struck Jamie that the ornament had been made just weeks after Fionnuala's death. Ryan noticed the look on her face, and gently removed the ornament from Jamie's grip, then glanced at the inscription. Their eyes met in silent understanding as Jamie's heart clenched at the lost look in those sad blue eyes. But Ryan shook her head and leaned over to offer a kiss, silently thanking her for understanding.

The tree trimming took a good two hours, with the boys taking charge of the lights while the girls organized the ornaments. When they were finished, it looked exactly like what it represented—a lifetime of fond family memories. A number of the hand made trinkets were far less than beautiful, but every one was authentic, and represented the best efforts of the small hands that had created it. As they stood back to survey their handiwork Jamie leaned her head against Ryan's shoulder and murmured, "That is the most beautiful tree I've ever seen."

Cal was playing in a weekend tournament at the Arena in Oakland, the home of the Golden State Warriors of the NBA. As befitted a pro team, the arena was huge—seating close to twenty thousand people. It was hard to sell the stadium out when the Warriors played, and when the biggest draw of the tournament was the Golden Bears women's team, attendance was absolutely anemic.

The sparse crowd in the cavernous stadium didn't aid the team's play, and they were routed, with Ryan determinedly playing every minute of the game. The three forward, two guard offense worked fairly well, with Cal scoring much more than usual. But on defense Ryan didn't do nearly as effective a job as Janae had, allowing the other team to score almost at will. "That coach should be taken in for a thorough mental examination," Martin glowered at the end of the disappointing match. "She keeps the best player on the bench for two weeks, then forces her to play a position she's not suited to. On top of that she doesn't give her one minute of rest. Those are human beings down there," he yelled to the diminishing form of the coach as she trailed behind the team on their way to the locker room.

"It's all right, Marty," Maeve soothed. "Ryan's a big girl, and she can ask to be taken out if she needs to be."

Martin gave her an incredulous look, then turned to Jamie for support. She smiled and shrugged her shoulders as Martin looked at his wife. "We're talking about Siobhán. She wouldn't ask for a break if she had a compound fracture."

"That trait must be from the O'Flahertys," Maeve said to Catherine, who was quietly watching the interplay. "The Ryans are a very level-headed people."

Martin's eyes rolled dramatically, but he chose to keep his opinions to himself, having already learned his lessons well during his short married life.

🙦

Just after six the phone rang in the O'Flaherty home. Jamie lunged for it to avoid waking her sleeping partner. She answered breathlessly, "Hello?"

"Hi," a soft soprano voice floated over the line. "This is Sara Andrews. Is this Jamie?"

"Oh, hi, Sara. Sorry for the way I sounded. Ryan's asleep, so I made a leap for it."

"She's okay, isn't she?" The concern in her voice was obvious. "She's so thin lately that I've been concerned about her."

"Oh, sure she is. She had a game this afternoon, and you know how hard she plays. We're working on getting some weight back on her, but she burns calories off a lot faster than she can eat."

"She's always been that way," Sara said with a fond laugh. "When we were in grade school she was the only kid who brought two lunches—one for recess and one for lunch."

Jamie smiled, dismissing the tendril of jealousy that flared whenever she acknowledged the history Ryan and Sara shared.

"Yeah, I'm getting a glimpse into Martin's troubles. These afternoon games are terrible. It's hard to get enough fuel into her to last her through the game while not having her too full to play."

"Is that the tournament in Oakland? I read about it in the paper today."

"Yeah. That's the one."

"Would it be okay if I came to the game tomorrow?"

"Sure. Why don't you come over here and ride with me?"

"Oh, gosh, I don't want to put you out…"

"Not a problem. Ryan's going to leave hours before I do, and I'm babysitting tomorrow, so it would be nice to have another pair of hands."

"If you're sure…"

"I'm positive. The game's at one, so I'll leave here at noon. Come anytime before that—and wear something that you don't mind getting drooled on," she added with a chuckle.

"I will and…thanks."

"Are you absolutely sure this is something you want to do?" Ryan asked for the fifth time.

"Yes, honey. I want to go to Mass, and Caitie is usually fine during the service."

"I know, but you've never had her alone in a setting like that…"

"If she gets to be too much, I'll leave. It's no big deal. Why is this bothering you, babe?"

"I don't know." She paused reflectively, trying to get a feel for what was bothering her. "Maybe it's having you and Sara spend time together this afternoon," she guessed. "That feels weird."

"Weird, like you wish I hadn't asked her without checking with you? Or weird like," Jamie shivered from head to toe, making a disgusted look, "That?"

"You are so cute," Ryan smiled, taking her partner in her arms and giving her a squeeze. "You have the cutest way of taking the slightest hint of a bad mood and whisking it away."

"I just love you," she sighed as she snuggled close. "I don't do anything special."

Caitlin had been playing peacefully with the new stuffed animals that Jamie had purchased, but when she saw the extended hug she got to her shaky feet and tottered over to the pair. "Uh…uh," she cried, her chubby hands reaching skyward.

Ryan leaned back in the embrace and gazed down at the baby fondly. "She's almost got another word there," she commented as she pulled away momentarily to bend and swoop the child into her arms. She snuggled her in between their bodies and chuckled as Caitlin let herself be enveloped in the tight clutch. Her blonde head rested under Ryan's chin, and Jamie dipped her head to plant tiny, soft kisses all over her giggling face.

"Who's kissing you, Caitlin?" Ryan murmured. "Who's kissing your face?"

She rubbed her face against Ryan's chest as the kisses started to tickle. Jamie's face was still inches from hers, and she stuck her hand out and patted her, in a gesture she had been making since she was tiny. "Jamie is kissing you," Ryan said slowly as the patting continued. "Jamie."

"Mmh mmh," she got out, trying diligently to imitate her cousin.

"That's right…Jamie," she tried again.

The look of concentration was so intense that Jamie had to bite her lip to not laugh in the baby's face. The child scrunched up her brow and gave it another try, "Mmhh mmhh," she huffed forcefully as Ryan congratulated her for her efforts by grabbing her legs and holding her upside down, high in the air. She giggled wildly at the sensation, always loving the somewhat rough treatment that she received from Ryan. But Jamie captured her and held her to her chest, giving her a tender squeeze and a final kiss on her wispy blonde head.

"You'd better get going," Jamie said. "I refuse to watch you run laps again if you're late. My poor heart can't take the stress."

Church went remarkably well since Jamie went against O'Flaherty tradition and dropped Caitlin off in the childcare center before Mass started. As much as she loved being with the baby, she really didn't believe that the child got anything from sitting still for nearly an hour, and she knew the people surrounding her were grateful for the break. She spent a good ten minutes in the child care area before the service to get her acclimated, but the tot quickly forgot that Jamie was with her when she met the other children that the three volunteer mothers were watching. There were five other kids being watched, and two were close to Caitlin's age. Jamie surveyed the whole set-up to make sure that it was safe, and was reassured when she got good vibes from the volunteers. Nonetheless, she made sure that each of them had her cell phone number in case there was any problem. "No one else is with me today," she warned, "so I'm the only one who will come to pick her up."

"Don't worry, Jamie," a woman named Lori assured her. "We know the O'Flahertys and the Driscolls. I went to school with Conor and Colm."

"Oh, that's a relief. Do you know Tommy and Annie?"

"Not well, since they don't attend many church functions, but I know Maeve quite well. Where is she this morning, anyway?"

"Oh, she's helping Martin with the big holiday open house at the fire station. She wouldn't approve of me leaving Caitlin here, but I think she'll be happier playing with other kids than fussing in church."

"Oh, I agree," Lori said. "My mother thinks Blake should be in church too, but this is so much less stressful for us both." She pointed to a dark haired boy that Caitlin was following around. "You know, we could always use another willing volunteer…"

"I need some solitude today, but I may take you up on that in the coming weeks."

Sara looked lovely as usual, Jamie thought with a smirk. She had always been a little envious of long legged, delicately boned women, and Sara was clearly a prototype for the species. Her hair was shorter than the last time Jamie had seen her: now the thick, glossy, chestnut strands ticked the tops of her shoulders when she moved her head. A very soft looking cream-colored sweater topped a cocoa brown skirt that looked like suede or moleskin. The skirt was long, nearly covering the tops of the dark brown leather boots which combined to make her legs look endlessly long. Jamie had to force herself not to snatch another quick look as Sara bent to fold herself into the Lexus. *Get your eyes off her ass!* she slapped herself in a mental rebuke.

There was really no doubt in her mind as to what attracted Ryan to Sara. Of all the women from Ryan's past, she had to admit that Sara would be her choice. Regrettably, being around her always brought out normally hidden insecurities, and not just because of the role she'd played in Ryan's life. Sara was everything that girls were brought up to emulate. She was tall and lean and graceful, with a walk that looked like it belonged more to a dancer than an athlete. Her voice was high and soft, making her seem both demure and very sexy. She exuded gentleness and softness, with a hint of playfulness, and Jamie spent a moment wondering what it would feel like to be in her arms. *Jesus! Will you stop this? What's gotten into you today?*

Sara snapped her out of her musings when she asked, "Has Jordan left for the training facility?"

"Yeah. She left on Monday morning. It was pretty hard for her to leave."

Sara turned a bit in her seat and said, "I've got to admit I was surprised that Ryan didn't get invited too. Her stats were better than Jordan's in some ways."

Jamie was surprised that Sara had obviously been perusing the team on the Internet, and even more surprised that Ryan hadn't told her the truth. "Uhm…she *was* invited. She chose not to go."

"Are you serious?" The shock on Sara's face was evident even though Jamie could only cast a quick glance at her. "How could she pass up a chance like that? My God, when I think of how much it meant to her to go to the Olympics. It was all she talked about."

Jamie nodded. "I knew it was important to her, but I don't think I knew it was that important."

"You have no idea," she said seriously. "You know how focused she can get." At Jamie's nod she continued. "She didn't have a computer when she was in high school, but I had one. After practice, she'd come over and plop herself down in front of that computer for any new bit of information she could get about the

Olympic team, or the national soccer federation. Every piece of information would go right into her memory bank," she said. "She knew every player on the team, and when I say she knew them, I mean it. She knew every camp they'd attended, how they did in high school and college. She knew how our stats stacked up against every player at the same age. It was really remarkable how focused she was. She actually seems very well rounded now compared to how she was then. Nothing...well, nothing more than her family, was as important to her as soccer. And nothing about soccer was as important as the Olympics."

"And you," Jamie quietly added.

"Wha...?"

"You were always going to be on the team together, weren't you?"

Sara's chestnut hair brushed across her shoulders as she nodded her head. "Yes, that was the dream."

"I've never been able to figure out why she quit soccer so abruptly," Jamie mused. "I mean, obviously it made sense to quit the team at Sacred Heart, given the harassment and lack of support from the coach, but she could have played in a city league or on a club team. It's also never made any sense to me why she wouldn't go to another college to play. Martin says Stanford would have been thrilled to have her."

"UCLA, North Carolina, Duke, Virginia, the Ivy League," Sara added. "Jamie, everybody wanted her. She was so heavily recruited by North Carolina that it was almost like she was being stalked—and they were national champs at the time, clearly the premier program." Sara shrugged her shoulders, and said, "For whatever reasons, she obviously had her heart set on Cal."

"Were you recruited by those schools?"

"No. No way. I was good, and I did well at Cal, but Ryan was great. She could have...no...should have been, on the World Cup team. She could have made it easily if you ask me. Cal was never very strong in soccer—it was really beneath her skills—but it's what she wanted."

"No, that's not it." A resigned sigh escaping from her lips. "She didn't have her heart set on Cal. She had her heart set on you."

Sara turned slightly in her seat and stared intently at Jamie.

"What do you mean?"

"She let you decide where you'd go—since you were a year older. Think back," she insisted, knowing her hunch was correct. "When did you both start talking about Cal?"

Sara was quiet for a while, a look of serious concentration on her face. She finally nodded briefly and said, "We started talking about Cal when I was a sophomore and Ryan was a freshman. The Cal coach came to a lot of our games, and it became pretty obvious that she wanted me for her team. As soon as Ryan heard that—we started daydreaming about it all the time." Sara's head dropped back and she took in a deep breath, letting it out slowly. "We took BART over to Cal to see all of their home games," she said, a smile settled onto her features. "It became our school. We learned the fight song, and we'd sing it when we walked home from practice at night." A few tears appeared on her cheeks, and her voice grew raspy. "She started to call me Bear, and when we'd part at night she'd give me a playful punch and say, 'Go Bear.'" Wiping furiously at her wet cheeks, she said, "You're right. She did it for me. It was all for me."

Jamie reached over and patted her knee, the emotion in the car nearly palpable. "You were such a vital part of the dream. When you weren't a part of it any longer, she didn't have a reason to continue. She wanted to go to Cal to be with you, and she wanted to be on the Olympic team with you. It wasn't attractive to her once you were gone…it wasn't worth the struggle."

Sara's eyes fluttered closed as her head tilted towards the window. "I was so unworthy of her," she said, sorrow choking her words. "I am so eternally grateful that she found you," she added as her hand reached out blindly to rest on Jamie's leg.

"Y…You are?"

"Of course. It's obvious how much you love her, and how much you have to give to each other."

"That kind of amazes me," Jamie mused quietly. "I guess I thought you were still…"

"I am," she whispered. "I still love her with everything I am."

Jamie shot her a wide eyed look, but Sara squeezed her leg and reassured her, "But all that I have is nothing compared to what you have. I've tried very hard in the last few months to face some hard facts about myself, and I have to admit Ryan pushed me to do that."

"How did she push you?"

Sara turned back, staring at the side of Jamie's face. "She told me why she'd choose you over me if she had the chance all over again."

Jamie's voice was a little loud even to her own ears. "She what?"

"Yeah." Sara let out a short, wry laugh. "God. My heart almost broke when she told me that, but I've spent a lot of time thinking about it, and she was right. She's surpassed me so far emotionally that she could never be happy with me. She needs someone who is her equal. That's you. And if I really love her, I need to want the best for her. I think she has it," she added quietly.

They were approaching the arena now, and Jamie was utterly silent as she pulled into the nearly empty parking lot and turned off the car. Her head dropped back as she sighed deeply, and composed herself for a moment. Turning slightly, her face curled into a gentle smile and she unlatched her seat belt as she leaned over. Sara allowed herself to be caught in a tender hug, broken only by Caitlin's cry demanding to be brought in to the embrace. "She hates to be left out," Jamie whispered as she pulled back, the light scent of Sara's perfume still filling her lungs.

"So do I," she admitted. "And I'm very grateful that you've welcomed me into your lives."

"You're very welcome," she said. "Anyone who loves Ryan is always welcome in our home."

Ryan's game was really on, and she had a stellar outing. She didn't score much, because their opponents put a double-team on her, but that strategy allowed one Cal player to be unguarded almost constantly, and they used that to their advantage throughout the afternoon. Even though she didn't contribute much offensively, she did a much better job with her defense, and her improved play sparked the other members of the team to kick their games up a notch as well.

At one point Jamie asked Conor reflectively, "Do you think it bothers her not to score?"

"Nah. She gets more pleasure out of playing good defense. What's important to her is making a contribution however they need it in a given game. She told me that she didn't care what happened the rest of the year, but that she wasn't going to have another trillion in the box score if it was the last thing she did."

"What's a trillion?"

"That's basketball lingo for nada. No points, no assists, no rebounds, no free throws attempted or made, and no fouls."

"But why is that a trillion?"

"Well, in the box scores they list all of the offensive and defensive categories next to one another. During the early games, Ryan would have two minutes played with a bunch of zeros after the minutes. Even though there aren't enough zeros to make it a trillion, the term stuck as a way of saying you played but didn't do squat."

"Her trillion days are over," Jamie agreed.

Sara, Caitlin and Jamie went down to the locker room entrance to greet Ryan after Cal's hard-won victory. They'd been waiting mere moments when Jamie spotted a familiar face from the corner of her eye. A very familiar face that she would have been happy to never see again. The thin blonde woman was leaning against the far wall, looking at Jamie with undisguised interest. Actually, she looked more like she was scoffing at her than interested in her, and that look alone made Jamie hand the baby to Sara with a quick, "Be right back." She stalked over to Cassie Martin, smiling inwardly as the smirk left the taller blonde's face, replaced by shock at Jamie's audacious approach.

"Hello, Jamie," she said with mock politeness. "I saw you upstairs with your mother. Interesting that she didn't go to Washington with your father. Trouble in paradise? Or hasn't she noticed that he's gone?"

Ignoring the comment, Jamie asked, "Why on earth are you here? You don't like sports." She acted as though something had occurred to her. "On second thought, you don't like anything."

"You're not the only one with secret interests. Actually I've gotten to be good friends with one of the players."

"Don't tell me, let me guess," Jamie offered. "Either Janet or Wendy."

Cassie blinked at her a few times. "How did you guess that?"

"They're the only ones who seem to be your type," she replied with a sickeningly sweet smile of her own.

"Speaking of types, I've been hearing all sorts of things about you." Cassie taunted, her attractive face curled into a very unattractive sneer. "Everybody knows."

"Knows what?" she asked, intentionally playing dumb.

"Knows that you two are dykes."

"You're kidding." she said with a completely shocked look on her face. "Everyone knows?"

"Yes, everyone." Jamie had seen her lanky lover emerge from the locker room, and caught her surprised glance. Ryan immediately changed paths and headed right for her. She was coming from behind Cassie, catching her unawares.

"My God," Jamie moaned, as if she couldn't bear the thought. Lifting her chin she said, "Well, if everyone knows, there's no reason not to do this." She opened her arms and pulled Ryan in close for an openmouthed, tongue-thrusting, spit-swapping kiss that continued long past any reasonably modest limit.

Knocking Cassie over with a feather would have been overkill at that point. Jamie could hear her try to catch her breath to make a comment, but after a few seconds of the passionate kiss, Jamie no longer cared who was watching; and by the time she could feel Ryan's mouth curl into a grin, she had almost forgotten why she had even begun the embrace. "You must have really liked my game today," Ryan murmured through her grin.

"I think I was trying to make a point, but now I don't remember what it was." She absently looked around and found the space previously occupied by Cassie blissfully empty.

Sara came over with the baby asking, "What in the heck was that display about? That woman you were talking to almost fainted."

"Old roommate," Jamie explained. "Doesn't like Ryan. Persona non grata."

"I'm starved," Ryan said as soon as she walked in the door to the house.

Jamie called out, "Hey, anybody home? I'm gonna cook."

When there was no reply she said, "It's just the three of us. We don't have a lot, but I could make vegetable frittatas. Would that hold you until dinner?"

Laughing, Sara said, "That would hold me for twelve hours."

"Hey, I'm a growing girl," Ryan said.

"Face it, you've always eaten like a teenaged boy. God, Jamie, you should have seen her when she was eleven or twelve. She would go home after practice and eat a huge sandwich that her Dad would have left for her, then we'd go to my house and my mother would make her another one. Then she'd go home to have dinner."

"I was a lot more active then," Ryan reminded her.

"Honey, you never stop now. How could you be more active?"

"Trust me," she said. "I just was."

"We really have to adopt," Jamie muttered as Sara laughed. "You can stay, can't you?"

"I've got no plans," Sara said, casting a tentative glance at Ryan. "I love being around the munchkin." She bounced the giggling baby on her hip. "The last home cooked meal I had was Thanksgiving. I usually grab a salad for dinner. It'd be nice to have something hot for a change."

"Okay, here's the deal. Ryan, go take a shower; Sara, you watch the baby—I'm going to the store for something more substantial than a frittata."

"Yes, ma'am," Sara said quickly.

❦

Jamie cooked while Sara and Ryan entertained Caitlin, with an assist from Duffy. Now that the baby could walk, Jamie didn't like to cook with her in the kitchen, even with Ryan watching her, so play was restricted to the living room.

"So...uhm...seeing anyone new?" Ryan asked.

Sharing a shy smile, Sara nodded slightly. "Yes. I've gone out with Ally a couple of times since Thanksgiving." She paused for a second and said, "She told me about how close you were."

Ryan lifted an eyebrow and asked, "What did she tell you?"

"Not too much, honestly. I think she only said as much as she did because it was obvious that I thought she was insane for letting you go," she chuckled.

Ryan nodded, knowing that Ally wouldn't reveal anything of their sexual history. "How do you feel about that?"

"It's a little odd," Sara admitted. "I uhm…I'm not sure if we'll keep seeing each other."

"Because of me?"

"No, not really. We're keeping this very casual. Ally has some very clear goals before she gets involved with anyone, and I'm not sure I'm ready for that yet." Sara was lying on the floor, her attention half focused on Caitlin and half on Ryan. "I'm a little scared by her."

"Scared?"

"Yeah. It seems like she's very clear about what she wants and how she wants to get it. I feel so muddled around her…like I'm still a kid, and she's an adult."

"I felt that way around her a bit, too," Ryan said, sharing a warm smile with her friend. "She has a very powerful personality, and she's quite determined when she knows she wants something." Cocking her head, Ryan asked, "Do you like her enough to try to go forward?"

"Yeah…yeah, I do," she said. "I like her a lot, but I'm afraid she'll think I'm too immature for her."

Ryan lay on the floor and put Caitlin on her stomach. The baby loved to sit on Ryan's belly and pretend that her cousin was a pony, sticking her feet into Ryan's sides as she jumped excitedly. "This is the best exercise for my abs," Ryan chuckled. She turned her gaze to Sara and said, "Ally gives the appearance of being totally in control. But she has as many insecurities as the next woman. She's really clear about what she wants from a relationship, but I guarantee she's not significantly more mature than you are. A lot of that is the image she presents."

"Really? Do you really think so?" She sounded tentatively hopeful.

"Really. Ally had to grow up quick. She's been on her own for a long time, and I think that makes her appear more mature than most people her age. But she's looking for someone to love—like most of us are."

"That's what I'm looking for too." Sara sighed, absently playing with Caitlin's foot.

"Well, my advice is to give Ally a chance if you feel any spark. She's a great person."

"We haven't even kissed yet, but I'm really attracted to her. It's funny," she said thoughtfully, "she's really not my type, but I guess that doesn't matter, does it?"

"Nope. I didn't recognize that my type was feisty green-eyed blondes until about a year ago. Who knew?"

Sara laughed mildly at her friend's joke, then, with a very serious expression, said, "Jamie tells me you're having a heck of a time with this coach. What's going on?"

Ryan shrugged. "She's a tough one, but I think I'm finally figuring her out."

"I've been on a lot of teams with you, and I've never known you to have a problem pleasing a coach."

"Well, I think the biggest thing is the fact that I'm a twenty-four year-old woman, playing with seventeen and eighteen year-olds. Coach believes in having one set of rules—and they're really inflexible. I think she does that to keep a very tight handle on the younger players—which makes sense, but she applies those rules to me too. I started off the season by trying to do what made sense—even if my decision didn't fall within the rules. She's quickly made me see that's not gonna work."

"And you're okay with that?"

"Yeah, I am. It's her team—her rules. I knew she was inflexible when I signed up—so I've decided to stop being a baby and go along with the program. From now on, I'm gonna ask permission for everything."

After Sara left, Jamie started to head downstairs, saying, "Time for my weekly attempt to cheer my father up."

"Good luck, honey," Ryan said, giving her a sympathetic look.

She marched downstairs and lay on the bed, dialing his number. "Hi, Daddy," she said when he answered.

"Hi, sweetheart. It's nice to hear from you. How are things?"

"Things are fine with me. I just wanted to see how you were doing."

"Oh, about the same." He sighed heavily. "I'm getting by all right. It's just that…I didn't expect to be at this place at this point of my life." He was quiet for a moment, then added, "It's so ironic. I can hardly count the things I've done that would have given your mother every justification to boot me out of her life. But when I make up my mind to dedicate myself to her and permanently stop cheating—she jumps to a faulty conclusion and tosses me aside." He sighed once again and said, "I can't complain—since God knows she's got plenty of justification. But it seems so ironic…do you know what I mean?"

"I think I do," she said quietly. "I know this is hard for you."

"Yes, yes it is. I wish I could get her to listen to me. I've committed myself to her, and I swore that I'd try to be the husband she deserves—if she'd only let me."

"I wish I could help, Daddy. I really do."

"I don't want to put you in a bad position, but if you ever get the chance, I'd really appreciate it if you'd try to get her to at least talk to me. This is driving me absolutely mad."

"I don't know if I can do that, Dad. I can't get in the middle of this…"

"You're right," he said, sounding thoroughly defeated. "I'm sorry I asked. I made this bed, now I have to lie in it."

Chapter Eight

On the first day of their Christmas break Jamie and Ryan decided to head down to Hillsborough to spend some time with Catherine. But first Ryan wanted to stop by her high school to have a chat with her old principal. Jamie watched with a grin as her partner stood in front of her closet in her underwear, debating the merits of her wardrobe. "Still trying to impress the good sisters?" she asked with a twinkle in her eyes.

Ryan turned a stern gaze on her, but couldn't maintain it for long. "I hate to get busted so easily."

"Well I think it's adorable that you still care what the nuns think of you."

"I want to look like an adult. I was such a gawky kid...I hate to look the same six years later."

"Honey," Jamie said slowly as she let her gaze travel up and down her lover's sculpted body, "gawky is the last word anyone would use to describe you. Gorgeous...sexy...devastatingly beautiful..."

Her litany was stopped abruptly by Ryan's lips gently pressing against hers. "You always make me feel special."

"You *are* special," Jamie assured her as she ran her fingers through her dark hair. "Will you let me pick out some clothes for you?"

"Sure. You do a much better job than I do, anyway."

"I don't agree with that, but you seem especially indecisive today, and we need to get going to avoid rush hour traffic." She jumped to her feet and quickly pulled out a pair of neatly pressed khaki slacks, a pale yellow turtleneck, and a marine blue wool sweater that looked particularly good on her lover. "Here you go. You'll look great in that."

"Thanks, babe," Ryan said, sliding into the slacks. "As long as you're there, pick me out something for tomorrow too, okay? And add some workout clothes so I can go on a run or use your mom's gym."

"Coming right up. Then let's rock."

"I appreciate you taking the time to speak with me, Sister Mary Magdalene," Ryan said when they were shown into the neat office. "Do you remember my partner?"

"Of course," the woman said. "It's good to see you again. After having had the pleasure of speaking with your mother, I'd better watch out if you share the same negotiating skills."

"Oh, my mother is far more skilled than I am."

"What can I do for you girls today?"

"I had a couple of things on my list," Ryan began, "but I may as well get the stickier one out on the table." She looked uncomfortable, but forced herself to take a breath and get it out. "Jennie's very excited about attending school here. And I have no doubt that the academic instruction she'll receive here will help her tremendously. But I'm worried about her socially."

"Is that because she's a lesbian?"

"Partly, yes. It's hard to be a lesbian-identified teenager almost anywhere, but I'm particularly worried about how she'll fit in here."

"I assume you're now referring to your own experience, Ryan."

"It's the only experience I have to go by," she said with a tight smile. "I want to make sure that Jennie will get some support from the faculty if any of the students start to harass her. She's very open about her orientation compared to how I was at her age. I hadn't even really acknowledged to myself that I was gay. And when I think of the harassment I got, I can only imagine what will happen to her."

"Ryan," she said thoughtfully, "given how you feel about your experiences here, why do you want Jennie to attend our school?"

"Because I know you well enough to believe you, Sister. And if you tell me you'll support her, I believe you will. Except for that one dreadful incident, Sacred Heart changed my life in so many positive ways that I want Jennie to have those same opportunities."

Sister leaned back in her chair and dropped her head back for a few moments. She got up smoothly and came around the front of her desk, perching on the corner, right in front of Ryan. She extended her hand and gently held Ryan's when she gave in to her unspoken request. "I promise I'll support her. I owe that much to every student who attends this school. I'm so sorry I didn't do the same for you." Her light brown eyes stared deeply into Ryan's, and Ryan knew that the woman was telling the truth.

"It's okay. It all worked out for me in the end."

"God works in mysterious ways," she said as she released her hand and went back to her chair. "Now what else did you want to cover?"

"I wanted to find out where to buy her uniforms and a list of textbooks she'll need. I want her ready to go on January the tenth," she said with a broad smile.

"My God!" Ryan cried as they turned onto Catherine's street. "Looks like half of the electric usage in the Bay Area comes from your neighborhood." Jamie laughed at her characterization, but she did have to admit that the gardeners had been busy. Most of the large homes were surrounded either by stone or stucco walls, or dense shrubbery. Nearly every hedge and fence was decorated by some form of electric light in honor of the holiday, and given the neighborhood, it was clear that the homeowners hadn't stood on rickety ladders to put them up. When they entered the property, Ryan was delighted to see that every Italian cypress that surrounded the Evans home had been neatly wound in tiny white lights, and a long double row of shiny silver luminaries bordered the gracefully curved drive. The roofline of the house was trimmed in white lights, and a pair of gargantuan wreaths hung on the front door. "Who was the poor sucker that had to get on that slippery slate roof?" Ryan asked.

"Mother hires professionals, honey. They have cranes."

"Whew. I could see some poor guy sliding down that thing, never to be heard from again."

Marta answered the door moments after they rang the bell, and she gave each woman an enthusiastic hug. "Feliz Navidad," she said as she motioned for them to enter. The high ceiling of the living room allowed for the placement of the largest Christmas tree Ryan had ever seen in a private home. It stood at least twelve feet tall and was perfectly, and professionally, decorated in ornaments that Ryan guessed were precious antiques. The selection of ornaments perfectly accented the furnishings of the living room, of course, matching both the warm, rich colors and the understated style. The tree also carried more lights than seemed wise when attached to a dead or drying tree. It was actually putting out as much heat as the cheery fire in the stone hearth next to it, and Ryan mused that her father would probably not be able to be in the room without a fire extinguisher in his hands.

The rest of the room was decorated with touches of green, red and gold, and the massive mantle was bedecked with a velvet cloth that matched the colors of the ornaments that graced the tree. Fresh smelling fir garland was wrapped around the banister that led to the second floor, and it was interlaced with tiny white lights that served to highlight Catherine's slim form as she gracefully descended the stairs. "It is so good to see your friendly faces," she said, remaining on the lowest step to hug her guests.

"Your house is magnificent," Ryan said in amazement. "I've never seen anything like it."

"I almost skipped it this year, to tell you the truth." She grasped each woman's hand to lead them into the living room. "But the decorators were so disappointed that I finally told them to go ahead. Now I'm glad I did it," she said with a small smile. "It brings some cheer to the old place." Ryan noticed the stress in her features, and observed that Catherine's gait was much stiffer than normal.

Ryan paused to run her hand over a large, elegantly carved Nativity scene. "This is beautiful," she said when Catherine came to stand next to her.

"That's our Nacimiento."

"Is it a family heirloom?"

"After a fashion," she nodded with a small smile. "It means a great deal to me. I'd like it to be in your house one day."

Ryan looked at her and caught sight of the depths of sorrow in her lifeless brown eyes. She grasped her hand and gave it a squeeze, saying, "I think you should keep it for the next fifty or sixty years. I want to see your great-grandchildren come down here to marvel at the beautiful decorations you have."

Catherine stifled her tears and took a seat, and soon Marta came bustling out carrying a tray with an insulated pitcher and a set of three heavy mugs. "I made some mulled wine for you to sip on before you go out," she said.

"Oh, I forgot what day is was," Catherine said. "Marta teaches her class tonight, so we'll have to go out."

"Nonsense," Jamie said. "You don't mind if we use your kitchen do you, Marta?"

"No, no of course not. I would be honored."

"We'll cook dinner. I don't think I've ever made a meal for you."

"That was one thing we had in common," Catherine replied with a sad look.

"Hey, come on," Jamie said as she handed her mother a mug filled with the spicy red wine. "We'll do it together—the three of us."

"Oh, honey, I can't do a thing in the kitchen."

"Not without instruction, you can't. Right, Marta?"

"Definitely. Anyone can cook with a little instruction."

<hr>

They sipped their wine as Ryan related the gist of her discussion with Sister Mary Magdalene. "Oh, I need to call her," Catherine said. "Kevin started today, and I want to make sure everything is going well on her end."

"That was incredibly thoughtful of you to hire Kevin to do the work, Catherine," Ryan said, "but he doesn't want to charge you."

"That's why I told him I wouldn't hire him if we didn't agree on his wages up front. I could understand if he wanted to do some small job for me, but this will take every hour he can spare between now and the tenth when school starts. He still tried to pull a fast one on me," she chuckled. "He quoted me a ridiculously low number for his hourly wage, so I called the union hall and asked for the going rate for electricians. He's going to be surprised when I pay his bill."

"You know, Catherine, most clients worry about being overcharged."

"Not with your family." she said with a dramatic rolling of her warm brown eyes. "You'd think you were communists."

When they got up to head to the kitchen, Ryan stopped to regard a framed picture of a very young Jamie sitting transfixed on the lap of a very credible looking Santa Claus. She was about three years old, and the look on her face made Ryan grin so widely that her cheeks ached. "I need a copy of this," she as she shook the frame in Catherine's direction.

Catherine walked over and leaned against her when Ryan slid an arm around her waist. "Wasn't she a beautiful child?" Catherine asked wistfully.

"Incredibly." They gazed at the image for a few minutes. Tiny Jamie was wearing an emerald green velvet dress, white tights and black patent leather shoes. She had her hair pulled back in a ponytail with a matching green ribbon tied around it. Her cheeks were flushed with excitement, and her eyes sparkled with delight and awe at the presence of the fabled St. Nick right next to her.

"Look at those chubby legs," Ryan said affectionately.

Jamie piped up. "I was only three. You're supposed to be chubby then."

"You're adorably chubby. Boy, Caitlin will be very lucky if she continues to look like you."

"Come on you two," Jamie said. "You've idolized me enough. I've hardly eaten all day and I'm famished."

After doing an inventory, they decided to roast a chicken and have some rosemary potatoes, asparagus and Pennies from Heaven, one of Ryan's favorite carrot dishes. She loved the sliced carrots sautéed with butter and brown sugar until they shone like copper pennies, and she asked Jamie to make them every time there was a bunch of carrots in the refrigerator. There really wasn't much to do except for chopping and slicing, so Ryan sat at the counter sipping her wine, while Jamie provided her mother with a short cooking lesson. After receiving her instruction, Catherine did a decent job of cutting up the carrots and the rosemary. Jamie checked on her frequently and praised her for her efforts, making her mother beam with pride.

Catherine loosened up as the evening wore on, but she still looked drained and pale when dinner was finished. Ryan got up to clear the table and offered, "Since you two cooked, I'll clean up. Why don't put on your suits, and we can go sit in the spa for a while."

"Excellent idea," Jamie agreed and Catherine seconded the vote. They left as Ryan began to work, and a few minutes had passed when a pair of hands grasped her around the waist.

"Catherine," she hissed sharply, "I told you not to do that when Jamie's here."

"Oh, you are such a naughty girl," Jamie scolded, squeezing her tightly.

"Hey, where's your suit?" Ryan asked, turning around to catch a look at her still fully clothed body.

"I had to go to the bathroom, so I came back to grab a handful of this delicious ass."

"You know, you get very randy when we're down here," Ryan commented as she stuck her butt out for Jamie to grab at will.

She grabbed Ryan's hips and pressed against her in a tight circle. "Do you mind?"

"Not in the least—since your father's gone." She gasped as one of Jamie's hands slid up her stomach and grabbed a breast. "But we're gonna have to give the spa a miss if you keep that up."

"Oh, you're so easy," Jamie whispered into a pink ear as she covered her body fully. "A simple touch and you get all flustered." She grasped the waistband of Ryan's slacks with her left hand while her right slowly slid her zipper down. "Now you'll be telling me that this excites you, too," she scoffed huskily as her hand slipped past the zipper and cupped Ryan's mound. "Mmm, I love you in your tight boxers."

Ryan's head dropped back against Jamie's shoulder as the

determined hand squeezed her lips together rhythmically. Ryan's feet moved apart and she shifted her hips forward to push her pelvis down against Jamie's searching fingers. "Mmm," she murmured in a strangled cry. Jamie suddenly realized that she'd bitten off more than she could chew at the moment. Hearing her mother's footsteps, she slid her hand out and dashed out the other door, leaving an astounded Ryan with her fly and her mouth hanging open as Catherine came into the room.

"Need any help, dear?"

She wanted to ask if Catherine minded if she put her hand into her pants and finished what evil Jamie had started, but her rational mind said in a voice at least an octave too high, "No, no, no help. Go get the spa ready for Jamie."

Catherine smiled at her companions when they were all relaxing in the spa. "What do you two have planned for your free time?"

"We don't have much free time," Jamie said. "We're not having formal golf practice until school starts again, but I've got to really start playing a lot. And Ryan's got to spend every spare minute getting her applications for grad school in, as well as basketball practice, of course."

"We haven't really talked about this, honey," Catherine said, cocking her head curiously. "Are you planning on attending school next year?"

Jamie smiled at her partner and said, "I make fun of Ryan for being unable to decide, but I'm even worse than she is. I can't make up my mind, Mom, and going just to stay in school seems silly."

"I suppose I assumed you'd go on for a masters in English. You used to talk about doing that."

"Yes, and I talked about going to a writing program, and I've toyed with the idea of getting a Ph.D. in psychology. Ryan thinks I should go to law school—because she thinks I'd be a natural." She paused to stick her tongue out at her grinning partner. "She tries to make it sound like a compliment, but I think it's a veiled way to call me argumentative and manipulative."

Ryan's eyes went round as she pointed to herself with exaggerated innocence.

Jamie smiled warmly and said, "I am manipulative, baby. Truth hurts."

"You're persuasive," Ryan demurred. "That's a good trait."

Jamie turned back to her mother. "So, my interests are all over the place. I think I'm going to pass on applying anywhere right now. Once we see where Ryan gets in, it'll be easier to narrow my own choices down."

Catherine looked to Ryan. "Well, fill me in. What have you chosen?"

"I'm still on the fence, too. I'm going to apply to Cal and Stanford in math and biology, and Stanford and UCSF for an M.D./Ph.D. program. Then I'll see where I get in, and make my choice."

Catherine blinked and said, "I had no idea you wanted to be a physician."

"I don't think I do." She shrugged. "I think research would let me make the kind of contribution I'd like, but at the higher levels there's a built-in bias against people who don't have their medical degree. I also can't conduct clinical trials on my own without an M.D. That's not such a bad thing if I work in an academic setting, but if I want to work in private industry, I really need the credentials. I hate to have to do it, because it will take me a long time to finish—but if I get in, that's probably what I'll do."

"How do you feel about locking yourself into more schooling?"

"I don't mind the schooling part. But we've decided to wait to have children until we're through with school. I'm bummed at the thought of not having our first child until I'm over thirty."

Catherine smiled and said, "You never know what will happen. You might be surprised with a baby before you expect one."

Now it was Ryan's turn to blink in surprise. "Uhm…we can't have an accident. We have to make a conscious choice to get pregnant. There's not a single sperm between us."

Throwing her head back and laughing heartily, Catherine said, "I know that. I meant that you might decide to get pregnant much earlier than you're planning. Goodness." she laughed again. "I sometimes forget that you're lesbians, but I've never given a thought to either of you having the ability to impregnate the other."

Ryan laughed as well, shaking her head. "Maybe that's what I'll do my research on. Wouldn't you like to have an adorable clone of Jamie running around the house?"

Smiling at her daughter-in-law, Catherine said, "Knowing you, I might as well get the nursery ready. I'm continually impressed by your talents."

After a relaxing dip in the warm water, Ryan said, "I'm in the mood to give two massages. And I choose you to go first." She poked her finger against Catherine's chest.

"Oh, Ryan, you don't have to do that," she demurred weakly.

"But I want to. You don't want to disappoint your guest do you?"

"I'm helpless around both of you," Catherine declared dramatically, but allowed herself to be led out of the spa and into the massage area in the pool house.

Catherine went to bed as soon as Ryan was finished with her, and Ryan did such a good job on Jamie that she was snoozing peacefully on the massage table by the time Ryan was finished. "I have got to plan better," Ryan mumbled audibly as she lifted the sturdy body and carried her into the house, smiling down at the serene expression as her partner woke enough to give her a lazy, satisfied smile.

Early the next morning, Jamie's nose twitched in Ryan's direction. "Why do you smell so sweet?"

"That wouldn't have been your question twenty minutes ago. But I smell sweet now because I went for a nice long run, stopped in the kitchen for a baked cinnamon roll, and hopped in the shower. I've washed my hair, shaved my legs and brushed every tooth. All of that adds up to sweetness."

"And why are you back in bed?" Jamie asked with a sultry tone to her voice.

"I'm here to collect. You left me with the female equivalent of blue balls last night, missy."

"Oh, let me see," Jamie teased, giggling as she ducked her head below the covers. "I don't see anything blue down here," her muffled voice called out. "Everything's pink and sparkling clean." She popped back up. "I'm gonna go get all sparkly too. I'll love you forever if you dash back down and get me one of those rolls while they're still warm."

"Do you think Marta will mind?" Ryan asked as she trotted over to the door, her firm breasts jiggling just the way Jamie liked them.

"I think she would faint dead away, you gorgeous thing. Put some clothes on before I have to call the paramedics."

When Jamie emerged from the shower Ryan was back in bed, contentedly sucking her fingers clean of the glaze that covered the sticky cinnamon rolls. "You'd better hurry," she teased.

Jamie leapt to the bed from at least five feet away, and only Ryan's quick reflexes saved the buns from winding up on the sheets. "Why do you do things like that?" she cried in exasperation.

"Because I know you're as quick as a cat, and I love to see the look on your face." She happily snagged a roll from the plate resting on Ryan's lap.

That comment merited her a gentle kiss…and another…and another until they were grappling together in a mess of sheets, down comforter and tangled limbs. Ryan had the presence of mind to secure the plate prior to her opening volley, but when Jamie was about out of control Ryan pulled the plate back and snatched another roll, idly commenting, "I'm hungrier than I am horny."

Jamie lunged for her and grabbed the roll from her mouth, stuffing the entire thing into her own mouth before Ryan could even bite down. "Hey, give that back!" Ryan tried to tickle it out of her. But Jamie leapt to her feet and danced around behind an upholstered wing chair, moving it quickly to keep a bounding Ryan at bay while she chewed noisily with a wicked look on her face.

She finished the morsel and opened her mouth wide to show

that it was all gone. Ryan leapt for her and managed to get both arms around her waist despite Jamie's fierce defensive moves, then she tossed her over her shoulder and lightly paddled her butt before dumping her back onto the bed. "As punishment for that, I'm going to lift weights instead of make love."

Jamie pouted, "Don't leave me…I'll be good, I promise," she added with her best innocent look.

"I didn't say I was going to leave. I said I was going to lift weights." And with that she grabbed Jamie by the waist and rolled onto her back. She used her powerful chest and arm muscles to power Jamie up and down amid screams and nearly hysterical giggles.

The game became much more creative as Ryan managed to perform a set of abdominal crunches with her partner straddling her lap and limply resting against her chest; twenty pushups with Jamie lying completely atop her; and another twenty with Ryan's body poised over Jamie's. The last pushup was aborted when Jamie snaked her arms around her partner and pulled her to her chest, refusing to allow her to finish. Jamie's warm, wet kisses made Ryan lose her focus, and they spent the next hour making love enthusiastically and athletically.

When they finally emerged from Jamie's room, it was past nine o'clock and they nearly collided with Catherine as she emerged for the first time. "Oh, how nice. You managed to sleep in."

"Yep," they answered in unison, with matching looks of innocence on their very satisfied faces.

Ryan ran off to practice while Jamie and Catherine sat in the sunny kitchen, idly picking at the last remaining cinnamon roll. "I'm worried about you, Mom," Jamie said as she gazed at her mother's drawn face. "I've never seen you look so sad."

"Christmas is hard," she admitted. "Harder than I thought it would be. I think back to our first Christmas together…how filled with promise and plans we both were. You were due to be born soon, and we were so much in love." She sighed and wiped at a tear with an irritated gesture. "It seems so long ago."

"Your mind is really made up, isn't it?" Jamie asked, her concern evident.

"Yes, I'm afraid so. I know this is hard for you, but I can't go on like this."

"Mom," she said gently, "I promised myself I wouldn't get involved, and I really don't want to, but I honestly think that Daddy's telling the truth this time."

Catherine nodded, a resigned look on her face. "I think there's a very good chance of that."

"But…"

"Honey, the issue isn't whether or not he's telling the truth this time. The issue is that I haven't been able to rebuild my trust in him." She leveled her gaze and asked, "Could you stay with Ryan if you were innately suspicious of every woman that she spent any time with?"

"No, no, I couldn't. Every once in a while I feel some jealousy and it drives me nuts. And that's with me knowing that she would never cheat. If I couldn't trust her…we'd have nothing," she said softly.

"That's exactly it. I didn't know that until this last incident. I thought we could start anew. But even if he could—I couldn't. I have too much resentment built up over his behavior. I can't let go of it. I wish I could—but I can't."

"I understand, Mom," she said, scooting her chair close and giving her mother a gentle hug. "I'd do the same thing. I've told Ryan that I have a 'one strike and you're out' policy on cheating. It's unforgivable."

"Thank you for understanding," Catherine sighed, her breath warm against her daughter's neck. "I was afraid this would be impossible for you to accept."

"You're a very generous and giving woman. If you could get past this—you would."

"I need to get on with my life. I've been in a holding pattern for years—like I was in suspended animation. I've had enough." She sat up and wiped her eyes with a napkin, then shook her head to clear it and said, "Goodness. Life is so much more painful without

Karma

a hearty dose of alcohol."

She got up and went to the refrigerator and poured herself a glass of orange juice. Jamie didn't ask the question—she cocked her head and waited to see if her mother wished to talk about it further.

"My therapist seems to have the notion that I drink to escape my feelings," she said lightly, sitting back down and gazing at her daughter with an unreadable expression on her face.

Again, Jamie didn't reply. She merely raised an eyebrow and waited.

"I've decided to limit myself to one drink a day—to prove her wrong, of course," she chuckled. She glanced at her watch. "It's probably a little early for my daily quota now, isn't it?"

Leaning in for another hug, Jamie merely said, "You're a very brave woman, and I admire how you're handling all of this. I know it's really tough for you."

"Thank you, sweetheart," she whispered. "I'm doing my best. Sometimes I don't think I can get through it, and then I remind myself that my daughter deserves a sober mom."

"I have a great mom," Jamie murmured, kissing her mother's cheeks gently and leaning in for another hug.

When Ryan came back, they were still at the breakfast table, and she stood in the doorway with her hands on her hips. "Have you two moved?" she asked, a scowl on her handsome face.

"Nope. We decided to be in place for lunch. Hungry?"

"Gee…when have I ever said no to that question?" Ryan grinned. "I'll make lunch."

As if she had the room bugged, Marta appeared and guided Ryan to a chair. "I'll make anything you desire. It is my pleasure."

Ryan cast a glance at her mother-in-law and asked, "Can Marta go home with us?"

"No way. Marta and I are a package deal."

"Oh, I'd be happy to have you come too. I'll give you my room." She had a big smile on her face, and Catherine knew that at some level the young woman was entirely serious.

"I think we'll keep the Peninsula branch of the family right where it is. We need the space for parties."

"Speaking of parties, you'll come spend Christmas with us, won't you, Mom?" Jamie asked. "We'll all get together on Christmas Eve for dinner, and then go to midnight Mass."

"You sound like an old hand at this," Catherine said.

Jamie dipped her head and admitted, "This will be my second Christmas Eve with the O'Flahertys."

"It will?" Catherine asked, clearly puzzled. "I distinctly remember you going to Mass at your grandfather's."

"I snuck out of Jack's apartment to sneak over to Ryan's. I told him I had to go to Berkeley to pick up something, and then I met him at church."

"You were with me all day," Ryan said, giving her a fond smile. "I don't think I knew you were a runaway."

"You've led quiet a secret life," Catherine said.

"I also snuck out of the firm's New Year's party to go find Ryan at hers. That was a tough one. If Jack hadn't been so busy kissing butt I never would have made it."

"And neither of you knew that you were attracted to each other?" Catherine asked in amazement. "I don't ever remember sneaking out of the house to go see my girlfriends."

"I was totally attracted to Jamie by that time," Ryan admitted, "but I'd convinced myself it was a wasted effort." She smiled at her partner and said, "I think she had a pretty good idea that she had feelings for me too by that point. I got a massive vibe from you at the New Year's party. It seemed really important to you to give me a New Year's kiss."

"Mmm, I still remember how my lips tingled when I kissed you," Jamie said with a dreamy expression on her face. She sighed heavily, tossing her head to clear it. "So, what's the verdict, Mom? Will you come?"

Turning to Catherine, Ryan commented, "You may as well agree. She always gets her way."

"That she does. All right, I'll come. But would you come home with me after church and spend the night? I hate to seem so needy, but the thought of waking up on Christmas morning to an empty house is more than I can bear right now."

"We'd be happy to, wouldn't we, honey?" Jamie said.

"We'd love to." Ryan reached over and squeezed her hand. Turning to Jamie, she said, "Do you want to spend some time with your father too? I know this is going to be hard for all of you to get through."

"Oh God," Jamie muttered as she closed her eyes tightly. "I… guess I…"

"It's all right," Catherine said. "I want you to spend time with him. He's going to be very lonely this year, too."

"I really appreciate that you still feel some empathy for him. That will make things easier."

"I love him, " Catherine said softly, tears forming in her eyes once again. "I'll always love him. But I can't be married to him."

After lunch the threesome sat out by the pool, trying to soak up the watery rays of the wan December sun. Jamie turned to her partner and said, "When you were gone, Mom asked what we'd planned for New Year's, and I realized that we haven't discussed it."

Chuckling mildly, Ryan agreed. "We've had so much going on that it didn't seem like it was that close."

"If you'd like to do something special, Mom had a brilliant suggestion."

"I like special. What is it?"

"I told Jamie that I knew about Mia and her newfound interest in Jordan," Catherine said.

"Oh, do you now?" Ryan teased. "How did you figure that mystery out?"

"It wasn't hard. I saw them dancing together at your father's wedding, but I didn't give much thought to it at the time. I know girls your age are often very affectionate with each other. But I was at your house after I took Jennie to Sacred Heart, and they came in. They were quite…affectionate, as well as very distracted, and they didn't see me, but they were a lot friendlier than I can remember being when I was that age."

"Oh, they're friendly all right," Ryan said with a chuckle. "But how does that relate to New Year's?"

"I told Mom how upset Mia is to have Jordan gone, and she suggested we all go somewhere together for New Year's. Since you'll be in North Carolina on the 30th, it makes sense to go somewhere on the east coast, and she suggested the Bahamas."

"Wow," Ryan said slowly. "That would be nice…"

"Warm water, sun, sand…" Jamie said.

Ryan's lips curled into a big grin as her eyes blinked slowly. "Mmm, I do love the water."

"Crystal clear water that actually looks aqua against the pink sand," Catherine added.

"Mmm." Ryan submerged herself in the thought for a moment before her eyes opened wide and she said, "Pink?"

"Pink," Catherine stated confidently. "My favorite place in the Bahamas most definitely has pink sand. Have you ever been to the Caribbean?"

"I've been to beaches from Los Angeles to Point Reyes in the States, and I've ranged as far as Dingle Beach in Ireland, but that's it."

"Then you are most definitely in for a treat," Catherine promised.

"But what about Jordan and Mia?" Ryan asked. "Don't we have to check their schedules first?"

"Well, Jordan will know if she makes the team by then, since they make the final cut on the thirtieth. If she gets cut, she can definitely come with us, and if she doesn't, she could go straight to Florida for their first tournament. I think Mia said it starts on January the fourth."

"That sounds great, and the thought of lying on a warm beach is extremely appealing—but how can we get in anywhere?"

"I have the best travel agent in the English speaking world, Ryan," Catherine said. "Let me see what magic he can work for you."

"That'd be great, but are you sure Mia's available?"

"What could you imagine that would make Mia pass up four days on the beach with Jordan?" Jamie asked with a puzzled look on her face.

"Good point. Make the call."

Catherine went inside to get her travel agent started, and after a minute Ryan asked, "Is today the twenty-first?"

"Yep. Why?"

"I've been trying to work out a schedule to get our training in. If we start as soon as we get back, we'll have exactly six months to get ready for the ride." She shook her head. "I've never tried to prepare with so little time, but I guess we don't have much choice."

"Pardon?" Jamie asked slowly, recognition dawning.

"The AIDS Ride?" Ryan said, giving her partner a puzzled look. "The one you and I are going to do together?"

"Back up a minute. You mean to tell me that you honestly think you have time to participate in the ride this year?"

Ryan blinked slowly and nodded. "I have to."

"You most certainly do not. I'll have to push you across the finish line in a hospital bed, and you know it, Ryan O'Flaherty."

Ryan's eyes filled with determination, and her chin jutted out enough to show she was not going to give in. "Then you'll have to do that, because I'm doing the ride."

By the time Catherine neared the pool, she could hear the raised voices, and see the flush coloring her daughter's face. Turning immediately, she started to head back to the house. "Mom." Jamie called. "Will you come here and help me convince this block-head that she can't possibly get ready to do the AIDS Ride this year?"

"No, I most certainly won't," Catherine said over her shoulder. "I'll never get involved in your squabbles. Call me when you're finished arguing."

Ryan called out, "Come on back, Catherine. We're not arguing." She turned to Jamie and narrowed her eyes. "There's nothing to argue about. I'm doing the AIDS Ride this year. I'd love to have you join me, but I'll understand if you don't."

"You make me so damned mad some times." Jamie's eyes were narrowed and she stared hard at Ryan. "How can you ignore the patently obvious facts? You're underweight; you're still lethargic from the flu; you've got a huge independent study next term that will take up a massive amount of your time; you're trying to play a varsity sport with a martinet for a coach; and you've committed to tutoring Jennie. When in the hell will you have time to ride?"

When Catherine reached the door she called out, "Let me know when you're finished not arguing, girls."

"We're not arguing," Ryan insisted, her face getting red as well. "There's nothing to argue about." Leaning closer to her partner she whispered harshly, "You can't tell me what to do. Others have tried—and failed."

Catherine's eyes widened as the door closed, determined to stay inside until there was a truce. *At least Ryan's shown she's human…I was beginning to wonder.*

"How can I get you to listen to reason?" Jamie fumed, not even noticing that her mother had departed.

"The same way I can get you to," Ryan said, with a withering glare. "Maybe you've not been paying attention, but the AIDS Ride means a tremendous amount to me. I've participated every single year—and this isn't going to be the year I break the string. You're free to make your own decisions. If you don't think you can get ready, you don't even have to try. But I'm doing it if June the fourth is the first time my ass is on a bike seat."

The sound Jamie let out was half scream and half howl. "You're positively infuriating." She leapt to her feet, and stormed back into the house, leaving Ryan to savor the blessed silence.

An hour later, Jamie went back outside, smiling gently when she spied her lover, sound asleep on the lounge chair. Her organizer was lying open on the ground next to her, and the breeze was making the pages flip noisily. Picking up the massive book, Jamie looked through the weeks, noting that Ryan had already neatly filled in notations for practically every available moment between January the fourth and June the third, with an estimate of how many miles she would be able to ride in the given time. She had to chuckle to herself when she saw that Ryan rode an hour later every day after daylight-saving time began, since she'd have that extra hour of light.

She sat down and gazed at her sleeping partner, her anger

forgotten. Ryan was often infuriating, but Jamie had to admit that she deeply admired her perseverance and dedication to a cause. The AIDS Ride was important to her, and she was going to participate—no matter the cost.

The sleepy blue eyes blinked open, and Jamie reached over and grasped Ryan's hand. "Mad at me?"

With a smile that could have melted the hardest heart, Ryan shook her head gently. "Of course not. Are you mad at me?"

"No. You know I can't stay mad at you. You're too damned adorable." She tweaked her nose and offered a hand up when Ryan tried to sit.

"You won't even try to get ready with me, will you?" she asked softly, looking into Jamie's eyes.

"I can't, honey. I have golf practice in the mornings and I have to practice or be in a tournament both days of the weekend. I don't have the time." She put her arms around Ryan and said, "I'll still contribute, of course, and since we signed up for this year at the end of last year's ride, I'll let them keep thinking I'm going to ride."

"Why's that?"

"So you get a tent to yourself," she teased. "No way I'm letting anyone get that close to you for a whole week."

※

Later that afternoon, Jamie found a quiet moment to put in a call to her father. Her talk with her mother about the divorce had been weighing on her mind, and she felt a strong pull to connect with him. "Hi, Daddy," she said when she reached him at his office.

"Hi, sweetheart," he said, and she could practically see the smile that graced his face when he recognized her voice.

"Daddy, I wanted to see if you had plans for Christmas. If not, I'd really like to spend some time with you—if you can come to California, that is."

"Are you sure, Jamie?" he asked hesitantly. "Of course I'd like to come, but I don't want to interfere…"

"You can't interfere with my life…you're part of it. Of course I want to spend some of the holiday season with you."

"I'm free after today, to be honest. I was wasting time in the office since I didn't have anything better to do."

She felt that statement tug at her heart, and she said, "Come home now. We have a lot of things going on, but I'll spend every moment I can spare with you. Poppa would really like to see you, too."

"Okay, baby," he said. "I'll come as soon as I can arrange it."

"I'm really looking forward to seeing you. I miss you."

"Thank you, baby," he said in a strangled voice. "That means a lot to me."

Chapter Nine

That night, Sara Andrews walked up a steep hill, wishing that she'd been able to find a parking spot closer to Ally's apartment. It wasn't that she minded the walk, she was just worried that she'd look like she'd been climbing hills, and it was very important to her to look her best.

She was unreasonably nervous, and had spent much of the day obsessing about everything from her haircut to her clothing.

She'd always been style-conscious, even as a young woman who dressed nothing like her peers. Her clothing choices were often far too sophisticated for someone her age, but she felt comfortable with her chosen style. And since she had to dress well for work, she didn't want to have to maintain two complete wardrobes. So, she usually wore stylishly feminine outfits for both work and play. That habit had always worked well before, but now she worried that she might have to change her style to better fit in with Ally.

Ally dressed in typical Bay Area lesbian fashion: cotton or knit shirts, jeans, khakis or cotton pants, and black shoes or boots. Sara had that type of thing in her wardrobe, but she didn't feel comfortable dressing that way for a date, particularly when she was consciously trying to impress. She knew that if one of them had to change it would have to be her since Ally would look ridiculous in a dress and heels.

She smoothed her chocolate-colored velvet blazer into place and twitched the matching short skirt so it was perfectly straight. Looking at her reflection in the glass panel of Ally's front door, she fussed with the collar of her pink angora turtleneck, nervously cleared her throat, then rang the buzzer, feeling her heart rate pick up when the front door clicked open.

An interior door opened, then Ally's soft, lightly-accented voice floated down. "Hi, there. Do you mind coming up?"

"No, not at all," Sara replied, following the lilting voice. When she reached the unit, she was met with a warm smile, and she almost leaned in for a kiss, reminding herself at the last minute that they had both agreed to take things very slow.

"Did you have any trouble parking?" Ally asked. She was lacing up her shoes, and Sara took the opportunity to check her out from behind. As she had on each of their previous meetings, Ally was wearing a long-sleeved cotton shirt, this one a light blue. Slightly faded black jeans hugged her hips, and Sara spent a moment fantasizing about peeling those snug jeans off her body.

"Uhm…no, no trouble," she replied once she remembered it was her turn to speak. "Where should we eat? Do you want to go somewhere around here?"

"Yeah, let's do." She stood up and let her eyes trail down Sara's body, her small smile growing larger as she progressed. "Boy, you look great."

"Thanks. Not too dressy?"

"Mmm…not at all. I love your look. Feminine, soft and sexy."

"Thanks. You look nice yourself. Blue is a good color for you."

"Well, I think pink suits you great," Ally decided. She leaned in and said in a conspiratorial whisper, "Don't let it get out, but I have a secret fondness for pink."

"I'll keep that in mind." Sara smiled to herself when Ally took her hand to guide her back down the stairs.

"How about Indian food?" Ally asked as they walked down Castro Street.

"That sounds good. Do you have a favorite place?"

"Yeah. I eat Indian a lot. I'm not a strict vegetarian, but I generally avoid meat. Indian restaurants usually have a lot of vegetarian choices."

"I should eat less meat myself. Maybe you can guide me towards some of the better dishes."

"I'd be happy to."

The place was a few blocks away, and as they walked along the moderately crowded street, Sara marveled that she didn't feel uncomfortable holding Ally's hand in public. Deciding not to overanalyze every element of their interaction, she tried to allow herself to go with it and feel comfortable.

"Here we are," Ally said, holding the door open.

Sara led the way, but when the hostess saw Ally she gave her a welcoming smile and showed them to a nice table in a quiet corner of the restaurant. After a short recitation of the specials, she left them alone.

As an aficionado Ally knew a lot about Indian food, and she patiently described her favorite dishes to Sara, telling her the pluses and minuses of each item.

Smiling warmly at her, Sara said, "I can see why you're a good trainer. You're very adept at explaining things clearly."

"Thanks. My parents are both teachers, so I guess I learned how to offer cogent descriptions early on."

Sara closed her menu and gazed at her friend for a moment. "Would you order for me? I have a feeling that you'll do a better job than I would."

"Sure." Ally nodded to their server, and gave him their order. Then she leaned back in her chair and said, "That was strangely reassuring."

"What was?"

"The fact that you trusted me to order for you. I've been worried that you might secretly be one of those fiercely independent lawyer types. You know, the ones who can't stand to let anyone lend a hand?"

"I work with a lot of them, but I'm not one of them." She gave Ally an inquisitive grin. "Do you have any more misperceptions that I can disabuse you of?"

"Uhm…yeah, I actually might." Their appetizers were delivered, and Sara's patiently waited for Ally to speak again. "I've been worried about how confident you are about identifying as a lesbian. I hate to be narrow minded, but I'm only comfortable dating women who are sure of who they are."

It took a few moments for Sara to respond. She touched her food with her fork, but didn't make a move to take a bite. She looked up again and said, "I'll be honest with you. I've been fighting my identity for years; but I haven't doubted who I was, if that makes any sense." Ally raised an eyebrow in question and Sara explained, "I've known I was a lesbian for years, but I've tried very hard not to have to publicly acknowledge it. But I also haven't tried to convince myself that I might be straight. There's no way that's true. So I'm going to be more open."

"Are you sure that you're ready?" Ally asked gently.

Her answer was immediate and decisive. "Yes. Without question. Telling my parents was, by far, the biggest hurdle. I lost what I'd been afraid of losing, and yet, I'm still standing. I wish they'd been more understanding, but they've done their worst. I have nothing to lose at this point."

"You have a lot to gain," Ally assured her.

"I know that. I really do know that."

Ally took a bite of her appetizer and chewed thoughtfully, with Sara doing the same. "Delicious," Sara said, holding her fork up near Ally's mouth. "Bite?"

Taking the morsel, Ally nodded. "That's always a good choice. Glad you like it." She offered Sara a bite of her dish as well, chuckling when Sara waved her hand in front of her mouth. "Mine's awfully spicy. I thought you might like a tamer choice."

With a twinkle in her warm brown eyes, Sara said, "I've been opting for the safe choice for too long. It's time to be a wild." With a flourish, she took a hearty bite of Ally's dish and proclaimed, "Delicious."

"Tell me about the safe choices," Ally said, her eyes locked with Sara's.

Taking another bite, Sara considered her answer. "I guess it started not long after I discovered that I was a lesbian." She didn't want to tell Ally about her experience with Ryan, so she intentionally jumped over it. "After I had my first lesbian encounter, I decided that I couldn't handle the whole issue. I took the coward's way out and avoided even a hint of temptation. I concentrated on school, and my sport, and tried to forget that I had a sex drive."

"Your sport?"

"Uh-huh. I played soccer at Cal for four years."

"Wow, I didn't know you were a jock."

"I'm gonna choose to think that's not a reflection on how out of shape I look." Sara laughed softly at the wide-eyed look Ally gave her.

"No. Not at all. You look great, really great. But you've never talked about doing anything athletic."

"That's because I don't at this point. I want to start playing soccer again, though. I have to do something more athletic than run along the Bay every morning."

"Hard to do because of your job, huh?"

"Yeah, but that's no excuse. I have to make time, like I do for everything else that's important."

"I have a few friends who play. Why don't I hook you up? You're not averse to playing in a lesbian league, are you?"

"That'd be great. I'd really like that."

"Consider it done. Now tell me more about these safe choices."

With a heavy sigh, Sara revealed a few of the things she was least proud of. "I still find this hard to believe, but I didn't touch a woman for more than three years after my first encounter. I went out with a few dozen men, but I refused to let myself even consider being with a woman again. I don't remember what caused me to finally break free, but when I was a senior, I took the plunge."

"In high school?"

Shaking her head, Sara said, "No, college. I was twenty-one, and I had yet to really have sex."

"But then you found a woman, right?"

Chuckling, Sara said, "You're jumping way ahead. I sucked up my courage and finally journeyed into the dangerous world of the Internet. I allowed myself the horribly guilty pleasure of going to a lesbian chat room."

"Wow," Ally said, shaking her head in sympathy. "You must have been terrified to hold off on your desires for that long."

"That's a very big understatement. My hands were shaking so hard I could hardly log in. I didn't say one word that night, and as I recall the conversation was completely insipid. But I was so damned proud of myself." She smiled at the memory as she recalled, "That night was the first time in a long while that I didn't feel disgusted with myself when I went to sleep."

"That must have felt great."

"It did," she agreed, then laughed softly. "I developed a pretty heavy Internet addiction after that heady evening. The minute my roommate left the room, I was lurking in a chat room. Over time, I forced myself to interact with people, and within a few weeks I created another alias that showed I was from the Bay Area. Finally, someone asked me to go into a private room, and much to my surprise, I did."

"Did you hook up?"

"God, no. I was way too chicken for that. I played around in chat rooms for months before I finally agreed to actually meet a human being."

"Hey, don't be so hard on yourself. Everyone has to go at her own pace."

"I guess you're right, but my pace was darned slow."

"So, did you have a date, or what?"

Looking a little surprised, Sara said, "Do you want to hear the whole sordid story?"

"Yeah, I do. I'm interested in you, Sara. Your past is part of you."

"All right," she agreed. "But don't complain if you're bored."

Ally rested her forearms on the table and looked at Sara with rapt attention.

"I arranged to meet a woman who was a student at Stanford. Damn, I was scared. But I forced myself to get on the train and go down to Palo Alto on a Saturday night. We agreed to meet at a coffee shop at eight o'clock, and I think I got there at seven." She laughed, but she didn't look like she thought it was funny. "I sat inside an ice cream shop across the street and watched the place like I was a police detective. Lee showed up at eight on the dot, and somehow I found myself walking across the street to meet her. I'm sure she knew how nervous I was," she said, rolling her eyes. "At one point I laughed, and I sounded hysterical."

"I bet she was nervous, too."

"You know," Sara said thoughtfully, "she really wasn't. She was only a freshman, but she'd been out to herself since she was fifteen. She was from Hong Kong, and her family moved to San Francisco when she went to college."

"Now, that's a close family," Ally laughed.

"You have no idea. We had a really nice time, but at ten-thirty she said she had to go to her dorm room so her parents could call her. Apparently, they called every night at ten-thirty, and she had to be in the room or they'd freak out."

"Even if that wasn't true, it's a good way to get a woman to go home with you."

"It worked," Sara agreed. "And I'm sure I wouldn't have gone if she'd flat-out asked me."

"So…did you enjoy yourself?"

Sara nodded decisively. "I've never made a decision that I was happier with."

"Wow, she was that good?"

Laughing, Sara said, "At the time, I had no idea if she was the worst or the best. All I knew was that I'd taken the biggest risk of my life and done something that I'd been mortally afraid of. The world didn't stop, the sun came up the next morning, and I didn't have a lavender 'L' tattooed on my forehead." She shook her head, still in awe of how she'd felt that night. "In retrospect, Lee was a wonderful lover for someone as inexperienced as I was. She was gentle, and considerate, and she really knew how to help me express myself. I've slept with women who were technically more proficient, but no one has ever made me feel as comfortable as she did."

Ally reached across the table and took Sara's hand in hers. Brown eyes shifted to meet the compassionate gray-blue ones gazing at her. "That was very brave of you. I know how hard it can be."

Her eyes darting from Ally's large, warm hand to her intense gaze, Sara's heartbeat picked up, and she felt a faint shiver roll down her spine. "It was brave," she admitted, "but my bravery didn't last very long. We got together two more times, arranging things like we had before. But when Lee wanted to exchange phone numbers and see each other more often, I panicked. I still can't believe I did this, but I changed my screen name and never spoke to her again."

"You weren't ready," Ally soothed, her fingers lightly caressing Sara's hand.

"That's no excuse. That was the second woman I'd run away from, and I can't imagine that Lee wasn't hurt." She looked up, her gaze level and intent. "I was a coward, and I let my cowardice hurt another innocent person." She shook her head, and said, "It took me a long time to forgive myself. But I finally did by promising myself I would never hurt someone like that again. I'm glad to say that I haven't."

"That's all that you can do," Ally said. "You can only try not to repeat your mistakes."

"I know. I made sure that from then on every woman I met knew that I wasn't in a position to be in a relationship."

"Did you go out with a lot of women?"

Sara's head shook, making her hair glide across her shoulders. "No, I didn't. I uhm…really didn't date at all. I'd chat with a woman until we decided that we wanted to get together, and then we'd go to her place and have sex. I got together with a couple of women repeatedly, but I wouldn't call it dating since we didn't go out in public together." She laughed ruefully. "I managed to find women even more afraid of disclosure than I was."

"Was the sex satisfying? Was it worth what you had to go through?"

Giving her a wry smile, Sara asked, "Wanna know the truth?"

"Yeah, I do."

"What I really needed was the closeness. I wanted a woman to hold me and kiss me." Her eyes fluttered closed and she sighed. "That was worth it. That was worth anything."

Ally's hand shifted, and she linked her fingers with Sara's. "I predict that you'll have a lot of kissing in your future."

Her chin dropped slightly, and Sara gazed at her friend through half-hooded eyes. "I hope that's true. And I hope you're the one kissing me."

Ally grinned, looking a little shy. "That was part of my plan…I mean, prediction."

On the way back to the apartment, Ally shot Sara a quizzical glance and asked, "I don't think you've ever told me what led you to become an attorney. Do you mind talking about it?"

"I discovered that I had a certain talent for law. Not an

overwhelming interest by any means, but I took the LSATs on a whim, and did remarkably well. I figured that I needed a profession, so I might as well pick the one that came easy to me." She shrugged and said, "I certainly don't dislike what I do, but it doesn't fill my soul."

"What would?"

"I'm not sure yet," Sara admitted. "I haven't been doing it long enough to know if I could carve out a corner of the law that I'd love. I think I'll discover that over time, if it exists at all. How about you? Do you love what you do?"

"I don't normally think of it in those terms, but I guess I do," Ally said thoughtfully. "Training people really suits me, and I have no plans to change careers now, or in the future." Tilting her head, she asked, "Are you bothered by the fact that I don't want to do something more challenging?"

"God, no." Sara gasped. "I respect people who find something they love, and then learn how to do it well. That's all that matters to me. I'd respect an expert ditch digger much more than an inept neurosurgeon."

Ally dropped Sara's hand, and slipped an arm around her shoulders, "I like you," she said softly, inclining her head until it rested against Sara's.

"Ditto, Ms. Webster. It's unanimous." Sara tucked an arm around her waist, and let her fingers play across the tight muscle she felt along her flank. "Good lord, how much do you work out? You're all muscle."

Ally laughed gently and said, "I'm gonna be in a competition the weekend I come back from San Diego, so I'm really reducing my body fat. Believe me, you're gonna be glad I'm gone. I'm a real bear when I can't eat any of my favorite guilty pleasures."

"Do you get a lot of enjoyment out of competing like that?" Sara was unable to keep her hand still, letting it glide along the shifting muscle.

"I haven't made up my mind, but this might be my last meet."

"Really? Why?"

"Mmm...a lot of reasons. I only compete in chemically free competitions, but in the last couple of years I've begun to doubt that some of the women are really clean. There are so many ways of tricking the system," she said, shaking her head. "It pisses me off to be completely free of banned substances, and lose to someone I have my doubts about. A lot of the other women are suspicious, also, and the meets have become big gossip-fests, where people spend their time guessing who's clean and who's not." She made a face and said, "I'm too old for that grade school stuff."

"I can imagine that's really frustrating," Sara sympathized. "You have to be confident there's a level playing field."

"Exactly. But even without the doping controversies, I think I might choose to hang it up. I've spent a lot of years working on my body, and it's begun to feel like I'm too self-obsessed. I want to focus on people other than myself at this point in my life." She looked at Sara and said, "Bodybuilding was the perfect thing for me when I started. It gave me the confidence I lacked at the time, but I'm past that now. So I think the odds are good that I'm gonna move on with my life after the meet."

Sara moved her hand, letting it slide up and down an incredibly well-defined arm. "You won't…lose this, will you? I mean, I hate to be small-minded, but I'd kinda like to see what a perfect body looks like."

"Come to my meet. If you like muscles, it's the place to be."

"Well, I was particularly interested in seeing your muscles. Kind of a private show."

Ally gave her a squeeze, thrilling Sara with the power she felt enveloping her. "They won't disappear overnight. I could be wrong about you, but I'd guess you're the sort who likes the feel of muscles rather than their definition."

"I'm not sure what I like," Sara admitted. "I've never gone out with a woman who was bigger or stronger than I am." She almost retracted her words, but then decided that she didn't want to mention Ryan's name.

"Well, we'll have to experiment, then, won't we?" Ally said in a husky, sexy tone than nearly caused Sara's knees to buckle.

Her voice was much higher than normal when she managed to say, "I love a good experiment."

Karma

It was ten o'clock when they found themselves back at Ally's apartment.

They stood in front of the building, but Ally didn't invite her in. Instead, she placed a hand on each of Sara's shoulders and pulled her close, tilting her head to place a gentle kiss upon her lips.

The kiss wasn't passionate in the least, but Ally's lips were so soft, so warm and welcoming, that Sara desperately wanted to throw her arms around her and kiss her for hours. But after a few seconds, Ally pushed her back into position and smiled warmly. "I had a great time. Can we go out again when I get back?"

Nodding automatically, Sara managed to say. "Have a good time. I envy you being down in the warmth of San Diego. It's supposed to be cold and rainy here over Christmas."

"Yeah, I'm looking forward to a week of warm weather. My sister and her husband live pretty close to the beach, so I might even get some surfing in."

"Have fun." She squeezed Ally's large, warm hand and watched her walk into the building. Ally paused at the door, and gave her a wink that made her heart skip a beat. Sara nearly floated back to the car, knowing that she'd wait as long as she had to for another one of those kisses.

※

"Hey, honey?" Jamie asked as she emerged from the bathroom that evening. As usual, Ryan was sitting up in bed, laptop perched upon her raised knees.

"Yeah?" she answered absently, her fingers never slowing their rapid pace on the keyboard.

"I'd like to keep our portfolios going. I think it's fun to have something we can compete with each other over."

Raising one eyebrow, Ryan's crooked grin settled upon her face. "You still have to buy me five shares of 3Com."

"I know," she chuckled, crawling into bed and settling close to Ryan's side. "E-mail?"

"Uh-huh. Writing to my cousin Cait. About done."

Knowing that was a polite way of asking for a moment of quiet, Jamie waited patiently while Ryan completed the note. As she hit the send button decisively, she turned and said, "I'd be happy to keep the bet going. But we need a new end-date. How about the last day of spring term?"

"Okay. It's a deal. I ask for one concession though. Can we start from the same point again?"

"Of course. That's the only way it's fair. I'll transfer some of my holdings to your account so that we're equalized. How's that?"

"As expected, you're generous to a fault."

⁂

Late the next morning, the phone rang and Sara picked up on the first ring. "Sara Andrews."

"Hi," said a warm, melodic voice. "I have the names of the friends of mine who play soccer. Would you like them?" Waiting a beat, she added, "Oh, this is Ally."

"I know your voice by now," Sara said. "It's nice to hear it again, by the way. And, yes, I'd love to have numbers for your soccer contacts."

"It'll cost ya," Ally said.

"Okay. What's the price?"

"Lunch. I'm free until three. Name the place and I'll meet you."

Sara let out a soft laugh. "You want to have lunch today? That's not much notice. It's nearly noon."

"Are you free?" Ally asked, ignoring Sara's complaint.

"As a bird. Do you mind coming to my office? There's a central reception area on the 25th floor."

"No, I don't mind a bit," Ally said, with a touch of hesitancy in her voice, "but are you sure that's what you want?"

"Well, I thought you might like to see my office. But it's no big deal…"

"I'd like to see where you work. But I want to make sure you're comfortable having me at your office. People who've never seen a dyke in their lives know that I'm one."

Sara was quiet for a moment, then said, "I wouldn't go out with a woman I was ashamed of or embarrassed to be seen with. I don't have the slightest reluctance to have you come to my office."

"Okay. Just checking."

"What I really think is that you're adorable."

"Adorable, huh?" Ally asked, her voice low and sexy.

"Definitely adorable. I could go on complimenting you, but I think I'll save them until I see you in person. Ready to jot down my address?"

Ally showed up about a half hour later, looking completely comfortable when Sara arrived in the reception area to pick her up. She was leaning against one of the huge windows gazing out at the view, and Sara snuck a moment of guilty pleasure enjoying the view of Ally's backside. She couldn't actually see her rounded butt, since Ally was wearing a black leather coat that came to mid-thigh, but Sara took a great deal of pleasure in the view, nonetheless.

She had never noticed how broad Ally's shoulders were, but the gleaming black leather highlighted them to perfection. Ally looked so confident, so completely at ease, that Sara immediately felt more at ease herself. "Hi," she said softly as she sidled up beside her and placed a hand on her back.

"Hi."

As usual, Ally's voice sent a shiver down her spine, and Sara found herself grinning like a schoolgirl. She had to remind herself to speak. "Ready to go? We can stop by my office on the way down."

"Sure." They started to walk towards the elevator, and Ally commented, "I think this is the tallest building I've ever been in. Actually, my apartment is as high as I normally get—since I stopped drinking—that is."

"I've gotten used to it, but it sways a on a very windy day, and I find that disconcerting. I try hard not to think of what would happen in the event of a major earthquake."

"Just stay away from the windows. The building would be fine, but the glass would probably pop." She started to look uncomfortable, then gave Sara a sheepish smile and said, "Could we take off now? I uhm…don't really feel like being in this building any longer."

Charmed by her honesty, Sara took her hand and gave it a squeeze. "You'll have to buy. I left my purse in my desk."

"I'll buy for the whole car if the damned elevator would come," she said with mock alarm.

"Hey, if it'll make you feel better, we can walk down."

Ally looked down at the short, snug skirt, longish jacket and medium height heels that Sara was wearing. Tilting her head, she asked, "Would you really walk down twenty-five flights of stairs to make me happy?"

"Of course," Sara said immediately. "Not a problem."

The elevator bell rang, and before the doors opened, Ally leaned over and whispered, "I think you're adorable, too. Perfectly adorable."

※

"You know what I was thinking?" Ally asked while they ate their salads.

"No. Not a clue. I don't know you that well—yet," she added.

"I was thinking," Ally said, ignoring the tease, "that you might need a training program if you're going to get back into soccer shape. I'd be happy to help you devise one, or even train you if you think you'd like that."

"Wow, really? That'd be great."

"We can get started as soon as I get back from San Diego."

"Okay, but I'll have to find a way to pay you back." Batting her eyes, she asked, "Do I have any skills or talents you think you might like to tap into?"

"Heh, heh, heh." Ally gave her a sexy leer and said, "I certainly hope you do, but since we're taking it slow, how about if you help me buy and set up a computer instead?"

"You want to upgrade?"

"Yeah. From a pencil and paper," she joked. "I've never had a computer, and it's long past time I got one."

"You've got a deal. We'll go shopping as soon as you come back." She looked at her for a long moment, then quirked a grin at her. "I'm gonna miss you."

"Why do you think I had to come over for lunch?" Ally chuckled. "I could have given you those names over the phone, you know."

Sara reached over and traced a few blue veins on the back of Ally's hand, concentrating thoughtfully as she did so. "Are you always so open with your feelings?"

"Nope. Actually, I usually don't reveal more than I absolutely have to. You seem so forthright that I feel compelled to be the same."

"Good," Sara nodded. "That's good. I uhm…have to admit that I'm not usually very open, but I've decided to turn over a new leaf. I want to do things differently this time. I want to do this right."

"That's exactly how I feel. I want to do this right—no matter how scary it is."

Smiling warmly, Sara said, "I can't wait until you come back. I think this is gonna be fun."

"If we do it right, it will be," Ally agreed, beaming a smile of equal intensity.

Ally insisted on walking Sara all the way back up to her office, shrugging off Sara's concern about her earlier jitters. "I was mostly kidding," Ally assured her. "I was pretty shaken up by the Loma Prieta quake, but I hardly ever think of it anymore. It just freaked me out a little to be in a big building and talk about quakes."

"You don't have to come up. Really."

"You know, one of my goals is to face each of my fears and try to break the hold it has over me. This is a little one, but little ones become big ones if you let them."

Sara reached down and gave her hand a squeeze. "Let me know if you feel uncomfortable, okay?"

"Will do," Ally smiled. They made it to Sara's floor, and walked into her small, but neatly organized office. "This is really nice," Ally said, looking around. "Very lawyerly."

Sara shrugged. "It's all right. I spend so much time here that it seems a like a tiny prison cell, but it's home."

"Speaking of home, I should get going." With a grin that was a little sly, Ally pulled the door closed with her foot, then stood in front of it. "How about a goodbye kiss?" she asked, her voice low, and warm and sexy.

Approaching her tentatively, Sara stood in front of Ally and waited for her to pull her forward for a kiss, as she'd done the night before. But Ally didn't make a move. She stood in front of the door, a half smile on her handsome face. Deciding that she'd have to act, Sara stood very close and rose up on her toes, holding onto Ally's shoulders while she inclined her head and brushed her lips across the soft ones that beckoned to her. She paused for a second, then lowered herself to the floor, keeping her hands on Ally's shoulders for another moment. "Hurry home," she whispered, then let her hands slide down the strong arms, enjoying the definition even through the thick leather coat.

"See you soon," Ally said, giving Sara a sexy wink. She opened the door and strode out, while Sara stood in the doorway, watching her until she entered the elevator lobby.

How can my knees be weak from such a tiny kiss? What would happen if she really kissed me? The smirk that settled onto her face at the mere thought of that scenario remained in place for the better part of the day.

Chapter Ten

Catherine walked into the kitchen on Wednesday morning as Marta answered the ringing phone. "Evans residence," she announced.

Catherine heard her say, "One moment, please, I'll see if Mrs. Evans can come to the phone." She hit the mute button and asked, "Will you speak with a Kayla Horwitz?"

"Kayla Horwitz? Who on earth is Kayla..." Catherine's face blanched, and she walked over to Marta, feeling her legs shake as she moved across the floor. "I'll take the call, Marta. Thank you." She placed the receiver against her ear and said, "This is Catherine Evans. What can I do for you, Ms. Horwitz?"

"I was sure you wouldn't take my call, Mrs. Evans. It's...very generous of you."

Catherine didn't respond to her compliment. Instead, she reframed her original question. "Is there something that you wanted?"

"Yes, yes, there is," she said. "I know this isn't my place, and I know that Jim wouldn't be happy with me for calling, but I feel like I have to clear something up."

"I can't imagine what that might be, but go ahead if you must," Catherine said, bordering on being rude.

"I know that you've called off your attempt at reconciling with Jim, and I think that you've misunderstood what was going on between us..."

"Ms. Horwitz," Catherine said, her voice crisp and businesslike, "I hate to be curt, but this really is not your concern."

"Yes, it is," the young woman said firmly. "It *is* my concern."

"And how is that?"

"It's my concern because I care very deeply for Jim, and he's in such a deep depression that I'm dreadfully worried about him," she said in a rush.

Catherine let her words sink in, then said, "I see. Well…I certainly don't want to cause pain to either Jim or you, but this is between him and me. It's not something I can discuss with you."

"I don't want to discuss it, per se," she insisted. "I want to assure you that Jim and I haven't been intimate for some time. He broke up with me early in the fall, Mrs. Evans. We weren't together when you saw me in the television shot."

"All right. Now I understand why you're calling. Again, I appreciate that you're trying to do something kind, but you're hardly the best corroborating witness that Jim could have."

"I know that—"

Catherine cut her off. "I don't know you, and I have no reason to trust you. But even if I did, that incident was merely the last straw for us. It wasn't the main reason I decided not to go forward."

"But you were working towards reconciliation until that happened," Kayla reminded her. "So it had to be an important reason."

"Ms. Horwitz, I'm not going to discuss the details of my marriage with you. This is an intensely private matter."

"I know that," the young woman agreed. "Really, I do. I'm only calling because I'm worried about Jim. Don't you have enough feeling left for him to be concerned about him too?"

Catherine didn't say a word. She let the silence continue until Kayla must have realized that she was not going to get a response. "He has a very good heart, Mrs. Evans," she said quietly. "When we broke up, he wanted me to go back to San Francisco. He was worried about how it would look if you knew I was still here with him. It's my fault that this happened, because I convinced him that it'd look bad for me to be sent home after a month. I was totally selfish, and he's the one who's paying for it now."

It sounded like she was crying, and Catherine found herself responding, against her better judgment. "How old are you, Kayla?" she asked gently.

"Twenty-six," she sniffed.

Karma

"Jim and I have been married since you were four years old. In all of that time, many, many things have transpired that have coalesced to destroy our marriage. I assure you, you had very little to do with it."

"But, Mrs. Evans, if I'd gone home like he wanted me to…"

"Kayla, I don't mean to be unkind, but if our marriage were important to you, you wouldn't have begun your affair. The same is true for Jim. It's disingenuous of both of you to have a sexual affair and then claim that you want to help salvage the marriage. The way to save it would have been to keep your hands off each other."

"I know," she said, her words obscured by her tears. "I'm so ashamed of myself."

"You deserve some blame for your actions, Kayla, but you didn't make a vow of fidelity to me. In my opinion, Jim wronged you, as well, by dragging you into this mess."

"No, no, it was me," she sobbed. "I was the aggressive one. I thought we'd have a quick fling. I don't know why, but I found him so attractive, Mrs. Evans. It's my fault."

"Nonsense. I've had many men show interest in me during our marriage. Jim could have easily refused if he'd wanted to."

Kayla was quiet for a moment, then said, "I guess there's enough blame to go around."

"Yes, we all have some level of culpability," Catherine agreed. "But the participants are still Jim and me. I appreciate what you've tried to do, Kayla, and I won't mention your call to Jim if we speak."

"Thank you. I know you'll have a hard time believing this, but I'm truly sorry for what I've done."

"No, I can believe that, Kayla. I hope, for your sake, that you never find yourself in my position. It's not very pleasant to always feel second best in your husband's eyes." Catherine shook her head, angry with herself for asking for this young woman's sympathy. "My mind is made up. Jim and I won't be getting back together. You have my explicit permission to start seeing each other again."

"Thank you," Kayla said, her voice shaking again. "You're treating me with much more courtesy than I deserve."

"I'm trying to move on. Holding on to my feelings of rancor for you, or even Jim, will only inhibit that process. I'm merely taking care of myself."

"I hope you take good care of yourself. You seem like a very kind woman."

Catherine smiled in spite of herself. "I have my moments. Take good care, Kayla. I hope things go well for you in Washington."

"Thank you again, Mrs. Evans."

"Call me Catherine," she said, then placed the phone back onto the cradle.

Chapter Eleven

After Ryan's basketball practice on Wednesday, the two young women sat in the otherwise empty O'Flaherty house, and tried to plan the rest of their day. "Do you have anything you want to do today?" Ryan asked.

"I have everything I want right here," Jamie stated decisively, climbing onto Ryan's lap to rest her head on her chest.

After a moment, Ryan wiggled her eyebrows and asked, "You know what would be fun to do?"

"Okay," Jamie said absently, standing to pull her sweater over her head.

"Not that," Ryan laughed, but she couldn't resist the urge to tickle the bare tummy that revealed itself. "I thought we could call Jennie's housemother and ask how they were fixed for Christmas."

"You mean the house?"

"Yeah, the house and the kids. My guess is that most of them won't be remembered by their families at all."

"And…"

"And I thought that since we're not exchanging gifts, we could try to make this a memorable Christmas for people who really don't have everything they need."

"Oh, honey, that would really be sweet. I'm going through withdrawal a bit since I agreed not to buy presents for you and your family, and it would really make a difference for those girls to have someone go out of their way for them."

"I think the kids need a ton of things. So let's call Sandy and get a list, and then go shopping."

"You're on, Tiger."

The six girls living in the house needed about what Ryan assumed they would: nearly everything. Sandy provided sizes and color preferences for each girl, and related that she'd not had enough extra money to provide a Christmas tree, either. Jennie was at home, so after talking to Sandy, Ryan spoke with her and arranged to take her and anyone else who wanted, to go pick out a tree after dinner that evening.

When she hung up, she turned to Jamie and said, "I think we can nearly make this a one-stop shopping experience."

"Sure we can if we go to a mall. Which one should we go to?"

"No malls. Let's go to Big Box," she said with a wild look in her eyes.

"Big Box?"

"Baby, you haven't lived 'til you've been to Big Box."

The early afternoon traffic allowed them to reach the massive discount store fairly quickly. Ryan immediately made a beeline for the junk food, and ordered two hot dogs for herself. Jamie took a pass, having had a nice healthy salad while Ryan was practicing, but she enjoyed watching her lover demolish the jumbo-sized hot dogs. The food was located outside the building, and when Ryan was finished, they went to the front door, where she pulled out her membership card and flashed it at the man guarding the door.

"You have to belong to get in here?" Jamie asked in amazement as she looked around the massive warehouse-style space. The floors were concrete, the walls were stamped steel with no insulation, and the open plywood-sheet shelving went almost to the ceiling, making it the least attractive store she'd ever been in.

"Yep. When I was little, I thought it was pretty cool that we qualified to join something," Ryan laughed. "Little did I realize that the membership requirements were only to keep out people with absolutely no visible means of support."

Karma

"What do you buy here?" Jamie asked as she looked around suspiciously.

"Lots of stuff. I buy my socks here, and sometimes sweats and stuff, household and personal products, tires, liquor. The best deals are on things like food, though."

They were walking down an aisle containing gargantuan boxes of cereal and jams and jellies, and Jamie started to ask, "Ryan, who on earth would buy…" but then she realized with a start that the O'Flahertys were the ideal consumers for such items. "Did you buy all of your food down here when you were growing up?"

"Yep. We would go through one of these boxes of cereal in a week," she said proudly, holding up a box bigger than Jamie could imagine eating in a year. "You couldn't get too attached to a particular brand though, because Da bought whatever they had that week. He would come down every two weeks or so, since we didn't have much storage room. He'd prowl the aisles and plan our menus around what was available. I guess that's why I learned to eat anything that was put in front of me. But after Brendan left home, and Rory was gone so much, we dropped down to a more normal scale. Da still comes down before every family party, though. We really like the meat they sell here, and it's a very good bargain."

They were browsing through the clothing tables where Jamie saw some cute pastel T-shirts and sweats. She started sorting through them to find the appropriate sizes for the girls. Ryan came back to the cart with bags and bags of white athletic socks. "So many?" Jamie asked.

"Two bags are for me. I throw all of my socks away once a year. Then I buy two bags of these, and I'm set."

"No wonder your socks always look nice. I thought you did a fabulous job with the laundry."

"No, my socks take a beating, and I truly hate to get blisters, so I make sure they're always nice and fluffy. The best way to do that is to cycle through them every year. Do you want some too?"

"Sure, I could use some." She examined the bag and marveled, "These are less than a buck a pair."

"I know. That's why I throw them out after a year."

"I sometimes pay fifteen dollars for a pair."

"Stick with me, sweetie and I'll show you where all the bargains in the Bay Area lie."

"Do you think the girls need jackets?" Jamie asked as she surveyed two tables full of lightweight winter jackets.

"Well, Jennie didn't have one on at the last basketball game, and it was cold out in my opinion, so my guess is she doesn't own one." There were three different styles of coats available, and each came in two color choices, so they picked one of each to provide some individuality for the girls.

"I think we need to get them something fun, don't you?" Jamie asked as they left the clothing area. "They're still kids, after all."

"That's why I wanted to come here, to tell the truth. Do you feel generous enough to buy them a couple of computers?"

"They don't have them?" she asked in amazement.

"Nope. Not a one in the house."

"Absolutely." They went to the electronics aisle and Jamie started to load six of the laptops into the cart.

"God!" Ryan cried. "Don't go nuts. I think two is plenty."

"Let's get three. Two girls to each one seems like a better ratio."

"All right, but only one printer for the whole group."

"Okay, but we've got to buy some basic software too."

"Deal. Let's get out of here before we go broke."

※

The store wouldn't take Ryan's debit card for such a large purchase, so she had to use the credit card Jamie had given her. As they waited for the manager to come approve the charge, Jamie opened her mouth to speak, but Ryan cut her off with a, "Don't you dare say, 'I told you so'."

"Who, me?" she asked with a face full of innocence. "Even though I did tell you so," she added as she danced away from Ryan's attempted pinch. Standing a safe distance away, Jamie said, "Many stores are funny about debit cards, hon. I was trying to protect my punkin by getting her a charge card."

The manager asked for another form of ID, but she was eventually satisfied that Ryan was who she claimed to be. As they pushed their two groaning shopping carts to the car, Ryan said, "It is nice having a charge card. It let me pay for the doctor when I had to take Jennie down, and it let us do this. Thanks for being so thoughtful."

"You're welcome." Jamie smiled at her. "You know what I was thinking of?"

"Huh-uh," Ryan replied.

"I was thinking of coming here when we have our big family. I want to need those massive boxes of cereal too."

"Baby, if our kids have O'Flaherty genes in them, we'll need to come here if we just have one."

"I hate to even suggest this, but we should stop at Bullseye," Ryan said with a sick look on her face.

"That's another place I've never been," Jamie said. "But why do you look like that?"

"Going to Bullseye the week of Christmas is a like going to the marketplace in New Delhi the day after Ramadan."

"Have you been to New Delhi?" Jamie asked in surprise.

"Well, no," Ryan said seriously. "Why would I go once I heard about the lines?"

The Bullseye was located not too far from Big Box, and Jamie was surprised when Ryan went to the farthest corner of the massive lot to park.

"Why way out here?"

"One—we've got an awful lot of things in the back, and I don't want anyone to peek. Two—there's a cart return right next to us so I don't have to take the cart far. Three—there aren't any cars next to us to ding my doors. Four…"

"Good enough, babe," Jamie interrupted. "I sometimes forget how much thought you put into every decision you make."

"Hey, being careful got me the best girlfriend in the world, so don't knock my methods."

"No complaints," she agreed as she grasped Ryan's arm with both hands and pulled her close. "You don't mind if I hold on to you in public, do you?"

"I prefer it," Ryan said as she leaned over to kiss the top of her partner's head.

Jamie had, in fact, been to New Delhi, and after seeing the crowds she thought that perhaps Ryan had not been forceful enough in her warning. "My God, this is total mayhem."

"Yeah, but the biggest crowd will be by the toys. Let's head straight for the Christmas decorations and hope they've got something left."

Their luck was holding because a clerk came out to restock the shelves with a large hand-truck full of tiny white and multicolor lights and sparkly ornaments. Jamie suggested they use either multicolored lights with only one color of ornament, or go with multi-colored ornaments and white lights.

"I'm glad you're here," Ryan mused. "I would have grabbed three of everything and hoped for the best."

"No, honey, you have to plan this too. I think it might look most festive to buy every color ornament and go with white lights."

"Okay," Ryan said as she started throwing lights into the cart. When she started grabbing a couple of boxes of each color of ornament, Jamie interrupted again.

"They've got three different sizes, babe. Buy one of each so the tree has more depth."

"Huh?"

"If you vary the size of the ornaments, it creates an optical illusion and makes the tree look bigger." Ryan shot her a dubious look, but did as she was told. Keeping with the Evans family tradition, they bought enough lights to illuminate Candlestick Park, but Jamie assured her that they were required. Some delicate multicolored garland was added to the now full cart, and they headed for the clothing area.

They decided that they'd buy a pair of jeans for each girl, and a pair of dressier pants as well. After a small debate, they also agreed on two blouses, three bras and seven pairs of panties for each. Ryan went to fetch another cart, then stopped for a box of popcorn, leaving Jamie fully in charge of the selections. When she returned, popcorn half eaten and a semi-guilty smile on her face, Jamie patted her side and said, "This isn't your favorite thing, is it?"

"Nope. It's bad enough buying clothes for myself. Buying them for others is torturous."

"You go over there and browse in the electronics," Jamie kindly directed. "leave me the empty cart."

"You do love me, don't ya?" Ryan grinned, taking her up on her offer before she could change her mind.

When the cart was groaning, Jamie signaled her partner and they threaded their way through the confusing lines, where Ryan took over and guided the carts to the shortest line in the entire store. "You're good at this," Jamie complimented her.

"Practice, practice, practice."

"Hey, how about if I ask Mom to come help us trim the tree tonight? I don't think she's ever actually done one herself."

"Great idea. See if she wants to have dinner first."

🦄

Catherine wanted to join them, but she insisted that they allow her to take them out to dinner, since they'd been running around all day.

Ryan heard Jamie's end of the conversation, and she asked for the phone. "Hey, Catherine?"

"Yes, dear?"

"How about that fabulous dim sum Jamie's always talking about? Isn't that place near your house?"

"You'd do anything to get out of going to a restaurant, wouldn't you," she teased.

"You've learned my tricks pretty quickly. But I'll behave if you really want to go out."

"No, dear, I love dim sum too. I'll bring enough for Mia, in case she's at home."

🦄

Since the vacation plans for New Year's were a surprise, Catherine addressed Jamie when she told her about her talk with her travel agent. "He found a room for you in a fabulous house on Harbor Island."

"Is that in the Bahamas?" Ryan asked.

"Yes, Harbor Island is right off the tip of Eleuthera, which is one of the bigger islands. Anyway, he can book you from the thirty-first through the second. You could fly home on Monday the third, and be back in time for practice."

"Can you take time off during basketball?" Mia asked.

"Yeah, we get Sunday and Monday off. And if we win both games in North Carolina I don't have to come home with the team," she added, waggling her eyebrows playfully.

"What?"

"I told Coach Hayes about this trip, and she said I could go directly to the Bahamas if we win both games."

"But, honey, what if you don't win?" Jamie protested.

"Do you really think I'd allow us to lose with that kind of carrot dangling in front of my nose?"

"Ryan, things happen that you can't control. We won't be able to cancel if you have to go home with the team."

"Then I'll have to run a bunch of laps," she declared defiantly, "because we're going."

"God, you guys are making me soooo jealous," Mia mused.

"Don't you have any plans for New Year's, Mia?" Catherine asked, trying to surreptitiously feel her out.

She looked down at her plate and muttered, "Not anymore."

"What about Christmas?"

She brightened up as she cast a smile at Ryan. "I'm going over to Ryan's for Christmas Eve. My parents are going to be in Rome, and they wanted me to go with them, but I wasn't in the mood." Looking at Catherine she asked, "What about you Mrs....I mean, Catherine."

"I'll be with all of you on Christmas Eve. Then the girls are coming down to my house for Christmas Day. You're more than welcome to join us."

"Thanks," she smiled. "I might do that. Do you have big plans for New Year's, Catherine?"

Jamie held her breath since she knew this would be a tough time for her mother. In all of the excitement, she hadn't stopped to think of how sad it would be to be alone at the start of a new year.

"I've decided to go to Italy. I'm leaving on the twenty-sixth and coming back on the tenth."

"That's great, Mom," Jamie said enthusiastically. "Are you... meeting friends there?"

"Ahh...yes. I won't be alone."

"It must be really hard for you right now," Mia said with sympathy.

"It is, but I'm dealing with it as best I can."

"You're doing a lot better than my mom did when she thought she'd caught my dad cheating," Mia laughed, blushing furiously as she heard herself give voice to the family secret.

Catherine didn't look perturbed in the least. "What happened, dear?"

"It was a long time ago—I was probably in high school," she mused. "It was early in the morning, before school. My brother came running down the stairs yelling, '"Hide! Mom's coming.' Of course, there were a million reasons for me to assume I'd done something wrong, so I started running." She laughed at the memory. "I ran out the front door with Peter right after me, and we were halfway down the driveway when my dad came running out in his boxer shorts."

Catherine's mouth gaped open at this revelation, and Ryan had begun to chuckle as Mia continued. "Two seconds later, the door flies open, and my mom is there on the front step brandishing a big knife. She starts yelling at the top of her lungs that if she ever caught him with his...uhm...member...in another woman, she'd cut it off and grind it up for sausage."

Ryan was slumped down in her seat, unable to hold herself upright through her laughter. But Jamie and Catherine sat unblinking with their mouths agape as Mia concluded, "I don't think she really would have." After a beat she added, "But you never know, do you? All I know is that if he ever fooled around on her, she never found out about it."

"Did he really have an affair?" Jamie asked, still stunned.

"Don't know. I don't think she knows either," Mia admitted. "I think she was just suspicious, to tell you the truth."

Catherine finally found her voice and said, "I think your mother had the right idea. If I had taken a stronger stand, Jim might not have had the nerve to keep it up."

"That's exactly what my dad was worried about," she said seriously. "He wanted to make sure he could keep it up."

※

The four of them drove over to Jennie's as it was getting dark. Jamie, Catherine and Mia decided to stay and organize the ornaments and lights, to allow for several of the girls to go with Ryan to pick up the tree. Jennie clearly had other ideas, because she grabbed Ryan's hand before she could get fully into the house and declared, "Nobody else wants to go. Come on," she urged when Ryan didn't move quickly enough to suit her.

"Okay, okay. Give me a half second." She let the young woman lead her back down the sidewalk and into the car. As she started it up she asked, "Something wrong?"

"No," Jennie said with a smile. "I don't get to see you alone much any more. I…kinda miss it."

"You know, I never stopped to consider that," Ryan said thoughtfully. Turning to Jennie she said, "I'm sorry for that. I should have asked you if you minded doing things with other people all of the time."

"I don't mind," she insisted. "I like to be alone with you, too though. There's stuff I can't talk about with other people around."

"Anything you need to talk about now?" Ryan asked as she steered the car towards the local tree lot.

"No, not a lot," she said.

"How are you feeling about the holidays?" Ryan asked gently. "Are you okay about being at Safe Haven?"

Casting a quick glance over at her friend, Ryan saw silent tears sliding down her pink cheeks. Turning the car onto a side street, she pulled to a stop and got out. Jogging around to Jennie's side, she opened the door and tugged at her shoulder until she got out as well. Then Ryan enveloped Jennie in a tender hug, rubbing her back at the same time. "I'm sorry, I know it's hard to be away from home," she whispered.

"It's hard at Christmas…" she began, but Ryan knew it was much more than that. Being fourteen and abandoned in various ways by both parents had to be a wound that would never truly heal. She thought of her own fragile psyche, scarred severely because of her mother's death. The thought of having her parents voluntarily leave her was more than she could fathom.

"I know, I know," she murmured as the small body shook against her. She knew there were no words to soothe the pain, so she didn't even try. She would just be there for her.

"I'm so glad you're my friend, Ryan," she choked out. "I don't know where I'd be without you."

"I'll always be your friend. I've never lied to you, have I?" she asked as she pulled back and made eye contact with the red rimmed eyes.

"No, never."

"I promise that I'll always be here for you. I don't make promises like that often, and when I make one, you can count on it. Do you believe me?"

Her eyes opened wide, and she nodded her head slowly. "I believe you, Ryan," she murmured softly as she leaned in for another hug. She took a deep breath and said, "I didn't ask the other girls if they wanted to come tonight. I wanted to be alone with you."

"That's okay, sweetie. I'd rather be with you anyway." She leaned down and kissed her head. "Hey, what's going on here?" she teased, running her hand through the fine blonde hair. "Did you run out of razors?"

"No. I uhm…kinda want to look like…"

"The other girls at school?"

"Yeah." She blushed as she asked, "Do you think I'll fit in?"

"I do, and I'll help you in any way I can. How about if I take you for a cool new haircut right before school starts?"

"Haircut?" I think I need more hair, not less."

"The guy I'll take you to can give you a trim that will make everyone ask where you get your hair cut," Ryan promised. "You can be a trendsetter."

The tree trimming party lasted until nearly ten o'clock. By the end of the evening, each of the girls had picked one of the older women to flirt with outrageously, save for Jennie. To Ryan's great relief, three of the others decided that Mia was the one for them, and she mused that the constant attention seemed to be a good remedy for Mia's doldrums, even though the girls were only sixteen and seventeen years old. The boldest of the group, J.C., still had a hankering for Ryan, and the older woman politely put up with the not-so-subtle flirting until Jamie actually got up and insinuated herself between Ryan and her young admirer. Jennie's friend, Callie, seemed to have a crush on Jamie, but she was much more subtle in her overtures.

On the way home, Catherine observed, "Do you really think that's a good atmosphere for Jennie to grow up in? Those girls seemed so overtly sexual."

"Oh, they are. Most of them have been tossed out of the house for some pretty outlandish behavior, and I'd guess that most have been sexually abused at some point in their lives. Jennie has been around that type of thing for a couple of years now, and she really hasn't acted out sexually. Sandy keeps a very strict watch on the girls to make sure the older ones are never alone with the younger ones. Hopefully she'll meet some average kids her own age at Sacred Heart who can be good influences on her."

"I worry about her," Catherine repeated. "She is such a sweet child."

"She really is. But wasn't it clear tonight why it's hard to place kids who've been abused? Those girls were practically in our laps."

"I was about to pop that J.C. character," Jamie mumbled.

"You can't let them get to you. They're lonely kids who don't know how to get love any other way."

"Oh, she knew how she wanted to get love, all right," Jamie assured her. "And she looked like she could teach you a thing or two."

"Uh-uh, no way," Ryan vowed. "You're my one and only teacher."

After practice the next day, Ryan dashed up the stairs to the

Karma

Berkeley house, water dripping from the windproof/waterproof jacket and pants that Jamie had purchased for her earlier in the year. The day was cold, the kind of damp cold that makes one's joints ache. Surprised at how dry she was, Ryan took off her jacket and pants while still on the porch, her T-shirt and tights keeping her from shocking the neighbors.

She heard some loud music coming from the living room, and after a moment rolled her eyes at hearing one of the pop bands that Jamie had an inexplicable fondness for. *I'll distract her and put something decent on,* she decided, opening the door to find her partner gently swaying to the music. *I'll never understand how she can like really complex classical pieces and this pabulum.*

Ryan had opened the door so soundlessly, and the music was so loud, that for a moment Jamie didn't realize that she was being observed. Ryan leaned against the door, her face twitching into a warm smile as she watched her partner move gracefully to the music.

Jamie had a beautiful, graceful style of dancing that warmed Ryan's heart. She often teased Ryan that she didn't really dance—she had vertical sex. Jamie however, had a much more demure, understated style that perfectly matched her personality. Smooth, poised, and refined—but with an undercurrent of passion that only someone who knew her well would notice. Ryan most definitely knew her well, and felt her mouth begin to go dry when the beat picked up and Jamie's hips began to twitch more forcefully. Ryan checked her watch, noted that they had two hours to kill, and decided how the time would die.

She started to take a step towards her partner, but as she did, Jamie moved under one of the warm lights, casting a golden glow onto her body. Ryan had never considered herself overly impressed by good looks. As adorable as she found Jamie, she had to admit that her outward appearance was not even in the top ten reasons that she was attracted to her. But every once in a while, she moved in a certain way, or had a particular expression on her face that made Ryan look at her as though it were the first time.

Ryan sucked in a breath as she considered what a fantastic-looking woman she'd chosen to spend her life with. From her spun-gold hair to her dark blonde eyebrows, and lashes that batted slowly, hiding her verdant green eyes—Ryan loved every feature. Her small, well-formed nose and her absolutely luscious lips, so full and succulent. And her skin…Ryan honestly had no words for her skin. As far as she knew, no one had ever been clever or poetic enough to conjure up words for the flawless wrapper that covered the most wonderful package in the world.

Without a word, Ryan kicked off her shoes and padded across the room, sweeping Jamie into her arms as she continued to move right along to the beat of the music. Jamie let out a gasp when Ryan's body wrapped around hers, but she quickly regained her equilibrium, managing to maintain the beat.

They moved together, neither speaking—neither needing to. Their bodies spoke volumes, and neither wished to interrupt. The next song was one that Ryan heard often, and she knew it was a favorite of her partner's. Surprisingly, when the lyrics began, Jamie started to sing along—but in Spanish. Ryan privately thought that the song was ridiculously sappy, but the perfectly accented Spanish gave the tune a mysterious flavor that carried her away. She closed her eyes and listened to her lover sing to her, while their bodies touched gently all along their lengths.

They began to caress each other lightly, Ryan's hands unable to remain at rest. Switching to English, Jamie looked into her eyes and sang not a lyric, but a promise.

> *You're the one for my life. The one I've waited for.*
> *This is our journey, the one we'll take forever.*
> *No matter what comes between us, I'm yours.*
> *And for the rest of my life, I pledge myself to you.*

Looking down into the beautiful eyes that held her heart, Ryan bent and covered Jamie's mouth with a tender kiss. As much as she loved hearing her sing, she couldn't hold back another moment, and they held onto each other tightly as their bodies became one.

With a hunger that had quickly grown to voracious proportions, Ryan sucked greedily upon the coral-pink lips, then thrilled to the sensation of Jamie's slick tongue filling her mouth. Their moans nearly drowned out the music, and when Ryan stooped slightly, Jamie read her signal and jumped, landing in her arms.

In moments, they were in their room and Ryan was placing her gently on the bed. Jamie wrapped her arms around Ryan's neck, and pulled her down. They grappled briefly, Ryan's body half off the bed—Jamie refusing to relinquish her hold. Ryan finally gained purchase and stretched out alongside her lover, covering her mouth once again, her hands simultaneously worked on buttons and zippers and hooks.

Lying there, blouse open, slacks unzipped, the front closure of her bra no longer an impediment, Jamie smiled serenely when the dark, damp head dipped and took her breast into a warm mouth. She was feeling particularly sensitive today—and fairly sensual as well, as evinced by her impromptu dance number. But when Ryan's mouth began to suckle her, she felt an explosion of sensation that was tremendously stimulating—and made her long for more.

"Yes," she moaned, with the first word of her own creation since Ryan had come home.

While her mouth worked the plump flesh, Ryan's determined hand slipped into Jamie's pants—creating a trail of fire wherever her short nails traveled. Ryan loved to touch her partially-clad body—finding it much more erotic than complete nudity. Her mouth moved to the other breast, squeezing it with the other hand. The pressure of her hand and the force of her sucking made Jamie growl with pleasure. She stuck her thumbs into her waistband and stripped off her slacks, the roomy cut of her khakis helping her to disrobe in moments.

As soon as her slacks and panties had been cast off, Jamie shifted her body and wrapped her legs around Ryan's waist, holding on tight as her partner ratcheted her desire higher and higher.

Pawing at the irritating clothing that kept her from feeling her partner's heated skin, she waited impatiently while Ryan yanked off her T-shirt. Jamie took over, unhooking her bra with care, revealing the twin prizes that her own questing mouth sought.

She took her time, savoring the variety of tastes and scents that buffeted her senses: the fresh scent of soap; a touch of baby powder; a faint note of musk, which would grow stronger with her arousal; and a bit of clean, salty sweat. And always, hiding under the artificial scents, was Ryan's own aroma—indescribable, but as familiar as the smell of her own home—permanently imprinted on her brain.

As Jamie's tongue swirled around the stiffening nipple, she felt Ryan's hands slip to her waist to peel off her tights. Then the long legs wrapped around Jamie's waist, holding her in place as she had done to Ryan moments before.

She reveled in the feeling of being completely trapped—of being subject to Ryan's absolute whim, to do with as she chose. Her free hand went to the neglected breast, and plumped the nipple that her searching fingers found. Ryan replied lustily, moaning as Jamie simultaneously sucked and squeezed.

Suddenly, their positions were reversed, and Jamie found herself on her back, with her legs dangling over Ryan's broad shoulders. Without warning, the dark head dipped and Jamie felt sensitive flesh pulled gently into Ryan's mouth, the warm, wet tongue and lips touching her everywhere. With a soft, determined sucking motion, Ryan consumed her, thrilling her to the core as she felt every part of her most delicate flesh disappear into that hungry mouth.

Jamie's jaw opened and closed impotently, her lips unable to form words. Ryan possessed her so totally that she couldn't move, so she consciously relaxed and let her lover caress her. As soon as she gave up any attempt at control, her climax built and hit her hard, the feeling washing over her in waves, each one more calming, more soothing than the last.

Ryan's hot tongue wasn't ready to release her, and the silky smooth organ continued to stroke and play with Jamie's sensitized flesh. Jamie's hands went to her partner's back and stroked her with the same slow movements, soothing Ryan's racing heart.

Gently releasing her captive, Ryan climbed up her lover's body and took her into her arms, rocking her gently until she had fallen asleep against her. "I love you," Ryan whispered, the first words that she had spoken.

Chapter Twelve

"I don't know if the baby will even fit in here," Jamie said in amazement as they loaded the mass of presents for Jennie and her roommates into the back of the Lexus. It was late that afternoon, and they'd been trying to wait out the driving rain, but when it became obvious that it wasn't going to let up, they finally decided to pack up and go.

Maeve was in charge of Caitlin, and when Ryan suggested that she might like to help play Santa, she was only too willing to release her young charge. "She's been a terror today," Maeve warned Jamie when she ran up to the house to collect the baby. "As Ryan would say, she's a adrenaline junkie."

"Oh, we can manage her," Jamie said as she accepted the gurgling child.

"Mmh mmh," Caitlin grunted with a frustrated look on her sunny face.

"Ryan's trying to teach her to say my name," Jamie said. "We've given up trying to teach her 'Ryan'," she laughed. "She can't get a handle on any part of it."

"She seems like she's not satisfied with yours either," Maeve observed.

"No, she's not, but I think she'll get to Jamie a lot sooner than Ryan."

"Oh, let me go pull her car seat out of my car," Maeve said as she grabbed her keys.

"No need. We decided it was time to invest in our own. We got it all installed this morning. Now we'll always be prepared."

"Marvelous." Maeve said. "I hate to take it out of my car in the rain."

"That silly niece of yours was out in the rain for hours. We finally got the bike rack we'd ordered months ago, and she couldn't wait a day to get it on, even though we won't be riding our bikes any time in the near future. Then she had to get the car seat set up, and put the license plates I finally got for her on the car, too. She gets so focused."

"She's been like that forever. Don't waste your time trying to change her." Sticking her head out of the door she asked, "What is your special new license plate anyway?" She had to crane her neck to read it, then she laughed and said, "Now isn't that the truth." Bending to kiss Jamie goodbye she said, "I hope you have a lovely time this afternoon, girls. We'll probably go over to your house later to have dinner with the children, so we'll meet you back there."

"Okay, wish us luck," Jamie cried as she tucked Caitlin under her bright yellow slicker, then dashed back down the stairs to the waiting car.

Traffic was awful so they cut across the city on Mission, trying to get to the Bay Bridge. The heavy gloom made the late afternoon even darker than normal, and everyone had their headlights on even though it was only four o'clock.

The baby was chattering away in the back seat, attempting to make an important point when they pulled to a stop at the corner of Howard and Mission to allow a Muni bus to pass in front of them. Ryan turned to say something to Jamie when a male face appeared in the window right behind her lover's head. Something about the look on his face caused Ryan's stomach to clench, and she had her mouth open to warn Jamie when the window behind her own head was abruptly struck with a very heavy object. Twin screams echoed through the car; Ryan couldn't have said whether or not one was hers. A large, powerful hand reached through the gaping hole and grasped Ryan roughly by the collar, compressing her windpipe when the fabric of her T-shirt was twisted forcefully. She felt something cold, hard and wet press against her neck as a voice ordered, "Unlock the doors and get out."

Very few viable options presented themselves. Glancing quickly past Jamie's fear-frozen face, she saw the flash of blue steel pointed through the window at her lover, so any thoughts of trying to escape were quickly abandoned. "My baby is in the back seat," she said as calmly as possible, her voice thin from the diminution of air. "Let me get her out, and you can have everything we've got—no arguments."

"You're not in any position to argue, bitch," the man growled. "Now get out, or you're gonna be breathing out the side of your neck."

Another glance in the rear view mirror showed no other cars directly behind them, and the traffic coming from the other direction was not terribly heavy either, allowing few possibilities for help. She lowered her voice, trying to make it as calm as possible and said, "Can you get out, Jamie?"

She was unable to speak, but her head nodded quickly. Her eyes turned towards the screaming baby in the car seat, but Ryan shook her head. "Get out," she said firmly. Jamie's hand was shaking so violently that she could hardly grasp the door handle, but as soon as the lock popped, the man on her side jerked the door open with one hand and shoved the gun against the back of her head with the other. She fumbled for her seat belt, managing to unlatch it as he started to drag her from the vehicle. He yanked hard and she hit the pavement, landing on her butt with her feet still in the car. Kicking Jamie aside like a piece of trash, he jumped in over her prone body and slammed the door, nearly catching her left foot when he did. "Caitlin!" she cried pathetically, trying to scramble to her feet.

The gun at Ryan's neck scraped harshly against her skin as the man jammed it under her left ear. "You've got three seconds. Then we take you with us. Dead," he added unnecessarily. Every instinct in her body told her to defy the order and stomp on the accelerator. But the man in the passenger seat looked even more nervous and edgy than the one at her side, and she thought the odds of him killing her for no reason at all were pretty high. She thought that if she got out, they might allow her to take Caitlin to avoid the aggravation of having a screaming baby in the car. So with her body resisting the powerful messages flooding her brain, she opened the door and started to slide out. "Please…please let me take the baby," she begged in her most plaintive voice. "If you take the car, the police won't even bother to look for you. It's just a car. But if you kidnap a tiny baby…" Her plea was cut off by her assailant's left hand striking her hard across the mouth. She tasted the metallic tang of her own blood as her knees buckled and deposited her onto the ground, but she kept begging for the baby.

Both men had their attention diverted for a moment, and in a move that seemed almost instinctive, Jamie grabbed the rear door handle and yanked it open as the larger man hopped into the driver's seat, intentionally stepping on Ryan in the process. A car came up behind them, and in a panic, he hit the accelerator hard. Jamie wasn't sure how it happened—all she knew was that long months of training her body allowed her to grab the car seat with her left hand and the seat back of the passenger seat with her right and haul herself inside. Gasping for breath, she let out a sigh of relief as she pulled the door closed and began to try to calm the hysterical baby.

Her relief was short lived as the passenger turned and glared at her evilly. "Somebody's in a hurry to die," he said, with what looked like glee.

When Ryan's ass hit the street, a young man frantically dug for his keys, determined to get into his apartment and call the police. But a blur of movement caught his eye, he whirled to look through the glass and saw Ryan leap to her feet, take off running at a remarkable rate of speed, and hurl her body through the air, her hands reaching desperately to grab onto the wind foil. The man ran back onto the street, forcing himself to witness what was sure to be the foolhardy woman's last act.

Unbelievably she somehow began to pull herself up onto the roof, using the bike rack as an anchor. Soon, she flopped onto the roof, leaving the witness to stare mouth-agape. The stunned man knew the police would never believe his story, but he felt obligated to recount the tale, since he was sure he was the only witness. The car accelerated rapidly, the wet tires spinning as the driver hit the accelerator hard. Watching intently, the man tried to cement the events in his mind, wondering how he would explain the happenings to the police. Going over the scene in his mind, he entered his building again, thinking, *That was either the bravest or the stupidest woman on earth, but no matter which, she doesn't deserve to die the way she's going to.*

Jamie's heart was thudding louder, faster, and heavier than she knew was possible as the car lurched down the street. She knew that Ryan was with them—the loud thump and even louder cursing had alerted her to her lover's mad leap, and since that moment she had been turned around in her seat, her eyes scanning the street, making sure that her beloved partner hadn't silently fallen off. But the reassurance that she felt from knowing her lover was close was abruptly quashed by the cold, hard tones that floated over to her from the front seat. "Once we knock her off—you're next."

Okay, two mean guys, two big guns, one slippery car, and a demented woman hanging on for dear life. I've got them where I want them, Ryan thought wryly. They'd been careening down little-traveled side streets for several minutes, trying desperately to lose the determined woman who clung so tenaciously to the roof rack. *Thank you, thank you, Jamie for buying me these gloves,* Ryan said in silent prayer. The tacky, weatherproof gloves were the only things saving her life at the moment, and she had never had an article of clothing that she was fonder of. Immensely glad that she'd taken the time to fully understand the make up of her new bike rack, she grabbed the sturdy pieces of metal designed to hold the front forks of their bikes. With a snap, they lodged into an upright position, giving her two good handles. The basic structure of the rack, which reminded her of a metal bed frame, helped provide a place to brace her feet, and she began to have some confidence that she'd be able to hang on.

"*Shit!*" she cried aloud as a wrenching swerve across two lanes of traffic roused her from her momentary reverie. The driver was trying to dislodge her in any way possible, and she had to admit that his plan was a good one. If she'd been him, she would have stopped the car, shot her in the head and driven like hell; but his plan was also sound.

The fact that they had not yet killed her gave her a burgeoning sense of security. She reasoned that she could probably survive a fall off the car, although another car would probably hit her after she fell. So the only choice was to hang on. She began to feel more and more confident that they were not going to hurt the baby, since the easiest thing would have been to take her from her car seat and toss her out. Ryan would surely jump off to protect her, and they'd be able to take off again without drawing much attention. But it seemed that they were now in a state of panic, and were not spending a whole lot of time considering their actions. She was also cheered that they hadn't forcibly thrown Jamie from the car, something she reasoned they would have done if they were utterly psychopathic.

Seconds later she began to reconsider her own conclusions when she heard the motor for the passenger door window whir briefly, then a shiny blue/gray gun poked out the top of the window and tried to point itself at her. She knew the guy couldn't aim the gun with any degree of accuracy at that angle, but the thought of a gun firing wildly was not reassuring, either. She wasn't sure where in the hell they were, since her stinging eyes couldn't blink fast enough to be able to focus properly, but as the gun came out, they started to descend an extremely steep hill.

Her body lurched forward and her feet started to slide, but a desperate stab allowed her to shove one foot over the rack, preventing her from sliding all the way off. Without taking the time to think, she removed her right hand from the rack and lunged for the gun. They wrestled over it for a few seconds, with the gun discharging twice during the struggle. The screams that she heard coming from both Caitlin and her lover assured her that they were both alive, but obviously terrified. Ironically, her position on the roof gave her an advantage over the man in the car, since his arm was raised at an extremely oblique angle. Twisting hard, she wrenched the gun partially free from his grasp, and kept twisting until he let out a startled cry of anguish as she felt at least one bone snap. She shoved the gun under her body, grabbing on to the roof rack and snagging the back bar with her feet as the car made another ascent. *Now the odds are getting better,* she thought, almost smiling at her small victory.

Jamie offered up a silent prayer of thanks that they were in the always-congested city, and not on the quieter, residential streets of Berkeley. On a less traveled street, it would be much easier to stop the car and shoot both of them without someone seeing the act occur. So she allowed herself a moment of relief when the passenger yanked his broken arm back into the car, now minus a gun. She knew that Ryan was still hanging on since she could occasionally hear her kick some part of the roof, and it was patently obvious that one less gun in the wrong hands was a good thing.

The driver didn't share her optimism, and that became painfully clear when he turned to look at her briefly. "Just your luck that the idiots of this state passed the three strikes law, honey."

"Wh...wha...what?" she finally asked, her throat raw from screaming.

"I've got two violent felonies on my record. This is my third. If I get caught, I'm gone for twenty-five to life. Probably life—without parole. My brother here is on his third already, so we're going away for a very long time."

She looked at him in utter confusion, wondering why he felt the need to relate his criminal history to her. But he clarified his point very quickly. "Death row at San Quentin is a lot nicer place to ride out the rest of your life," he said in an almost conversational tone. "We've got nothing to lose, so we're gonna go for broke here. Witnesses are definitely not a good thing." He had turned his big, mean-looking face in her direction as he said this, and the chilling, matter-of-fact tone he used made it clear that he viewed this with as much concern as he gave to his choice of breakfast cereal.

"You're going to kill us?" she asked with much more calm than she felt.

"Yep. Sure am," he agreed. Looking at his brother he asked, "I bet you want first crack at the one on the roof, huh, Wendell?"

"With my bare hands," Wendell agreed, fire sparking in his beady eyes.

"Hand." the driver barked with an evil laugh. "You've only got one that works, dipshit."

"Fuck you, Elmore," he spat, and Jamie mused for a moment that their first names could have contributed to making them antisocial killers. "Find a quiet street and let me at her."

"Oh, whatcha gonna do, Wendell?" he asked in an evil cackle. "Don't you wanna fuck her first? That's the only way you ever get any," he added, laughing uproariously at his jibe.

"Oh, I'll fuck her all right," a thin sting of drool running down his face. "While I'm strangling her."

There was no doubt in Jamie's mind that Wendell was truly psychotic, and that he would indeed attempt to strangle her beloved Ryan if he had the chance. Elmore, on the other hand, didn't seem as unstable as his brother, even though he seemed as evil. Her mind raced, trying to think of anything that would get them out of the situation, but she wasn't able to come up with any clear thoughts. Her mental review was broken, however, by the welcome sounds of a siren; and when she turned and spotted the cruiser right on their tail, she nearly cried with relief.

"Pull the car to the side of the road," a disembodied voice ordered.

Elmore obviously had not received high marks in "follows orders well" in elementary school. He slammed his foot on the accelerator, laughing maniacally. "This might be our last ride for a long time, Wendell. Let's go out big."

Jamie was busy reassessing her initial more charitable assessment of Elmore's mental state when he turned and grinned at her with the most chilling look she had ever seen in her life. "It's your final ride too, baby. Any last requests?" Her wide eyes and inability to catch her breath were the answer he was looking for, and he threw his head back and laughed in a manner that would have been worthy of Satan himself. Ironically, now that the car was speeding faster than Jamie thought possible, Caitlin had not only quieted down, she began to enjoy herself. It was evident that she knew

Karma

Jamie was upset, and she knew that Ryan wasn't with them, but her "need for speed" caused her to ignore all of these details as she started making her usual moves in her car seat, jumping up and down and giggling wildly.

The siren was wailing incessantly, but the closer the squad car got, the more risks Elmore took. Jamie was practically out of her mind with panic for her lover, but she was certain that she was still on top, from the occasional burst of Gaelic profanity she heard from her when Elmore intentionally bottomed the car out on a particularly large hill.

"What kinda turning radius ya got on this?" Elmore asked in a casually conversational tone as he took an almost ninety degree roll, skidding for half a block and slamming the side of the car into a fire hydrant, before he hit the gas and sped into an alley. The cops couldn't keep up, and they lost them as they sped on by. "Hmm, not bad, not bad at all," he decided.

Once again Jamie screamed, perversely reassured when she heard Ryan bang into something hard and curse lustily.

Elmore seemed to be enjoying himself, and he grinned evilly as he turned to Jamie. "Hey, the kid likes it," he added, nodding in Caitlin's direction. "She's cute," he said, acting like he'd noticed her for the first time. "I don't think I'll kill her." He turned his attention back to driving for a moment, asking Wendell, "You think they'd go easier on us if we left the kid alive?"

"Fuck no." Wendell spat. "We never catch a break."

"Ehh, good point, brother. Let's kill 'em all." He hit the accelerator again with a vengeance, laughing heartily as Jamie and Caitlin screamed in unison—one from fear, and one from delight.

Martin and Maeve had arrived at the O'Flaherty home, and gone into Martin's former room to watch the evening news. With a boyish grin, he sat in his favorite old chair and patted his legs, inviting his bride to sit on his lap. "Oh, Martin, you are such a tease," she chided. Nonetheless, she sat down and made herself comfortable, ruffling his hair as she did so. "What if the children come home?" she asked as she checked her watch.

"Ha. The girls are constantly knotted around each other like a pair of pretzels, so they can't say a word. Conor and Kevin aren't due for an hour, and Rory's in Los Angeles. We can snog to our heart's content." He proceeded to do that, stealing several sweet kisses from his very receptive bride.

The television was playing softly in the background, and a tiny part of Maeve's brain was listening, and that tiny part heard the breathless announcer say, "Repeating our breaking news, police are in pursuit of a late model, beige Lexus LX 300, license number JDSE SRO. The plate is a vanity style, and the JDSE is separated from the SRO by a heart."

His co-anchor opined, "Most people use those plates to express their love of something or someone, Chuck. So that might read JDSE loves SRO."

"Oh, that makes sense," he said, enormously pleased to have that mystery revealed. "The car was traveling at a high rate of speed, and an unidentified person was seen hanging on to the roof rack. Boy, Wendy, some people have a very strange idea of fun. Probably some pranksters pledging a fraternity."

Maeve's grip had loosened as the announcers babbled away, and by the time Chuck was finished with his statement she was on her feet, staring at the television with a stunned expression. Martin hadn't heard a word either anchor had said, so intent was he on his partner's lips, but he knew something was terribly wrong from the look on Maeve's chalk white face. "Darlin, what is it?" he said, leaping to his feet and grasping her by the shoulders.

"The girls…Caitlin…Caitlin!" she screamed as the realization hit her.

Martin's head snapped around and tried to focus as the announcers said, "We have News-chopper Five located over the financial district, where the Lexus was last seen. They're in pursuit, and we'll stay with this fascinating story until it's resolved. Again, police are in pursuit of a late model Lexus RX 300, license JDSE heart SRO."

Martin's nerveless hands dropped from Maeve's shoulders as he sank onto the bed. "How…why…Maeve?" he finally got out.

"Call the police, Martin," she ordered. "Tell them that Siobhán is not on that roof by choice."

"*Roof?*" he cried as she pushed him in the direction of the phone.

Both felons, even though they lacked formal schooling, were well trained in the ways of the police. "They'll be all over us like flies on a turd," Wendell muttered as they sped along.

"Mom always said you were the smart one," his loving older brother replied. "Any bright ideas, genius? Your first one about carjacking sure went well."

"You're the one who picked fucking Tarzan up there," Wendell reminded him. "I woulda picked somebody older and weaker."

"Sure you would, candyass. You always like the helpless ones."

"I'll tell you one thing. I might go down, but that bitch on the roof is going down with me."

Chuckling harshly, Elmore opined, "Well, she won't go down on you without a gun to her head. That's for sure."

"I got plans for her," Wendell said, spit foaming out the side of his mouth.

"Well, you don't have long; and knowing you, you'll screw it up once or twice, so you better come up with a good idea quick."

Ten minutes after Martin and Maeve were alerted to the emergency, the house began to fill with members of the O'Flaherty clan. Maeve steeled her courage and made the most difficult call of her life—telling Catherine that her only child was in grave danger. Kevin was immediately dispatched to go pick the distraught woman up and bring her to the house.

While she waited, Catherine stood in the kitchen slugging down vodka as quickly as Marta could pour it for her, though the cook was partially successful at trying to put less and less vodka into the glass. As she paced alongside her employer, her fingers silently worked the beads of her rosary.

As the alcohol started to take the raw edge off, Catherine took a breath and dialed her husband, telling Jim of their child's predicament. He was at his apartment, and his voice quickly turned warm when he heard her familiar tones. "Hi, Catherine. It's a nice surprise to hear from you."

She felt as though a sword had lanced her heart as she forced herself to say, "Jim...it's Jamie." Fighting for composure, she said, "She and Ryan have been...carjacked."

"What?"

"They've been carjacked. I don't know what happened, or why, but there's a news helicopter that's been following them. It's on every channel."

"I'll be right down, Cat," he said immediately. "I don't want you to be alone..."

"No, no, I'm going to Ryan's house. One of her cousins is on his way to pick me up. Call your father, and let him know. I...I couldn't do it." She started to sob, her legs giving out as Marta managed to maneuver a kitchen chair under her. "Oh, God, Jim. What will we do if anything happens to her?"

"It won't," he vowed. "I'll get on the phone with the police commissioner and make sure every officer in the city is out there, tracking them down."

"Promise me," she begged. "Promise me that they'll be all right. Please?"

Her pleading tone of voice nearly broke his heart, and he did his best to sound confident. "They'll be fine," he insisted. "They have to be."

⁂

Conor came bursting into the house, his mouth set in a grim mask. He brushed past every member of the family and grabbed the police scanner from the kitchen, turned and started back towards the door. Brendan leapt to his feet and chased him down the stairs, opening the door to the truck and barely making it in as Conor brought the big V-10 to life and slammed his foot onto the accelerator, determined to bring his baby sister back home.

⁂

Karma

The Lexus was zigzagging around near the Moscone Center, and as they passed old St. Patrick's church, Ryan offered up a prayer to both the patron saint of her homeland and also to her mother. *I'm not ready to see you yet, Mama,* she said as she closed her eyes tightly. *I've got a lot to accomplish here, and I've got to stay alive to keep Jamie and Caitlin safe. Please help us get through this,* she prayed, her tears mingling with the icy rain that pelted her body relentlessly.

At the same moment Ryan was saying her prayer, Wendell finally came up with his bright idea. Elmore had turned onto 7th Street, and after a few blocks hung a right on Leavenworth. He hit the gas hard when they got onto the level but crowded street, switching lanes and veering into oncoming traffic wildly. "I got it," Wendell said thoughtfully, oblivious to the cars and bodies scrambling to get out of their way. "We can't shake her off, so let's shoot her off."

He looked very pleased with himself. "Not bad, brother. Be my guest." He reached between his legs and handed his brother his gun, paying only partial attention to the oncoming traffic. "Whoa," he cried with a wild laugh. "We almost bought it that time." They had missed an oncoming MUNI bus by inches, and as Jamie lurched and vomited onto Wendell's back, the baby laughed with glee.

"Fuck!" the vomit-covered, broken-armed man cried. "Stupid bitch."

He turned and aimed at Jamie's head, but his prudent older brother grabbed the gun as the shaky index finger of his broken arm tightened on the trigger. "I've only got four rounds in there, dipshit. Don't waste 'em. You can always strangle the one in the back."

"Fuck," the disappointed man grumbled. "I can't fuckin' strangle her with a broken fucking arm. I can't even shoot," he pouted. Wendell fidgeted with the gun, moving it to his left hand, but finding it very difficult to hold it and aim, since that hand was missing the index, third and fourth fingers.

"Told ya not to make that pipe bomb," his helpful older brother taunted, laughing hard at his own humor.

"You are one funny asshole," Wendell muttered as he tried to

243

hold the gun with his painful broken arm and pull the trigger with the thumb of his other hand. Jamie's eyes nearly popped from her head as she saw the gun negligently aimed out the windshield—pedestrians filling the sidewalks. "Fuck! I can't do it."

"Give it here, dipshit," Elmore insisted. Wendell looked like he wanted another try, this time aimed at his brother, but he dutifully handed over the weapon. "Watch and learn," Elmore drawled.

As he lifted the piece towards the roof, Jamie cried out in the most bloodcurdling voice that anyone in the car had ever heard, "He's gonna shoot you through the roof."

"Sure am." Elmore laughed and peeled off three rounds, accompanied by an even louder and more pathetic scream from their passenger.

Ryan was only partially thankful for her partner's warning. She really didn't have a lot of options at the moment, and since she couldn't guess where the shots would come from, she couldn't brace herself or move. But she was thankful that she could squeeze off a prayer, even though it was only, *Save me, God.*

The first shot pierced the roof and flew through the sleeve of her new jacket, managing to miss her skin completely. Number two was about an inch from her right cheek, a scaldingly hot piece of shrapnel nicking her skin; and number three would have hit her right between the eyes if they hadn't been climbing Nob Hill and her body had not shifted back a good five inches.

"He didn't get me!" she cried, as elated as she was astounded. Then the car lurched right and started to descend towards the Embarcadero.

"Fuck!" Elmore snapped. "One fucking round left. At the bottom of the hill, I'm gonna jump out and waste the bitch. This is personal."

That decision made Wendell even angrier. "I owe her," he ground out. "I wanna blow her fucking brains out."

"I wanna be an only child," Elmore snapped. "Get over it."

Deciding that the time for prudence was over, Jamie rolled down a window and shoved her body through until she was sitting on the door. Reaching up with both hands, she grabbed Ryan's leg and cried, "He's gonna get out and shoot you at the bottom of the hill."

"The fuck he is," Ryan shouted as she released her left hand and grasped the gun that had been gouging her stomach during the ride. "Hang on to me." she demanded. Jamie lunged and put every bit of her strength into hanging onto Ryan with her left hand, grabbing onto the waistband of her jeans, while her right held onto the handle atop the passenger door. She had never understood why car manufacturers put those handles on cars, but she promised to send Lexus a thank you note as soon as she had a moment.

Ryan leaned over the left side of the car, and aimed as carefully as she could. They had just turned onto Mission and were approaching the turn onto Embarcadero, and Elmore had to make a hard right to avoid going into the drink. As he turned, Ryan fired the weapon, the recoil stunning her as red-hot fire flashed from the barrel. The bullet hit Elmore in the right shoulder, passed through his body and hit Wendell in the left arm, causing both men to scream simultaneously.

The bloodstain blossomed on Elmore's shirt as he tried to control the car through the tight turn. Wendell reached for the wheel, madly trying to steer the car, fighting with his brother for control. Ryan shoved the gun back under her stomach, and grabbed on with both hands again. "Get back in and put your seat belt on!"

Wendell gave up on his attempt to steer, groping madly for the gun that had fallen to the floor, determined to at least kill the bitch who had made his simple plan go so horribly wrong. But his wounded left arm, deformed left hand, and broken right arm did not make the task easy. As first one helicopter and then another flew overhead, he grasped the gun, but the car lurched to the left. Elmore had obviously taken his foot off the accelerator, since the car was going no more than ten or fifteen miles per hour; but even at slow speed, Elmore couldn't control the car. Ryan screamed when she saw where the laws of physics dictated they would land. "We're going into the bay. Unbuckle Caitlin's carsea…"

Her words were cut off by the surreal sensation of having the car leave the pavement and head straight into the water. Elmore yanked the wheel desperately, but he only managed to keep the right wheels on the pavement a few moments longer than the left. As the nose of the car hit the water, Ryan leapt from the roof and slammed into the ice cold, jet-black water at the same time the vehicle did. Her body urged her to scream, but the water was so unbearably cold and hard that she was unable to. She fought with every fiber of her being to stay conscious. Every shred of her determined personality decided that she was not going to drown—and no matter what—she was not going to lose her lover or her cousin.

She fought through the water until her head broke through the inky surface, glad beyond belief when a San Francisco Fire Department helicopter hovered overhead, shining a hundred thousand candlepower lamp onto the scene.

※

Amazingly, the twenty-two people jammed into Martin's bedroom and living room were absolutely silent as the news helicopter captured the entire scene. Hands blindly gripped the nearest hand as the entire group willed the young women to keep fighting. The camera caught Ryan's dark head as it burst through the water, and Martin's legs gave out to deposit him unceremoniously to the floor.

Jim and his father came running into the room, the younger man looking about wildly until he found his wife. He grabbed her and wrapped his arms around her tightly, holding on for dear life as they watched their only child fight for her life.

※

Ryan's wild leap had left her a few feet from the rapidly submerging car. She swam the short distance and scrambled across the roof, crying out as Caitlin and her car seat poked out of the water. Grasping the seat with one hand, she blindly stuck the other underwater, grabbing onto Jamie's shoulder, then she yanked as hard as she could, pulling the gasping woman up at least a foot into the air.

Jamie sucked in a lungful of air as she fought to tread water. The helicopter was rapidly lowering a sling, and as it passed by their heads, Jamie grabbed it and held on for dear life. "Grab the baby carrier and climb in," the voice of the rescue worker boomed.

Karma

Ryan handed the car seat to Jamie and ordered, "Go on up with Cait. I've got to get the others."

"What?" she screamed over the whine of the engines.

"I can't let them drown." Ryan insisted, her eyes filled with determination. As her dark head voluntarily submerged, Jamie closed her eyes for a second, grasped the sling, snuggled the car seat into the harness, and secured the shackle. Taking a lung-filling breath, she dove right down behind her lover.

"For the love of God, what are they doing?" Martin cried from his spot on the floor.

"They're drowning." Catherine sobbed, unable to look, as her husband held her in his arms.

"No! No!" Martin cried. "My baby's too strong to go down that easily. Please, Siobhán. Please come up!" he begged the inanimate television.

Seconds later both heads surfaced, sucking air in as quickly as it would come. A third head bobbed between theirs and Ryan gasped, "Can you hold him?"

"I can't let you go back!"

"I have to, baby," she cried as she dove down again. The sling was lowered again and this time Jamie helped their assailant climb in, ignoring his strangled cries when she grasped his arm roughly to push him away from her.

"My God!" Martin cried. "They're trying to rescue those dirty feckers."

As he said this, a powerful Fire Department speedboat swung onto the scene. The assembled throng watched in horror as Jamie rebuffed the firefighters' attempts to pull her into the boat. She wrenched her arm free and dove again, determined to bring her lover to the surface, or die with her.

※

Ryan's hands flailed blindly as she felt the open window of the car. Her right hand felt a body, and she gripped it and refused to let go as the form tried to push her away. They tussled briefly, but as they did so a powerful scuba light hit them, providing blessed illumination. Ryan was below him trying to propel him up to the surface, and once Jamie saw this she grabbed him by the shirt and started to kick. By the time she surfaced, she felt a million tiny stars obscure her field of vision, seconds before everything turned black.

※

The roar of the crowd was nearly deafening as Ryan bobbed to the surface, her left hand firmly holding the now limp body of her attacker. Half a second later, the cheers stopped abruptly, and all of the air was sucked from the room when it became clear that Ryan cradled her partner's body in her right arm. No one breathed—no one moved—as the fire fighters leaned over the gunwales to lift Jamie's still body into the boat. The only sound was a dull thud as Catherine joined Martin on the floor, slipping limply from Jim's firm grip.

※

Ryan knelt next to her lover's prone body as the paramedic examined her. "CPR!" she cried, ready to do it if the paramedic didn't.

"She doesn't need it," the woman said calmly. "Her lungs are clear, and her pulse is good. She fainted from lack of oxygen." Turning to Ryan, she smiled briefly and assured her, "She'll be fine." Climbing over Jamie, she turned to Elmore, calling out to her partner, "Gunshot wound to the shoulder. Radio ahead to prepare two units of O-positive blood."

Karma

When the boat smoothly pulled up to the end of the pier, Ryan felt hands grasping for her. She was pulled to her feet before she knew what was happening, slowly realizing that two of her brothers were standing in the boat with her. Without a word, they assisted her out, Brendan going up behind her on the rope ladder the fire fighters had dropped into the boat. After Conor checked with the paramedic, he gently picked Jamie up and placed her over his shoulder, climbing the ladder with one hand. Brendan grabbed her, and cradled her like a child in his arms as Conor reached the pier. The women were quickly loaded into the waiting ambulance, with both boys climbing in as well, ignoring the instructions to the contrary.

"She's fine." Martin cried. "She's fine." he yelled again as he stumbled to his feet.

No one else understood his jubilation as the faces in the crowd stared at him. "How do you know?" Jim cried, his eyes wild with panic.

"The paramedics on that boat would never—never—have let those boys carry her if she was injured. They obviously had their hands full with the other one," he added, unwilling to even dignify the man with a pejorative term.

"Are you sure, Martin?" Catherine's weak voice floated up to him.

He dropped to his knees and faced her, eyes inches from hers. "I swear it, Catherine. I promise you. She'll be fine." He wrapped his arms around her and they cried together, sharing the whirl of emotions that passed between them.

By the time the ambulance pulled up to the emergency room, Jamie was conscious, although very sick to her stomach from the virulent combination of seawater and terror. She vomited several times, missing Ryan by bare inches each time. Waiting for the attendants to open the door, she beckoned Ryan closer. Ryan leaned over the pale face, only to hear her say, "If we'd drowned tonight, I'd be kicking your ass all over heaven right now."

Chapter Thirteen

As the back door of the ambulance opened, the phalanx of photographers nearly prevented the stretcher from being wheeled into the E.R. Luckily, the police were also on the scene, and they did their best to clear the path.

Conor and Brendan went with the baby, and Ryan stayed glued to Jamie's side, refusing to budge when they reached an examining room. An attendant strode into the room, took one look and her, and said, "Sorry, you'll have to wait outside in the lounge."

"I'm not leaving," she muttered, grasping Jamie's ice-cold hands. "Can you cover her with some blankets? She's freezing to death."

He put his hands on his hips and glared at her. "You have to leave."

"Call the fucking cops," she spat, her patience at an end. "I shot the last guy who tried to separate us." She turned and gave him a stare that made him gulp. "Now get her a goddamned blanket."

A calm looking young man strolled into the room. "Problem?" he asked, sizing up the standoff between Ryan and the orderly.

"She won't leave," the orderly accused, equally angry.

"It's okay, Robert," the doctor said. "I think I can handle her." Turning to Ryan, his face broke into a grin as he stuck out his hand. "Rick Marshall. Some display you two put on tonight. We were all watching in the doctors' lounge."

Ryan didn't extend her own hand. She actually barely seemed to have heard what he said. "She's freezing," she stated once again, leaning over Jamie's body to check on her. Her own body was shivering so roughly that it was hard to decipher her words, but her concern was only for her lover. "Can't somebody get her a damned blanket?"

Ducking out of the room, the doctor returned with several. A nurse came in and tried to get Jamie's clothes off of her, but the waterlogged garments didn't lend themselves to removal in the usual way. "I'm gonna have to cut them," she decided, and Ryan backed up enough to let her work, still chafing one icy hand with both of her own equally cold ones.

As the clothing was cut away, Ryan's eyes landed on her partner's stark-white body, Jamie's entire form shivering violently. Her extremities had a bluish cast to them, and as Ryan stared at her, she was overcome with a rising sense of panic which quickly turned to horror—her imagination causing her to view the shivering body as still and lifeless. Her mind began to race, and she forced herself to recognize that she was nearly hallucinating. But her relief was short-lived when she realized with shocking clarity that because of her decision to save the men who tried to kill them, she'd done as much as the felons had to put Jamie's life at risk.

Struggling with the horrible realization, she grasped the small, cold hand harder and harder, until Jamie's weak voice finally said, "Ow."

Ryan immediately released her grip, then practically fell onto her to cover her torso with her own body, holding her so tightly that Jamie could barely breathe. The doctor could see that Ryan was on the verge of hysteria, so he held onto her shoulder and spoke soothingly. "Get up now," he said quietly. "I have to look at her." Another tap—this one harder, brought no reaction. Ryan was sobbing incessantly, and Jamie's shaky hand had risen to pat her on the back. The doctor could hear Jamie's soft voice trying to calm her partner, but it wasn't doing much good.

Conor poked his dark head in, and the doctor started to order him out of the room. But when the man saw his sister bent over her lover, sobbing hysterically, he raced in and cried, "My God. Is she…?"

"I think she's fine," the doctor interrupted, staring at him helplessly. "I don't know what's wrong here, but I can't even get a look at her."

Finally understanding that Ryan was losing it, Conor wrapped his strong arms around his sister and started to pry her away from her lover. Ryan was holding on so tightly that Jamie's body started to rise with her, and he urged, "Come on. Let her go. She's okay, but the doctor has to look at her. Please, Sis, let her go."

She looked up at him as her hold loosened, and he saw the utter confusion and raw pain in the red-rimmed eyes. He turned her and held her tight, soothing her while he tried to guide her out of the way. But as strong as he was, and as terrified, upset and fatigued as she was, she wouldn't leave Jamie's side. "No!" she cried, doggedly grabbing onto the examining table.

Conor met the doctor's eyes and shrugged his shoulders. "We'll try to stay out of your way," he offered helplessly.

"Fine," the doctor agreed, deciding that he wasn't going to be the one to remove this determined young woman from her partner's side.

Now that they had some room to move, the doctor and the nurse worked together to remove the clothing from Jamie's body. He then wrapped her in the blankets, moving the covering around as he examined her.

With her frozen clothing off, Jamie still shook, but she started to feel a tiny bit of warmth suffuse her body. She was fully conscious, albeit mentally slow and hazy on details. Her biggest injury seemed to be her ribs, where Wendell had kicked her as he pushed her from the car. Rick palpated the area, and gasped as Jamie cried out in pain and Ryan grabbed his arm. "Don't you dare hurt her," she growled, making him shrink back from her wild glare.

"Ryan, it's all right," Jamie soothed, her voice still weak and shaky. "He's got to examine me."

Looking at her own hand as though it had moved involuntarily, Ryan shook her head and said, "I'm so sorry. I...I don't even know what I'm doing."

"It's okay," the doctor said. "I'm finished now." He patted Jamie's shoulder, and said, "You seem fine. There's no sign of internal injury, and your lungs are nice and clear. You're the luckiest pair of people I think I've ever met—and you seem perfectly healthy."

Jamie looked up, "Don't let Ryan get away until you look at her. She has a history of head trauma."

The doctor wanted to say that he didn't doubt that in the least, but thought he'd better keep his opinions to himself. He examined Ryan with her standing up—since he didn't want to argue with her any more than he had to. Her pupils were normal and exactly the same size, and she was able to track his penlight without difficulty. She had a nasty cut on the inside of her mouth, a small slice had been carved into her cheek, and her lip was swollen, but those few superficial injuries seemed to be the only ones that her head had sustained.

He put his warm hands under her shirt to palpate her belly, finding nothing out of the ordinary. She was, of course, covered with bruises, but her main source of pain seemed to be her still-shaking muscles. Her joints didn't appear to have sustained any injury, much to his surprise, and he soon pronounced her fit as well. "I'm going to prescribe some muscle relaxants, and something to help both of you sleep. I'll give you enough so you can get some rest tonight and tomorrow. I don't want either of you to develop a dependency," he added. "You're both going to have some emotional repercussions from this. Take my advice and try not to rely on substances to get yourselves through it."

Jamie nodded, thankful that the doctor seemed to understand how horrible the entire event had been for them, and that he also cared enough to urge them to care for themselves properly.

"Thanks," she said. "We'll take care of each other."

"I can tell that," he said, smiling.

She tugged on his coat, and he leaned forward. "Can you give her a shot of something to calm her down? I'm afraid she's going to have a stroke."

He gave Ryan another lingering gaze, seeing the wild look in her eyes. "Uhm...level with me," he whispered to Jamie. "Is she on something? Crack, crystal meth?"

"No, nothing," she insisted.

Ryan's strong hand gripped the doctor's shoulder and she pulled him upright. "What are you hiding from me?" The look in her eyes was absolutely frightening, but her pupils were not dilated, and she seemed lucid otherwise. "What's wrong with her," she demanded.

"She's fine," he said, trying to soothe her. "She's worried about you. Quite frankly, you're acting hysterical."

"*She almost died!*" Ryan cried at the top of her lungs, forcing the doctor back a step.

He shot Jamie a look, nodded once, jerked his head at the nurse, and they both left the cubicle.

Ryan shrugged off Conor's loose embrace and went to her partner, wrapping Jamie in a bone-bruising hug.

"Honey...?"

Ryan lifted her head to look at her, sorrow filling her eyes.

"Your clothes. Please take them off and cover yourself up in one of the blankets."

Ryan shook her head and went right back into the hug, but Jamie persisted. "They're making me wet. I'm starting to warm up—don't get me wet again." She would have been willing to sit in an ice bath to feel her partner's embrace, but she didn't want Ryan to stand there in her dripping clothes for another moment, and she knew she'd comply if the request was framed properly.

Ryan stepped back, looking even sadder as she released her. "I'm sorry...I didn't realize..."

"Hey," Jamie whispered, "we're all right. No one was hurt. Try to remember that."

Ryan couldn't give voice to the guilt that filled her soul. She nodded and started to remove her clothes, not noticing when Conor stepped from the room to give her some privacy and a nurse brought in a set of extra-large and medium scrubs. Ryan insisted that she could dress her partner. The thought never entered the nurse's mind to argue, and she quickly departed as well.

Tenderly, Ryan slipped the loose garments onto her partner's clammy body, then covered her with the blankets once again. When she was finished, she continued undressing with Jamie observing her carefully as she peeled the sodden clothing off. She had red welts all over her torso from lying on the gun, banging into the bike rack, and wrestling with the felons in the water. She moved slowly, but didn't seem to be in too much pain—which was reassuring. The nurse came back in with a muscle relaxant and an anti-inflammatory for Ryan, but she insisted that Jamie take it.

"Ryan," she said, "I don't need it. The doctor wants you to have it for your muscles. I was sitting in the car, baby, not holding onto the roof."

"Oh." She opened her mouth and swallowed both pills, Jamie's worry increasing when she saw how confused and slow she was.

Ryan looked at the nurse and asked, "Can you tell me where my cousin is?"

"Your brother is with her. I was in the room during the examination. She's cold, but other than that, perfectly fine."

"Thank God," Jamie murmured, almost under her breath.

"Oh, the doctor wants to know when your last tetanus shot was," the nurse asked.

"Mine was a couple of years ago when I was traveling in the third world," Jamie recalled.

Ryan shrugged, looking confused.

The nurse left the room, and a minute later the doctor returned, this time with a burly security guard. He gave Jamie a look and she grasped her partner's hand, saying, "The doctor has to give you a tetanus shot. Will you let him?"

Her eyes flitted between Jamie and the guard, trying to figure out why the huge man was in the room. Finally she let Jamie tug at her to get her to sit, and then lie on the table, while Jamie scooted off. "She won't give you any trouble," she told the doctor.

He looked dubious, but her prediction soon proved accurate, as Ryan's eyes rolled up into her head before the needle even pricked her skin. His eyes grew wide and he started to withdraw the needle, but Jamie assured him, "She always faints at the mere sight of a needle." He shot her a warning look, but she insisted, "I promise you, she's not on drugs. She's desperately afraid."

"She doesn't act like she's afraid," he mused, looking carefully at the perfectly composed features of the unconscious woman.

"She's afraid for me," Jamie quietly informed him, sparing a deeply sympathetic glance at her lover. "There's nothing worse for her."

※

When Ryan's eyes fluttered open, Jamie was gazing at her from close range. "How do you feel?" she asked. Her voice sounded strangely muddled and her image wasn't quite sharp to Ryan.

Ryan reached up and rubbed her eyes. "Fuzzy. How long have I been out?"

Karma

"Not long."

Ryan started to get up, but immediately lay back down. "Dizzy," she muttered.

"Honey," Jamie said, leaning over her, "I asked the doctor to give you something to relax you. He gave you an injection of Valium. It might make you groggy."

Her blue eyes blinked slowly, then a flash of pain flickered through them. "Did I scare you?"

"No, no," Jamie whispered, placing soft kisses all over Ryan's bruised face. "Never, sweetheart. You've never frightened me. You're very, very anxious, and I wanted to make sure you could calm down a little. That's all," she soothed.

Ryan blinked again, then slowly nodded. "I feel okay now. Help me up?"

Jamie lent her an arm, and Ryan slowly sat, then waited until she was sure she was steady. Confident that she was, she got up from the table, standing still for a moment. To Jamie's eye, the Valium had taken the edge off, leaving Ryan relatively close to her normal state. Conor poked his head in at that moment, carrying a perfectly contented baby. Ryan's entire demeanor softened and she held out her arms. "Hi, punkin," she murmured as he handed her the child. "Miss me?"

Caitlin was dressed in a disposable diaper and a tiny cotton gown. She tossed her arms around Ryan's neck and cuddled furiously, while Ryan cooed to her and kissed her head.

The unhappy orderly came back in and sniffed, "Someone from the hospital administration is coming down. Wait right here."

"We're going home," Ryan said firmly. "They can bill us like they do everyone else."

"That's not what the police say," he said with a smirk as he turned and left the room.

When Ryan poked her head out, Brendan was having a highly agitated discussion with a man in a rumpled suit. "You can have them all day tomorrow," he promised, "but they're too exhausted and beat up to even give you a cogent statement tonight."

"Look, I've got a report to write, and I can't write it without any information. Every reporter in the city is parked outside, and they're demanding answers."

Ryan strode across the floor, her paper slippers shushing quietly. "What's the problem?"

"Detective Bettis," the man said, extending his hand. "We need a statement, ma'am. I know this is tough for you, but we can't put off police business."

Brendan decided to play his trump card, surprised at himself for even thinking of it. "You probably don't know this yet, but the other woman involved is Senator Evans' daughter. I think the department would want you to handle her with kid gloves, don't you?" His big blue eyes were giving the detective a very meaningful gaze, and the man allowed his shoulders to slump.

"How about we let you go home and get warm and dry? We'll come to your house to interview you in…two hours?" he asked, looking to Brendan for approval.

Glancing at Ryan, Brendan nodded. "That will be great. Thanks for your understanding."

He turned and smiled at his sister as the officer left and said, "I've turned into a name dropper."

Ryan wrapped her arms around him, and he felt the strong shiver that shook her body. He walked her back into the examining room, the enormity of the situation finally hitting him. When he caught sight of Jamie, looking so rumpled and small in her roomy green garb, he let some of his feelings out, and tears began to stream down his handsome face. His display of emotion caused Ryan to relax the scant control she'd managed to find. Brendan wrapped an arm around each of his sisters, and the threesome stood huddled together, crying helplessly, all relieved beyond words that they had managed to survive.

※

As the O'Flahertys emerged from the treatment room, a distraught Tommy came running down the hall, eyes wide with alarm. "Where is she?" he cried when he spotted then.

"She's with Conor," Ryan said, pointing to the waiting room. He careened around the corner, and when his eyes landed on his child, a strangled cry flew from his lips as he leapt for her. He enveloped both Conor and Caitlin in a bear hug, rocking them back and forth as he sobbed.

In her twenty-four years, Ryan had never seen such a display of raw emotion from her cousin. Of all of the boys he was the most reserved, even though she knew that he was fairly demonstrative with Annie. He was usually even-tempered and calm, and she privately thought that he was more like her maternal grandmother than anyone else in the family. Perhaps it was because of his job, but he always behaved dispassionately when faced with traumatic events. But seeing him standing in the waiting room, crying his eyes out, gave greater testimony than she could have imagined to the place his daughter held in his heart.

After a very long while, he lifted his head and spotted Ryan, seemingly for the first time, even though they had already spoken. He lifted one muscular arm in invitation, and she willingly let him include her in the group hug. "Thank you, thank you, thank you," he murmured in a soft chant.

Caitlin had been concerned since he'd arrived, and now that they were all hugging her and crying, she began to get a sense that something was wrong. When she scrunched up her tiny body and began to wail along with the adults, they broke apart, more to preserve their hearing than anything else. "Take her home," Ryan advised. "Annie has to be out of her mind with worry."

He smiled faintly at Ryan. "Your father had to be physically restrained to keep him from coming down here. But it's such a zoo outside, I begged him to stay home. He'd likely spend the night in jail after decking a few of those jerks."

"Good call," Ryan said, knowing that her father wouldn't think twice before taking out a few reporters with his bare hands.

They were about to leave, when a perky young woman came in the room and announced, "We're getting set up for the press conference. Would you like to freshen up a bit, Ms. O'Flaherty, Ms. Evans?"

Despite the sedative, Jamie saw every shred of Ryan-the-intimidator return with a vengeance. She stood up very straight, and leveled her gaze at the woman. "We're not participating in any such thing. As a matter of fact, I'd be home in bed right now if I felt I could leave without being arrested."

"But…" she said as her eyes went wide, "people are dying to get to know you both. You're heroes."

"Ridiculous," Ryan scoffed. "We have no intention of giving up our privacy to become a news bite. If we're done here, we're going home to our family."

"But the police…"

"I've spoken with the police," Brendan assured her. "They've allowed us to leave."

The woman looked disappointed, but she was powerless against a bevy of determined O'Flahertys, so she stood aside and offered no further comment. Conor placed a supportive arm around the back of each woman and helped guide them out of the room. But the news media had packed the entrance to the E.R. so tightly that a number of security guards were on hand to allow emergency patients to get inside.

Brendan led the way, trying to clear a path, but the crowd of still and video camera operators descended on them like a swarm of locusts, with each person shouting out a pithy question—mostly along the lines of, "How does it feel to be a hero, Ryan? What do you want to say to America, Jamie?"

Ryan shot a few murderous glances that she was fairly sure wouldn't make it to the local newscast, since her scowl did not fit the image they would try to create for her. Brendan used his powerful body to push roughly through the crowd, caring not a whit if he crushed a few of the lemmings on the way. They finally got to the police cruiser that was to take them to the truck, but when half of the media scrambled for their cars and trucks, Brendan asked the officer to drive them home. "I don't think they're going to give up easily, Sis," he said worriedly.

His prediction proved all too true, when they pulled up to the house and gawked at the legion of trucks, generators, and photographers waiting for them to arrive. "No fucking way," she muttered. "We're talking to no one that we're not related to."

"It's gonna be tough."

"This is where it comes in handy to have a police officer with a nice big gun," she said as she stared at the officer's blue-clad back.

※

Minutes later, they were locked in a crushing embrace with dozens of relatives, thanks to the strong-arm tactics of a dozen O'Flaherty men who had pushed the crowd of reporters off the deck. Brendan appointed himself family spokesman, and he went back out and spoke over the railing. He announced that neither woman would be giving interviews this night or ever, and asked that their privacy be respected. He knew that the gesture would fall on deaf ears, but at least he was on record as trying to be polite.

After the crowd had calmed down, Martin and Maeve and Catherine and Jim each grabbed their respective child in a desperate embrace. All six cried helplessly as they clung together. Jamie looked around the room, found her grandfather, and invited him into the hug. She cried even harder when she felt his arms close around her, sinking into his embrace as she had when she was a child. Eventually, Martin pulled away and ordered, "Downstairs with the both of you, and don't come back until you're warm and dry."

※

By the time they got downstairs, the drugs had really kicked in and Ryan was even slower mentally than she had been at the hospital. She grabbed Jamie from behind, and they tumbled to the bed in a jumble of arms and legs. By the time they hit the mattress, Ryan was crying again, an element of hysteria to her sobs that worried Jamie deeply. Struggling against the force of the embrace, Jamie pulled away to turn and face her. Clutching the damp head to her breast, she soothed, "Tell me, honey."

Ryan's mouth opened slightly and immediately shut tightly. Two more times she tried to speak in a calm fashion, but she finally gave up and gasped, "I almost got you killed tonight. I know you know it. You said yourself that you'd kick my ass in heaven if we died."

She started to cry again, remorse over her actions overwhelming her.

Jamie felt sick to her stomach, her words coming back to haunt her in a way she hadn't anticipated. She'd assumed that Ryan would be cavalier about her actions—chalking it up to doing what one had to do when another human was in peril. It didn't dawn on her that Ryan would not only take her seriously—she would hate herself for what she had done. "Oh, sweetheart," she sighed, holding Ryan close. "I...I don't...I didn't mean that. I'm so sorry." She tightened her hold and rocked her lover for a few minutes, kissing her dark, fishy-smelling hair repeatedly. Pulling back, she looked into Ryan's sorrow-filled eyes. "You have to be who you are. The woman I love is so generous, so filled with love for others; that she does things that are—to most people—very foolhardy. If you asked one thousand people if they'd risk their life to save someone who was trying to kill them—most of them wouldn't be able to keep a straight face. They'd think you were crazy for asking the question."

"I am crazy," Ryan muttered. "I'm fucking insane."

Jamie grasped her chin and held her still, forcing Ryan to meet her eyes. "You are not. I don't want to hear another word like that out of you." She kissed her firmly, trying to make Ryan feel how much she loved her—exactly as she was. "One of the things I love most about you is how much you value human life. That's who you are, and you could no more stop being that way than you could stop being tall or left-handed. It's part of what makes you you—and I love you with all of my heart."

"I would have died if you'd drowned, " she sobbed pitifully. "I would have died."

"Look," Jamie said, still holding her chin. "You're more athletic than I am...you're stronger than I am...you're a better swimmer than I am...hell, your lungs are bigger than mine," she insisted, recalling a breath-holding contest in her parents' pool that she had lost by almost a minute. "Going after those two didn't risk your life nearly as much as I risked mine by going after you. Are you angry with me?"

Ryan blinked slowly, her eyes round and looking puzzled. "No... I'm not angry with you."

"You should be," Jamie said firmly. "You didn't want me to follow you…you told me not to…but I did it anyway. I made the decision to die with you if I couldn't bring you back. But instead of saving you, I passed out from lack of oxygen. If you hadn't pulled me to the surface, I would have started to breathe underwater—and I would have drowned. My death would have been from my own hard-headedness," she insisted. "You're a risk-taker. I'm not. Trying to follow you was crazy—even though I'd do it again in a heartbeat," she said, sparing a small smile for her beloved partner.

"I love you so much," Ryan sighed, holding her close. "I'll never be able to tell you how much."

"You show me every day. I know exactly how much you care for me. I hope you understand how I feel about you."

"I do," Ryan said, a smile curling one corner of her mouth. "I do."

Ryan stood in the shower with the comfortingly warm water cascading down her body. Jamie stood behind her, washing her with a reverence normally reserved for royalty or deities. Finally, Ryan turned and whispered into her lover's pink ear, "I'm okay. You can be more aggressive. I proved tonight that I don't break easily." Ryan was obviously trying to act like things were back to normal, and Jamie did her best to contribute to the illusion.

"You certainly did that," she agreed, with a small smile. "Those idiots had no idea who they were fucking with. They had an argument because of you."

Ryan really didn't want to hear the details of what went on in the car, but she was embarrassed to admit that, so she gave Jamie a blank look and waited.

"When they were almost out of bullets, the crazier one of the pair pointed the gun right into my face," she said, shivering violently, despite the heat of the water. "I could honestly see his finger whiten on the trigger. But his brother reminded him that you were still up there on the roof, and he agreed that he hated you worse." She smiled up at her partner and said, "So, remind me to never complain about you being a pain in the butt, okay? Your ability to annoy them saved my life."

Ryan leaned down and turned off the water, managing to get out of the shower before her knees gave way. She fumbled around, her wet body almost causing her to slide off, but managed to sit on the closed toilet lid and catch her breath. Jamie cursed herself for relating the story, her plan to lighten the mood having gone horribly wrong. She wrapped the shivering woman in a towel and then stood in front of her, holding her head against her belly until she calmed down slightly. "I'm sorry for telling you that," she whispered.

"S'okay," Ryan nodded. "You had to live through it. I should know these things."

"Maybe someday," Jamie sighed, "but not now."

※

Jamie was warm and dry before Ryan, since her hair was so much easier to finish. "You go on up and reassure your parents," Ryan told her. "I'm afraid to come up with one drop of water still in my hair—Da will check."

Three minutes later a soft knock on the door announced Martin's presence. "Can I come in?" he asked when she turned around.

"Of course." She turned off the dryer and faced him, waiting for him to speak.

"Come sit," he indicated, moving to the love-seat. When she did, he placed a hand on her shoulder and pulled her to his chest. "We're all so proud of you, sweetheart. Not only that you saved Jamie and Caitlin, but that you did so with so little bloodshed."

Her eyes grew wide and she started to shake her head, "I don't want to talk about it."

"Shh," he soothed, tightening his hold. "I know it was hard for you to shoot that man, sweetheart." He rocked her quaking body, saying, "As angry as I was when I watched it on TV, I'm very proud that you dove back in to rescue the feckers. That's what makes you such a wonderful young woman. We're both so very proud of you, Siobhán."

She nodded. "Aunt Maeve told me how she felt."

"She's proud of you too, love. But I wasn't referring to your aunt. I was speaking of your mother and me. She was with you tonight, you know."

"I know," she croaked through her tear strained voice. "I could feel her when we went by old St. Patrick's. I said a prayer to her right before we hit 7th Street—before they started to shoot through the roof at me."

He grasped her tightly to his chest, realizing that he didn't know all of the details of the travails his baby had been put through.

She sat up a bit and pulled her hair out to the side. As she ran her fingers through it, an inch-wide clump fell from her fingers to drop next to her neck. The clump was at least four inches shorter than the rest of her hair, and as he looked at her in question she explained, "One of the bullets hit the sleeve of my jacket, but didn't scratch me. Another would have hit me in the head, but we were climbing Nob Hill and I shifted backwards; and the third hit so close to my head that it shot right through my hair. Is that luck?" she asked helplessly. "I think Mama convinced somebody upstairs that she wasn't ready for company yet."

"She could charm the slither out of a snake," he whispered, his voice choked with tears. "I'm glad to know she hasn't lost her touch." He rocked his child in his arms for a long time, humming the lullaby that Fionnuala had always sung to her. After they'd both cried themselves out he said, "I'm so glad your mama didn't call you home tonight, Siobhán. I don't know how I'd go on without you."

"You won't have to, Da. I'm going to do my best to never come that close again. Life is too precious to give it up without a damned good reason."

When Ryan emerged from the stairway, Mia pushed through the crowd and wrapped her in a hug. Finally lifting her head, she smiled up at Ryan and said reverently, "You rock."

Ryan started to reply, but Mia kissed her again and turned to dash back to the corner. "I volunteered for phone duty," she said as she picked up the phone on the third ring. "Hello, this is Mia Christopher. How can I help you?"

Blowing Mia a kiss, Ryan looked around and found her partner sitting in the corner of the dining room, leaning heavily against her grandfather. Giving them their privacy, she went into the kitchen and found Maeve making sandwiches. She entered quietly sat down on a stool and gazed at the older woman until she looked up and noticed her niece. Without a word, Maeve walked over and pulled her into her arms, holding on until both of them were unable to shed another tear.

After her aunt force-fed her a sandwich, Ryan went into the living room and found her partner, grasped Jamie by the hand and made her way to the center of the crowd. The occupants of the couch immediately vacated to let the young women sit. "Beer or whiskey?" Kieran asked as soon as they were settled.

"Nothing for me," Jamie said. "My stomach is still too upset."

"Wish I could," Ryan said, "but I'd be on my ass if I drank anything with the drugs they gave me."

"You'd be in good company," Kieran assured her. He bent to kiss her head and said, "I predict most of this crowd will be on their asses before the night is through."

※

When Jamie left to use the facilities, Catherine spied the opening and took her spot on the couch. She didn't say much, and Ryan guessed that whatever she said would be slurred, but she wrapped her arms around Ryan's neck and squeezed until Ryan let out a gasp of pain. When Jamie returned, her mother didn't look like she was in any condition to get up, so Jamie sat on Ryan's lap. Catherine captured her legs and put them up on her own lap, removing her socks and beginning a tender, if drunken, foot rub.

Jim spotted the threesome, and came to sit on the arm of the piece behind his wife, placing a protective hand on her shoulder. "I missed a lot of the detail here," he said. "Why were the three of you out on a night like this, anyway?"

"We were taking a huge load of presents to Jennie's group home," Jamie said. "The car was packed with clothes and computers…" She looked up at him and said, "It's all gone now."

Catherine's gaze sharpened, and she assured them, "Don't give it another thought. I'll take care of it tomorrow."

They both smiled at her, assuming that her promise would be lost in the drunken haze in which she currently resided.

An hour later they hadn't moved from their spot. Jamie realized that not one member of the family had said much about the incident, and no one had asked them to recount anything that had happened. But, one after another, they would come stand by them and pat them gently on the head, or touch a face, or a shoulder. It dawned on Jamie that the O'Flaherty way was not to talk about upsetting events at all. They all had a good idea what had happened, since they'd seen most of it on television. They all assumed that the incident had terrified them both to the core, so there was really no sense in making them talk about it again. But they all offered physical affection, which seemed so much easier for Ryan to accept. *I wonder if this is genetic*, she mused as Donal came by and kissed her on the top of her head. But when Annie came over and sat on the arm of the love-seat and pulled Ryan's head down to rest in her lap, she reasoned it must be learned behavior, since Annie wasn't related by blood.

"You're hair's still a little damp," she chided Ryan. "And you still feel cold." As she spoke, she was gently trailing her fingers through Ryan's hair, but all at once her calm demeanor collapsed completely, and she broke into nearly hysterical sobs. Ryan reached up and gathered her in her arms, as Jamie scooted off her lap.

"It's okay, Annie," Ryan soothed. "She's all right. Not a scratch on her sweet head."

"Because of you two," she sobbed. "Only because of you. If you hadn't done everything…I mean everything, right…"

"You don't know that," Ryan murmured. "You don't know that we made the right choices, and you don't know what would have happened if we'd done something different. You don't know, Annie. We don't know. The only thing we're sure of is that she's absolutely fine now. That has to be enough."

Ryan got up to take a call from her family in Ireland, the news reaching them as soon as they woke. CNN had been heavily running the story of the senator's daughter and her harrowing brush with death, and a neighbor of Ryan's grandparents had gone running to their door to inform them of the incident.

Speaking to her family upset her more than she would have guessed. Perhaps it was the distance—perhaps it was because she so longed for a hug and a snuggle from her aunt—but whatever the reason, she was feeling very shaky after she hung up.

To have a moment to herself, she climbed the stairs to the upper floor, going up halfway to avoid being noticed. When she didn't come back, Jamie got up to look for her. It took a while, since the stairway was the last place she expected to find her, and when she caught sight of her, tears sprang to her eyes again.

Ryan was sitting on a stair-tread, her arms wrapped around Duffy's neck, the big, black dog tenderly licking the tears as they fell from her eyes. Jamie could see that her lips were moving, and that Ryan was obviously sharing something with her beloved pet. Duffy was, as usual, the soul of understanding—and Jamie left them to their embrace, knowing that there were things Ryan felt safe sharing with Duffy that she wouldn't share with anyone else on earth.

✦

The police arrived at nine o'clock, and after some discussion, they decided to conduct the interview in Ryan's room. Both Jim and Brendan insisted on being there as their representatives. But Ryan's eyes goggled when Conor stepped in and insisted that he was representing Ryan also.

They went downstairs, and a few minutes later they began the questioning. When it became clear that each woman's perspective was different, they decided to split them up. One officer, Jamie and Jim went up to Rory's room, while Ryan and her brothers stayed downstairs. Conor pushed his chair back a bit and tugged on Ryan until she sat sideways in her chair and leaned back against his broad chest. He rubbed her shoulders and arms briskly, ostensibly trying to bring some feeling back into her appendages; but in reality, he couldn't touch her enough. Conor had considered his baby sister his personal charge since the day she was born, and this terrifying brush with death had affected him profoundly. He found the image of her going under to rescue her attackers flooding his mind, and every time it happened he held on a tighter, until she finally whispered, "You're bruising me, Con."

"I'm sorry, " he said quickly as he released his grip. "I…I…"

"I know, Conor," she said as she kissed his cheek. "I know."

He gave her a small smile, and wrapped her in a gentler embrace for the duration of the interview.

When they were finished, Ryan was dismayed to learn that the officers wanted to switch places and question them all over again. She was bone tired and emotionally drained, but she didn't feel that she had much choice, so they submitted to a second bout of questioning, this one a quicker than the first.

It was after midnight when the gathering started to break up. As the last of the cousins departed, the news media finally got the message, and began to pack up their equipment too. Mia agreed to sleep in Rory's room since he was in L.A. and wouldn't return until the next afternoon, and after a quiet discussion, Catherine agreed to go with Jim to his apartment.

Before they left, Jim pulled Ryan aside, placed his hands on her shoulders and stared into her eyes until she began to feel uncomfortable. "I'll never—ever question your love for my daughter again. I know that we'll probably never be friends, but I want you to know that I feel a level of gratitude towards you that I can't even begin to put into words. Thank you," he said, a few tears dotting his cheeks.

She leaned in and gave him a hug, the very first one in their relationship. "She's my life," she said simply, putting a motivation to her heroic actions.

Before leaving, Jim called the San Francisco police department and explained his situation. A few minutes later, three squad cars pulled up in front of the house to escort them to the apartment. "Is this necessary?" Catherine asked.

"I don't want to speak to any reporters. The police will keep them away from us until we get into the building."

They said goodnight to everyone, with Jamie worriedly watching as her father and her grandfather practically had to carry her mother down the narrow staircase.

※

The police escort worked perfectly, and after dropping Charlie off, Jim and Catherine entered the gold-toned elevator of the building. When they reached the unit, Jim flicked on the television, and was dismayed to see that the story had morphed by the time it had reached CNN. Now the headline was "Senator's daughter taken on wild ride." "Great, great," he muttered as he sank into the sofa to watch the story. Catherine sat beside him, and he found his hand captured by hers as she leaned against his shoulder. Once the announcer made clear that Jamie was his daughter, the story focused more on Ryan's heroics, showing dozens of shots of her hanging onto the car, and a few of her diving repeatedly into the bay. When the footage of Jamie's limp body being lifted into the boat appeared, Catherine buried her head into Jim's chest and cried until she was physically exhausted.

Eventually he got her to her feet, and led her to the second bedroom. She paused in the doorway and asked in a shaking voice, "Will you stay with me? I can't bear to be alone." She looked so fragile and helpless that he would have agreed even if he hadn't felt as great a need for contact himself.

"Let's go in the bigger bedroom," he suggested, and she followed his lead. He started to remove his sweater, but saw that she was standing in the middle of the room, looking completely lost.

Going to her, he placed his hands on her shoulders and said, "Let me help you get undressed."

Again, she nodded, looking up at him with grateful brown eyes. Her alcohol intake had been so moderate lately, that the massive infusion she had imbibed since the incident began had served to render her more helpless than she could remember being. He removed her sweater, and fumbled with the zipper on her slacks for a moment, finally freeing it and sliding them down her legs. It dawned on him that she had no clothes in the apartment, so he hurriedly unbuttoned his blue dress shirt and handed it to her. She still made no move to help, so he unclasped her bra and slid it from her shoulders, then tossed it aside as he eased her arms into the oversized shirt. He smiled at her as he rolled the sleeves up time and again, finally freeing her hands.

He kicked off his loafers, and shucked his slacks, then pulled back the covers and guided her into bed. Unsure of how much contact she wanted, he got into bed on the other side, maintaining a respectful distance until she scooted across and wrapped her body tightly around his.

"She's okay, Cat," he soothed as his hand ran through her hair. "She's home in bed…perfectly safe. Ryan will protect her," he said confidently, realizing with a sharp blow of recognition that Ryan had taken over his role as his daughter's protector—and had performed that role better than he ever could have.

Before she went up to bed, Mia handed Ryan the phone tally. Jamie leaned over her shoulder to review the ridiculously long list, marveling at the sheer number of people who had called.

"Wow, she's from grade school," Ryan murmured as she surveyed the pages. "Cool, the entire volleyball team called. And looks like almost the entire basketball team—wow, even Coach Hayes. I wonder if I broke any rules tonight," she idly mused. "Hey, when did Jordan call?"

"You were in the shower," she explained. "But she said to tell you she loves you."

"The feeling's mutual."

Despite the muscle relaxant, Ryan's body began to stiffen up as the night wore on. After making sure that she took another pill as well as the sleeping pill, Jamie gingerly began to remove Ryan's clothing. There were no obvious injuries on her partner's body, save for scrapes and bruises and the swelling and cuts on her cheek and lip, but she winced every time she moved.

"Are you sure you didn't tear a muscle or a ligament?" Jamie worried.

"No. I'm stiff and sore. There aren't any exercises I do that replicate hanging from a roof rack for an hour," she said with a crooked grin made slightly more crooked by her swollen lip.

Jamie felt her stomach grip again, but she tried to maintain her outward calm. "Maybe we'll have to devise a new workout for you," she mused. "It could be all the rage. Berkeley matrons will be hanging off their SUVs in droves."

"Thanks," Ryan murmured quietly, acknowledging her partner's attempts to normalize the situation.

"Don't mention it." She helped Ryan into a turtleneck and sweat pants, a telling concession to the numbing cold she had been forced to endure. She climbed into bed with a grunt, and a sharp intake of air when Jamie curled up against her side. "Come lie on my chest," Jamie urged gently.

Rolling onto her side, Ryan placed her head on Jamie's shoulder, letting out a deep sigh in the process. "This is perfect," she hummed in pleasure. "You're the best pillow in the world."

"Everyone would want to be a pillow, if you were the head that rested on them." She held her as tightly as her own bruised ribs would allow, but Ryan was too restless to settle down.

With a frustrated sigh she sat up, gasping when she did. "It's gonna take a lot more than a sleeping pill to knock me out." She sat up against the headboard and drew her knees up, draping her arms around them and resting her chin atop a knee. "I can't turn it off."

"The movie?" Jamie asked softly.

Ryan breathed out heavily. "That's what it's like, isn't it?"

"Yeah." Jamie sat up, too, also wincing from the effort. "It's like a really terrifying movie that's on some kinda loop. It repeats and repeats and repeats."

Nodding quickly, Ryan said, "I bet our movies are different."

"Yeah. I'm sure they are. We had very different experiences."

"In a way, I bet it was easier for me," Ryan mused.

"Yeah, sure. It's a lot easier hanging off a car in a driving rainstorm."

"You were with them," Ryan said, her voice growing dark. "I can't imagine that wasn't its own level of hell."

Jamie gazed at her partner for a few moments, then said, "We were each in hell. But we got through it." Gently pulling Ryan's hand from its grip she held it in one of her own and traced the veins and tendons with her index finger. "There's only one way to get though the night, sweetheart."

"What's that?"

"To summon up some of our powers of denial. I think we need to try our best to stop the movie from repeating and stop obsessing about what we did, and what they did, and what might have happened."

"Easier said than done," Ryan commented quietly.

"I know that. I know that we've been through a horrible ordeal and that our brains are trying to deal with it. But I think we'd be much better off if we stopped obsessing about what did happen and try to focus on what didn't happen."

"Go on."

"I know this is an 'Is the glass half full or half empty' kinda thing," Jamie said, "but in this case, I think it might help us."

"Uhm…you wanna go over all of the injuries we could have right about now?"

"No. That's the last thing I want to do," she said, shaking her head. "All I want to do is thank God that you're in this bed, and I can feel your warm body, and hear you breathing." She took in a breath, trying to avoid crying again. "We're alive, Ryan," she whispered. "By any account that shouldn't be so. But we are." She brought Ryan's hand to her mouth and placed a dozen kisses upon it, caressing each long, graceful finger in turn. "This might sound funny, but I keep thinking of how I'll feel when I give birth."

"You lost me."

"Well," she said thoughtfully, "giving birth is probably the most dangerous thing that most women ever do, right?"

"Uhm…sure, I guess that's true."

"So, it's dangerous and frightening, and extremely painful," she said, shivering a little, "but when you hold that new life in your hands women almost uniformly report that they don't think of any of that. All they do is marvel at their child, and thank God for giving them the miracle that they hold." She smiled at her partner, tears running down her cheeks again. "I don't want to think of the pain, or the fear, or the danger. I want to thank God for letting you lie next to me in this bed. I want to count your pink toes and your chubby fingers, and assure myself that you're the perfectly healthy creature that you appear to be."

"I am," Ryan said, smiling through her tears. "I'm your perfectly healthy creature."

Jamie wrapped her arms around her precious bundle and whispered roughly, "Thank you, God. Thank you for giving me this wondrous gift."

Ryan was sobbing softly, her head nuzzling against Jamie's neck. "I love you so much. I'm eternally grateful that you're whole and safe and that we're lying in our own bed, holding each other." She shivered violently and started to add, "By all rights…"

Jamie shushed her by placing her fingers upon her lips. "By all rights we're where we're supposed to be. I don't know how we made it. You don't know how we made it. But none of that matters. We did make it, and I'm so overcome with gratitude that I'm about to burst." She hugged Ryan tightly again and whispered, "We've been born again. Share my joy."

The dark head lifted, and Ryan let her eyes settle upon her partner. For all of the terror of the long night, Jamie's face bore a peacefulness—a look of true serenity that absolutely amazed Ryan. She opened her heart to the emotion that was spilling from her partner, letting in as much as she could bear—allowing it to soothe her tortured soul. She felt like she was draining the very lifeblood from her lover, but Jamie was gladly offering the transfusion—trying to share the grace that made her spirit soar. Slowly, Ryan began to nod, a smile so faint that it was barely visible starting to blossom. Bit by bit it grew and brightened, until it nearly mirrored Jamie's. Eyes glistening with unshed tears, feeling her lover's spirit filling her own body, she wrapped her arms tightly around Jamie and let the energy continue to flow between them. Finally, she released her enough to gaze into her eyes and speak. She managed one sentence, but it was the distillation of every tender emotion that coursed through her body. "You're my miracle."

Karma

The End

By Susan X Meagher

Novels

Arbor Vitae
All That Matters
Cherry Grove
Girl Meets Girl
The Lies That Bind
The Legacy
Doublecrossed
Smooth Sailing

Serial Novels

I Found My Heart In San Francisco

Awakenings
Beginnings
Coalescence
Disclosures
Entwined
Fidelity
Getaway
Honesty
Intentions
Journeys
Karma

Anthologies

Undercover Tales
Outsiders

To purchase these books: *www.briskpress.com*

To find out more visit Susan's website at
www.susanxmeagher.com

You'll find information about all of her books, events she'll be attending and links to groups she participates in.

All of Susan's books are available in paperback and various e-book formats at www.briskpress.com

Follow Susan on Facebook.
http://www.facebook.com/susanxmeagher